Vivian in Red

KRISTINA RIGGLE

Copyright © 2016 by Kristina Ringstrom
Cover and jacket design by Georgia Morrissey
Interior designed and formatted by E.M. Tippetts Book Designs

ISBN 978-1-943818-16-7
eISBN 978-1-943818-38-9
Library of Congress Control Number: 2016937092

First hardcover publication September 2016 by Polis Books, LLC
1201 Hudson Street, #211S
Hoboken, NJ 07030
www.PolisBooks.com

POLIS BOOKS

Books by
KRISTINA RIGGLE

Real Life & Liars
The Life You've Imagined
Things We Didn't Say
Keepsake
The Whole Golden World

For Bruce
It had to be you

1

Milo

S he called me a vine; said I twisted into all her spaces, wrapped around all her branches. I remember she was missing one round-toe shoe, which made her stand at an odd, broken angle. Her hat was twisted into a ball of felt in her hand. She'd torn the hat from her head, turning her neat curls into a spray of hair something like a halo.

She said that to me, then she was gone out of my life, and for half a century I'd forgotten her, same as I'd forgotten the name of my Hebrew school rabbi and the minute details of what my father had really looked like.

Until yesterday, my God.

My son Paul had asked me to come in to the office to discuss business. Always business with Paul, holding down the fort at Milo Short Productions. So far, we're holding our own, even with the falling chandeliers and rotating stages and all that mishegoss, not to mention Mickey Mouse storming Broadway now with his productions of movie cartoons that mainly existed in the first place to plug cheap plastic toys. I mean, some of those songs are all right, but everyone's already heard them. Say "Tale as old as time" to anyone and see if they don't start singing along like Angela Lansbury as a teapot of all things. I prefer Mrs. Lovett and the worst pies in London, if it's all the same to you. Now Sondheim. That's writing for you.

If my granddaughter Naomi gets her way, we'll be making *Star Wars: The Musical.*

Anyhow, I was up early, and Esme knocked and said, "Good morning, Mr. Short, it's a hot one out there already," and began to make up the bed as I was fixing my tie in the mirror. My son David was forever telling me that I don't need to wear a suit to the office anymore, that a shirt with an open collar is fine, and these awful tan pants he liked to wear. "You'll overheat wearing all that," he would tell me and I'd laugh, because you want heat? Try banging out tunes on a warped old piano in a tiny box of a room with an aging vaudeville act dripping sweat on you with nothing but a clacking metal fan stirring maybe three hairs on your head. Nowadays the buildings feel like the North Pole and it's the contrast that's a shock to the system, if you ask me.

Thinking of David made me start to feel my age properly. Eighty-eight years old I am, and David himself was fifty-seven, rest his soul, but there's no age at which losing a child doesn't knock you to the floor.

So I turned from the mirror and sang to Esme, "It's a hot one already, fair to melt me down to size, you better go it steady, or end up eulogized!"

She tossed her head back and favored me with a laugh. "Oh, Mr. Short."

"I probably wrote that in thirty-five or something. I don't got any new ideas anymore. Just an old man and his greatest hits."

She put one hand on her hip and smiled at me. "And you know exactly how charming you are when you're modest. Would you like me to call for the car?"

"I think I'll walk part of the way," I told her, and began my slow amble out of the room. I've missed being able to hurry. I like going places, that's why I'll never leave New York. Everyone's always going because there's always somewhere to go.

Her smile fell. "It's really hot, are you sure? I sure wouldn't want to in this heat, and I'm a year or two younger than you are, Mr. Short."

She bit her lip. This means she's torn between what Paul wants her to do, and what I want her to do. It's my company, my house, my legacy for lack of a better word, but Paul runs it most days, yet I can put the kibosh on something if I don't like it. So who's in charge? It's poor Esme and the kids down at the office stuck in the middle.

"Just a few blocks. I am perfectly capable of getting a cab when I get tired. I have a wallet and everything. Hey, even an old goat like me needs some exercise."

She smiled, shaking her head, and her thin shoulders drooped with defeat. For the umpteenth time I felt how bizarre it is, this slight girl from somewhere in Central America doing physical work in my house while I sit idly by, though as Paul tells me, she could no doubt wrestle me to the ground in under a minute. She's no weakling, this girl. And it's a good job. We take good care of her. What good is money if we can't take care of people?

I could hear her footsteps as she came to the stairs to watch me descend, which is awkward, because it takes forever and a half these days. I always go one step at a time: one foot down, then the other, so I've got both feet on a step at once. Always with a good grip on the rail. God forbid I fall and they make me move out of my room to the main floor or even worse, some god-awful soulless box of an apartment like those ones Paul buys and sells all the time in Midtown and the financial district. I love my grand piano across the hall in the library, and the big canopy bed that my wife picked out, rest her soul. A grown man alone sleeping under a frilly canopy is only strange if you don't feel like your late wife is still with you on the other side of it.

Step, step, step. I could tell Esme hadn't moved, and her stare was prickling the back of my neck. I watched my loafers slide across the dark red stair runner with its floral design, another thing of Bee's I could never bring myself to change, no matter how many times my daughter Rebekah sniffed at me about how outdated it was. "I'm outdated, too," I'd fire back, "and it suits me fine."

It's a comfort to look around and see my Bee everywhere, in all these things she lovingly selected, looking to me for approval though I never could see the difference between one shade of mauve and another.

It always felt like a milestone when I reached the landing without so much as a wobble, able to take a breath. That's one thing about being old, you revel in life's little victories. There's a picture on the wall of the landing, our wedding picture, with Bee draped in lace and me with my giant ears jutting out like wings off a stage, the yarmulke mercifully covering up the early bald spot that I didn't yet know was there. I'd had to stomp twice to crush the glass, so nervous I was, while Bee smiled next to me, serenity pouring out of her, waiting patiently enough because she knew I'd get it eventually.

Having gained the ground floor at last, I lifted my hat off its hook, stepped carefully down the stoop, and headed down toward the office. As was my habit, I glanced back at the stone façade of the townhouse, which I still think of as Bee's house. I can still see her face when she clasped her hands in wonderment, unable to believe it was really ours, just a block from Central Park and not so far from where we came as the crow flies, but it might as well have been across the globe. You'd think I'd have built the thing myself I was so proud.

Nope. Four floors, narrow rooms and all, I'll stay in my own house. It just takes me a while to get around, is all.

As I ambled down toward Midtown, I returned all the smiles the passersby sent my way, touching my hat brim even, which seemed to tickle them. I'm like a living museum piece—don't think I don't milk it sometimes. I've discovered this late in life that it comes in handy to be cute, and cute is something I've never been until lately. Apparently old men who dress like it's 1945 are a cute bunch.

Not that they recognize me. They may have danced at their wedding to my biggest hit song, or gone to see a show or movie made from a Milo Short Production, but not a one of them could name me or recognize my face, and that's okay with me. Composers are overshadowed by the star singing the song, and lyricists don't get half the credit composers do. Invisible is something I got used to, before I was cute.

I hadn't gone two blocks before I had to admit that Esme was right. It was brutal out there.

I settled onto a bench and fanned myself with my hat, and thought of dinner the night before. My granddaughter Eleanor was staring so hard at her plate it's like she thought it would sit up and start a conversation with her. I knew better than to just ask her direct so I grabbed Eva as she blew by toward the parlor to yell at one of her kids, and asked her what gives.

"Boy trouble," she'd muttered to me, the way a person complains about tax day or the snow in January, with a fatalistic, *what else is new?* shrug. I didn't let go of her forearm right off, so she had to elaborate. "Daniel moved out."

This here was a surprise; I'd figured he had a rehearsal or something, was why he didn't come over. Not that I was so excited about them living together with no wedding—poor Bee would've had a fit—but we all had figured an announcement was coming any day. And he was such a mensch, far as we could tell. For an actor, anyway. Poor Ellie couldn't catch a break. That mother abandoning them like she did, mother a term I use loosely, mind you. And then David dying on us way too young before Eleanor had a chance to even start her life.

It was one of the great-grands that got Eleanor to quit with the staring at her plate. Joel and his wife had twins and Joel being a doctor had gotten paged and Jessica looked like she was near to coming apart trying to deal with them. Then Eleanor scooped one twin up, and the baby jammed a fistful of her hair into her little gummy mouth and Eleanor walked to the front window to watch the people and cars go by and the little girl just settled. She has that way, Ellie does. I meant to talk to her and say something wise like grandfathers are supposed to, but then she slipped away to go home to that apartment while the rest of us argued about whether Rudy Giuliani was ruining the city or saving it.

As a taxi went by with strange pulsing music coming out the open windows it was a reminder that I was expected at the office, and if I didn't turn up soon they'd send out an all-points bulletin for my whereabouts. I had to brace myself to push off from the bench, and I didn't feel much refreshed for the break. The July heat seeped into the shade even, crawled down my neck and wrapped around my chest. I'd have been better off staying upright. It took me an age to stand up again, so some fleet youngster jumped in front of me and hopped into the first cab that passed.

The next one came by quick and I figured it was my lucky day, then. Once I was inside, the driver turned so sharp I slammed into the door. Now that would have been ironic, if I got hurt or killed in the cab meant to keep me from dying of heat stroke.

But I survived the drive to the Brill Building. That's how we knew a music publisher was moving up back in the old days, when they made it to this place from the old Tin Pan Alley way down on Twenty-eighth. The Brill was always where I wanted to be, once I started coming up in the business myself.

I had to nudge through a pack of tourists taking pictures of the shiny doorway. Mostly the tourists don't upset me too much. They spend a lot of money on Milo Short Productions, and don't ever forget it, I always told my employees when I heard grumbling about how they stop in the middle of the street and open up their maps, or lumber along in clumps covering the whole sidewalk.

But even I, sometimes, want to sock one in the head with a walking stick, though I don't use one. Makes me wish I did. I believe I would carry one with panache.

Anyhow, they finally parted for me, and I suffered through the blast of freezing air inside and made my way upstairs to Paul. His cute office girl greeted me like I hung the moon, again with the cute old man thing. Plus I'm the boss and all. I flirted with her, naturally.

To think I took all of that so casually, not knowing what was coming. But does anyone ever know what's coming? Ask Cole Porter if he knew a horse would crush his legs, maybe he'd have never gotten in the saddle.

Or maybe he would've still. Hard to say. I didn't really know him too well, and it's not the kind of thing you ask a person.

When I went into Paul's office, I was surprised by the presence of my oldest granddaughter, Naomi. "You look sharp," I told her, and she smiled because she took that I meant she looked fashionable, which she always did, usually in black, sometimes—like today—in a bold red. This was a girl who'd never wear a flower or pink. She might go crazy and wear a pinstripe. Naomi had cut her hair after graduation and I never got used to it, how short it was, when she'd had tumbles of curls down her back for her whole life. Even Naomi's bones looked sharp. Her collarbones poked out from the round neck of her blouse.

Paul told me that he and Naomi had been talking about an idea. They exchanged a long look before turning to face me.

"Pop, we want to put on *The High Hat* again."

"Nope. And you must really have wanted me to get some air and exercise to have me come down here for this. You could've asked me this on the phone, or at dinner, or remembered every other time I've told you I don't want to rehash the past and saved yourselves the trouble."

"Hear us out," Naomi jumped in. She'd remained standing behind Paul's desk, and now she stepped in front of him, upstaging him. "We could combine it with the release of your biography!" At this she spread her fingers wide, like she was about to break into jazz hands, and drew out the word: *bi-AH-graph-eeee...*

"That's supposed to make it more appealing? Hi, have we met? I'm your grandfather, who doesn't like to talk to strangers about myself. Remember me?" I stuck out my hand for her to shake it. They ignored me.

Paul leaned forward now, almost having to elbow Naomi out of the way to get back in view. "It wouldn't be a stranger. I'm thinking of asking Eleanor."

Before she turned away to the window, I caught a grimace from Naomi. She did not like this part of the idea. Clear as day she didn't.

"Eleanor wouldn't do it," I answered. "Anyhow, so I tell my story to Eleanor but she publishes it so strangers can read all the gory details. Same difference. I'll repeat my line in case you're getting senile in your old age, kid, but I don't intend to dig up my old 'success.'"

"C'mon, Pop, how gory are your details?" Paul folded his hands, leaning forward toward me. "People love you. They would love your life story. Other people have written it and done a crummy job. Remember that putz who said Irving Berlin practically wrote your first song, just because you were in the same room once? And don't get me started on how many people wrote that you came from nothing, as if your father couldn't rub two pennies together, just because it made a better story than his tailoring business doing well for so long. Eleanor would do it up right, and we'd premiere the show the same time as the book came out. Mark my words: Best Revival of a Musical."

Naomi had turned back from the window by then. "To put it plainly, we need a hit because we need the money. I'd love it if a fresh undiscovered property would be the next *Rent* for us, but that hasn't happened and the balance sheets show it. Production costs are through the roof, but people will only pay so much, and the number of seats in the theater never changes. The tourists are coming back again, thanks, Mayor Rudy, but they want family-type shows they know they'll like. Revivals are perfect, so why not yours?"

"I told you a hundred times. I didn't build this company to coast on moldy old revivals, and that includes my own moldy old stuff. Find something new. Find me a latter-day Sondheim."

"Sondheim's not dead, you know."

"I know he's not, but we can't afford him. I'm saying, stop dredging up the old."

Naomi thumped her index finger on Paul's desk, mussing the papers he'd just straightened. "People love nostalgia, even people who can't remember it firsthand. What about this? You could even write a new number. That would be dynamite. The press would go nuts. They love old people doing stuff that young people do. No offense."

I waved my hand at her: none taken. But I didn't budge and we went around in circles for a while, and they made me promise to think about it, then turned me down for lunch because they had a meeting.

Maybe that was why it happened. Because Paul and Naomi brought up *The High Hat*. With that song that I would never sing, never play, never listen to. A song unwritten, time unspooled... I was thinking in lyrics again. I shook my head hard, shaking away cobwebs and old times and buried things no one can change.

I was strolling back uptown, pondering whether to stop for a bite or get a cab home so Esme could make me a sandwich. Then what I saw made me stop so quick the top half of me wobbled forward, even though my feet had stuck down hard.

Her shiny dark hair peeked out from under her hat, and she had one gloved hand touching the brim, like she was adjusting it, or keeping it from blowing off in the wind. Her long dress was the scarlet of lipstick and stoplights; the hem was fluttering even though I didn't feel a breeze at all. When I raised my astonished eyes from her rippling hem to her smooth face and her red, red lips, she winked at me. Took those arresting green eyes, angled her delicate chin slightly away, and winked at me, with a tiny one-sided smile in the bargain.

And that's the last thing I remember seeing, because that's when everything went dark, and all I heard were cries of alarm and surprise, and at first I thought all of them had seen the same thing as me: Vivian, winking on Broadway and 52nd, looking as gorgeous as she ever did in 1934, but here in 1999, when she should've been ninety or dead.

2
Eleanor

With my phone in my hand, and Uncle Paul's voice terse on the other end—not his secretary, not Aunt Linda, usually in charge of all things family—I think of the time I saw a scaffolding fall, because of the sensation in my chest: a raucous collapsing. I can almost hear the clanging. *Someone's dead.*

The guy on the scaffolding had been up there doing something to the masonry on one of those woebegone crumbly old buildings which seem to have been forgotten amidst all the jutting glass and steel. The man was fine, other than that he probably pissed himself with fear. His harness thing caught and he grabbed the side and sort of rode it down. No, the amazing thing was the sound, a series of metallic clangs as the platform smashed its way along the metal supports and bounced off that stone façade. The racket was loud enough and long enough for pigeons and pedestrians to scatter. We—the other commuters and I safely across the street—stood mesmerized by the slow-motion nature of the destruction. For a while I got nervous walking under scaffolding but like everything else, you get used to it again.

"Eleanor," Paul says now, jerking me out of the memory, into the grim reality of whatever news he has to deliver. "Your grandfather collapsed this morning."

"Oh, no. How is he? He's not...?"

"He's at Lenox Hill Hospital now. They're not sure what happened, but apparently he was walking home from the office and he just fell down on the sidewalk. It looks like he had a stroke."

"It's so hot today! Why didn't he take the car?"

"You're telling me. I don't know why not. I'm on my way down there."

"Is anyone with him now?"

"Joel was already there on rounds, so he's checking on him. I'll be there soon. Don't feel like you have to rush right over right this second. They're running tests and things now and it'll be some time before you can see him, I just wanted you to know right away, because... Well, you know. Anyway. Gotta go, Ellie."

My fingers dial before I can decide not to, before I've even realized the note with Daniel's new phone number is in my hand.

"Eleanor?"

I loathe caller ID. Daniel's voice is already rich with suspicion, even dread.

"Grampa Milo collapsed today."

"Oh, geez, honey." His voice instantly softens. "Is he okay? Are you?"

"I'm not sure, and I don't know."

"Umm..."

He could have an audition, but he might be headed to a temp job. His degree is in English and so far that's gotten him proofreading gigs here and there, sometimes he answers the phones and makes copies. Better than pouring Budweiser for tourists, he always says. I also know he pushes back against actor stereotypes, and that includes the standard-issue actor-waiter. In this suspension of time I wish I hadn't called. He's an ex now, and what am I supposed to expect from him?

"Which hospital?" he says now, and I tell him Lenox Hill.

"I can be there in an hour. Do you have your cell phone on you?"

"No, forget it, I shouldn't have troubled you…"

"You called me for a reason, Ellie. I'm not going to leave you hanging like this. See you soon." He hangs up, and it requires two shaky tries for me to replace the receiver back into its cradle before I sink into my desk chair.

I know he won't leave me hanging, and somehow his kindness makes this worse.

It was not quite a week ago that Daniel greeted me with the famous "Can we talk?" line.

I'd been at my desk then, too, chewing the tip of my pen to a flattened, gnarly triangle as I stared at notes for my next interview. What followed was one of those tedious, excruciating talks where one just wants it all over with, and the other wants to understand. I played the role of the one seeking understanding, though I really did know. It just felt necessary to ask, anyway, like we really were on stage somewhere, and the audience was expecting certain things from us before curtain.

This feeling was heightened when I made some remark about, "Can't believe you're leaving me" and he retorted, "You've been leaving me for a long time."

"Ha," I answered back, though it came out lifelessly, without the sting that I'd wanted. "That's from a play. I know because I ran the lines with you."

Finally, Daniel rose and said he was sorry for hurting me by leaving, but that he didn't think I'd hurt so long, anyway. And he closed the door carefully and locked it from the outside, because he was always considerate like that. Even though we lived in a doorman building, he wasn't going to leave me vulnerable behind an unlocked door.

When I finally hauled myself up out of the chair, dazed like I'd been sucker-punched, my gaze lighted on a slip of paper on the coffee table. *Staying at Tom's,* he'd written, and then included the phone number. He hadn't written it during our talk. He'd prepared it ahead. How far ahead? How many nights did he sit with me over takeout, watching *Seinfeld*, planning this?

I tried to tell myself Daniel couldn't be expected to memorize my work schedule, that he had no idea he was ripping my life in half just before an important assignment.

Daniel likely didn't realize that I'd spent the previous five days talking myself up for that interview like a prizefighter, all but dancing back and forth and jabbing the air. That this assignment from *Skyscraper* magazine was a coup. I'd be interviewing a grieving mother in Brooklyn, who was demanding police take action in the supposed accidental death of her son. The authorities had written off his death by car crash as a sadly common tragedy: kids don't look where they're going, do they? But his mother smelled something rotten in how fast they came to that conclusion in favor of the wealthy driver of that glossy black BMW. It looked to be my toughest interview yet, by a mile and then some.

Perhaps it wouldn't have mattered, anyway. Maybe it was already written in the book of life that I'd start shaking as the mother started yelling at me.

My editor, John, had reminded me that I couldn't just accept her rendering of the facts, sympathetic though she was. I had to be as thorough with Mrs. Ashanti Greene as I would with the police later. It was because of this coaxing from John that I'd written the questions in my notebook like a script, so I could read the words one by one and not chicken out. So I read from my script and asked, "How can you be so sure it wasn't simply an accident that your son was run over? Kids do get run over sometimes, especially if they dart out in the road."

So that's when she started with the yelling, and I started with the shaking and crying.

She hollered, "How dare you cry when it's my son that's dead? When all I'm saying is truth, how dare you?"

Breakup or not, perhaps it was already ordained I'd bolt from that grieving mother's kitchen without another word. That I would throw up in a garbage can and wipe my face with a piece of paper from my notebook before running through Bed-Stuy until I could find a cab.

So when John fired me—much as anyone can fire a freelancer—perhaps that was inevitable, too. I thought he might give me an easier assignment, one like I'd been doing before. Everyone loved my profile of a guy who gave popular, impromptu performances from his West Village fire escape. Likely because it was Rat Pack jazz and not rap, the cops yelled out requests instead of shutting him down.

No nice, friendly profile assignments for me. John said I needed a good long break.

I'd been making a paper clip chain while John made me wait for him in his office, and I'd for some reason still had the thing in my hand as I drifted out of the offices and plopped down under a tree in Bryant Park to get my bearings. It would have been foolish to return a handful of paperclips, and would I unlink them first? It seemed wasteful to throw them away. So I carried them home with me, into the apartment, here they still are, strewn over the notebook I'd clutched in that Brooklyn kitchen with its curling linoleum and faux wood grain table with the one short leg.

Now I pick them up, those paperclips, and I find myself passing them through my fingers like a Catholic with a rosary, as I pace this apartment in front of the floor-to-ceiling windows meant to give the illusion of space in this city where we're crawling all over each other like ants in a hill.

Since Uncle Paul's call just minutes ago, I'm bowled over with regret that I bolted from the last family dinner so quickly; if I'd only known that Grampa was about to… I try to absolve myself: *how could you have known?* But then: *he's almost ninety. Any day could be the last day.* Grampa had been holding court as usual, recounting the funniest opening night mishaps he could recall, including the time a corpse started giggling on stage. The actor had apparently felt a sneeze coming on, and was holding it in while making like a dead body, and somehow it struck him funny what it would look like if he did indeed sneeze. The sneeze, the nerves, trying not to breathe too obviously, it all struck him so hilarious he could no longer stop himself. "The schmuck should have just sneezed!" Grampa cried, and everyone roared with laughter. I should have stayed and enjoyed the fun, even though I'd heard that story maybe a dozen times. Instead I chose to evade family interrogation over the absence of Daniel.

Anyway, soon enough they'll get a hold of me, and it will go like this: What could have gone so wrong? He was such a nice young man, and worked so hard (implied afterthought: *for an actor*).

For the sake of something like dignity, I would refuse to divulge the existence of lithe, pretty Moira with her cap of black hair and her eyes blue like lapis. I'd come back weakly with, "We've grown apart" and my aunt would retort, "Nonsense! You have so much in common!" by which they mean, "You're both nice Jewish kids and you'd make adorable babies so get to it already."

Daniel had already taken his things, which we'd arranged in one brief, brittle phone conversation. I'd arranged to be out at a show so he'd have several hours. When I came back to the apartment—really Uncle Paul's place, he lets me live here at a laughably low token rent—and saw it denuded of my ex's scripts, leather jacket, books, and vinyl records he never played but liked to thumb through, I sighed, dusted my hands, and thought, *that's that*. This wasn't painless for me, of course, but had anyone seen me, they might have thought so. Daniel has accused me more than once of too easily shutting down. I could never convince him that some people—those of us not actors, those of us not show-offy hams who advertise every fleeting emotion to the world—feel things quietly, internally. I feel plenty, I just don't feel it's everybody's goddamn business.

Now I'd gone and ripped off this particular scab by calling Daniel because Grampa had a stroke. But else could I do? When everything goes wrong, you reach for those who know you best, who know you at your worst.

Here in my empty, quiet apartment, I stroke the glass of my late father's watch, torn in two by my equal impulses to fly to Grampa Milo's side, and to hide under the bed rather than go into another hospital. My father should have died at home, in hospice care, but the cancer played a mean trick and jumped out and got him when we weren't expecting it. As if cancer wasn't bad enough all by itself.

"This isn't the same, and Grampa needs me," I remind myself out loud, my voice ringing hollow in the still air. And so I am moving with determination and speed now, as if I could outrun the death of my father, as if I wouldn't carry the memory with me all the way to Lenox Hill.

I STARE AT the brick across 77th Street until the mortar lines start to waver and look like something out of Escher. I half-wish I still smoked so I could have a reason to be out here in the heavy July heat, instead of in the artificial cold next to Grampa Milo's hospital bed.

But nausea had been crawling through my guts and my hands wouldn't stop shaking. Clenching or relaxing, either way made it worse. In my twenty-three years, I had plenty of experience with older generations putting a brave spin on things for my benefit, but staring into Grampa Milo's confused face, I saw this privilege would be afforded me no longer. He was letting me see his fear; he'd never looked so sick and lost. When Naomi and her husband, Joshua, swooped in a few minutes ago, I made a dash for the outside, just for a bit, just to breathe and think.

Over my left shoulder appears a shadow I can't ignore, so I look up into the soft brown eyes of my cousin Joel, who snuck up on me so quick he might have grown up out of the sidewalk.

"You okay?"

"I guess."

My doctor-cousin, biggest success story of all the Short progeny, puts on his "reassurance face." "He's going to be fine, we think. His vitals are good."

"I know. You said. So why can't he talk?"

"The CT scan indicates an embolic stroke, and there's an area of deficit around the infarct that appears to be causing his expressive aphasia."

"For God's sake, Joel."

"Sorry. He had a stroke which is keeping him from speaking. That's what aphasia means. He can think of the word but can't get it out. The stroke also affected motor control; in this case his right hand and leg are weak, especially the hand."

"Oh, my God. Will he ever be able to write again?"

"We hope so. He's a tough old gent, and therapy can help him get these things back."

"Even at eighty-eight?"

"I've seen it before."

"Now what happens?"

"He has to see the neurologist, and all the various therapists will come in to see him. A speech path, physical therapist, occupational therapist, et cetera. They want to evaluate him and determine placement."

"Placement where? What does that mean?"

"They will likely recommend a nursing home setting for the time being, to keep an eye on him and for therapy, but it sounds like Aunt Rebekah is on the war path about it and he'll probably come home with twenty-four/seven nursing care."

"Well, good. Grampa Milo would hate those places."

I finally look away from the brick to face my cousin, and his shiny forehead is creased. He's tall and prematurely balding, and the combined effect is to make him look like he's growing through his own hair.

"There are some excellent facilities with wonderful staff. But yeah, El. I know what you mean."

A familiar movement in my peripheral vision snags my attention. Before I even turn my head all the way I can tell who it is. Daniel has a distinct, loping gait that I've always been able to pick out of a crowd long before I can even read his face.

Joel utters one confused syllable: "Huh."

"Never mind," I tell him, my voice full of warning.

By this time, Daniel has approached us. He thrusts out a hand toward Joel, makes his inquiries, and my cousin gives an abbreviated version of what he just told me.

After he sums it all up, and Daniel nods his sad commiseration, Joel doesn't seem to be leaving, though he must have someplace important to be. I wish for his pager to sound off, to make him stop giving Daniel that "sizing up" look.

Daniel breaks the silence. "So Joel, how are those babies?"

"Hungry, my God. Either Jessica or the nanny are feeding one of them at any given moment. How do the families where kids outnumber the adults ever do it? Oy, I can't imagine."

I break in with, "You mean you haven't heard the Eva Monologues on Proper Parenting?"

"I always make sure I get paged. Look, I better get back in. Hang in there, Ellie. Bye, Daniel."

And so he's sucked back into the building, looking at his watch, his white coat flapping away behind him.

Daniel steps closer to me and asks me how I am, and I answer with a shrug.

"So Joel knows? About us?"

"I had to explain why you weren't at the family dinner. He's trying to figure out why you're here now."

"I told you, I wouldn't just abandon you at a time like this."

"Well, he's going to live, so you're in the clear now."

"Don't do that, El. You called me, I came. I'm not the bad guy. But seriously, are you okay? I can't tell, when you get like this. When you go all 'statue' on me."

By this time I'm facing him, but he's enough taller than me it's easier to focus on the flaking print on his Pearl Jam concert T-shirt than it is to crane my neck to look him in the face. It's bright, too. The sun is pouring out rivers of heat and light, and my head has begun to throb.

"I'm scared for him. He can't talk, his right hand is affected, he can't write. What kind of life is he going to have without words?"

Daniel turns so we're shoulder-to-shoulder, both staring at the same masonry wall, and he drapes his long arm loosely over me, tucking his hand under my hair. For a moment he's uncharacteristically still. I almost hate to break the spell.

But in the quiet, I answer my own question: at least it's life of a sort. At least Grampa Milo is still here.

I reach up to briefly clasp Daniel's hand where it rests on my shoulder, and step away from him. I lead the way back into the hospital, where my grandfather lies mute and scared, but alive.

3
Milo

At my piano, I should be comfortable. It's the first place I ever felt so, after all, way back in the Bronx days when my father finally made enough money to buy us one. It was meant for Leah, but she never took to it, not like me.

And it shouldn't be so bad, either, playing one-handed. But it's my right hand that doesn't work, leaving only my left for harmony, unless I try to force my left hand fingers into straining awkwardly to play the melodic line.

Haltingly, messing up the phrasing, I plink out, *The way you wear your hat, the way you sip your tea....*

It sounds wrong to me, worse than silence. I stare down at my right hand, frustrated. No one seems to get why I can barely move it. I should be able to do something or other by now, what with the therapy. And my voice, too, that therapy lady Marla keeps encouraging me to make sounds, even sing little nursery tunes like "Twinkle Twinkle Little Star," but there's nothing there. She's trying her damndest to pretend not to be disappointed, but I've spent a lifetime watching people act and she's no Ethel Barrymore.

Some of them think I'm exaggerating somehow, or maybe just too depressed to try. I overheard my daughter-in-law Linda mention Prozac and if I could've, I would have laughed out loud.

Ha, Prozac. Please, in my day when you felt down you had a belt or two of Scotch and felt calmer, if maybe a headache in the morning.

Not that Scotch is always the greatest cure, mind you, I know that from up close and personal experience.

I drop my left hand onto the keys, a soft, pathetic, sick-sounding chord seeping into the air. They're trying, my family. They really are. The hospital people talked them into putting a genuine hospital bed in here, as if I'm an invalid. My walking's not so bad, thank you very much, stroke or not. My leg strength came back pretty quick in fact, which is another reason they think I might be malingering about my voice. As if I would do such a thing!

They brought a TV in from the living room, and the old record player, so I've got something to do other than watch the Yankees or cable news. While still in the hospital, I saw my own collapse reported as a quick bit before cutting to commercial: *Noted Broadway producer Milo Short collapsed on a Manhattan sidewalk yesterday.* That made me imagine the *Post* headline: "SHORT NOT LONG FOR THIS WORLD?" Those schmucks can't resist a pun.

There's a nurse off in the corner, a rotating clutch of them, all quiet and professional and none too chatty, of course what would I say back anyhow? I scowled and shook my head about the constant nurses, but Paul informed me the hospital wouldn't spring me unless they knew for sure I was going to be monitored. For how long? I'd like to ask. Forever? Until I kick it? Until another stroke gets me and then I start drooling and stumbling for real, like that poor bastard Marty?

So I guess it could be worse.

Except it's hard to imagine worse just now. I'm beyond mute, I'm rendered wordless entirely: speech, writing, even playing proper music, it's all gone. Marla the therapy lady gave me a board with pictures and a pointing stick. It's all I can do not to throw that garbage across the room; it's infantile, something you'd give a clever chimpanzee, and yet even that seems to confound me, somehow.

The family has begun to talk past me, over me, as if I'm deaf, for that matter. I saw this with poor Marty after his stroke. He was alert as ever—I could see the spark in his eyes—but he was so impaired they treated him after a while like a potted plant. I never was great at praying, and maybe praying for someone to die is wrong, but I did it anyhow, then. I felt like he wanted me to.

I put my left hand on the keys again, trying something slower. *I hope that he turns out to be…*

"*Someone to watch… over me….*" Eleanor laughs as her voice cracks over the "watch." I turn on the piano bench to see her coming over to me. I finish the musical phrase with as much panache as I can.

"I'm no great singer, am I, Grampa Milo?" She comes to settle next to me on the piano bench. I shrug and wave my hand side to side: *eh, not bad.* It's true. All us Shorts have sturdy, serviceable voices with a range of about six notes.

"Should I play the right hand for you? I think I can manage that." She looks around a moment and remembers. "Oh, you always play by ear. That's something I cannot manage, sadly. Maybe we'll find some songbooks. I'd love to be your melody."

She drapes her arm around my shoulders and gives a squeeze.

Eleanor is the last one in the family to talk to me like I might answer. Well, her and Esme.

Ellie's been around plenty these last days. While I'm always glad to see her, I also know it means she's not busy, which is not so great. I remember from the night before my fall how Eva had whispered to me about her nice young man leaving her, "no reason at all that we know of," she'd said, though from the look she shot Eleanor's direction I figured she'd imagined a reason all her own. For Eleanor's whole life they'd been trying to glam her up—my daughter Rebekah, my other granddaughters. They'd put her in bright colors, style her hair, do her makeup. She'd sit politely through their ministrations, then go home and wipe it all off and go back to her dark plain colors. If they would ask me—not like they ever did, or would—Eleanor doesn't need all that stuff. All she needs is someone to make her smile. That smile, when it comes out, gleams like sunlight on the sea. No one is immune, especially not that Daniel kid, who I really thought would stick it out with her. But it's been weeks now, so it seems he's really gone.

Eleanor nudges my shoulder just slightly and starts the right hand part of Chopsticks. I oblige her for a few minutes, then feign tiredness. Or maybe it's not so feigned, I realize as Eleanor helps me stand up and we head over to my favorite chair.

Esme pops her head in the room. "Miss Eleanor? I'm sorry to interrupt, but Mr. Paul is upstairs in the office and he'd like to see you."

Eleanor sighs and pats my hand. "I've been summoned. I'll be back in a few, Grampa Milo."

And so I'm alone again, as alone as I ever am, with the nurses, of course. This one looks busy with a book or some papers, so I try to whisper to myself. I go with my wife's name: Bee. I keep thinking the next time will work, that since it vanished so quick it will come back quick, too. No such luck, so far. I try not to mutter to myself too much, because then I look crazy instead of just mute. As it is, they're all treating me like I'm made of dust and if they sneeze in my direction I'll blow apart.

I fell flat on the sidewalk and only had a bruise. That's fragile for you.

Thinking of the sidewalk makes me think of her. I could have sworn I saw her there, Vivian in red, just like in 1934, touching the brim of her hat, and I blink away the memory. It feels like bad luck to dwell on that time, not to mention how she ended up, poor kid.

That's when I notice the albums. Old photos were more Bee's thing than mine. She'd bring them out sometimes, and we'd leaf through, have a few laughs.

Bracing on the arm of my chair and leaning forward, I raise myself up with only moderate exertion, and begin my progress across the floor toward the shelves that hold the albums, which are next to the bay window. There's a window seat there; that's a pleasant place to rest, and I could see the people outside, if I cared to watch them. Yes, these here albums only begin after 1937 or so, and that suits me fine, as certain events in years prior I'm not inclined to recall. I reach for one, and it's heavier than it looks, but I can handle it okay, even one-handed.

When I make it to the window, what I see there makes me drop the album right to the floor.

Vivian is sitting on my window seat. Legs crossed, cigarette in her hand. I can smell the smoke and her flowery perfume woven together, that cloud was always around her, and I'd know she was coming without even turning from the piano.

I'm torn between crying out for help—from what I don't know—and talking to her, my God, she's here after all these years, how and why...? I open up my mouth, but my voice is still gone.

That's when Vivian smirks and shakes her head at me, just a little. It's a look of, *Not so fast, buster...*

Esme comes trotting in, and the nurse is standing here with me all of a sudden, and I point at Vivian, I point hard, I'd be poking her if I were closer.

"Mr. Short, what's wrong?" asks Esme, as she picks up the album and looks in the direction I'm pointing. "What's wrong? I don't see anything there."

Vivian from sixty years ago turns away from us to gaze out the window at New York in 1999. Still smoking, not making a sound.

I allow Esme and the nurse to guide me back to the chair I'd been sitting in. Once settled, I raise my gaze back up and half expect her to be gone, but no, Vivian is still there, looking out the window.

The pair of them, my tiny Hispanic housekeeper and this bland blonde nurse, start asking me questions about what I saw, what was wrong, along with the nurse checking my pulse, frowning at her watch as she times the rapid beats.

I play it off with what I hope is a sheepish smile, something like, "Oops, silly me," with a shrug of one shoulder, as if I'd seen a shadow that startled me is all. They ask me a few different ways if I'm okay, if I need anything, until finally they fade away to their respective posts, the nurse jotting notes in a book, no doubt recording this little incident.

I close my eyes for a moment, knowing Vivian will be gone when I open them next. She's just a trick of my old brain, something on the fritz up there. That same stroke that made me collapse, made me lose my voice, also made me see a person from my long ago past. That's all.

When I open my eyes, she is halfway across the room, sauntering toward me.

The cigarette is gone, I notice, but the smell lingers, the way smoke always does. Vivian is swaying her hips as she walks. She always had some extra curve in her steps but this is a bit much, even for her.

Even for her! Thinking of her as real when she couldn't be.

Yet my heart is thudding harder as she gets closer. I'm feeling dizzy, my heart still lugging away in my chest, and I think, oh now I'm gonna die. I was half-dead before and here it comes. I wonder why I'm seeing Vivian instead of my Bee, or my dear David, or poor Allen, all of them gone before me.

She's so close. If I were sitting up straight, I could touch the hem of her dress, which I now notice is different than before. It's a chocolate brown suit, in fact, one like she would have worn to work. It ends past her knee and is in that way modest, but it hugs her body so nicely I can't fail to notice her curves even as I'm dying. Her brown curls are pinned behind one ear, brushing under her tapered, sharp chin. She's got that same smirk, one that says, *I know something you don't know.*

I could bawl that I won't get to see my kids and grandkids one more time, not to mention the great-grands who barely understand what I am but that I give them candy, with their round red cheeks and giggles about anything and nothing—

Then Paul's heavy feet come clomping down the steps. "Hey, Pop, I have to head back to the office."

And she's gone. The space where Vivian was standing, just inches from the toe of my shoe, holds nothing but dust motes winking in the sun.

4

1934

The elevated train roared over Milo's head, startling him into grabbing his hat, interrupting his fingers' rehearsal of sorts on his pant leg. His right hand had been tapping out "Alexander's Ragtime Band" with such concentration he was nearly run down by a policeman on a motorcycle as he crossed the street.

His mother couldn't believe what he had planned for the morning.

"People can't give up wearing clothes!" She'd bitten off the words hard in Yiddish, abandoning English as she always did when she grew emotional and frustrated, though newlyweds Yosef and Chana Schwartz had emigrated at the turn of the century. Rapping the wooden table in their apartment for emphasis, she leaned in and continued her harangue. "In fact, they go to a tailor more because they have to mend things when they might have bought new. Letting down the children's hems to go another few months. Your brother says business is better this month than last! But music? It's pretty, yes, but we don't need new songs. We can keep playing the old songs." She jerked her arm back toward the wireless in the front room. Milo didn't point out that it was in fact playing new songs all the time, and someone was out there performing them, and getting paid, too.

Instead, he sipped his watery coffee and sighed. "We need them even more now, I'd say." Milo couldn't help adding, "You loved it when I learned to play."

She threw her hands up in the air as her only response, and went back to kneading her dough. Milo's father and brother were already at Schwartz and Sons tailor shop a few blocks away, which was where Milo would be too, if he hadn't decided to quit kidding himself. The shop was getting along just fine without him, and whatever his mother might insist, he was doing no one any good screwing up the hems or buttons in the shop, requiring Max to fix it all. He charmed the customers, and helped with the figuring and sweeping, but he was no tailor. And whatever else Chana Schwartz might insist about the shop "doing better than last month" Milo was no dummy. He could sense the frustration rolling off his father like fog, while he and Max had whispered conversations and thumped numbers in their ledger books with rigid forefingers.

He knew how much his father had stretched in '29 to get them into this apartment, "just one block off the Grand Concourse" as Yosef Schwartz never tired of saying. The day they moved in, Mr. Schwartz swept his arm to indicate the shiny parquet floors, walked up and down the step into the sunken living room like it was a party trick, and kept turning the faucet in their very own bathroom like Moses himself striking the rock.

Money was tight even then, his father shutting down fast any talk of buying their own automobile. To make their "one block from the Grand Concourse" rent, he went on mending their own clothes long past their prime, putting the kibosh on going to shows, even the Yiddish theater he loved down on the East Side. Since the Crash? It took no great leap of imagination to understand why his father grew more pensive and solemn by the day.

Just last week at the newsstand, Milo heard men grumbling to each other about "Prosperity is just around the corner," like Hoover kept carrying on about and had been laughable for years by now. Not that it looked like FDR was fixing everything, either, and his big campaign song was "Happy Days Are Here Again." Milo liked to mutter new lyrics to himself while he cleaned up the shop:

These so-called happy days, my friend
Should like to drive me 'round the bend!
I build my shack, line up for bread;
These happy days just never end!

No, it was time Milo Schwartz earned his own keep, and since tailoring wasn't for him, he'd take the only thing he was good at and find a job doing that: he'd be a piano player.

When he first mentioned it, his mother had gasped, grabbed the table, pounded her round, dimpled fist that her son might be playing for coins in a dirty speakeasy. Milo had reminded her ever so gently that the Volstead Act was over and done with, and everyone was getting tight respectably in public now, which truth be told, didn't ease her mind so very much. In the end, he promised her no saloons or taverns or barrooms. Even though none other than Irving Berlin himself had started as a singing waiter at a Chinese restaurant back when he was Israel Baline.

As the elevated rumbled away downtown, Milo tried to shake off the morning's conversations and his mother's objections, lest this distraction get him killed before his audition.

Milo felt he had miscalculated by waiting until midday to head to the theater district. His shirt was so sweat-soaked under his jacket it was probably transparent, and he smelled worse than any given alleyway in the city. But he'd figured showbiz people would get up none too early. And with any luck they'd all smell just as bad and no one would be the wiser.

The theaters and marquees loomed up ahead of him, then, and if his mother had been there he'd have said, "Look, see? All those people putting those shows on. They're still getting paid, so why not me?"

He sucked in a breath, puffed out his chest, and swung open the door to the 51st Street Theatre, better known to Milo just then as the home of Jerome H.

Remick and Company, Music Publishers.

After getting directions from a bored and skeptical boy at the box office, Milo huffed up the stairs, as sweat tickled a line down his back, and the din of pianos and muffled singing grew louder in cadence with the crescendo of his thudding heart.

Inside the lobby, a few people working in nearby half-glassed-in offices glanced up at him, but went back to their work, no doubt assessing he was no performer and therefore not worth knowing. Milo approached an office girl, a young woman tapping at a typewriter. "Miss? I'm here about a job."

"Mmm-hmmm," she said, still typing.

"Playing the piano?"

"Yes, sir," she answered, but hadn't yet looked up at him, still typing. Finally she reached over and slapped the machine silly by way of slamming the carriage back. Milo jumped.

She looked up at him and said, "So what is it you want to do here?"

"Play the piano."

She moved her mouth around a little, and Milo realized she was trying not to laugh at him. She lowered her voice and leaned over her typewriter, and Milo noticed her bosom lightly depressed the keys. This tickled his funny bone somehow, so he bit his own lip to keep from laughing.

"It's called being a song plugger. You plug the songs for the acts. Sometimes here, sometimes around town. That's what a piano player does here."

Milo would have proposed to her at that very moment. Having never been in love before, he assumed the torrent of gratitude was close enough. He cleared his throat and spoke with theatrical volume and diction. "Yes, of course, that is exactly what I meant. And whom do I see about such an important job?"

She laughed at this. "I'll check if Mr. McHenry will see you."

She leaned into an office doorway. Milo noticed several of the men stop their conversations or paper shuffling to watch the shape of her derriere as she bent slightly at the waist to talk to Mr. McHenry.

She gestured lightly with her hand. "Go right in, Mr....?"

"Schwartz."

"Mr. Short."

Milo shrugged. Once he had the job, there would be plenty of time to get his name right.

Mr. McHenry was a voluminous man melting behind a desk that seemed not large enough for him. He mopped his brow with a soaking handkerchief in a gesture that struck Milo as awfully optimistic. He jerked his thumb at the piano.

"Let's hear you."

Milo nodded, and rested his hat on an empty office chair, for lack of a better place. He settled onto the piano bench, sucked in a breath, closed his eyes, and let his hands do their thing.

His fingers danced along like they didn't belong to him, really. They just went right ahead and had a party, and this terrific song came out, and it felt like great good luck that one of his favorite songs to play, the one he'd probably learned earliest, thanks to his mother's frequent requests for him to play it, happened to be authored by Irving Berlin himself, and surely that would impress Mr. McHenry. He was swinging back into the bouncy refrain when he heard, "Hey, pal, I said that's enough!"

Milo turned around on the piano bench. "Sorry?"

"I've been hollering at you for eight bars. I said thanks, I got the picture." McHenry heaved himself up by way of planting both massive palms on his desk, and stomped over with some papers. He slapped some music onto the piano. "That was nice and all, pal, but it's old-fashioned. Play this and let's see how you do."

Milo swallowed. The marks on the page looked like ants crawling around on a white floor. With a hand nearly trembling, he pulled his glasses out of his inside pocket and used his necktie to polish off the dust.

He slipped the frames into place, and his hands hovered over the keys. Even with the lenses, the notes wavered. The glasses were old, his eyes were worse.

He turned back to McHenry. "You know, my eyes don't see so well. I'm really more of a player by ear."

McHenry, who'd settled back behind his desk by now, raised one eyebrow at Milo. "Really. So how do you suppose that helps us here? When your job is to read the music we give you? Any music we decide? New music, that no one's even heard yet? So that the acts and producers can put it over big and sell sheet music by the ream? Have a nice afternoon."

And with that, McHenry went back to scowling at the music on his desk as if Milo had fallen through a trapdoor and vanished.

And he might've. He certainly wanted to. Instead he slunk back out, then back in again, to pick up his hat. McHenry appeared not to have noticed.

He nodded to the office girl, who gave him a shrug and mouthed "sorry" before returning to her typing.

Out on the street, he looked down the long block of music publishers and theaters and realized the same fate would greet him inside each office. His one talent was useless for anything but after-supper entertainment in his parents' apartment, unless his eyes were magically cured, or his father received some windfall that made Milo unafraid to ask him about money for new glasses. And even then, so what? What made him so special?

Milo was too hot and tired just then to walk back to the platform, too embarrassed to show his face at home besides. He stood in the shade of the building, and for a few moments stared down at the worn and scuffed tips of his shoes, as people with better places to be hustled past.

What an ignoramus he'd turned out to be, not even thinking one step past his masterful playing of a song that had been first published twenty-three years ago in 1911, the year he was born, in fact.

Milo sighed and began his hot, sticky trudge. He wondered how many suits his father and Max would have to sew, how many cuffs they'd have to make, before the shop made enough money that he could get some better specs.

He'd missed out on all the fun before the big crash in '29. He'd been a diligent, obedient son struggling along in the shop and going to school and doing his arithmetic, because his mother insisted he not drop out to work, like his father had done. He pounded away on their badly tuned piano at night, playing by ear the songs they heard on the radio. His wilder classmates and neighbors would swill bootleg gin in speakeasies or house parties, but Milo figured his day would come when he got a little older.

Then he was eighteen years old, and suddenly nobody was having any fun anymore. Whatever his mother said about the Depression being good for business, he wasn't fooled for a minute. He could see with his own terrible eyes how bad business was. No one wanted custom-made suits in fine fabrics these days. And people could make do with their own home sewing for repairs and fit easily enough. It wasn't so hard to fix a seam for most people, and if your hem wasn't perfect, well, who was going to complain? You wouldn't, not if it meant more money in your pocket. And even if you couldn't manage that, plenty of newer immigrants would take in your sewing in their homes, for cheap. Which was just how Yosef Schwartz got started a generation ago, on Orchard Street.

Milo was a block from the train station when he saw it: a snaking gray line of men, three or four abreast. They were quiet, ordered. The bread line rocked gently as the men shuffled forward. Some wore suits and fedoras, others open-collar shirts, with flat caps pushed back over sweaty brows. They muttered a few words to one another, but mostly seemed to stare only at the collar of the man in front of them.

Milo kept looking at the line of men as he waited for the traffic to clear with a few other men in suits. One, with a fine hat and a newspaper under his arm, observed to someone near, or maybe to anyone in earshot, "I'd jump off the Brooklyn Bridge before I'd do that."

"You might get the chance to test that out if things keep going the way they are," someone else said.

The traffic light changed, and the men continued uptown, but Milo remained on the curb. He cast a look back over his shoulder, toward Broadway, and TB Harms, Jack Mills and Company, and Jerome Remick. He stood there as people jostled around him, as somebody asked him for a dime. Stood there looking back, and thinking.

A WEEK LATER, Milo slogged through the sodden streets of Manhattan in a storm, everything below his hip pockets soaked with windblown rain, his vision obscured by the black umbrella he held low enough to keep the gale out of his face. He'd almost stormed back to Remick's that same boiling hot day, but when he pictured facing the cute secretary again and her adorable smirk, and McHenry's impatience, he lost his nerve. His nerve had failed him one more time at home, when he told his mother that no one had time to see him, and he was supposed to come back the next week. He assumed she'd be relieved that her younger son's brush with the entertainment industry was over, but he thought he heard her sigh quietly before asking him to chop some onions.

Once again, in terrible weather, he made his way toward Times Square, the rain drenching him thoroughly even in the few blocks from the 42nd Street stop of the Third Avenue El. This time he walked right past the Hollywood Theatre and picked up the Brill Building instead, home of TB Harms Music Publishers, recently acquired by Warner Brothers, and as good a place as any.

But he hadn't counted on having to wait very long, and his resolve was cracking with each tick forward of the second hand. Once installed in a wooden chair, Milo began repeatedly polishing his glasses like a sacred rite.

He saw some fading vaudeville acts and hopeful dewy-eyed girls come in and out, but nobody famous came by. No Kate Smiths, no George Cohans. Of course, they probably had music pluggers chasing them all over town banging out tunes and waving music at them, why would they bother showing up at a place like this?

The secretary this time was a stiff-backed woman with hair wrestled into a tight knot behind her head, and who was disinclined to give him any helpful hints. Milo's confidence was thinning out by the minute, especially when he cast sidelong glances at the other piano players he could see go into nearby offices and start pounding away at the music like they were born to it.

When the clock ticked over to three o'clock, he stood up and put his glasses back in his coat, and tried to shake out his damp pant legs for the slog back to the train. He'd head into Schwartz and Sons and help with the customers, maybe joking around enough to convince them to spend a little extra. Smiling people always did spend more; this much, at least, he'd learned at the shop.

"Short? Is there a Short in here?" Again with the Short. It didn't sound so bad, though, Milo thought, and went well enough with his adopted first name, too. He'd dropped his given name, Moshe, while still in high school, though his parents would never call him anything else.

He whirled around in time to see an elfin-looking man with tired eyes and a necktie all askew. Milo pointed to his own chest.

"Okay, get in here, pal. I'm not even supposed to do this, my boss is. But my boss has a hangover, see? So, lucky me. I've got about one minute to hear you, so go."

Milo summoned up his tailor shop charm. "A minute is all I need."

He put his glasses back on and smiled broadly, pumping the smaller man's hand with enthusiasm. The man introduced himself as Mr. Bernard Allen, and pointed Milo to a piano in the corner. "What have you got for me to play?" Milo asked.

Allen walked over to his desk and retrieved a piece of music. It was handwritten on manuscript paper, and Milo gulped. The pencil was soft and it was even harder to read than the printed music he gave up on at Remick's. Allen said, "This right here is a piece of garbage. It's the worst thing I've seen in this place all week and that's saying something. But I want you to play it like it's the greatest thing you ever heard in your natural life. Play it in a spotlight. Pretend you're on Bing Crosby's radio show. Get me? Now, go."

Milo nodded and inspected the music. It was awful, all right. Milo couldn't say why exactly, not exactly being a learned student at a conservatory. He just knew it the same way his brother could tell a hem wasn't straight with one quick glance, even if was off by just a hair.

"You gonna go, or what?" Allen prodded.

"Sure, sure." Milo waved his hand. He squinted hard at the notes and pretended the pounding in his head at the effort was the bassist in the band, giving him the beat. By the time he put the music on the piano, he wasn't so much seeing with his rotten eyes as picturing it in his head what the notes looked like when they briefly wavered into clarity.

And he went for it like pigeons at bread crumbs. He smiled at Allen, he moved his hands with flourish. He almost danced off the piano stool, which was on wheels and rolled around on the floor a little. He even added a run up the keys and a tink on the high C just because, to finish it out with panache.

He turned around and hoped to see Allen looking delighted, but he only looked more tired. Milo wanted to run all the way home and hide under his bed.

"Yeah, okay, sure. Come back tomorrow at nine."

"Sure? You mean, sure I got a job?"

"If you can put over a garbage song like that so well, you might make our good songs sound great. You looked like you actually liked that sappy mess."

Milo shrugged with one shoulder. "It wasn't so bad."

"Sure it was, and I oughta know because I wrote it. Now beat it, I'm busy. Come back in the morning."

With that, Allen strode over to the piano and balled up the music in his fists as if the melody had been a personal affront to all of music history, leaving Milo blinking in stunned disbelief.

"You waiting for me to demand an encore?" Allen said, without looking up.

Milo scurried away.

Despite the ongoing rainy onslaught outside, and the splashes from the automobiles and the wind turning his umbrella inside out, Milo caught himself whistling "Happy Days Are Here Again" as he made his way over to his father's shop. Schwartz and Sons Tailoring was about to become just Schwartz and Son, singular, and forever, if Milo had his way.

5

1999

Eleanor

When Esme pulls open the door to my grandfather's limestone townhouse—his home since the biggest Broadway hit was *Kiss Me, Kate*—she gives me the sad smile, complete with head-tilt.

How I hate that look, that practiced, silent "poor you" I've seen my whole life. What's wrong with just looking sad? That smile is like saying "chin up," which is something else I hate to hear. I'll put my chin up when I damn well please and not a moment before.

She steps back and I pass into their foyer, making for the steps up to his office with his grand piano and his reams of sheet music dating back to FDR.

"Miss, he's in the parlor today."

Of course, I'd forgotten. This literal lowering of Grampa Milo seems irrevocable. The elderly don't gain back freedom they've lost.

I hover in the entry for a moment while Esme makes her way off to wherever she was working. I can see the back of his head over the top of a tufted, embroidered chair. A familiar and favorite melody lilts around the room: Fred Astaire's unassuming tenor from the old scratchy record player. *Someday, when*

I'm awfully low, I will feel a glow...

Grampa Milo is different, and I have to be different in his presence. He is no longer the funny chatterbox who taught me pinochle, which I thought for years was spelled pea-knuckle. He used to play any song I wanted on the piano, even Top 40 songs, by listening once or twice and replaying them by ear, making like a human jukebox. It didn't seem that long ago he was plinking out the melody to George Michael's "Faith," and I was giggling into my hand hearing the naughty lyrics in my head. His price for that parlor trick was for me to sit and listen to him play the sumptuous melodies of his day, all but his own most famous song. Like any proper teen-ager, I pretended to hate that part.

He can't do that now, and may never again. And though I've been visiting him all along, each time I step into his presence is akin to walking into a punch.

I suck in a breath and push my glasses up, and walk in, eyes on the carpet for as long as I dare without being rude.

"Hiya, Grampa." He looks much the same as usual, except for being downstairs. This was Grandma Bee's room, really. He looks at me with downturned eyes, too, along with a smile that's vague and pretending. He's happy to see me, and sad he can't say so, and I have to look away before I weep.

I take a seat in the other tufted chair. A table between us holds a copy of a glossy coffee table book about Broadway, the black cover faded to the gray of a foggy morning. While seated, I tug and haul the chair over the thick rug, leaving behind deep depressions.

When I look up again, having settled closer, Grampa waves at the air around his head.

"Yes, I love this song, too. Jerome Kern and Dorothy Fields. A female songwriter was unusual back then, huh?"

He opens his mouth to answer me, and his face crumbles as he remembers. I rush to fill in the silence: "She was a genius at making vernacular sound beautiful. 'Awfully low' rhyming with 'feel a glow.' Just perfect."

We both look up, as if we can see the notes unspooling into the room.

Maybe Grampa is picturing Dorothy Fields. He might well have met her.

Uncle Paul and my doctor cousin, Joel, have been worried, so I hear. Joel said the speech pathologist, Marla, seems puzzled by his utter lack of progress of any kind; he should be making some improvement with his right hand, or his voice, or even that silly pointing board with the alphabet, pictures, and a stick. After all, the strength in his right leg came right back, even more quickly than expected. Why won't the rest of his right side catch up? Why can't he speak, even a little? Joel thinks he doesn't even want to try, that he's too depressed and overwhelmed. No other explanation would make medical sense, and for Dr. Joel everything has to make medical sense.

I don't agree that Grampa is depressed, but I don't bother to contradict the good doctor, as no one listens to me, anyway.

My grandfather's continued silence echoes like a vibrating cymbal crash. I'm not the most talkative in the Short family, which is a fact that usually drifts by unnoticed. There are too many Shorts hollering over each other and making a fuss to realize that I'm quiet. Now, I'm the only one in the room who can talk and in fact I must.

The alternative is to look over at Grampa Milo and watch the tragedy of his situation settle over his face and weigh him down.

I look around the room for a prompt, anything to talk about other than myself, which would be a short conversation, wouldn't it? That's when I see the photo albums my grandmother kept down here, in order by year, on a shelf below the window seat that looks out over the park.

I jump up and pull out the oldest one, using my cardigan sleeve to brush off dust. In walking it back to my grandfather, I notice he seems a little wary, but I've got the album now and nothing else to talk about, so I settle down with it and open it on my knees, turning it as close to him as I can.

In the first photo I open to, a trim young woman is standing in front of a marquee for a revue called *George White's Scandals*.

"This must be Grandma Bee." Of course it must be. Grampa Milo was famous for proclaiming that my grandmother had been his first and only love. "She saved me from a life of barren spinsterhood!" he'd joke, and Grandma Bee would laugh and flick her hand at him, *Oh you, you're such a card.*

Grampa Milo nods, but he doesn't seem to be looking directly at the photo. It might be hard for him to see, of course, given that his eyesight was always poor. He never liked wearing glasses that were thick enough to work as well as they should, though now of course they make lenses so much lighter. I think he just got used to the world being indistinct. Maybe he'd find the clarity jarring, or maybe he's just vain and doesn't like how glasses look. To this I relate. If you lined up every person who ever told me "You are so pretty without your glasses" you could span the Brooklyn Bridge.

A clock ticks off echoing seconds. "Funny name, 'Scandals.' Now a scandal is President Clinton and that intern. Can you imagine that being in the papers back then? Horrors."

I admire the picture of my grandmother in her demure, below-the-knee dress, gloves, and pretty hat, consider how they all went by Mrs. and Mr. then, and dressed in suits all the time, and wonder if I wasn't born in the wrong decade.

"Is this picture taken in what, 1940?"

Grampa shakes his head, points his thumb down.

"Oh, earlier." Their fiftieth anniversary was in what year? And this must have been a bit earlier than that… "1937?"

Grampa smiles and puts a fingertip on his nose. Bingo.

"She's so pretty. Her hair's so long, I thought everyone bobbed the hair back then."

Grampa Milo shrugs, and I can read in his face: *what do I know from hair?*

Minutes pass like this, with me trying to retell the anecdotes he's told me down through the years, though that meant stretching my memory back a decade or more, using the pictures as a prop. Grampa, I can tell from the corner of my eye, leans on his elbow in the chair and closes his eyes. I'm about to take my leave and let him rest when he snaps up, staring fixedly at the corner of the room near a wooden globe on a stand.

"Grampa? Do you see something?"

He reaches over to the coffee table book and sweeps it onto the floor with a quickness I couldn't have imagined. I set the album down on the floor and put my hand on his knee, but he turns away as far as the chair will allow.

Esme sweeps in then, as if she'd been waiting in the wings this whole time, scooping up the album and the book. A nurse I'd almost forgotten about appears as well, checking over my grandfather, who submits to this investigation with a droopy, sulky acquiescence. This nurse is a man, with dark skin and an Afro-Caribbean accent which trills musically along as he narrates what he's doing for the sake of my grandfather, or maybe for me. I wish I knew his name and I'm embarrassed that I don't, but can't rouse myself to ask.

Esme speaks up. "Mr. Short, I will make you a whiskey and soda, it's just about cocktail hour anyway. Miss Eleanor, your uncle wanted to speak with you, could you come please?"

I mumble a goodbye and follow Esme as she leads me from the room with a big, confident stride.

In the kitchen across the entry, I sit down at a counter stool and Esme busies herself making two drinks. Her dark braid has fallen over one shoulder and I wonder that it doesn't bother her like that. I give my own ponytail a self-conscious pat, and feel it frizzing out, bristling under my hand.

"It's difficult," Esme says, filling the quiet with her own thoughts as I'd tried to do for my Grampa just minutes ago. "Sometimes he is in spirits, then he gets frustrated. He uses up all patience. I think he enjoys it for a time, like that game? What's it's called? Where you act out something and people guess?"

"Charades."

"Yes, that one. But then he gets tired of the game and boom, something hits the floor, or maybe he just slumps. Oh, nothing valuable. He would never ruin anything Mrs. Bee had picked out."

Esme pushes the drink across the counter to me. "Now, there you are. Cheers."

"You should have one too, for a proper 'cheers.'"

"No, miss, this is not for me."

"Oh, Grampa wouldn't mind, he'd probably make you one himself."

"No, I mean I drink nothing more than communion wine."

"Good for you, then. L'chaim." I down half the drink and it slams into my chest. "Does Uncle Paul really want to see me, or was that an excuse to get me out of the room?"

"No, he does. He's in the library."

I sneak a glance into the parlor as I ascend the stairs. Grampa Milo is leaning on one hand again and if he noticed me walk past him in the foyer he didn't acknowledge it.

Grandma Bee decorated the library in red and gold to look like the inside of a theater. The grand piano in the corner bounces the stark August sun into the room, and Uncle Paul, rubbing his temples behind Grampa Milo's desk, looks so much like his dad that I could be back in time with two braids holding back my frizz and the taste of grape Popsicle on my tongue.

"Hi, Uncle Paul."

"Hey, El, have a seat. I was just doing some work while you two visited downstairs. I don't like to leave him alone, but it's so hard to communicate with him for very long. At work I feel bad I'm not here, but here I feel pointless and like I should be at work. Anyway, your aunt should be along soon, and I think Naomi said she'd drop by."

Taking turns. Like with my dad at the end. When it was my time, I'd be motionless in a hard chair, pulled apart by agony and guilt, as I watched the second hand tick along.

"So, what did you need?"

Uncle Paul looks up from his papers. "Right. So. This is a little strange, given everything. But I wanted to talk to you about it before, and anyway, it appears time is ticking. So we want to get it all teed up."

"Get *what* teed up?"

Uncle Paul folds his hands and leans over them. "Your grandfather's biography. His definitive life story, complete with full-color, never-before-seen photos and behind the scenes anecdotes."

"I thought Grampa hated that idea."

Paul waved his hand through the air and shrugged. "We were talking about it. He was coming around. See, I think it would be a great idea to mount *The High Hat* again, in grand style. You know, try to get Bernadette, wouldn't she be terrific? Just imagine. We give the book the same title, have the show premiere in New York the same week the book comes out. I was even going to try and get him to write a new song or two for the revival. It would be a smash, I can feel it. I've already got investors sniffing around."

"Wow. Good luck."

"I'm not just making small talk here. I want you to write the book."

"Me?" I grab the arms of my chair like I might be flung out of it otherwise.

"Of course! Strangers have written about him before and it's always been boring as shit and half of it wrong. Maybe you can be the one to find out why he quit songwriting after *The High Hat*, and switched to producing. Never made any sense, to have one huge hit and give it up. A writer in the family and we should ask someone else? Please."

"No, I can't write it. It's a conflict of interest—"

"Only if we hide it, which we won't. We'll be perfectly up front about it. 'By Eleanor Short' on the New York Times bestseller list, tell me that doesn't sound good to you."

"But I've got work…" My voice fails me in the lie.

"I know, you've got your own things going but it's a bit of a lull, isn't it?" Does he know for sure or is he just guessing? Either way, I can't refute it.

"But I'm just a nobody. I've never written a book. Get someone from the *New York Times* or something. They'll jump at the chance. Why would anyone want me?"

"Look, people already want this. I've got editors calling me all over the place, especially this one fellow, practically waving a contract at me."

"Contract?"

"Book contract, darling Eleanor. The fact that you're young and Milo Short's granddaughter is a bonus, not a problem. Trust me."

I've been staring at my lap for all this conversation, twisting my father's watch on my wrist. I keep looking down as I ask, "How can I do this without… When Grampa can't talk?"

"I think he'll come around, what with that therapy, right? Joel says there's nothing medically wrong that should stop him. I think he's just shocked or something, like writer's block. Maybe we'll mash up some Prozac in his oatmeal."

"Uncle Paul!"

"I kid! Look at you, you're white as a ghost. I would never drug your grandfather, please. And if he doesn't…. Ellie, he's eighty-eight. He might not wake up tomorrow."

I wince at the bald correctness of that statement.

"What I'm saying is that we should do this while he's still around to see it all. Yeah, I know he hasn't been so wild about a book before, but that's another reason it's perfect that you do it. You're his favorite, and you'd never write up something tacky. You're probably the only person on the planet he'd trust to write about him." Paul pauses and stares hard at me, his large hand frozen in the act of tapping a pencil restlessly on the desk. I sense he has more to say, and so I wait. He tosses the pencil down and continues. "And actually, there is one other thing."

"What other thing?"

"Look, Naomi's been busy lately, since this book idea came up. She loves it, you know. The revival tie-in, the whole deal. But she's got this reporter fella she wants to do it, and she wants him to do it right now, without waiting for Dad to get better. She wants him to start interviewing all his old friends and such, and then come in here with flashcards and whatever, whether he can talk or not. And in fact it sounds like they'd milk the hell out of the 'sad old stroke victim' angle." Paul cringes, shakes his head. "There's nothing wrong with the writer, somebody-Bernstein is his name I think. But can you imagine what Dad would think of that? A stranger coming in here to quiz him? In his condition?"

"Just tell her no. You're her uncle. Or tell her Grampa won't go along with it."

"When was the last time you tried telling Naomi 'No' about anything? I may be her uncle, but she's also a grown-up, and if I don't have a writer picked out for this book idea, she'll stick in her own guy. But you'll do it right, I know you would. You'd be sensitive to him, you'd treat him gently. You'd make it a classy project. Naomi, she thinks big, see? She thinks, 'What do the people want, so we can give it to them?' and she'd get her writer to dig up whatever kind of gossip she can find, hand over some family pictures so it looks authoritative and real. Or worse, if we refuse to help at all, maybe she'll nudge him to do an 'unauthorized' book. That's got its own appeal, you know, but it would be a hack job."

"Would she do that?"

"She's not a bad person, El. She's looking out for the company, and the company needs help. Publicity, revenue, excitement."

"Does Naomi know you're asking me?"

"Sure. I told her."

I can well imagine the ticker tape parade she wanted to throw, complete with bandleader and baton twirlers.

"Can I think about it? Does the offer expire?" The daytime whiskey is making me feel both tired and jumpy.

"I wouldn't wait forever, what with Naomi and her writer pacing at the starting line. But sure, think it over. It's a big deal, writing a bestseller."

"Well, we don't know that..."

"Of course it'll be a bestseller. It's Milo Short, everyone loves him and they'll love this book. He has so many stories that have never been told."

Naomi's voice brays at us from the doorway. "Ah-ha! The book, at last." The thick carpet must have masked her steps as she approached. Either that or she tiptoed on purpose. Growing up, all the cousins knew not to bother keeping a journal or writing a secret note in her presence.

"Hello there," Paul said, his swallow visible even to me, across the space of that vast wooden desk. "Didn't hear you come in."

Naomi nods and strides over to lean against the front of the desk and look down at me. Her heels are shiny patent and she'd be looming over me even if I were standing up, though I'm still in the chair. "So, the family writer is going to take on the family legacy. I hope you're up to it."

"It's not definite…"

"I don't blame you for hesitating. It's a tall order, after all." Naomi crosses her arms and regards me with the mechanical smile of the salesman. "You lucky thing. All my contacts would be so jealous. This one fellow from the *Post* has been bugging me for years for some kind of angle to do a new book on Grampa. That's what the publishers want, of course, is something new. Who did that book, Uncle Paul? The one that covered Grampa's history and *The High Hat*? Fifteen years ago or something."

"That was a fella named Miller, but…"

"Obviously this will be a Short family project, of course. Assuming it's accepted in the end. When's the deadline anyway?"

She directs this last to Paul. I hate that she knows I didn't ask.

Paul answers, "People have been saying about a year."

She lets out a low whistle. "Whew. Including research. I'd better let you get to it. I do have some business to discuss with Uncle Paul, anyway."

"I was just going." Somehow I tangle in the chair legs and stumble as I try to get out the door. I'm accident-prone around my cousins, always have been. At no other time—not at school, not at magazine interviews, not with college friends—am I likely to drop things, trip, or walk too fast into a revolving door.

But under the steely gaze of Naomi, or the amused and tolerant smirk of Eva, and I shapeshift to fulfill their expectations: poor hapless Eleanor, poor mongrel child of that horrible shiksa who abandoned her husband and child and moved to some godforsaken place like California, Colorado, somewhere several time zones away. You should expect something else, with a mother like that?

I leave behind my cousin and Uncle Paul—their mutterings growing louder and more agitated in my wake—as I hurry down the staircase, trying not to hurry so much I tumble down the length of it.

I find Grampa Milo in the chair where I left him, frowning at some kind of board in his lap. As I come around, I can see it's made of cardboard, with bold letters of the alphabet at wide intervals. There are punctuation marks, and along the bottom, some simple words and phrases: *I'm hungry. I need the restroom. I'm tired.*

In his good hand is a pointer of sorts, a bit like a conductor's baton, only shorter. As I have now grown close, I can see that he's grimacing at the board, his face turned half away from it. It's like he doesn't want to get caught looking.

"Hi, Grampa."

He glances up, then sticks out his tongue at the board.

"I know, it must be so frustrating. But it's better than nothing? Isn't it?"

This must be the "communication board" the speech pathologist was talking about, when I overheard her talking to Aunt Linda.

Grampa Milo begins rapping the board with the pointer so fast with his good hand it's hard to believe he's impaired at all anywhere else. It takes me a few moments to catch up with him and understand: N-O-T-A-C-H-I-L-D.

"I know you're not. No one thinks that."

He then aims the pointer at me, squints to indicate his interest in something, then looks back down to the board. I follow the pointer—this reminds me oddly of a Ouija Board—and he taps out "D-A-N-I-E-L" with an emphatic thump on the question mark.

"Ah. He's not here."

He taps the question mark again, then twice more, rapidly. I understand he's not simply asking Daniel's location.

I smirk at him, just a little. "And here I thought with you I'd at least escape the interrogation."

He replies by tipping his head back a little, like someone might for a chuckle, though he doesn't. Why can't he even laugh? Then he taps the question mark again, and taps my arm with the pointer.

"Okay, okay, fine. I guess I can trust you not to gossip, huh, Grampa?" We share a bleak smile. "We split up. Now, if Naomi were grilling, er, asking me, I'd make her work to get her information, but that wouldn't be kind of me, under the circumstances. So, why did we split up?" I slouch in the chair a little, gaze at the ceiling. It needs some repair; I can see a crack threading its way across the ceiling. How best to explain? I push myself back up and face Grampa Milo again. "He thinks I don't love him enough. That's the whole boring answer. He can't get over how I don't like to look him directly in the eye. What kind of farkakte reason is that to dump somebody?"

Grampa Milo exaggerates a cringe at my Yiddish.

"I didn't say it right? It's just such a great word: farkakte. Still no? Oh well. What can I say, I only got half the good genes."

At this Grampa Milo frowns and shakes his head. I know what he'd say because we've had this exchange before, anytime I would joke about my half-and-half heritage. *Kid, don't say that about yourself, it's not right.*

"I'm just kidding, Grampa."

Now he starts tapping the D, as shorthand for going back to his original question. Least, that's what I assume.

"I'm not sure what else to say. See, I thought he liked me because I'm a little reserved, a little quiet. He used to say he loved my 'thoughtful silences.'" I turn in my chair to more fully face my grandfather, feeling more animated by my subject. Truth is, until Grampa Milo asked just now, I hadn't given the split much more thought than registering Daniel's absence with the usual feelings of loss and nostalgia, and a sense of inevitability. *Of course this gregarious, charming actor wouldn't stay with me.* Having been asked directly, having decided not to dodge the question, I realize that this explanation is exactly on point. "But after a few years I guess he thought I'd change. That for him, with him, I should be different. I think this whole time he's been waiting for the real me to show up, some vibrant, secret Eleanor I'd been hiding. But all along it was just me. Only me."

Down the side of Grampa's board is an assortment of cartoon faces showing an array of emotions. He taps the angry face, then the sad face. Then he drops the pointer in his lap, reaches over with his good hand, and wraps his knotty fingers around mine. He squeezes with surprising strength.

"Thanks, Grampa. I love you, too."

He begins to tap out another question, but he doesn't get very far before something draws his gaze. The piano. He appears to be staring at the piano. He's so still for several seconds I'm afraid briefly he's having another stroke. I look again, following his gaze, and see that it's actually more like the piano bench. The space where a person would sit.

I touch his elbow, as gently as I can manage so I don't startle him. I keep my voice low, asking, "Grampa? Do you see someone?"

He flinches away from the piano, his gaze in so doing landing on the contraption in his lap. He upends it, a gesture that might have been dramatic had the board been heavy, but it just flutters inoffensively to the floor. Grampa Milo takes the pointer and flings it with more energy, back over his shoulder, toward the foyer.

The nurse and I make eye contact, and we, too, speak without using words. I send him a reassuring nod and stroke Grampa Milo's arm.

"I know," I tell him, so quietly I'm not sure he even hears me. "I know."

Naomi and Paul thump down the stairs, as Grampa Milo continues to look askance at the piano bench. He seems a little pale, and this time I wave over the nurse, who approaches to check him over, take his pulse, and so on.

The nurse's invasion seems to snap my grandfather back to himself. He shakes his head hard, like a dog shaking off water, and then throws me what looks like an apologetic smile. Naomi and Paul come in to say their goodbyes; they both have an appointment at the office. I watch Naomi's glossy assurance, how comfortable she is in the rightness of everything from her shoes to her career to her brilliant, piano-playing, ballet-dancing daughter. I can easily imagine her shaking hands with a publisher and her hand-picked author, waving away any minor concerns about Grampa Milo's health, in fact using his health as a reason to expedite the progress.

Then this stranger would be in the parlor, and this stranger might witness Grampa Milo's fixed stares, his throwing and dropping of objects. He'd add a chapter to the end of his book, something like "The Curtain Falls: The Sad Decline of Milo Short." Without Grampa's participation, the book would be nothing but a rehash of what everyone already knows, maybe some gossipy anecdotes about his stars and productions.

Paul and Naomi are talking to each other now, and to the nurse, all three of them standing up and talking over my grandfather's head as if he's deaf as well as mute.

I swallow hard, as if to choke down the rising sense of panic, which in fact has a voice and it goes like this: *you can't do it, you're not qualified, what's wrong with you, what do you know anyway,* and I approach my uncle, interrupting their conversation as forcefully as I can manage, and leading him away into the foyer.

Uncle Paul looks down at me with his unruly gray eyebrows in twin arcs of surprise.

"I'm writing the book. Just tell me how we start."

6

Milo

shift in this lousy hospital bed, but every position I choose drives some spike of soreness somewhere. I resent every moment in this crummy thing, which does not much help with my sleep. All the money we've got, and this cardboard-feeling thing is the best we can do?

Esme forgot to draw the front room curtains and the room glows silver and gold from the moon and streetlights, depending where the light falls. The night nurse is in the living room next door, reading or watching television between her stealthy intrusions to "check your vitals"; in other words, make sure I haven't croaked.

Down in the theater district, no doubt it's still hopping. Everyone would be out at late dinners, having cocktails. The show people would be just starting their own happy hours, those young enough to still coast on a few hours of sleep and give a slam-bang performance the next night. In here it's so quiet I can just about hear my own heart stubbornly thumping away, paying no mind to my fouled-up brain.

Just now it looks like a well-lit set, truth be told, and it's something like beautiful. Maybe Esme should just leave the curtains open all the time. I wouldn't mind. Not that I could say the words, and all the charm of playing charades is long gone, never mind that damn alphabet board.

I crane around to see the edge of the stairs just outside the parlor door. It doesn't seem so far.

A wicked idea takes hold of me. Well, why the hell shouldn't I? It's my damn house and my own damn body.

They have clipped this little alarm thingy to my pajamas, and the other end to the bed, all of them pretending like it's not a dog leash, basically. "In case you fall out of bed," Rebekah explained it, not looking me in the eye. Who was she trying to kid? However it's easy enough, even in the semi dark, to unclip it from myself and clip it to the pillowcase.

I push the covers off and swing my legs down toward the floor. It's a tiny jump down, but no higher than my bed upstairs. I land harder than I expected, but the thick rug makes it nice and quiet. There's no movement from the nurse in the room next door. She was just here a few minutes ago, so likely won't be again for a short while.

I rest a moment at the edge of the hospital bed, collecting my breath and my bearings. I'm surprisingly dizzy from being upright all of a sudden. Then I straighten up my posture as much as my creaky body lets me and just walk across the floor like it's nothing, which it isn't, of course. I smile to myself and try a little laugh, though all that comes out is a light cough. Still. A sound I intended to make, it's progress of a kind.

The progress to the foot of the staircase is unremarkable. Now that I'm here, the staircase looks taller than I remembered it, before I fell. Or maybe it's being in the dark. Everything's scarier in the dark. Also, I left my glasses on the small table next to the bed.

Motion from the corner of my eye startles me just as I raise my foot to the first step, and I gasp and grab for the railing.

I chuckle at myself the moment I can tell it was simply headlights turning onto the street outside, which briefly glowed into the entryway. As for the glasses? I don't want to walk all that way back and anyhow, it's too dark to make so much difference.

It's been a few days since a Vivian sighting, and that combined with my ability to sort of laugh-cough has got me feeling more optimistic again. Whatever has gone awry in my brain is healing over. I can picture it up there, knitting away like when Bee made a scarf and it would stretch further down her lap night after night, as she stitched.

The progress up the stairs, though, is slower than I thought. I'd conveniently managed to forget how little I used the stairs during the day. Even before my fall, I'd come down in the morning, and only go up after supper and spend the rest of my evening and night on the piano or in bed. And often, Esme would take one arm as she walked me up after dinner.

So I put two hands on the railing, my arms pulling me up along with my legs pushing. Now I'm starting to feel sleepy. Fine time for that at this point, as I reach the landing at the first bend in the stairs. I'm committed now. I might as well push on through. I imagine my soft canopy bed and push toward it like I'm climbing a mountain, which it actually feels like just about now. I guess I'm having what the grandkids call a "what was I thinking" moment.

I smell her before I see her: roses and smoke.

Vivian is leaning on the opposite stairway railing. She's wearing a shirtwaist now, and a hat set on a jaunty sideways angle. Her arms are folded and she's just looking at me, with that amused, slightly haughty expression I remember when we first met.

She stands up from the wall and walks toward me, growing larger in my vision, making me think she's going to keep walking up until she walks right into me like mist.

Unspoken words are dancing around on my tongue like grease in a hot pan. All I can do is mouth them, so I do, helplessly, pathetically.

Why are you here? What are you? Leave me alone.

She has stopped in her forward progress, in a dark patch of the landing between pools of outside light, such that I have to strain to tell if she's even there.

What do you want? My lips form the sentence, my throat choking on the words that won't come.

That voice! It's deeper than it should be for someone so slim, resonant like the inside of a finely tuned instrument. It's not coming from her, though, because her, its—the apparition, vision, hallucination—the lips aren't moving.

I just want to be heard, is what purrs into my mind, vibrating in my own chest as if I'm the one speaking. *Don't we all just want to be heard?*

My legs buckle and I fold down, hitting the landing first with my knees, then my palms, then I hope to God I don't tumble all the way down and break my neck, all for the sake of a canopy bed. As my blurred, dark vision goes all the way black I'm thinking how different it all would've been if only I'd bought that goddamn coat somewhere else.

7

1934

"Hey, Milo, you listening?"

Milo sprang upright from where he'd been resting his head on his desk. Allen's hands hovered over the piano keys. "I'm gonna play this one time, so pay attention."

Milo closed his eyes and let the notes wrap around him, through him. He moved his fingers across the desk, an invisible keyboard. It was hardly an elegant system, but so far it worked better than Milo squinting himself sick at the music. He'd listen to Allen play it through one time, and between his memory and what his eyes could decipher, he'd lock it into his brain.

Allen had spotted him curled into a C with his pounding head between his knees after squinting at music all day.

"What's your problem?" he'd asked. "You got a hangover?"

"Headache. My eyes aren't great, makes the music hard to see." As soon as Milo said it, his instincts dulled by exhaustion and the tight pain across his head, he felt a dart of fear that Allen would get him canned, make room for a piano player who could read music properly.

Allen hadn't replied, which Milo found hardly reassuring. Instead, he began to pace their tiny office, a comical task in that box-shaped space. Then he nudged Milo's shoulder hard enough that he almost knocked him off the chair. "So, how are you with playing by ear?" Milo squinted up at Allen, his vision wavering into focus on his friend's smile. "Because I've got an idea," Allen said.

And thus was born their partnership in keeping Milo employed.

Milo was afraid the bosses would figure it out and send him packing, soon as they realized he couldn't actually see the music he was plugging. But no one paid him all that close attention once he got hired, and the bosses—who now answered to Warner Brothers, which pillaged the catalog for their films regularly after buying them out—had other things on their mind than whether their newest plugger could see.

So as long as Allen kept helping him out like this with the new material, things were swell. And for his part, Allen seemed fond enough of Milo not to mind so much. They all seemed to help each other out, Milo noticed. The office girls would cover answering the phones if one of them stepped out for a bite, or the fastest typist, Helen, would sometimes do some of the other girls' work for them if they were having a tough day.

There was no acknowledgment of this. They just went ahead and did it. Milo suspected that none of them wanted to see one of their own out there on a bread line.

Milo was practicing the newest tune—sentimental slop rhyming "love" with "dove"—when he nearly jumped out of his chair. "I don't have time for this!" bellowed the manager at Mrs. Smith, the head secretary with her brown hair slicked back on her head and pulled into a tight knot at the nape of her neck. "Get me another girl, and one that can type this time!"

He saw him stomp his way back to his office, and Milo figured it was time for a lunch break, anyhow. He paused by Mrs. Smith's desk. She was a widow, poor thing, a waif of a creature, of indeterminate age. She carried herself with an air of weary maturity, and her hairstyle was old-fashioned, but when she flashed a rare and cheerful smile, she could be a fresh young girl of twenty.

"You okay?"

She sighed and glanced briefly up from the carriage of her Corona. "Swell. Know any girls who can take dictation, read music, and type like the wind? If so, send them my way. Miss Jones got herself engaged."

"Another one bites the dust."

"Poor dear found herself the last of a dying breed: an independently wealthy man who goes fishing for a wife in the steno pool."

"I'm off to lunch. Want me to bring you back a sandwich?"

"Sure, I'll live the high life today with a pastrami on rye."

"Your wish is my command."

Milo himself wasn't going just to eat lunch. He was going to Macy's to buy his mother a present.

He had never given his mother a proper present that he could remember, not even when the tailor shop was in the money; he never earned his own keep before, is why. And with a few paychecks now, and a few lunches skimped on and coins set aside, Milo was prepared to buy his mother something nice, something just for her, that couldn't be given to anyone else like the last piece of brisket that she would never take.

He strode at a rapid clip through the silky cool of middle September to Herald Square. As he passed under the awning of Macy's, he stepped into a whole other world, where the Depression didn't exist, or everyone liked to pretend so, anyhow. And if a person pretended hard enough, couldn't he almost make it true? After all, with those stout pillars supporting floor upon floor of merchandise, you just had to know that people were buying these things with some kind of money.

Milo had already made up his mind, so once inside the store, it was a simple matter of finding the ladies' overcoats. His $18 weekly pay wasn't enough to afford an extravagant item, and his mother would never wear anything too fancy anyhow, these days. Just last week the Shapiros nearly got evicted, after all, and it was only passing the hat around the neighbors that kept the locks off the doors for a little longer. It wouldn't do to flounce around in fancy clothes, considering.

But a nice, new, warm overcoat for about $10, that much he could do, and Chana Schwartz would probably even wear it.

Soon enough, a headache gripped his face from east to west. He was standing, in all places, in front of perfumes, instead of overcoats. He suspected that he would need the elevator, but had no idea where it was.

"Who's the lucky lady?"

"I'm sorry, miss?"

That voice chimed in him like a bell, so familiar, yet he had never set foot in the store before. He turned away from his search for elevators and brought his nearsighted gaze to the shop girl leaning on the glassy perfume counter in front of him. The posture was familiar, too, somehow…

"Who's the lucky lady receiving a gift from a good-looking fellow like you?"

"Ah, well, my mother, if I can find the overcoats, that is. It's getting cold soon, see…"

"How nice for her to have such a thoughtful son." The girl stepped away from Milo and he thought that was the end of that, until she walked to the end of the counter, lifted a section on a hinge, and stepped through. An older woman behind the counter barked at her, "Miss Adair! You come back to your post, right now."

Miss Adair paid the woman no mind, despite the other lady's reddening outrage. Milo began to stammer, "Miss, I don't want you to get in any trouble, I'm sure I can find—"

"Right this way," she said, moving past him without seeming to have heard. He was able to easily keep an eye on her dark green dress, and the sway of her hips as she wound through the crowd brought more attention than just his. She paused before the elevator. "I'll tell you a secret, Mr.…"

"Short," Milo replied. It was already automatic to say so. He'd decided to go ahead and keep the new, American-sounding moniker that he'd gotten accidentally.

Miss Adair went on, watching the elevator doors and tucking one errant curl behind her ear. "I'm getting fired any time now, Mr. Short. I'm quite sure that the only reason I haven't been told this news is because they need me to stand behind the counter and gush rapturously about all the various eaux de parfum until a new girl can start. In fact, I couldn't care less if I were selling tin cans of beans, which is probably why they're firing me."

The elevator door slammed open, and the dark-haired Miss Adair preceded him inside. "I might as well see you all the way to your destination, wouldn't you say?" She turned to the elevator man. "Ladies' coats, please."

"Please, don't do this on my account," Milo replied, loosening his collar and swallowing hard.

"No, no, I'm getting canned on my own account entirely, I assure you."

At the appropriate floor—Milo didn't even notice the number, he was too busy feeling ashamed of helping this pretty girl get sacked—Miss Adair preceded him out onto the floor. "Mr. Short? Are you coming?"

He hurried along beside her. Her low heels clicked along the shiny floor. "You see, I used to have a job I enjoyed very much. Only I had a few bad days and a boss who was none too indulgent, and so I was out on my keister and ended up a salesgirl."

"What job was that?"

"I was a secretary at Jerome Remick. Now that was a job. Seeing the performers come in and out, listening to the pianos all day, of course I did take more than my share of aspirin, between the typewriters and the pianos—"

"We've met before!" exclaimed Milo, gently touching her elbow to get her attention. She stopped indeed, looking pointedly from his hand on her arm up to his face. Milo released her arm and flushed. "I apologize. I just—I remember you. A few months ago, you were kind enough to explain to this naïve young man exactly what a song plugger was."

She squinted at his face and Milo felt a warming flush creep up his jaw. This close, he could see she was just about the same height as him. "Oh yes. I should have remembered: Mr. Short. What an interesting name."

"Used to be Schwartz." Milo did not elaborate on the circumstances of the change.

"I see, Mr. Used to Be Schwartz. You didn't get the job, alas."

"No, but I got another one down the block. I'm plugging for TB Harms."

"Well. Good for you. Now, the girls up here can help you find the perfect coat, and I'm off to resume getting fired."

"Thank you, Miss Adair. I hope you don't get fired."

"Oh, I wouldn't waste your hope on that. Because I don't think I mind at all." She'd begun to walk backward, though this meant the shoppers had to scatter out of her way as she went. "And you may call me Vivian, just in case we happen to see each other again someday."

BACK AT TB Harms, Milo presented the sandwich to Mrs. Smith with a flourish and a bow, then slammed his office door shut and about knocked Allen right off his seat with the shock of it.

"Watch it, would you? A fella can't even think."

"Sorry. Guess I decided to be extra energetic today." Milo propped the coat box in a corner, his mind replaying that backwards walk of Vivian the perfume girl, the dame sauntering away with the faintest smile playing over her lips.

"The hour that I first knew you were mine…" Allen mumbled.

"Gee, Allen, I didn't know you cared."

"Shut up. Trying to rhyme it."

Milo tilted back in his wheeled office chair and chanted the line to himself a few times. Then he sat up and blurted: "Softly came a melody divine."

"Heh. Not bad." Allen leaned forward to scribble.

"What are you up to, anyhow?" Milo stood up from his chair to come look over his friend's shoulder. From this vantage, he could see the pink of Allen's scalp through his wispy blond hair. In front of him on the desk was some manuscript paper, and a melody scrawled in smeared ink.

Allen looked around; though they were alone in their office, it had glass walls starting halfway up, and the blinds were open. "Don't tell the boss, eh? But in between plugging I've been working on something of my own. Only, I'm rotten with the words."

"You gonna cut me in on the credit now?" Milo walked away, shaking his head.

"You just became my lyricist."

"Wisenheimer."

Milo put his hands on the keys and played the song again Allen had just taught him that morning. He was already thinking of who might like to hear it. There was a new act that had been coming around looking for material, a boy-girl set of cousins from St. Louis… He said out loud to Allen, "This one might be perfect for the Debonairs, you think? I heard that they're auditioning for George White…"

"I wasn't kidding about the lyrics. Why not? You go around making up words to songs all the time, and you come up with rhymes without even trying."

"Ha, you did it just now."

"Must be contagious. C'mon, it'll be a few laughs, maybe. We'll work on it in slow times here, or maybe after hours."

"Where we gonna do that?" Milo continued to play, the tune settling into his fingers like they had a memory of their own. "I don't want to sit around here any more than I already do."

"My apartment. I've got a piano even."

"No kidding?" Milo paused the song. "Well, sure. After work tomorrow we'll make like the Gershwins and be rich and famous in no time."

"Ah, don't make fun."

"I'm not, at least not very much. But look, I feel so lucky just to get this far, I'm not gonna get my hopes too far up."

"Well, as long as you're sure of failure, we've got nothing to lose." Allen bent back over his music.

"That strategy seems good enough for the government, eh?" and Milo switched tunes on the piano: *"These so-called happy days, my friend, should like to drive me round the bend…"*

"Suit yourself, Short. I'm going to aim a little higher than that if it's all the same to you."

"It is all the same to me, now shut up so I can do the work I'm getting paid for." Milo switched back to the tune he was learning, for the Debonairs or some other hopeful musical act, also likely to fail but with a faint spark of a chance at stardom. It seemed to him that the whole system was powered by that little spark: his own job, plus the costumers, set builders, singers, actors, producers. He glanced around at Allen, hands still playing the tune, as his friend scowled over his song. *Hope away, pal. Keeps us all in business.*

8

1999

Milo

wake up like crawling out of a long, narrow cave.

Voices. Daughter-in-law, Linda: "Terrifying. The nurse found him curled up on the landing. He could have fallen down the stairs and broke his neck."

A voice I don't know: "Of course, that must have been terrible for you."

For you? I'm the one ... And I was on the floor?

Awareness dawns on me that I'm once again in that stiff, flat mattress hospital bed contraption. My eyes snap open the same moment I remember seeing Vivian, and worse this time, hearing her voice in my head. And next thing I knew I was on the ground and a young nurse with a blonde ponytail was interrogating me and checking me over and sticking me back in bed, at which time I crashed right back into sleep.

The people in my parlor don't notice that I'm awake right away, though, so I close my eyes again, to eavesdrop about myself.

"I am so sorry about this. We've already spoken to the nurse on duty, I assure you."

Oh no, I hope they didn't fire her. It wasn't her fault.

"I should hope so," Linda sniffs. "I mean, I realize he unclipped the alarm, but honestly, she didn't notice him walking up the stairs? This place is older than old and everything creaks!"

"Of course, you have every right to be upset."

"I just hate to see him like this. Just a couple of weeks ago he was so vibrant and active, like he'd live forever."

I'm not dead yet. You're all acting as if I'm three-quarters deceased.

"He may yet live a long time." This was said by the stranger. Head nurse I guess? Some kind of boss lady. And she didn't say that with any kind of reassurance. She pronounced it like a sentence of doom, and this makes me feel as cold as a corpse already.

I leave my eyes closed so I can better remember what that—vision, apparition, whatever, said. What Vivian said.

I just want to be heard.

But she was heard by me, boy was she ever. They could hear her in Hoboken, that one.

The nurse and Linda continue talking about my "care," like I'm a finicky house pet.

Why can't I just get back to normal? I swear I'll appreciate being able to get around without being watched, I'll make good use of my voice and be nicer to everyone, tell my kids and grandkids I love them all day. If only I could rid myself of this Vivian-vision, and...

What if? Now that's the ticket. What if when I get my voice back, Vivian goes away? I only started going crazy in this particular way since the day I fell, the day I saw this impossible Vivian.

I vow to myself to be nice to Marla when she comes by, and really look at her flashcards and things. I'll try to sing along with her silly songs, and when she says "Cat and ..." instead of looking at her like she thinks I'm an imbecile, I'll actually try to say "dog." I'll be a good sport for the physical therapist trying to make my good arm work. I can come back from this, sure as hell I can.

I open my eyes, then, and elbow myself up to sitting, feeling for my glasses on the side table. Linda rushes over. "Pop! There you are, oh, it's so good to see you awake and alert. You gave us quite a scare. What were you doing up? Oh, I'm sorry, I know you can't say. I don't mean to…"

The nurse I can now see is a gray-haired lady with tortoiseshell glasses and the severe shape of an arrow: all straight up and down. She interjects, "No, it's good to keep talking with him, asking him things. Don't treat him like a child. He will answer if he can, when he can, in what way he can, right, Milo?"

I nod, but I'm biting back a grimace. People these days are so familiar, right off. I can't get used to how people who barely know me, people half my age, use my first name like it's nothing. But I know this is one of the many ways the world has moved on without me.

I point to her and tilt my head, squinting my eyes a bit. The arrow lady gets me.

"I'm sorry, I didn't introduce myself. I'm Caroline Bates, and I'm with Companions Home Health, the agency providing the care for you now. You won't often see me, you'll see our care workers, but I promise they are all attentive and professional. The very best in the city. And we won't have another lapse like tonight."

"And you won't unclip the alarm and go traveling at night, will you?" Linda asks. The two ladies are like sentries, the boss with the glasses and Linda with her erect dancer's posture, which seems, impossibly, even taller and straighter than usual. "We'd hate to have you in a nursing home, but if that's what it takes to keep you safe…"

How dare she! This… girl, not even my own blood. I decide she's bluffing. No one wants to do that to me. She's trying to threaten me, like with her kids.

Still, it's safer, no doubt, if I play along. At least until all this is over.

Linda goes on, "I don't know why you were headed upstairs anyway, Pop. There's a bathroom on this floor, and you've got a little buzzer there if you need help and…"

I shoot a gaze up the staircase, trying to evoke longing, sadness. I never was much of an actor but I've sure seen enough stage people hamming it up to make like a copycat. It feels a little ridiculous, truth be told.

"Oh!" Linda says. "Oh, you miss your own bed, don't you?"

I nod, again with the sad face, though maybe laying it on a bit thick.

Linda says, more to herself than to Ms. Bates, "I wonder if we could get some movers to bring his bed down here? Could that alarm thing be used on his bed? We'd have to move things around, it's a narrow room here... Or hell, just walk him up the stairs at night. Esme used to do that before he fell, even. There's a bathroom up there, too."

The Bates lady is getting ready to speak, but Linda raises a slim hand to stop her. "He won't be clomping up and down the steps all day. Just like before, he'd come down in the morning and only go up at night. His leg recovered quickly from the stroke, after all. We're keeping him at home to keep him comfortable and in familiar surroundings. The hospital bed is overkill." Linda looks down to address me. "And you won't be trying these solitary journeys at night anymore, right, Pop?"

I shake my head emphatically. Hell no, if this means I get to sleep in my own bed like a normal person.

A slam of the front door telegraphs my son's entrance. Paul is a slammer, always has been. He comes around through the door and I can't believe he looks so old all of a sudden. He comes in and when he sees his wife he stops short, and something comes over him. It's a rigid posture that looks unnatural, but most of all it's the distance between them he chooses not to close.

Ms. Bates takes her leave to look over the schedule for my "care."

Paul stares at his wife a moment. Linda stands without speaking, her hands loosely clasped, and her face a mask of passive waiting. It's easy to imagine her in this posture in the wings, wearing her toe shoes, listening for her cue to come to life.

Paul approaches me and pats my hand like he's petting a snake and isn't too sure I won't bite him. Physical affection was never very much his thing. "You gave us quite a scare," he says, parroting his wife's words almost exactly.

Linda interjects to explain how I want to go back to sleeping in my own room. "Oh, sure, fine, whatever you want," Paul says, as if we'd asked for his permission.

And I'm tired again, suddenly, though I've been sleeping for who knows how long. So I lie back down and close my eyes. The good part about being close to ninety is that no one cares if you nap at any given time, all the livelong day if you want. Like a housecat.

I roll onto my side, too, on my left, which was the side I always slept on with my dear Bee in our big four-poster bed. I could see her sleeping form, rising and falling in the faint light from outside: the moon, city lights, lampposts, all of it, the constant seeping glow of the greatest city in the world.

"He must be exhausted," Paul says, but his voice has an absent quality to it. I bet he's looking at his little electronic scheduler whatsit.

"It's so strange." This from Linda.

"What?"

"How he seems to have recovered so well, in almost every way. He walks well now, his left hand can play the piano. His face isn't droopy or anything like that. But even with all the therapy, he's just made no progress. Not on writing or speaking."

"Well, he's old."

"He didn't seem so a few weeks ago. Are you listening to me? Can't you put that gadget down for five minutes?"

"Sure I'm listening, but what? What else am I supposed to do? We're already hemorrhaging money for all this. I'm spending as fast as I can."

"God, Paul. That's not what I meant."

"You'll forgive me if I've got it on the brain. Pop always acted like Short Productions would go forever, but it's not like magic, you know. We haven't had a hit in too long, and this…" A pause. He's probably waving his hand over me, *this problem here*, "… is taking a bite out of the one solution I had in mind."

"*The High Hat.*"

"Yes, *The High Hat*. Book and show, and what the hell? Maybe even movie. Can you see it? I wonder if Leonardo DiCaprio can dance."

"All our problems solved by a dancing DiCaprio? How convenient."

"You joke, but it would probably do the trick."

"You never talk like this in front of him."

"He won't listen anyway, is why. Anyway, I'm not talking in front of him. He's out like a light there, and no wonder after his little adventure. Did you threaten him with the nursing home?"

"I mentioned it, yes, though I got no pleasure out of it. I'm not ready to parent your father. I do that enough with my parents."

"Oh come on, you love being in charge of everything."

"That's not fair and no, I don't. Hardly. But it's not like I have much choice."

Their conversation devolves into bickering, and I've gone from a harmless, sleeping elderly stroke victim to something even more insubstantial. They don't even concern themselves now with waking me.

Their argument breaks off quick, like a tape reel that's snapped. I hear the quick clicking of a woman fleeing in pointy heels. I wait to hear Paul's footsteps follow, but instead I hear him flop into one of those chairs by the fireplace, and he doesn't move.

Go after her, I'd like to say. Make up, apologize even if you're right, because so what? This little argument is worth so much to you? I'd say the same to her. Who cares who started it?

I care.

You again. Go away. Are you a dybbuk now? I've heard the stories.

Ha, a shiksa like me? I hardly think that's allowed.

You're nothing. You're stroke damage in my brain.

I'm nothing, am I? So why am I the only one you can talk to?

I scrunch my eyes tighter shut, resisting the urge to plug my ears with my fingers, knowing that it won't help.

9

Eleanor

spot Daniel from halfway around the pond. He moves with pacing energy, slicing along the path in his severe dark clothes. When he picks me out of the crowd he brightens, that look of "There you are! Happy to see you!" that was always one of my favorite things. Now this brief zing of happy comes with a fresh crack across my heart, and I am starting to believe this is not worth it. This generous emotional support, this thoughtfulness and consideration held out from a distance by an outstretched hand with no obligation or promise, with him only lingering at the doorway of my life—it's worse than a Daniel-shaped absence. Perhaps that is only bravado. I haven't been brave enough to test it.

"Hey." He grips me around the shoulders in a brief hug before falling into step, matching my unambitious amble. Joggers trot past. Nannies, mothers, and children flow around us like leaves on a current.

"Going to see Grampa Milo today?"

"Yes," I answer, patting my shoulder bag with its notebook and tape recorder, though why I'm bringing the tape recorder I'm not sure I could even explain, considering.

Packing my bag this way did feel more solid and believable, as if I'm a real reporter on the job and not just a kid following her uncle's orders. My spurt of chutzpah in taking on this book has been thinning out by the day, and it's only the humiliation of calling to change my mind that has prevented me from doing just that.

"I'm in over my head," I tell Daniel.

He waves his hand over the empty space above my skull. "That's not exactly hard, Shorty."

I elbow him lightly. "I'm not that short. Just compared to you."

"Anyway, it will all work out. It always does."

I don't even bother to reply to this. I used to waste my breath correcting him: me with the absent, rejecting mother and dead father. He'd counter with a heap of small disaster predictions that never came to pass. Maybe his point was that my orphaning was a weird outlier, an exception to his blithe "always." Or maybe he thinks because I'm still walking and breathing, this too has "worked out." Just now I'm tempted to ask if things "work out" for suicides, but that could alarm him uselessly. It's not nihilism as much as scoring rhetorical points. Only in my head, though, which I suppose makes those points somewhat less than rhetorical.

"Ellie? You in there?"

He used to ask me this all the time. I reply with my usual answer: "No, but you can leave a message."

"I really mean it. That you can do this book. I know you think it's just me being glib, but it's true."

He's answering as if he can read my mind. After two years together, I suppose he can.

He goes on, "You're a great interviewer, and look, this is your grandfather. It's not like it's going to be all hardball and stuff."

"Gee, thanks."

"I'm trying to be reassuring. I know the last time…"

I'd eventually told him about my freakout in front of the mother in Bed-Stuy. I'd edited the story to remove the exact reference to the timing. Not so much to protect his feelings. I just didn't want to endure his agonizing apology that would churn up that whole day again.

"I know," I say, letting him off the hook. He's not even mine anymore, no reason he should be on that hook in the first place.

"It's not like you were bad with tough interviews, anyway. You just needed strategies, is all. Eye contact, rehearsing how it would go mentally beforehand."

"No more coaching, thanks. Anyway, that's all over."

"Why? I mean, after this book, your name will get back out there…"

I tug on his elbow to stop his walk so he will face me. "Didn't I ever tell you how I got into this magazine thing in the first place? Eva did it. I was all set to do another summer making copies and answering phones at Short Productions, having a blast and staying out of the way. I used to tag along with Grampa when he went to check on shows in rehearsal, or at auditions, and that was the best, watching something creative get born right in front of my nose. But then Eva said I was 'wasting my talent,' and went and got me a magazine job with one of her college friends. It was the same thing, making coffee and such, but they gave me little writing assignments, too, about cosmetics and new romance novels. And then Naomi all but wrote my resume for me, did all the work preparing my clips on sheets of paper—I mean, she probably had Shelly do it at the office—and she got me my first freelance assignment after I graduated, interviewing some tech startup guy she dated once. All because Aunt Rebekah happened to read an essay I wrote for sociology and said I had a way with words. All because I didn't want to be a little Junior Naomi in pinstripe suits sitting in human resource meetings, and I wasn't sure what else I wanted to do. Don't ever say you're 'not sure' in front of my cousins. It's like chumming the water."

I turn toward a bench facing the glassy stillness of Conservatory Pond and flop down.

Daniel settles down on the bench next to me with a strange, unnecessary level of care. "All I'm saying is that you'll be great at whatever you want to do, Ellie. Whenever you figure that out."

I lack the energy to argue. It just ends up in this crazy loop where I say things about myself meant to be reality checks, and he keeps marshaling his ninny optimism, until I'm painting myself as a drooling nincompoop and he's awarding me the Pulitzer. I suppose it's meant to be nice, but you know what else would be nice? If someone listened to me.

I lean back on the bench and bump into Daniel's arm, which had been stretched along the back. He lifts his arm out of the way, crosses his arms over his chest. Not so long ago he would have wrapped that arm around me, stroking my shoulder with his fingers.

I watch a mother pick up her crying toddler. She covers the child's sore elbow with tiny kisses like bird pecks. My mother may have missed years of my falls and scrapes and mishaps, but I know who was there to pick me up, alongside my dad. My Grandma Bee, and Grampa Milo. I take in a deep, fortifying breath and then beam out a prayer of sorts to the memories of my grandmother, my dad. *I'll be good to him, I promise. I'll do my very best.*

"Hi, Grampa."

Grampa Milo looks up and waves at me, with his fingers opening and closing like a child who doesn't quite know how to do it yet. He seems downcast and frail, even more than he'd been right after his collapse.

When Esme let me in, she warned that "Mr. Short is not feeling in spirits today," and raised her dark eyebrows in an ominous look.

In the corner of the room sits one of the day nurses, reading a book. I'm hoping she'll step out and give us privacy, but she doesn't even seem to have noticed me.

I settle in the other embroidered chair, which remains in its new, closer position to Grampa's chair. The rug still holds depressions from the chair's former position, after all this time. "So, Grampa, did Uncle Paul explain to you about the book?"

His gaze appears to be on the floor ten inches in front of his feet, which are in slippers. He's always worn shoes in the house, and nice ones, too, having often said that his first purchase for himself after his first big hit was a decent pair of shoes. I'm about to repeat my question, when I detect a slow nod.

"I hope it's okay. I promise I'll do a good job. People are interested, you know. Why should we keep all those great stories to ourselves?" I had already decided to leave Naomi and her less-sensitive plan out of the picture. Grampa loves her, too, I know. Every brash, ambitious inch of her.

He turns his head slowly to face me, then gestures to his face. He shrugs, and turns his gaze back to the same spot on the carpet.

"Oh, I know, Grampa, but your voice will come back. Meanwhile, we can do a lot with yes or no, and gestures, don't you think? And Uncle Paul gave me a list of people to start with, you know, your friends who are still... I mean, those who... Oh hell, this is off to a flying start, isn't it?"

I'm rewarded with a sly smile.

I hadn't phrased it right, anyway. It wasn't a list of not-dead-yet friends. It was a list of relatives of those friends. Nephews and sons and grandsons. Most of the primary sources had gone ahead of Grampa to whatever there is after death. Of course there were younger people who had worked with him, but everything about the far past, the parts of his life that Grampa Milo always waved away with a grimace and a shrug? All of those people are already pushing up the daisies.

"I know you weren't always crazy about this idea, but I won't do a bad job, honest I won't. I'll be respectful."

No reaction. Maybe a nod, I can't even really tell.

"Excuse me a minute, Grampa. I have to go get something I'll be right back."

When I hustle across the entry, I interrupt Esme in the kitchen. She startles and turns away from the window, and that's when I notice a cigarette in her hand, near the cracked kitchen window. "I'm sorry, miss. I know I'm not supposed to. Just once in a while, when I feel worried… I felt so bad the other day when Mr. Paul said he smelled it. It must have been in my clothes." She stubs it out in the sink and closes the window.

"What did you mean when you said he's not in spirits?"

Esme sighs and bites her lip. "He had a burst of good mood last week, where he was working hard with the therapist on his words, and smiling at the nurses. He brightened up at Mrs. Linda's plan to let him sleep in his old bed again. But one night he seemed to get frightened, then very agitated, and tried to … push something. But just the air. There was only air. I was bringing him a drink while the nurse was in the restroom, and I was glad it was just me."

"Why is that?"

Esme looks over both shoulders, then leans across the kitchen island. "I'm afraid Mr. Short might be seeing things. And I'm afraid if Mr. Paul sees it, or the nurses, they will think he needs to be in the hospital. And I think that would suck the last of the life out of him, to be away from his home, from Mrs. Bee's home."

She straightens back up. "He has not done that again that I have seen, and no one else has noticed. But ever since, he has been sad and quiet and won't work with the therapists anymore. It's like something is vexing him, something even more than the not speaking."

"And he can't explain it to anyone. How terrible."

A chill crawls across my neck, though the apartment is stuffy in the summer heat that creeps in each time someone opens a door. It's more than terrible, it's eerie. Like a curse.

"This is ridiculous to do a book now. I must be out of my mind."

"What book, miss?"

"Oh, never mind, I'm just mumbling to myself. Thank you, Esme. For telling me this."

"And miss, please don't tell anyone what I saw Mr. Short do. With the pushing air. I'm worried for him to end up in the hospital, and of course Mrs. Linda would be upset with me if she knew I saw but did not say. I would speak of course if I thought the hospital would help. But I think... I think that it would not."

"Well said. I think that it would not, indeed."

"And I'm so sorry about the smoking. I promise I won't do it in the house again."

"Well, it's not *my* house, so I don't much care as far as that goes. But it's probably wise, for the sake of your lungs if nothing else. I won't tell, don't worry."

I step into the foyer, where I can see the back of Grampa Milo's drooping white head. I'll have to wait for the interviewing. Another day, when perhaps he is "in spirits."

As I say goodbye to Grampa Milo—I can't help but wonder each time if it will be the last—a worry squirms into the back of my mind. What if he was "pushing air" and pushed something else and was hurt? What if he became a danger to himself, if he's getting agitated at nothing? Was he hallucinating?

What if a terrible thing happened, and I helped it happen with my silence? Though, if I told Aunt Linda, she might fire Esme for not saying anything earlier.

If I've learned nothing from my aborted career as a journalist, I know this: the way forward is only obvious if you blind yourself to half the facts. When you fully think through both sides of an issue as a reporter should, when you can actually understand and believe all of the arguments for going one way or another, decision-making becomes impossible. After all, either path could lead to disaster. Maybe half-ignorance is where bliss truly lies.

I let myself out and realize I've left my carefully packed bag behind, with its useless recorder and fresh clean pad of paper. It hardly matters; they are props for a charade, and I'll have to resume the charade another day.

I SPEND THE next weeks dutifully going around to apartments around the city, and sometimes borrowing Uncle Paul's town car to motor out to the suburbs, visiting with those who had a touchstone with the past. When I can blot out the strange circumstances, I can almost enjoy these interviews.

Then someone will make a remark, like how very much I looked like my grandfather, and it crashes back over my head.

Uncle Paul was right about one thing: there is an advantage to my family name. Everyone is forthcoming to Milo's granddaughter, telling anecdotes and sharing remembrances, and digging out old photos. In talking with a frizzy-haired twenty-three-year-old about her grandfather, they forget that their words will be typed up in a manuscript and printed thousands of times. That's always when the good stuff shows up.

On a late August day when a cool wind whips up some early withered leaves amidst the usual street trash blowing around, I take the subway to SoHo, to meet the son of my grandfather's old songwriting partner. He might help me solve a mystery of sorts: why Grampa Milo stopped writing after his one huge hit show, to devote himself entirely to producing. He always said it was a matter of not ever being able to capture lightning in a bottle again, and not wanting to follow up his best work with a flop. That was the Milo Short line on the issue, and I'd never had the opportunity—in fact, never had the urge—to pry before.

The subway crowd spits me onto the sidewalk, and I consult my scrawled directions to the loft apartment of Jerry Allen, son of Grampa Milo's long ago composing collaborator, Bernard Allen. Jerry's building is a former cast iron factory now built into trendy loft apartments.

Jerry himself answers the door, a pink silk scarf draping casually over the shoulders of his unremarkable white dress shirt. "Well, if it isn't the Short family scion, do come in."

"Hardly a scion, and hello, it's nice to see you again."

"I'm not sure how I can help you exactly since I'm not my dad, but I will do my best to assume his persona while we speak. Which means I should be two and a half sheets to the wind and wobbling on the piano bench right about now. But I'm trying to cut back on my drinking while the sun is up, so we'll have to fake it, what do you say?"

"I say that suits me fine. Great place, here." The ceilings are high, the wood floors gleaming, and two walls of windows drown the room in sunlight.

He waves his hand as if to dismiss its existence. "Eh, it's not bad. My partner prefers it down here, but I'm old-fashioned and mostly just old, and I'd rather live uptown. ... Have a seat over there, if you would."

He points to a modern white couch that looks like it's folded from stiff paper, but is surprisingly comfortable when I perch on the edge of its pristine surface.

"Tea?"

"Sure," I answer, just to give myself a minute to organize my thoughts, though I'm afraid to stain the couch with tea. I always accept when a beverage is offered at an interview. It makes a pleasant bridge into the business of the day, and it creates a small domestic bond, if only for a few minutes.

There's a grand piano near the window, and I am drawn to the photographs propped on its glossy surface. As I grow closer, I can see that rather than the show-off celebrity photos I would have imagined—Liza Minnelli, Patti LuPone—they are all intimate candid shots of friends and family.

And there's Grampa Milo, looking his usual dapper and gregarious self. In the picture, he's laughing, a three-quarter view of a great guffaw, standing next to Bernard Allen and a large broad-shouldered woman who might be Mrs.

Allen; I'm guessing the picture is from the '50s or so. He looks comfortably middle-aged here, fortyish, with merry crinkles by his eyes and only the faintest glints of gray in his hair. The dapper look, I know, is entirely a function of his clothing, which was always finely made from the day he could afford it. Coming from a family of tailors, he knows the value of a good suit. But without the suit, if one should happen to catch a glance of him, he's actually a funny-looking fellow with features a bit large for his face and his hair never quite behaving, no matter how often he has it trimmed.

"Ah. You've seen my gallery, there. I'll get you a copy of that picture."

"Oh, that would be wonderful, thank you."

We get through the usual pleasantries, Jerry asking after Grampa and promising to visit, then we move back to the couch and chair.

Jerry is all charming host, but he's stiff and won't look me in the eye.

My recorder has got plenty of batteries and a fresh tape. With that in mind, I put away my notebook and pen, and angle toward him like we're two pals having a nice chat. He relaxes right off, as I figured he would, once I put the pen and pad away.

Jerry is telling some story about his dad that had little to do with Grampa Milo, but I've got nothing else to do this afternoon, and I'm in no hurry. In a lull, though, with Jerry gazing out over his piano, but not focused anywhere in particular, I blurt my question.

"Why did they stop writing? Together, I mean?"

"Well, my dad drank himself to death, one reason."

I blink hard, and shift on the couch.

"I meant before that. There were many years before that." Poor Bernie Allen. He could never get back the success of his one big hit, try as he might. Hollywood ate him alive and he fled back to New York, where he wrote flop after flop for the stage.

Jerry doesn't answer, and goes to his little rolling bar cart. "You want something?"

I shake my head and purse my lips to keep from filling the empty silence. That's one of the few tricks I've picked up: don't fill the silence. Let your source do it.

"You're going to sweat this out of me, eh?"

I laugh, but it comes out high-pitched and nervously girlish.

Jerry shrugs, walking back with the ice clinking in his amber drink. "I don't know for sure. But something happened way back then, I'm sure of it. Something between your grandfather and my dad that made them both quit. I mean, they could have found other writers if they didn't want to work together. Look at Richard Rodgers, going from Larry Hart to Hammerstein, and he did okay. It happened all the time. Except maybe for the Gershwins, God bless 'em. But that's brothers, and there's not much that can break up brothers, short of a brain hemorrhage, and hell even then, Ira kept writing." He raises his glass, toasting the poor young George Gershwin, cut down in his prime.

"So you think it was a breakup, then. Not just that Milo didn't want to write anymore."

"Who doesn't want to have a second success? You know any baseball players that quit after winning one World Series? Any opera divas who decide one perfect aria is enough? It makes no sense."

"But that's what he always said."

"I know that's what he said. But I don't believe him."

"Are you saying he's lying?"

At this Jerry settles back in his chair, crosses one knee over the other, and looks at me wearily, down his aquiline nose. "Are you writing a book, or are you writing an ode to his greatness?"

I flinch away from the judgment in Jerry's expression.

"Hey, look, I didn't mean to sound so tough. I know he's sick, and you love him, hell, we all do. Everyone loves Milo. And they should. Even my dad never stopped being his friend, even though they couldn't work together, but listen, if you're going to write a book you have to hear it all, not just what makes you feel good. And now I'm treating you like a child. Your dad, rest his soul, would probably kick me in the keister."

I glance at my dad's watch on my wrist with its big, friendly numbers that he never had to squint at, even when he wasn't wearing his glasses. "He'd probably agree."

"So, you want to hear my theory, or what?"

"That depends. You going to fix me a drink after all?"

"Now you're talking, toots."

At this I laugh. "Toots? Really?"

"I was watching some old movies and maybe the lingo is in my head. Your call made me feel nostalgic. Some of Dad's Hollywood stuff wasn't so bad, really. He just couldn't take it out there, the way they acted like songwriters— the songs themselves—were nothing."

"Grampa didn't like it there, either, I remember. I think he only went once, and didn't even finish the movie."

"Well, and he had that sick sister. That didn't make it any easier. If they had to hurry back for a problem, can you imagine? Days on a train." Jerry walked back with the drink. "Cheers to the bygone days of Allen-Short."

I raise my glass again. "Tell me what you remember, then. Tell me what you think."

Jerry takes a long pull of his drink and plunks it down. "Okay. I'm a rambler, so bear with me.

"After *The High Hat*, my God, were they flying. I was only a pipsqueak then, but I remember my father coming in late from these parties where he was schmoozing all the famous people. I remember moving uptown, and crying because I was going to miss my friends down the block. My mother used to tell me all the time how my father would twirl through the door, right through the door like frigging Balanchine, grab her by the waist and spin her around to music only in his head. But then Milo only wanted to produce other shows, instead of writing their own, and as you well know he was pretty damn good at sniffing out a hit. Somehow he just knew, as the great ones always do. Anyway, as I got older, I saw my dad around home more and more, but it was like he grew into the piano. He was sitting there when I left for school, and sitting there when I got home, his ashtray overflowing and a bottle beside him growing more and more empty. The angle of the sun when I got home used to light up those bottles and for a while I thought it was pretty, because I didn't really get what was happening.

"So, now I've never told this story before, so listen up. Get your notebook back out. I was, what, sixteen years old, I guess, when I told the teacher I had a headache and left school early. I was always a rotten student. My mom was out shopping, and the other kids were still at school. And I come in the door, and without even really noticing, I was whistling 'Love Me, I Guess.' You know it, obviously. That song had legs; people kept recording it for years. My dad hollered at me. I couldn't believe it. My dad was nothing like a yeller, ever. But he hollered at me to 'quit whistling that goddamn tune' and said 'that goddamn Short cut me loose and let me drift and it's all his fault.'

"I was scared, I tell you. I froze right in the middle of the room. He hadn't shaved, and he smelled bad. I don't think he'd bathed in a long time. He was so puffy, too, and looked sorta yellow. Now I know it was his liver giving out, but I didn't understand then. I'd never heard him talk bad about Milo before, so that made me stick around, instead of running back out the door or hiding in my room. So then he tells me, 'It was all because of that broad. She ruined Milo and ruined everything. She made him nuts and ruined him and that ruined me. Look how ruined I am!' He banged the keyboard then with his left hand, and these deep, booming clashing notes came out, and seemed to startle him as much as me. It was like he suddenly remembered who exactly I was, who he was talking to. He shook his head, real slow, and started plinking out notes like he did all day, every day, all the time, looking for a song that would never come."

I let out a breath I didn't realize I was holding. "Then what?"

"Nothing what. I scooted away to my room, and put on an Elvis record and tried to pretend I hadn't heard a thing. Two weeks later he was dead."

"I'm sorry."

"That was years ago, of course, but thank you."

"I wonder who that could have been? The 'broad'?" The old-fashioned word feels strange in my mouth. Grampa Milo always said Grandma Bee was his first and only love. It was family legend, affirmed at every anniversary, every time someone else got married, anytime weddings came up in conversation, for that matter.

"That I don't know. But you're literally writing the book, so I hope you can figure it out. I've always wondered, all these years."

"Why didn't you ask him, ever? My grandpa, I mean."

"Well, I was a kid, wasn't I? I was just some kid and I wasn't about to go grill the famous impresario about why he'd let some broad ruin his writing and drive my dad to his early death. Then I got older and I still wondered, sure, but what did it matter then? My dad was gone, and honestly, he picked up his own bottles." Jerry waggles his drink and the dregs slosh. "Same as I do my glasses."

I take a sip of my own drink, watery now from the ice. "Then why tell me now? If it doesn't matter."

"Because you asked. Because you seem like you really want to know, because I'm getting old myself and things I never knew are starting to bother me. Because I'm starting to wonder if it could happen to me."

"If what could happen?"

"If I could be ruined by someone else. See, we like to think we set our own course, but that day, drunk at the piano, my dad told me how your gramps and some lady were at the wheel and steered him into the ditch."

I straighten my spine. "As you said, he picked up his own bottles."

"That's right. As I said."

The loft door swings open, and a younger man strides in, how much younger shocks me. The wiry rope of his arm muscle is visible all the way to where I'm sitting on the couch. His dark hair flops forward as he bends down and kisses Jerry full on the mouth. I glance away, then feel stupid for doing so. But it wasn't squeamishness that made me look away. It was the possessiveness, with a dash of aggressive intimacy: *I'll kiss him if I want, and to hell with you.*

Jerry sighs when his boyfriend lets go of his face and disappears into the partitioned off bedroom at the far end of the loft. Jerry's face registers no love, no passion, no happiness. He looks tired, and haggard. The pink scarf has slipped down his arm. "As if he cares so much, him with his strange phone calls and coming and going at all hours."

"Oh," is all I can think to say.

"Yet I don't want him to leave, so I pretend I don't notice, and he goes along with the pretending that I don't notice. That's off the record, please."

"Of course. It's not your life I'm interested in."

"That makes two of us, dear. Cheers."

The entrance of the partner has ruptured the intimate cocoon we'd formed over whiskey and soda and memories of Milo. I begin to pack my things up. "I wonder if I could find her."

"Who?"

"The broad. The one that your dad thought ruined everything."

"Ask my mother."

I freeze with my recorder over the top of my bag. "What?"

"My mother is still alive and kicking. Well, alive anyway. She's a little nuts and not always herself, but you might catch her lucid."

"My uncle didn't…"

"Oh, he probably forgot her. She's so old most people assume she's dead. I mean, you did."

"You really think she'd know?"

"If my dad told his teenage son on a drunken rant two weeks before he croaked, it's entirely possible he was sober long enough to tell his wife at one point in the many years before that."

A voice sings out from the bedroom. "Jerry!" the boyfriend calls. "Could you send your little girlfriend home, please?"

Jerry sighs again and straightens his scarf. "I'll see you out, dear."

10

1934

Milo didn't register the knocking at first; he was too busy amusing his sister by playing on the piano whatever song came over the wireless on Bing Crosby's show, and doing his best—which meant scrapy and cracked—attempt at crooning. In his months at work, he'd gotten better yet at hearing a song, identifying it in a few bars including the key, then jumping into playing it. It was both parlor trick and damn good practice.

So the knocking was obscured at first by Milo tinkling away at "Paper Moon." Max and his father were next to him going on about the shop and how to make more profit without skimping on the parts that mattered. Leah coughed and laughed along with Milo's playing, though soon enough she'd get tired of the game and tell him to hush up so she could hear Bing.

Finally his mother called, "Moshe! Answer the door before they break it down!"

Milo hustled to the door wondering who would be knocking this time of night, and yanked it open to see his friend Allen, wavering on the doorstep like a sapling in a buffeting wind.

"Milo! Mrs. Smith gave me your address."

"If you just came from work, why do you smell like a still?"

"I didn't. I phoned her. She's a little perturbed with me because I interrupted her bath."

"Why does she have my address?"

"Will you invite me in already, or do you want me to stand in the hallway and have an interview?"

Milo waved him in, frowning through the introductions. Leah perked up: a real live songwriter! She wanted to know which famous people he'd met and Allen rattled off a list that Milo knew was at least half fabrication. Allen may have been recently promoted to junior manager at TB Harms, but he wasn't exactly rubbing elbows with Al Jolson.

Mrs. Short performed an obvious sniff in Allen's vicinity, and disappeared back into the kitchen with a curt nod. Max and his father nodded but resumed their discussion, poring over the accounts kept in Max's precise, tiny script.

For lack of space, he pulled up a chair close to the sofa in the far corner from where Leah sat swooning next to the wireless, and finally asked Allen what he wanted. Allen asked for a drink and Milo shook his head.

"Okay, like I said," Allen began, his hands working themselves into a frenzy as he talked, pulling at his own fingers, threading them through each other, kneading his own palms. "Like I said, Mrs. Smith told me where you live. That gal remembers everything she ever typed, I swear, it's uncanny. Anyhow, this is why I'm here. I got us a job."

"We got a swell job already."

"Not like this we don't." In the yellow light of the table lamp, Allen's eyes glittered and crinkled up with his gleeful smile. "I got us a job writing a Broadway show."

"What? Go on."

"Not kidding. Listen up: the big bosses were going to this party over at the

Gershwins.'"

"Wait—"

"Yes, those Gershwins. You thought I was lying just now when I told your sister I'd met them, eh? Now listen. So the bosses ask me to tag along, probably because I happened to be at the office later than anybody, course I was working on my own stuff but they were none the wiser about that part. So I call my wife and she's hopping mad because it's her birthday, but listen. So I'm there and I somehow get to talking with all these fellas, including one Max Gordon, and before you ask, yes, that Max Gordon. And he's telling us about this revue he's working on and how he wants to tear his hair out, how he had to fire two sets of songwriters, and he's only got enough tunes for half a show, only they open in eight weeks out of town. And no one wants the job, he rattles off names of every songwriter you can think of who all told him, 'Not on your life would I take that job.' But he's got enough money sunk in already hiring the cast and already building sets that he doesn't want to give up. Says he wants it to be topical, current, smart. I tell him, half-joking, but not all the way joking, that I'll do it. He turns to me and says, 'Oh yeah? What do you write, pal?' So I sing to him..." Allen paused, held up his arm, and giggled into his elbow, "...I still can't believe I did this, I think I was a little tight already. So I sing to him, 'Let's Live On Hilarity.' And he laughed! Said he'd hire me to do it if I could stand the situation."

"Stand what situation?"

"I told you. They open in eight weeks. They got a few tunes they can use, but they need almost a whole show's worth of songs, immediately. Yesterday, if they could. We'll have to work nonstop, then go along to the out of town tryouts to fix it up it as they go..."

"Where's the 'we' come in? Seems to me this was offered to you only, my friend."

"You have to do it with me. Write the lyrics. You wrote 'Hilarity,' didn't you?"

"Sure, and it was rejected by Harms and Remick and Berlin ... shall I go on? I'm not a lyricist, I just make up silly words. I did that Hilarity thing to humor you."

"Consider me humored. C'mon, you humored me into hiring a half-blind piano player."

"Are you quitting TB Harms to do this?"

"Haven't you been listening? They need this music pronto. Unless I give up sleep entirely, it's one or the other: a shot at writing a Broadway revue, or continuing to churn out sugary old-fashioned slop so that the lyrical geniuses over there can rhyme June, moon, and swoon."

"I'm just a plugger. There must be a hundred better lyricists than me who would jump at this."

"Maybe there are, but I don't want them. I want to work with you, and only you."

Milo became aware of silence filling the room around their discussion. The wireless was off. His dad and brother had stopped talking to each other and were now nakedly staring. Even his mother had come in from the kitchen with a dishtowel in her hands.

"C'mon, Allen. Let's take a walk"

"It's cold out there."

"It'll be good for the constitution. Let's go."

Allen took his wavering farewells, oblivious to the figure he cut with his ruddy face and alcoholic emanations. Only Leah was impressed by him, and she didn't know any better, hardly seeing anyone outside the apartment or the deli down the block.

Milo pounded down the stairs well ahead of Allen, who had to pick his way carefully, no doubt having to determine which one of the wavering staircases in his drunken vision was the real one.

Milo turned on him out in the sidewalk. "Whaddya mean by coming here to my family's place and saying all that?"

Allen's brow knitted up, and he bit his lower lip. "What? Offering you the chance of a lifetime?"

"Chance to give up a steady job for the likelihood of making a fool of myself and subsequent ruination. You saw my little sister in there, who thought you were so swell? How'd you like to see her coughing her guts out in a shack? My piano getting rained on out on the sidewalk after we all get evicted?"

"How'd you pay the rent before you got this job?"

"The shop was holding its own. But the landlord just raised the rent again, and people aren't coming in like they used to. We've got customers in the neighborhood but they can't always afford to pay us right off, and we aren't exactly putting their feet to the fire."

"All the more reason."

"I said, get someone else. Plenty of people could do it better."

"Even if I grant you that—which I don't—I don't care. I don't want anyone else."

Allen's words were puffing out into clouds in the frosty December night. Allen was staring right into Milo's eyes with such pleading and hope that it liked to break his heart.

"I can't."

"I won't do it without you. And my big chance will go up in smoke. Poof!" Allen puffed out a cloud on purpose then, laughing at his own joke, steadying himself on a lamppost. "Could you hurry up and agree with me? I think I'm sobering up, which is a deplorable state of condition to be in condition of."

"Why'd you go and get so liquored up anyhow?"

"I told you, I was at a party. And I stopped for a belt on the way here. Courage."

"You needed courage for the West Bronx?"

"What if I needed courage to ask you?"

Milo plunged his hands deep into his coat pockets. There was a hole in the bottom of the left one; he'd have to ask Max to stitch it up. "I still don't understand why it has to be me."

Allen grabbed the lamppost in both hands like he was going to throttle it, then regarded it with passionate ardor: "It had to be you, it had to be you, I wandered around, and finally found somebody who..."

Milo looked up and down the block to see if his neighbors were seeing this nonsense. He grabbed Allen's arms and yanked them down from the lamppost; it was surprisingly hard given his lubricated state.

"All right, Miss Marion Harris, that's enough."

"So you will?"

Milo looked up at the glowing windows of his family's apartment. "We'll be failures. You know that, don't you?"

"And what if we aren't? Jeez, Milo, if you thought like that before, we'd have never even met and I wouldn't be here bothering you now. But you showed up for that job that day anyhow."

Milo sang to himself, almost whispered, really, bits of the song that caught the ear of Max Gordon.

When a guy comes by to give you a dime, just say no to that charity! Tell us a joke, sing us a song, and let's live on hilarity!

"I think I could tinker with the rhymes a bit..."

"'Course you could, and you will, and it'll be a smash. I'm getting out of here before you change your mind."

And with that, Allen hustled off into the night, slipping in the slush but somehow not losing his footing, as if his ebullient mood had wrung the booze right out of his body.

Milo shook his head. A Broadway show, with him as lyricist. He'd just agreed to do it—more or less, at least he'd stopped objecting, which Allen took as a victory—yet it seemed as likely as having dinner with Clark Gable.

His brother greeted him at the door, talking low to him. "What is the matter with that man?"

"Other than being a little tight? Nothing at all."

"Was he offering you a job?"

"More or less."

Max shook his head. "Madness. You got so lucky to have the job you do, and now he wants you to throw it away on the stage."

"I'm not saying I would quit Harms."

"No? Two jobs, then?"

The rest of the family had drawn into their conversation. Milo felt surrounded, so he stepped down into the sunken living room and allowed them all to gather around him. By the end of ten minutes, he had them convinced he'd keep his job at Harms during the day and work on the show at night, with Allen, over at the theater.

Leah was enraptured, demanding to know who would be starring. Max harrumphed and sewed Milo's coat pocket. Yosef Schwartz nodded, and bent back over the ledger book.

Milo's mother folded her arms across her chest. "With all this working and songs, don't forget to eat."

Milo chanted to her,

> *Forget to eat, how could I! The food you cook is so good I*
> *"Can never stop 'til I'm stuffed to the brim*
> *And so fat they say, 'Why, it can't be him!'*
> *Perish the thought, I'll never forget to eat your scrumptious...*
> *uh..."*

Fish eye?" giggled Leah from her corner.

Max handed back Milo's coat. "Your pocket's fixed, genius."

THE NEXT DAY at Harms, Milo was whistling the tune to "Hilarity" as he sauntered through the door and hung up his hat and coat. He'd been thinking up new verses all night, seeing how he couldn't sleep anyway. He smiled broadly at the newest secretary, former Macy's perfume salesgirl Vivian Adair, who'd turned up to visit Milo at the office after she had been well and truly canned. Vivian looked up from her book she'd half-hidden under some files, and cocked one slim eyebrow at him.

That day she stopped in at Harms, Milo had been shocked to see her, but delighted. His gratitude for her long-ago advice to the aspiring song plugger caused him to think of her warmly, and it's not like her shapely legs and sparkling green eyes hurt her case. The other office girls had gaped at her suspiciously. Even the reserved Mrs. Smith had given her a long, appraising stare before looking down her nose again at her Corona.

Allen had been irritated at the disturbance when Milo brought Vivian into their little cubby of an office, and she didn't help matters by sitting on the edge of his desk, messing up his papers. She crossed her legs and tapped one foot in the air, as if to a rhythm in her head. That's when she explained her current jobless condition, and how she wondered if Milo had heard of any positions available? "I do so miss the music," she'd sighed. They were standing close enough—of necessity, in that cramped space—that Milo could see a tiny brown mole above her collarbone, and smell her aura of roses and tobacco smoke.

"As it just so happens," Milo replied, a grin spreading over his face, "a certain young typist just got herself hitched."

Vivian could type fast as a speeding train, which warmed Mrs. Smith to her right off. She landed the job on the spot. Vivian had been starting Milo's day on a pleasant note ever since.

Except today, when she regarded him with wide-eyed surprise, and shared glances with all the other secretaries.

Milo checked his reflection in the window in case he'd forgotten to put on clothes, or walked out with a face full of shaving lather. All normal.

He cast a sneaky look around for Allen, though he didn't figure on seeing him before the sun came up over the skyline after a bender like last night's.

"Milo!" bellowed Keenan, the manager, who'd blown through his office door like a typhoon. "You have nerve showing your face here now."

"Nerve? Sir, I don't have much nerve. In fact, I'm terrified right now. What gives?"

"I was under the impression that you and Allen are going to be big Broadway hotshots now and don't need to work in a dump like this."

Milo felt his blood rush right into his toes, and probably through his shoes and right out all over the floor. He looked down as if he thought he'd actually see it.

"Sir, there's been a misunderstanding…"

"Damn right there has. I want people here plugging our own music, not out there trying to get all they can for themselves."

"Hey, that's not fair. I'm here, aren't I? I'm all set to put in a good day's work, same as I always do," though Milo's heart sank at having to work without Allen. They'd gotten such a good system going, even after Milo finally sprung for some better glasses. Playing by ear suited him, simple as that.

"So is Allen crazy, then, for saying you're going to do this?"

"No, see… I want to keep both jobs. I'll just work on the show songs at night, is all…"

An unpleasant smile curled into place across Keenan's wide, pale head. "That so?" He pivoted on his heel, stomped back to his office and back out again, proffering a piece of manuscript out ahead of him as he walked, like a newsboy. *Extra, extra, read all about Milo Short's career going up in flames….*

It was a handwritten draft of "Let's Live On Hilarity," which they'd worked on in their office, during a slow, rainy afternoon.

"So," Keenan drawled, "you did this on your own time, did you? And just happened to leave it lying around the office?"

"Well, yeah, as it happens. That's exactly right."

"Far as I'm concerned, you quit this morning. Beat it."

"Wait, Mr. Keenan! I didn't—"

The door slam cut him off, and Keenan yanked down the window shade on his office door for good measure.

Milo turned to the gawking office girls. Vivian was glaring with murderous fury at the closed door of Mr. Keenan. Mrs. Smith had her hand lightly on her chest, her eyes wide. "Where's Allen?" Milo demanded.

Mrs. Smith just shook her head. "Oh, Milo," she said.

Vivian grabbed her coat and pocketbook. "I bet I know where. I'm taking a coffee break, Mrs. Smith."

Mrs. Smith protested, "Vivian, you can't just—" but Miss Adair was already pushing through the door and clattering down the stairs.

Milo scurried after her. "Wait! Just tell me where, don't get yourself in deep with Keenan, too…"

She banged open the door onto Broadway. "I'm so angry, I could spit. How dare they!"

She hadn't bothered to button her coat, and a gust flapped it open, pushing her dress against her, outlining her legs up as far as they went. Milo rushed to stand in front of her, to shield her from the breeze. He took her coat lapels and pulled them together, trying to button them for her. "You're gonna catch your death."

She batted his hands away and did her buttons up herself. "I bet he went right to the theater. He was so disgustingly proud he crowed all the way out the door about it."

"Which theater?"

In Milo's shock of the previous night, he realized he'd never asked where this supposedly brilliant show was supposed to be mounted.

"The New Amsterdam, I'm pretty sure he said."

She began to forge ahead through the crowd. "Vivian! I can get there myself. Please, go back upstairs. Keenan is in a firing mood and I don't think they'll take you back at the perfume counter. I'm begging you, kid, just go."

"Kid? How young do you think I am?" The heat of her anger was burning off, and now she gave him a lopsided smile of sorts, one corner of her rouged lips tipped up like a crescent. "I bet I'm older than you."

"Older than me or not, you look beautiful, now get upstairs, please, before I get you fired twice."

She gazed up at the building. The wind mussed her neat curls. "You know, I didn't want to come today at all."

"Bet you want to eat, though. Are you going back in or what?"

"Fine, Mr. Short. I'll go. Just pop Allen a good one for me, will you?"

Without waiting for an answer, she turned abruptly, causing two ladies with shopping bags behind her to cluck and shake their heads as she plunged between them.

Milo leaned against the building, putting his hands on his knees to stop them shaking. Leah had been up half the night coughing, and Chana Schwartz sat up with her, and Milo had listened to the cacophony, congratulating himself on not letting Allen talk him into quitting his job.

Milo pushed his hat firmly onto his head and sliced through the crowds as fast as he could manage without actually knocking people over. Over his shoulder he saw another theater that just last year had premiered a lavish musical revue, but now was a movie house showing *Tarzan and His Mate* for twenty-three cents a ticket.

He got to the front door of the place, and a great wash of stupid swamped him. He didn't even know how to get into a theater this time of day. The box office wasn't open. The front doors were locked, the lobby dark. How could Allen think he was capable of being a lyricist when he couldn't even find the door?

He walked around the block until he saw a side door on 41st Street, opening and closing to let in people in dribs and drabs. He figured no one would know him from Adam, so he sauntered up the block, trying to time his arrival at the door with someone else's entrance. This took him a few tries and he peered up and down the block for a policeman who might haul him off for loitering. But eventually a gal swung the door open hard enough, at the right time, that Milo caught it before it swung shut again.

He pulled his hat low as he snuck in, in case the girl should happen to look back over her shoulder. He braced himself for a scream if she discovered she'd been followed in by a stranger.

Soon enough, it was clear he needn't have bothered. People were rushing this way and that, no one going any particular direction. It put him in mind of ants after you kick over their hill.

He stood in the winding halls of this theater, not having thought of a next step, feeling the stupid creeping up on him again, when he heard that voice, that booming laugh that he knew was Allen, knew even more when it was accompanied by the careless tinkering of piano keys.

"When I get my hands on that schmuck…" he muttered, following the sound, ignoring a "Buddy, you need something?"

His trail led him to the wings, and the quickest way to Allen, from what he could tell, was to go right onto the stage itself, so that's just what he did. He burst out of the wings and onto the same stage where just last year, the lovely Tamara had performed "Smoke Gets in Your Eyes."

Allen's laugh cut off short, and he switched his light piano tinkling to villainous chords.

The house lights were dim, and the stage—while not lit for a show—was bright enough that Milo felt cornered by the dark, and confused. His bleary eyes finally sought out the stage's edge, and he leapt off into the dark, teetering on landing.

"What do you mean by quitting my job for me?"

The men who'd been laughing with Allen, and a pretty little thing Milo assumed was a chorine in this lousy songless revue, scattered like bugs in the light.

Allen finally left the piano alone. He had just enough beard growth to make his face look dirty, and his hair was sticking up in odd points, mostly on one side of his head. He still smelled like drunk, though his eyes were clear and bright.

"Hey, I thought you were with me. Last night…"

"I'm surprised you remembered how to get home last night, much less what I said or didn't say."

"I didn't remember. I mean, I probably coulda, but I slept in the office. That's how I caught Keenan so early. Things were a bit frosty on the home front yesterday, anyhow."

"I didn't want to quit! I was gonna work on the songs after hours, but then you went and got him so mad that I'm out of a job now."

Milo dropped onto the piano bench next to Allen, and plunked his elbows into the piano keys with a jarring, dissonant clang. Milo ran his hands through his own hair, gripping by the roots like he might rip it out, as the sickening echo rang out into the house.

"You know, you never even asked me how much we were gonna make off this gig."

Milo let go of his hair and pivoted just enough to see Allen from the corner of his eye. "Okay, I'll bite. How much?"

Allen told him, and Milo grabbed the edge of the piano bench. "No fooling?"

Allen laughed. "Nope, no fooling. You think Mr. Max Gordon is gonna pay you in peanuts? We're gonna do fine, I told you."

"Course if we fail, we might never work again."

"That's the spirit." Allen began to plink out ominous chords again, then swung into a jazzy rendition of "Hilarity." "So, whaddya say, pal? You said something yesterday about a better rhyme? I happen to know you've got nothing else better to do at this here moment."

"I came here to slug you."

"I know you did. And I did you the courtesy of sobering up first. Aren't I swell?"

"How am I going to tell my family I'm fired? Oy, my father. I've got to explain this to Keenan. Will you come back with me and explain it? Tell him I was always going to be loyal. Maybe he's cooled off enough now and he'll listen."

"Milo, what's your beef? You've got a job, and a job that pays well enough I saw your eyes bug out just now. And you don't have to report to that bully Keenan, and you can work anywhere and anytime you want."

"'Anytime' as long as it's right this minute, and all day and all night, isn't that it?"

"That's about the size of it."

"You've either ruined us both, or you'll make us famous."

"Probably both! Now let's get to work. Gordon is in a rush, seeing as he's paying all these people to rehearse songs he hasn't got. There's paper and a pencil right over there," Allen said, pointing with his head at a music stand next to the piano.

Milo hauled himself up off the piano bench, and walked with a resigned step to the music stand. He looked up to absorb the soaring grandeur of the theater and it hit him all at once, like a wrecking ball, that his brother had taken him to see the Follies here in '27. And now it would be his words filling up all this beautiful air, soaring out of some ingénue, or maybe even a star, dare he imagine?

He began to drum up some rhymes, then tried them out on Allen. Hours passed before he realized he was hungry, and by then it was three o'clock. He shook his head as if coming to from a dead faint, and violently started when he spied, a few rows back sitting in the theater seats, Vivian, her hair still mussed from the wind, her coat draped over the seat in front of her. She waved at him with a flutter of her fingertips and shrugged, smiling, by way of saying that she'd lost another job, and such is life.

11

1999

Milo

smile at my granddaughter as she walks in, a huge backpack hanging off her narrow shoulders. Bee would have fussed at her to have something to eat, and would have set about cooking her something. Bee could have employed a cook; we could afford it, of course. For a big enough party she would hire someone. But someone else should cook for family? Not on your life, she declared, and that was that.

Eleanor kisses my cheek, her hair tickling my face a little. She mostly misses my face actually, but she doesn't go back for a second try. Just as well. I'm worried I'm getting that old man smell. I mean, I shower and all, even if it takes me an age one-handed and a nurse has to hover outside the door, which is humiliating all by itself. But there's something about being in a bed or chair all the time that I think must create its own scent. Eau d'Invalid.

Eleanor makes small talk of the cooling weather, leaves turning, as she pulls a notebook out of her bag. She notes that Rosh Hashanah is next week and says she plans to come with the family to services. Her voice keeps trailing off and then she shakes herself back to what she was saying. Something's on her mind. Something more than usual.

"Grampa, I heard a name that might mean something to you. Vivian Adair?" The name hits me in the chest like a sandbag.

I can't help it. My eyes go to the window seat, the corner, the stairs, I know I'm looking like a crazy person, looking everywhere like this, but she keeps popping up. The other day I saw her at the piano, though she never played, so far as I knew. She was sitting on the bench, and her fingers were skating over the keys. She was looking down, her head tilted sideways like a curious child. She was wearing a glossy dress with fluttery sleeves, the waves of her hair covering her ears, her nose looking pert in profile. The nurse had been sitting right in the corner of the room, none the wiser.

"Grampa? What's wrong?"

I shake my head at Eleanor and shrug, like I thought I'd seen something and was mistaken. I smile, but I have to close my good hand tight to keep it from trembling, which will look strange to her I know. My heart feels like it's beating both harder and slower. Ominous drums in a film score.

"I know," she says, cringing, "you can't say exactly, but… Do you remember her?"

I bite my lip and look down at my knees, feigning an attempt to recall. This is also the perfect excuse to break my gaze away from my granddaughter's earnest eyes, which look even bigger behind her thick lenses—sorry, kid, you got that from me.

Why is she asking? Who the hell mentioned Vivian? Anyone in the city who would've known her is dead now, and that's sad but also just as well.

I look back and bunch up my forehead like, "Who?"

Eleanor looks down at her notebook, tapping it idly with her pen. "I was talking to Mrs. Allen. Bernie Allen's widow."

Oh jeez. Dorothy. I kinda figured she'd be dead by now, too. How on earth did she think to talk to Dorothy? I shudder to think what she might've said. I was never in her good books, after…

This is the precise reason I didn't want any damn biography written. Maybe I'll die before it gets published. Then they can put on my show and everyone will go see it as a tribute and they'll make a bajillion dollars and Paul and Naomi will be thrilled.

Eleanor's still looking down at her notebook. Now she's swirling doodles all down the margin. "She said her husband could never stand her for some reason, and that she was from Chicago?"

I swallow and shrug, to indicate I don't really know. Then I narrow my eyes, tilt my head. I'm getting good at telegraphing my thoughts with my face. Who knew I'd have to pantomime my whole life someday?

Eleanor gets it. She was always good at reading these little non-verbal things. Like with babies and toddlers, before they could talk. Eleanor would always seem to know what they wanted, sometimes even faster than their mothers. Drove Naomi and Eva crazy, I could tell.

She says, "She might not be important at all, but I was just curious. Mrs. Allen, and well, her son, seemed to think she was significant. In your early life. But you don't look like you even remember?"

I take a deep, slow breath, otherwise willing myself not to move, not to shift expression, not to betray a thing. I shake my head, sighing, eyebrows up, as if to say, *whaddaya gonna do?*

"Hmm. Well, maybe something will come to you. I'll ask next time, just in case. Well, then, I have this list of yes or no questions, to double-check my library research. Got enough energy for this?"

I'm so relieved to be off the Vivian topic that I nod emphatically, and lean forward in the upholstered chair.

Eleanor begins to ask. Her hair keeps sliding in front of her face, and she keeps pushing it back, until she finally ties it back with a hair thingy, sticking her pen in her mouth as she does this. The yes questions are easy, of course. When I shake my head no, it takes some doing to zoom in on what the wrong part is, but Eleanor asks enough details that she hones in on it quick. Smart girl, that one. She could be a superstar, career-wise, right there with Dr. Joel and businesswoman Naomi, though she's made it clear as crystal she doesn't want to be some executive in a suit. She might yet be that superstar, of course, though I overheard Paul saying she's not doing her journalism anymore. I wonder why he assigned her this book, if perhaps it was at least partly to give her a job. Well, why not? A family business should help the family.

Then Vivian is right next to Eleanor's chair. She's looking down, even, as if she's reading what's on the paper. The fright of this apparition so close to my granddaughter fills my head with a screaming white noise.

Don't touch her! I want to holler, though I'm not sure why that scares me so.

Vivian is wearing a brown wool suit, and a hat with a little piece of net coming off of it. She bends down to adjust her stockings, the net of the hat almost brushing Eleanor's cheek.

Eleanor looks up to me and I force myself to snap my gaze away, toward the piano. I pretend to be thinking, then cup my hand to my ear, waving my hand at her.

She pulls a sweater out of her bag, remarking lightly that she feels a sudden chill.

She repeats her last question, which I still didn't hear. I sink deeper into my chair. My breathing is fast and shallow, and the effort of trying to act normal while a ghost or hallucination or demon is hovering near my darling granddaughter is only making my old ticker pump harder.

A voice, that smoky voice, drifts into my mind: *I used to depend on you, Milo. And look what happened to me.*

I told you not to quit that job. I didn't ask you to follow me around.

"Grampa?"

Vivian perches on the arm of the chair now. If Eleanor were to sit back, she'd bump right into her. Through her? I've never seen the Vivian apparition get so close to another person. I have no idea what might happen—maybe not anything, since I'm probably just losing it, a stroke-damaged brain coughing up stuff just to make me crazy.

Vivian's voice again, purring: *You loved the attention.*

When you were nice, sure, who wouldn't?

That word, "nice." Seems to me it's usually used to describe a quiet girl, who will do whatever you like, without question. Like a loyal, devoted worker bee...

Don't. Don't you start. Leave her out of this.

"Grampa!"

I jerk my attention back to Eleanor, and that's when I realize I'd been staring just over her left shoulder, at the space where until one split second ago, there was Vivian. A movement out of the corner of my eye makes me startle violently. In an instant she's in the window seat, without ever seeming to have crossed the room. Well, why should she—it—have to walk?

"Grampa, you look terrible. Are you not feeling well? Can you hear me?"

I pantomime headache, fatigue. I grip my head, grimace, wipe my brow with my good hand, and in doing so notice I'm genuinely sweaty.

By this time the nurse is at my side, today a male nurse named Alejandro, who is taking my pulse.

"His pulse is rather fast," he says. "Were you talking of anything upsetting?"

"No, just boring stuff, like what year his first show was produced, double-checking the names of the co-stars... All stuff he's heard a thousand times."

"It's not your fault. I was just wondering."

Eleanor hugs herself tight. I've seen that gesture pass down from my children now to their children. My daughter Rebekah used to be famous for it. She'd told Bee that she started doing it on her first day of kindergarten because her mommy wasn't there to do the hugging.

Poor kid Eleanor never really had a mother for that, lousy woman taking off like she did.

Focusing on Eleanor, my flesh-and-blood, vulnerable granddaughter, seems to have distracted my mind from its own hallucinating. My pulse is calmer, I know, without Alejandro saying so, though he does.

He brings me fresh water. When I dare look up to the window seat, it is nothing but a lovely frame around a city scene: the fading green of early autumn, and pedestrians strolling by in hats and smart jackets.

I take in another deep breath and puff it out audibly, glad I can at least make noise of a sort. I snap my fingers so Eleanor will turn around and look at me again. I make a "sorry" face, and beckon her back.

"Grampa, were you really okay? I wasn't upsetting you, was I?"

I shake my head, hard as I dare.

"I'm tired of this for now," she says, dropping her notebook into her bag. "How about we just sit for a while?"

At this I nod, and smile. Alejandro has returned to his corner. He appears to be working diligently on something. Paperwork? Night school? Maybe he's writing up a detailed account of my attack of sorts.

I resolve to be master of myself next time the Vivian-thing appears. After all, what is it but a vision? She's not even real, and by this point I should not be surprised so much. If I keep reacting like this, I'm going to land myself in some kind of hellish combination of bug house and nursing home, not to mention upsetting every loved one I have who happens to witness my distress. Hell, there are worse things to see than a vision of a pretty girl. And don't I know it.

Eleanor gets up to wander across the room, and as I follow her progress toward the stereo, my gaze passes over Vivian striding toward me now. Same brown dress. No hat, though, and her lipstick looks a little blurred, like a photograph that didn't turn out right. Eleanor bends to look through some records stacked on a low table, and I turn my stare back to Vivian now, raising my chin.

I am also gripping the arm of my chair harder than I need, but what of it? *So you can look me in the eye after all.*

Her eyes are green, a deep gold green. People used to say she could be in pictures but until color movies were a regular thing, a person in a theater would never fully appreciate what she looked like, would never see those eyes the way

God meant them to be seen.

I steal a look at Alejandro. He's still bent over his work, chewing on the end of his pen.

I lift one eyebrow at her.

See? It's not so bad having me around.

Flash of memory: she said that once, in the New Amsterdam Theatre, out in the house seats. Back then I was writing the lyrics, trying to keep Allen dry long enough to write the tunes, all with the director breathing down our necks to work faster, faster, more songs, more songs…we had to throw out half of what we wrote. My stomach curls up in a pretzel just to think about it. All the while my father running out of money and trying to pretend like we didn't all know…

Vivian crosses her arms and stares up and away, like she's watching a performance beyond my head in the far corner of the room.

They're writing songs of love, but not for me… swirls into the air. Eleanor stands up from the record player and walks across the room. I nod to her; good choice. She's walking back to her chair, and that's when I see that Vivian is sitting in it. She's got her legs crossed, and she's smiling at me with a kind of playful, nasty glee I've come to recognize in these last weeks.

My resolve to play it cool is fading away with each step Eleanor takes. I can't explain why this panics me, but it does, and I make to stand up out of my chair, stop her, save her, and because Eleanor sees me start to stand, and so does Alejandro, they snap to attention like good little cadets and go right to my side.

An earthy chuckle, only for me.

I thought I wasn't real. Then what are you so worried about?

Go to hell, Vivian.

Beat you to it, Milo Short.

I point with my chin toward the piano. Eleanor and the nurse walk along next to me, each set of hands resting lightly under my forearms, until I reach the bench and they pull it out for me.

Eleanor switches off the music, and I apply my good hand to the keys. It's awkward like this; my left hand is used to harmony. But it's probably the only thing I've improved in the weeks since my fall: left hand melody. I play the first tune that leaps to mind, which happens to be the song that got me into the whole mess to begin with: *Herbert Hoover said he knew our bleak Depression wouldn't last...* But of course I can't sing the words. It's only Allen's jaunty melody that spills out of the old upright, filling up this tall, narrow room that's all too crowded lately, if you ask me.

12

Eleanor

The name beams up at me from the screen, the glowing pixels piercing my tired eyes. I take off my glasses, rub my face and the bridge of my nose, then put them back on. A long moment passes before the letters sharpen back to clarity.

This record came to me via genealogy research, helped along by a slight white lie that I'm researching the Adair family tree for a friend. My source, a lady named Joan from Springfield, Illinois, was overly apologetic she didn't know more, because this branch of the family was tangential to her own father's Adairs. Still, it was more than I had before: Vivian Adair, born 1909 in Chicago, died 1938 in some town in Michigan called Ludington.

Vivian never married.

One sister, Estelle Mann, née Adair, also settled in Ludington, who had one child, name of Millicent, who married and had one child, Alexander Mann Bryant. The records have little information about Estelle, other than that she recently died, and almost nothing on Millicent, either.

I do the math and note that Vivian hadn't even made it to thirty years old.

"So young," I whisper. I didn't realize how much I'd hoped to find her still alive until I saw that death date, and drooped under the weight of my disappointment.

Mrs. Dorothy Allen had been unnerving in her venom on the subject of Vivian Adair, all these years later. When I'd gone to interview her in the upscale nursing home in Connecticut, I'd imagined a doddering wisp of a creature, covered in papery wrinkles, tiny hands gnarled by arthritis. After all, Bernard Allen had been older than Grampa Milo, so his wife must have been older yet than my eighty-eight-year-old grandfather.

As I rounded the corner into her private room, I saw I was only partly right. Papery skin, yes, gnarled hands, somewhat, but broad and thick. Mrs. Allen, despite a slight stoop in her upper spine, cut an imposing figure, even from a wheelchair. She fixed me with a stare over the top of her glasses as I came in. She had knitting in her lap.

"What do you want?" she demanded.

I raised my chin and tried to remember Daniel's patronizing advice about exuding confidence. I told her I was writing about Milo Short, and that her son had told me something about a woman in Milo's life, around the time he quit writing lyrics.

"Vivian Adair," she'd sneered, drawing out the last name in particular, biting off the "R" hard instead of letting it fade softly away, as one might imagine for a Continental-sounding name. I asked her how to spell it, but this aged woman snatched my notebook right out of my hands and demanded my pen.

In penmanship that once was impeccable, now made shaky with age, and perhaps indignation, she wrote Vivian's name, with an added note: "Sister. From Chicago."

She thrust the notebook back toward me with the force of a dagger. Curiosity had swallowed my nerves by then. "You sound like you can't stand her. Why?"

"My husband"—she also sneered the word husband, I couldn't help but notice—"seemed to think she had something to do with why he and Milo never worked together again. He'd get drunk and rant and rave, and say things... I can't remember what things now, so don't ask me."

Her eyes seemed clouded, and I had an urge to reach out with a handkerchief and wipe them for her; they were leaky. All the same, those eyes bored into me, daring me to challenge her. I did not, in fact, challenge her to recall these rants. But there were a couple of other questions that needed asking.

"At the risk of offending you, I have to ask. Did Vivian and your husband have an affair?" I spit it out and held my breath, waiting for outrage.

"Ha!" she barked. "No."

"Or..." I tapped my pen in my notebook. "Maybe she and Milo...?"

"How the blazes should I know? Like I kept track of that rat's love life."

I straightened my spine at the "rat." I'd given Mrs. Allen my name when I made the appointment, with the aid of staff at the nursing home. I figured it was equal chance that she'd forgotten I'm his granddaughter, or just didn't give a rip.

Either way, I was none too disappointed to get out of there, and spent the drive back to Manhattan, in the back of Uncle Paul's borrowed town car, wondering what the hell all this meant.

My phone rings now, its metallic bleat so shrill into my quiet apartment that I yelp out loud, then chuckle at myself. I glance at my watch and blanch. I had plans with my old roommate Jill, who'd emerged from her law school torpor to make a happy hour date. I was a half-hour late already.

"Hi," I answer, "I'm sorry I'm late..."

"Oh, got a hot date, do you?"

Daniel. I should join modern times and get caller ID. "Oh, sorry. A hot date with Jill, if you count margaritas in Midtown as hot."

"Oh. I was just checking on you, and your grandfather."

I find myself rolling my eyes in impatience, wanting to get back to my computer and my notes. I can hear my dad's voice reminding me: *He's being kind. You should appreciate it.* Dad was so good at reminding me to consider others' good intentions. And it's true: breakup or not, Daniel was showing he cared.

I gave him a quick update, wondering if Jill had a cell phone, wondering if I should bother calling the restaurant to get a message to her.

"Hey," Daniel says. "You hungry? I could get Chinese at our usual place and bring it up."

Not once since the breakup has he suggested setting foot in this place again. I am hungry, I realize suddenly. Famished. I'd been so lonely in the immediate aftermath of the split, I'd have invited him up, tossed aside the food, and ripped off his clothes. A girl has needs, and I miss having wrinkles on more than just my side of the bed.

But I'm wearing a ratty Columbia shirt, pajama pants, and my breath smells like the onion bagel I had hours ago. Besides that, his sudden interest in spending time with me outside his ex-boyfriend mercy mission to support me in Grampa's stroke and recovery strikes me as a complication.

"No, thanks. I'd better catch up with Jill." It's easy to lie on the phone, even to him. I don't intend to see Jill, either. I'm going to order in and get back to my keyboard.

"Oh," he says, his voice rich with wounded surprise. I choose not to notice and hang up as soon as I'm able.

Back at the screen I reread the email from my genealogy source. Born in Chicago in '09. I wonder at the odd gaps in Mrs. Allen's memory. She knew this name, knew the spelling, but claimed not to know if Vivian had been dating her husband's best friend. She remembered Vivian had a sister in Chicago, but nothing else about her. In my last few questions before I gave up and left, I'd pressed her to elaborate on their connection, on the specifics of what actually happened. She could not, or would not, say. The most I could get from her was: "I don't think she *did* anything but cause trouble, and that's all I needed to know."

I was prepared to leave it alone, after asking Grampa Milo and getting answers some way or another—charades, yes/no questions, that alphabet board—and then moving on to more pertinent biographical details, like how exactly he landed that first revue gig, the *Hilarity* one.

But then Grampa Milo acted like he never heard of this girl. How could this be, when she was remembered so clearly, and with such venom, by his best friend and writing partner?

I was deciding, in the parlor yesterday, whether to question Grampa further on this point, when he seemed to have a kind of attack, staring at different points in the room, growing pale. I abandoned the interview at the time, but my train of thought since has hardly wavered.

Esme saw him "pushing" things. I've seen him several times now staring at nothing, especially yesterday, when talking of Vivian. Vivian, whom he seems not to remember.

I sit back in the desk chair, letting the screen blur in my vision, as I idly unfasten and refasten the strap on my father's watch. There's something about Vivian that disturbs my grandfather enough to pretend she doesn't exist.

13

Eleanor

duck out of the dining room into the gleaming white kitchen, breathing easier in the brightness of the space. Grandma Bee had redone the kitchen in the year before her heart attack. It's like she knew whoever used it next would want it updated with the latest appliances and bright, new finishes, though she herself was merrily accustomed to her comfy, outdated things.

I miss the old kitchen, much as this space feels more spacious and airy. I miss it because I could easily conjure Grandma Bee in here, smiling at me and kneading the challah. This new kitchen she barely got to use.

Esme has the night off; Aunt Linda and Eva have done most of the cooking. In other years I've enjoyed Rosh Hashanah. A new year in the fall has always made sense to me. Refreshing cool air, starting school. I relish the apples in honey, get chills at the sound of the shofar in the synagogue, and even enjoy the festive family dinners.

But tonight, I've had to endure pitying or interrogating looks from my cousins and Aunt Rebekah, having run into Daniel at the service. I nearly collided with him, in fact. I'd been looking down to my left, chucking the chin of one of Joel's twin baby girls. Daniel must have been watching my approach as he stood there on the sidewalk. "Shana tovah," he told me, and I clumsily replied, "You, too," so quietly he had to ask me to repeat myself.

My heart was still aching with the absence of Grampa Milo in the synagogue—having been deemed by the aunts and uncles as too frail to come— and so my farewell was distracted, and sounded pained, and I think my cousins have all interpreted this as enduring heartbreak. There was maybe some of that, too. It was strange, in any case, how avid Daniel's greeting was, his presence there at all. It was jarring in the midst of my melancholy about Grampa Milo's absence tonight presaging his absence forever.

Here now, at dinner, my grandfather is restless and sullen. He refuses to use the alphabet board, and grows impatient with our attempts to understand his gestures. A few minutes ago, his "good" left hand not particularly dexterous, he'd fumbled his wine and spilled it all over his lap. Eva was the fastest to get to him and begin mopping him up. I think I was the only one who saw the rough way Grampa Milo rubbed his face, so he could wipe away a tear without anyone seeing.

Eva barges into the kitchen hip first through the swinging door, hands full of red-stained cloth napkins. "Help me out here, El."

I wordlessly take a wad from her, as she heads for the fridge. "Is there club soda in here?"

I shrug, though her head and shoulders are in the refrigerator and she can't see me. It doesn't matter, anyway. She's only thinking out loud. She emerges with a can, holding it out to me. "Would you, hon? I just got my nails done."

I oblige with my short, unadorned nails and together we stand at the sink, pouring and rubbing. This is not a two-person job, not really, but I sense Eva is none too excited to go back in there, either.

"It's so hard," she says, scrubbing with fervor now. "I mean, he's almost ninety, it's not like he's gonna live forever, but…" She props her hip on the counter, and with her forearm pushes her frizzy curls out of her eyes. "Is it awful to say I'd rather he have just died in his sleep, rather than live out his life without control over himself?"

"No."

"You think it's awful."

"No, I don't. I'm just tired." People are forever thinking I'm mad at them, or critical, or depressed, when all I am is tired.

"And you poor thing, bumping into Daniel, that must have been a shock. I didn't even know he went to Emanu-El."

I smirk at this, as I set aside one mostly clean napkin. "He rarely does. He also called me up offering to bring me takeout the other night."

"Huh. This is a good thing?"

"It's a complicated thing and I don't want to deal with it."

"Relationships are complicated," she intones gravely, catching my eye. I catch her subtext clearly: *You just don't want to bother.*

After we have scrubbed every last napkin—and really, I'm sure we could have afforded new ones—Eva and I prop the club soda cans to fully drain in the sink and give each other a fortifying glance. Back into the fray.

Before we push through the doors, Eva grasps my elbow, her manicured nails pinching me a bit and forcing me to stop.

"And hon? Listen, he's a good kid, Daniel. If he comes back to you and says he made a mistake, will you give him a chance? People make mistakes all the time. If we could never correct our screw-ups, how grim would that be?"

Before I can answer, she grabs me around the shoulders, and for the first time tonight it occurs to me she's a little drunk. "Shana tovah, Eleanor."

Back in the insulated quiet of the Midtown apartment, I stare at the dark computer. I should go to sleep; I'm so tired and full and a little buzzed. But checking my email will only take a few minutes, and there's something I'm hoping to see.

It's been a couple of days since I looked up Alexander Mann Bryant online, and found him right away, where he's the director of a local community theater in Ludington. I printed a newspaper article, which stares up at me now from my desk surface. The muddy black-and-white printing shows a serious-faced young man staring meaningfully into the camera, a funny contrast to the obvious canned quotes in the article about how excited he is to be bringing *The Sound of Music* "once again" to the good people of Ludington. He hardly looks thrilled to be urging angel-face cherubs to chirp "Do-Re-Mi."

The theater website listed an email, and I figured, what could it hurt to ask? I'd sent something simple along the lines of, "Dear Mr. Bryant, I'm writing a biography of my grandfather, and it seems he may have known Vivian Adair, who I believe is related to your family. Do you know much about her? Eleanor Short."

I've checked my email more often in the last few days than I had in the previous month. I'm not sure what I'm waiting for, exactly. What would he know about a great-aunt who died more than half a century ago?

As I'm waiting for the modem to log on, I sort through my paper mail. There's a note in here from Uncle Paul. I frown at it, confused.

Dear El,

Listen, I'm not worried about the rent money. I know your freelancing is in a dry spell, and now without Daniel chipping in things might be tight. You're doing me a favor taking care of the place, it's an investment property anyway, like I always said. Hang in there, kid, and I know you'll do a great job on the book.

Paul

He's enclosed my September rent check, uncashed. I groan; he had to have known if he'd tried to refuse my rent check in person, I'd have refused his refusal. None of the Short kids coasted on our family money, at least, once we got our educations. I don't intend to be the charity case of the crowd. That's why he mentioned the book, obviously. A reminder that I'm not a freeloader in the long run. The advance money should be coming along soon, now that we've hammered out the fine points of the contract.

But as has been true all along, Uncle Paul could be raking in rent on this place from a proper tenant. For people who know me so well—who know I'd bristle about the returned rent check—they understand me so little. What I want most is to be taken seriously by them as a real grown-up person, not as their pet misfit. *Poor Eleanor.* Poor nothing; I'm plugging along, aren't I?

The Internet connection shrieks to life at last. Spam messages, goofy email forwards, political harangues, an exasperated note from Jill about me standing her up… Ah! AlexB1974@AOL.com.

> *Eleanor,*
>
> *The timing of your email is rotten, because Estelle, who was Vivian's sister and just about the only living person who would have known her, just died a couple of weeks ago.*
>
> *But the timing of the email is also kind of spooky, because of what Estelle told my mother, Millicent, before she died. My mom spent her whole life raised by Estelle—in order to speak nicely of the recently departed I'll just say that their relationship was 'difficult' and 'distant'—but it turns out poor old dead Aunt Vivian was her mom. See, Vivian was alone, and as Estelle put it, "It was a different time." Since Estelle and her husband didn't have any kids, they took my mom in and raised her. They found a friendly local doctor to put their names on the birth certificate and avoid public shame, and no one ever knew. At least until Estelle was about to meet her maker and maybe thought better of a lie that lasted longer than sixty years. Personally, I wish she'd just kicked it before she had the chance to throw my mom's whole life into the air like confetti, but we don't always get what we want. Obviously.*

So anyway, that's the Vivian story. Single mom, gave up the
baby to her sister, and died young. No one who knows the details
is alive anymore. That's not helpful to you I'm sure. Good luck.

Alex

I seize my papers and start rustling through them, looking for the genealogy printout, searching out Millicent's year of birth.

There! Millicent was born in 1937, when my grandfather would have been twenty-six years old, the year before he married Grandma Bee.

I look back at the email. Despite his belief that he was no help to me, Alex had typed his phone number, a few carriage returns after the sign-off.

The phone is in my hand, my fingers dialing before I even think to check the time. Eleven o'clock. Even on a Friday night, that's pushing it for a call to a stranger. Wait, what time is it in Michigan? Well, not earlier enough to matter.

I pace the apartment, pausing before the floor-to-ceiling windows, for lack of anything else to look at. I stare down at the glowing parade of headlights clogging the streets; shows are just getting out, couples are heading out for late drinks. Millicent doesn't know her father. Vivian was alone in Michigan, no man in sight.

It might not be the same person, I remind myself. All I've got is batty old Mrs. Allen's word that Vivian's family came from Chicago. There might be nothing more than a coincidence of name and approximate timing, assuming Vivian was close to Grampa's age.

So, why is my heart pounding?

I know now sleep isn't coming, not for hours at this rate. I waste twenty minutes channel flipping before I retreat to my bed with an earlier biography of Milo Short. I've been working through it, marking up facts and stories to confirm or correct, noting areas of his life I might explore in a different way, so I don't just copycat what's been done.

It's painstaking, and could very well settle me down. Instead of picking up where I left off, though, I instead flip to the glossy photograph pages, at intervals in the book.

There aren't many pictures from the thirties, but I study what ones there are, thinking back to my grandfather in the earliest days of his career, when he was not much older than I am now.

I've learned so far that he lucked into a job writing songs for a revue called *Let's Live on Hilarity*, when other songwriters failed to deliver. I've learned that it was mostly Bernard Allen's contacts that got them the gig, contacts he made through his job managing and composing at TB Harms. What remains a mystery is why my grandfather quit writing lyrics. I've got the songs from *Hilarity*, though not a script, and no recordings. Not even any still photos of that show survived. His songs are funny, sharp, the rhymes amusing and inventive. The lyrics don't age well, with all their references to Herbert Hoover and automats and such. But there's a liveliness that I recognize in my grandfather even today; well, until he collapsed.

Speaking of liveliness, as I turn past photos of the exteriors of buildings where my grandfather worked, and the Orchard Street tenement where his father first emigrated and where he'd have spent his youngest years, I smile at a picture of Grampa Milo and Bernard Allen in their prime. Allen's got one arm slung around my grandfather, and they're both holding drinks with their free hands. Allen's got that unfocused, woozy look of the tipsy, though I might be projecting, based on his reputation. The caption says it's a gathering at the Stork Club of people working on *Let's Live On Hilarity.*

I trace Grampa Milo's face with my finger, as if in a caress. Another picture from the same night shows him alone at a table, gazing at some point across the room, relaxed and pensive. I turn the page, then something makes me turn back and look at the photo again.

A woman with wavy dark hair is in the background of the photo, one arm across her chest, supporting the opposite elbow. In that hand she's got a cigarette balanced in her fingertips with the nonchalance of an era long before the Surgeon General's warning. A man in a suit leans in for conversation with the woman, but I can't imagine she heard a thing he said. She isn't even looking at him. Her expression is curiously intense. Her jaw seems clenched, her eyes slightly narrow. And she's staring straight at my grandfather.

14

January, 1935

"Geez, will you get a load of this place?" Milo took in the draping on the walls, and the vertical mirrored panels, but mostly, he was looking for famous people.

Allen jabbed him with an elbow. "Close your mouth, what's wrong with you?"

Vivian squeezed Milo's arm. "It's out of this world. Oh! I think that's Ethel Merman!"

Milo could barely keep his feet under him he was so tired, but back at the New Amsterdam, Allen had insisted that he show his face, since their producer, Max Gordon, wanted to treat them to drinks. Allen had hissed into his ear as Milo slumped over a music stand near the rehearsal piano, "Half of staying afloat in this business is staying in front of people's faces, people that matter. So they think of you later when they have work to give. Now look alive, Milo"—at this he raised his voice and slapped him on his cheek just lightly enough to be considered playful—"because we're painting the town."

Vivian had heard this last part and asked to come, too, and what could

Milo say? Allen's face had pruned up when he saw Milo walking up to him with Vivian on his arm.

In the club, having deposited their coats and hats with the check girl, Vivian excused herself to find the powder room and fix her hair, because the breeze from the walk over had disturbed her curls. Allen whirled on Milo. "Why is that dame here? They almost didn't let us in out there because Max had only put in a good word for us two. They don't let nobodies into the Stork Club unless a somebody wants them here."

"Because she wanted to go and I've got nothing against a pretty girl on my arm, and apparently the man with the golden rope out there didn't mind the pretty girl, neither."

"She's got no business being around this show at all. She's distracting."

"Oh, go on. And why are you talking to me about distracting? I gave you the words just yesterday for the torch song and I'm still waiting for the melody for that dance number they added. I can't write the words if I don't even know how many beats to a phrase. Can you give me that much, eh? How many? Seven and a rest? Gimme a hint, I'm begging you."

Allen snorted. "I just don't understand why she's got to be underfoot all the time. Even that chorus girl who took a shine to you doesn't follow you around half so much. I should be so lucky."

"You're a happily married man, now straighten your tie, you look like you got dressed in the dark."

Allen turned to one of the many mirrors and yanked the knot into place. "I did. I was in a rush."

Vivian was approaching them now, sashaying along in her silky dress that seemed expensive for an errand girl hanging around their rehearsals. Milo had gone to the director and asked if they needed help somewhere on the show for his friend. The man had taken one look at Vivian from afar and told Milo he didn't have the budget "to be giving jobs to everyone's piece of tail." Milo had let fly with his indignation and said he hadn't so much as kissed her hand, but that he'd been "sorta responsible" for her losing her last job. The director raised one eyebrow on his tired, unshaven face and declared that if she could make herself useful he could probably pay her a little, "but if she intends to be 'discovered' as a singer or a dancer, or goes around batting her eyes at the talent…" He made a slicing motion across his throat. "Don't think I haven't seen girls try to get on stage all kinds of ways. She's not hanging around you for your good looks, pal."

Max Gordon waved them over from his table, so Milo, Allen, and Vivian began to wend their way through the crowd as the band played a foxtrot, and the glittering crowd swelled to and fro like waves.

Max beckoned them to sit down, and launched the evening with a toast to "the newest Rodgers and Hart!" If he was put out at having to rustle up an extra chair for Vivian, he did a fine job of acting like he wasn't.

At one point, Allen grabbed Milo around the shoulders and pointed him at a camera, which flashed painfully in his eyes. "If we were somebody that'd be in Winchell's column tomorrow, and everybody'd be talking about us."

"Was that him taking the picture?"

"What are you, a moron? He sits at his table and watches all the beautiful people and writes it up the next day, and everybody in the city hangs on his every word, for good or ill. Ill, often enough. Nah, what we saw just now was the Stork Club's own photographer. Billingsley will have all the pictures of the famous people in all the papers tomorrow. J. Edgar Hoover's here somewhere, I bet."

Gordon shouted, "Hey, Short! Dance with your girl here, or I might have to."

Milo swallowed a golf ball in his throat. "I'm not much of a dancer—"

Gordon shrugged as if to say, *then I guess it's up to me,* and rose. Milo remembered the director's warning about Vivian tangling with the fancy people and figured the producer of the whole show would count in that forbidden group.

He stood up so fast he bonked the table and spilled his martini. A passing waiter swooped in with a cloth, and Milo bobbed in the tide of his embarrassment.

Vivian rose and accepted the hand that Milo had started to offer before the spill. "I'd love to dance."

She all but dragged him onto the dance floor, where the tune was a slow, lulling rendition of "Smoke Gets in Your Eyes." Milo relaxed by a degree; he could get by with shuffling in a rough square shape rather than actually dance. He held Vivian at a respectful distance for a moment, but she stepped so close she could bite him on the nose.

"It's too crowded to take up so much space," she said to him, her eyes level with his. "That would be quite rude, don't you think?"

"Sure," he replied, and then looked over Vivian's shoulder because to look straight in her greenish-gold eyes was like to give him a stroke. He'd never seen a gal stare so hard before.

"Why don't you like me?" Vivian asked him, raising her voice to be heard over the band.

"I like you fine, Vivian. You're a swell girl." Her curls were almost tickling his face. In her shoes they were the same height.

"You don't take me out anywhere."

'I don't take anyone out anywhere. I'm too busy writing and rewriting an entire show in just a few weeks. Allen tells me a chorus girl liked me and I didn't even notice."

"Oh well, chorus girls," she said. "You should take a night off and take me to a show. Or even a picture, if you want to save your pennies. A picture and a soda, how about it?"

Vivian tried to pull away to get a better look at Milo's face, but he continued to hold her close so he could look past her shoulder. It was easier, that way, to say it. "I don't think your family would like it if you were seeing a Jew."

"My family is a thousand miles away and if I cared what they thought I wouldn't be in this goddamn city."

"But my family's just a short ride on the El."

Vivian froze in place, and pushed back away from him. "You won't take me out because your family wouldn't like it?"

"No one would like it. We should either dance or move, we're blocking up the floor here."

Vivian whirled on her heel so fast she stumbled, and began to carve a path on a diagonal to the other side of the floor. Milo tried to keep up with her without knocking people down, keeping up a stream of "Excuse me" and "pardon" as he tried to keep Vivian's glossy brown hair in view.

At the other side of the dance floor, she jabbed a finger at his chest. "Irving Berlin's wife isn't Jewish and no one cares."

"I'm sure plenty of people do care, but he's Irving Berlin so they don't talk about it, not to his face, anyhow. Don't you read the papers? You heard that Father Coughlin on the wireless ever? You shoulda seen what someone scrawled on our awning at the shop the other day; I won't repeat it to a lady. I don't know what you see in me anyway. I'm a funny-looking Jew with almost no money of my own, in a career that's not exactly respectable and at which I will most likely fail. I'm working all the time, too, so I'm no fun, either, as you yourself pointed out. You're a beautiful girl and a hundred guys would fall at your feet if you so much as blinked in their direction."

"But not you."

"Maybe someday I'll get married and have a family but it'll be a Jewish girl that probably my mother picks out, and only after I have enough money that I could afford a wife, and that's nowhere near right now."

"That sounds dreadful."

"It's normal. I've never expected anything else and why should I? Kid, I don't mean to insult you. You're a beautiful girl but I'm the wrong guy. I promise you that."

"Some promise."

Quick movement caught Milo's eye. It was Allen striding toward them.

"Milo! Get back here already! Gordon wants to talk about staging and might need more verses in the swing number. And he says Bell doesn't like the melody in the duet."

He looked over his shoulder but Vivian had dissolved into the crowd. Allen grabbed his arm. "I knew she'd be a distraction. This is a working dinner, pal."

Allen staggered as he swerved around a pert cigarette girl in her red and blue outfit, swiveling his head as he passed to ogle her gams.

"No thanks," Milo said to the girl's tray of smokes. "I should make sure Vivian's all right."

"She's fine. What, is she going to get mugged in here?" Allen stopped short, wobbling as he did so, and seized Milo by his upper arms. Allen was shorter and smaller, and Milo had a crazy moment of wanting to laugh at how they must have looked just then. Allen said, "Forget her, look. You didn't hear what I heard just now. Gordon's worried. Shows are closing all up and down Broadway and people are losing their shirts. No one wants just a bunch of flash and girls with hardly no clothes on, and they can't afford to put that kind of show on anyhow. It's all up to us. It's gotta be the songs."

Milo nodded and shrugged his arms away from Allen, who led the way in a looping, twisty path back to their table. Allen sat down hard, nearly coming out the other side of the chair, and slugged back his drink.

"Short! Welcome back. So tell me about this last song you're working on…"

After an hour or so, Gordon ran out of steam for work and Milo felt he could breathe freely again. He knew Leah would sweat him for information on the Stork Club, so he glanced around some more to take a full report back. He wasn't much for reading the society pages, so he was probably seeing all sorts of famous types without knowing it. He did recognize Ethel Merman, first by hearing her brassy voice even over the sound of the band and the chatter, then by her huge smile and great swath of red hair.

The band swung into "Blue Skies." *Nothin' but blue skies, from now on …* He'd heard Irving Berlin came into the club sometimes. He craned his neck to scan the tables nearest, though Milo couldn't be sure he'd recognize him, anyway. Seeing no one he thought was Berlin, Milo leaned back in his chair and tried to imagine what it would be like to have dinner in a club, and hear the band strike up your very own song. Probably happened to good old Irving all the time, these days. Milo remembered Vivian's argument about Irving Berlin's gentile wife. How could he make her understand about obligations? She apparently felt none at all, having taken off from her family with not a single regret.

Milo put out his cigarette in the black ashtray, the words STORK CLUB in vibrant, blocky white. Earlier, Allen had told him that the ashtrays get stolen constantly. Milo didn't have the nerve to pocket one himself. He did pick up an extra couple matchbooks, figuring it would make Leah smile. A white cartoon stork stood on one leg, looking both rakish and ludicrous in a top hat and monocle.

He'd have to choose his words carefully if his father was in earshot when talking to his sister about this place. If Yosef Schwartz heard Milo going on about expensive suits and the prices of drinks—Milo had chanced to see a menu and wanted to grab his chest like he was near to die—he'd stomp around the apartment. The expense of replacing that awning ruined by some hoodlum had set Schwartz and Son back a goodly amount in a month where they could scarce afford it. But his father would not hear of not replacing it, snapping that his customers would not be rained on as they walked into his shop.

Meanwhile, they'd come home the week before after a picture at the Paradise Theater to see the Kleins' furniture all in the street, getting rained on. The Schwartz men had joined their neighbors in busting down the bolted door and putting their furniture back, but most of it was already ruined, and it was only a matter of time before the marshals came to enforce the eviction.

Milo craned his neck again, looking for Vivian, trying to remember the color of her dress. But it was smoky and dark inside, and his eyes were bad, and it seemed hopeless. She'd probably caught a cab and gone home, the thought of which made Milo shift in his seat. He should've gotten her the cab himself if she'd wanted to go, and called it for her, and seen her into it properly. He hadn't ever been much for taking girls out but he knew how to be polite and he sure hadn't been that.

Milo set down his glass and shouted across the table. "Mr. Gordon! Thanks much for tonight, but I'd better shove off so I can write you some more terrific lyrics."

Allen clapped Milo on the shoulder and regarded him with an unfocused, woozy gaze. Milo told his friend, "You'll take a cab home? You take a train and you're like to get on the wrong one and end up in Yonkers."

Allen promised and Milo untangled himself from his friend's droopy arm. He decided to make one more circuit of the club before leaving, just in case.

He walked past her at first, and it was her voice that made him double back. She was laughing, but the sound was strained, nervous. He squinted through the haze until he saw her face yellowed by a candle at her table. A man was next to her, having pulled up his chair so close he was practically in her lap. He had one hand on her chin, and in the heartbeat that Milo was looking, he saw that hand grip, and crank her face toward his. Vivian was trying to pull away, grimacing with the effort.

Milo stomped up to the table and used the deepest voice he could muster. "Hey! Pal, do you mind? That's my girl. Vivian, where'd you get to, I've been looking everywhere." He was holding out his hand and stepping forward as he said this as if there was no doubt at all the man would relinquish Vivian to him. Perhaps because the initial loud "Hey" had startled him into loosening his hand, the man sat back from her, glaring up at Milo with malevolence.

Vivian took Milo's arm and he whisked her through the crowd, jostling people and not bothering with the "excuse me" this time. They burst onto into the lobby by the hat check and both looked behind them, then chuckled in a giddy, nervous way.

Milo set Vivian back from him and looked her over. Her dress seemed shifted funny, and wrinkled. Her hair was a mess as if she, or someone, had been running their fingers through it. Her hat was missing, as was one glove. "Are you okay?"

Vivian patted her hair. She looked pale, except for a pink flush just at her cheekbones. "Just fine. I lost my hat, I think, but best to leave it. I'd never find it now."

"Who was that fellow?"

"Oh, someone who I thought was the right kind of man. I was wrong that time, too. Seems like I'm wrong quite a lot."

Milo cleared his throat and presented the tickets to the hat check girl. "Good thing I found you again. I had your ticket."

When he turned back around, Vivian had her arms crossed and was facing away. "Yes, good thing."

Milo collected their coats. "Should I get you a cab?"

"I'll walk."

"Oh, you'd better not, you'll freeze out there."

"Then the train."

"Look, let me get you a cab, see you home…"

She snatched the coat out of Milo's hand, knocking his own to the floor in the process. "God forbid someone see me in a cab with a Jew, it would be a scandal!" She was out of his sight in three long strides while Milo was still trying to collect his things off the floor.

He chased her out into the night and saw, to his great relief, that she was slamming the door of a cab after all. He shrugged into his coat and lit a cigarette, waving on another cab that had slowed, hopefully, by the Stork Club awning. He'd take the El.

He glanced back in the direction Vivian's cab had gone, annoyed that she made him think she would walk home alone in the dark, in this weather. So maybe they'd never get married or anything. Still, he'd never want anything bad to happen to the girl, especially on his account.

15

1999

Milo

'm straightening my bow tie in the mirror downstairs, while Esme fusses behind me with a lint roller all over my tuxedo jacket. My father would've given his eyeteeth to have one of these roller things for the shop.

In the mirror behind Esme's frowning concentration, I see Linda's somber face appear. I raise my hand in a wave, and then smile broadly, tugging my tie from both sides.

"You look great, Pop," she says, but her voice is limp and tired. "Now you be sure to let us know the minute you are too tired and want to go home. Joel made me swear on the family silver that I wouldn't tire you out."

I wave my hand at her. Yes, I know, I know.

She's got this long silvery dress that swoops down to the floor. It looks sharp on her. It reminds me of the gowns all the ladies used to wear way back when. Bee used to have such a fit when hemlines went up so high you could give a girl a physical just by walking past her on the street, and I can't say she was wrong. There's something so unimaginative about hanging your parts all out.

Not that the men didn't like to look at skin back in my day. Look at Ziegfeld.

He didn't exactly go broke by putting girls in sparkly nude stockings. No, he went broke by losing his keister in the stock market like most everyone did back then.

I'm so glad to be getting out somewhere, anywhere. I've been starting to feel stir-crazy in this place, and lonely. I let them tell me to stay home on Rosh Hashanah, and as soon as everyone left, with me and a nurse all by our lonesome, I regretted it. Sure, it saved me from having to deal with all the pity faces, and it spared me from the exhaustion of being out in public for hours. But I missed it, turned out. Yom Kippur. I'll definitely go on Yom Kippur. I mean, if I can go to this AIDS charity gig Paul lined up, I can get myself to temple on that day, of all days. My poor mother, rest her soul. She used to hate it when I'd work on Shabbat, and miss dinner, too, not caring a button that the theater world doesn't exactly grind to a halt on Friday nights.

I'm almost looking forward to this party. No one can hear anyone talk at those places anyhow, not hardly. I can stand there with my drink and smile at all the girls and I won't have to go numb with small talk.

Linda's been quiet, picking invisible lint off her own dress. She says now, "Okay, I'll go have the car brought around. Paul will be down to help you with the stairs."

She catches me roll my eyes. "Pop, we always liked to give you a hand no matter what, and it rained today, the steps are slick. You don't want to end up in the hospital with a broken hip, I'm sure of that."

Damn if she isn't right. Fine, then.

Esme pats my shoulder. "You look fine, Mr. Short. And don't you worry about them fussing over you. It would be worse if they didn't care, yes? I'll be off for home now. No gala for me, just checkers with my son. Maybe helping him with homework if he didn't bother to do it yet."

I wave goodnight to her and stand back from the mirror. I look snazzy in a tux. I remember the way Max used to appraise me, when I first could afford to start dressing sharp. He'd tug at my cuffs, inspect the sewing, offer his approval with a curt nod. I could've worn suits he made, but I couldn't bring myself to make him crouch at my feet to get the pants hemmed right. It seemed wrong to me. He might've liked to, I don't know. It's not a thing we ever talked about.

I come out the bathroom door, and a dark shape out of the corner of my eye startles me. I look around quick: Eleanor! I clap my hands so she sees me. She'd been staring at photos lined up on a table near the window seat, but she looks up now, and I know her happy face is a reflection of mine. It takes me two seconds to figure what's different: no glasses tonight. She's got most of her hair behind her head but some curls are squirting out. She's wearing a plain black dress that stops at the knee but looks quietly elegant. Not sophisticated like Linda's sleek gown, or bold like Naomi would wear, but lovely in its way.

She has reached me now and gives me a careful hug, hardly any pressure at all. I squeeze her tighter to show, c'mon, we're not made of porcelain here. She chuckles and gives me a firmer squeeze. I'm tempted to ruffle her hair but don't want to muss it up.

I pantomime delight and surprise to her.

"This isn't my usual kind of party, Grampa, but when they told me where you were going, I decided to be your date. Naomi called in a favor to make sure I got a seat so late. I think I might owe her a kidney."

I indicate her dress and give her a nod and a smile.

"Thanks. It's Eva's. I haven't been to a society thing in a while and didn't have anything suitable, so they tell me. Esme had to take it in a little, which just between you and me, drove Eva a little nuts." Eleanor giggles behind her hand, then pulls at the corner of her eye. "Goodness, these contacts. I shouldn't bother but if I have to hear 'You look so pretty without your glasses' one more time I might jump in front of the F train."

She's joking, but a chill crawls over my neck anyway.

She takes my arm as if I'm supporting her, though I know it's the other way around. "Shall we? Our chariot awaits."

From the corner of my eye like this, she could be my Bee, and this thought makes my heart cave in a little.

Paul is waiting on the steps and between them all they get me down the wet stone without incident, and loaded into the car, which is not our usual town car at all but a limo. Of course, it's a *gala*, after all, and there are a bunch of us going anyhow.

Linda and Paul are seated as far away from each other as they can manage, which in this big car is pretty far in fact. Eleanor is staring out the window as the limo pulls into the halting traffic.

Vivian smiles back at me from the front seat, next to the driver. She gives me a fingertip wave, then blows me a kiss.

I stare back at her long enough to show she doesn't bother me, and then I stare out my own window, and we all sit in silence like a bunch of store mannequins.

I'm getting a handle on this Vivian-apparition business. I might startle if she really sneaks up. But mostly I just look at her like, so what? You're there. Enjoy yourself.

It's not terrific that she's hanging around. I've stopped thinking of her as "the thing" or "it" or "hallucination" because it's tiring to make my mind think that way when my gut just calls it Vivian. I still figure she's stroke damage, in any case.

My stroke damage turns around in her seat and looks from one of us to the other. She looks from Paul to me and nods with a knowing look. Then she puts her slim hands on the back of the front seat, near the little privacy window, and rests her chin on those hands, inspecting Eleanor.

I look over at Eleanor, too; she has turned toward the front of the limo and is gazing out the window closest to her face. Not much to see out there she hasn't seen a thousand times before. It's that time of evening where some of the city is fully dark, shadowed by the buildings, but then the setting sun spills gold down a street, bright and thrilling as could be, for just a moment, as you glide past.

When she's not pulling at the corner of her eye, she's tugging on a curl, and there's a softness around her eyes that makes me think she's so very sad. I hope it's not for me. That's the thing I'll hate the most when I kick it. Whatever happens I'll either be fine, or just dust, but either way, I hate to think of them sad. I wish I could tell her not to be sad, that I'm old and when I'm gone it will be fine because old people are supposed to die. Not like her dad.

And not like me.

I reach out and slam the little door shut, Vivian disappearing from view. I can't tell if the door closed over formless fingers, or if she moved, but in any case I can't see her. I listen for that husky alto in my head but there's nothing.

I glance around and they're all staring at me. Paul has his portable phone to his head. Linda's mouth is frozen in an oval, a lipstick stilled in her hand, her compact open in the other. Eleanor touches my knee. "You okay, Grampa?"

I nod and look out the window, and I'm glad for once that I can't explain, because what on earth would I even say?

It's a fine fall night, cool but not cold, the boiling heat of August blown away. I'd have loved to stride up the steps of the New York Public Library past all the flash bulbs, right between those two stone lions, but the limo pulled right up to the 42nd Street entrance; either the driver knew the old geezer couldn't manage the stairs or Linda gave him advance word.

I try to look around casually as Paul gives me a hand out of the car, to see if Vivian would appear out here, too. No sign of her, for now anyway. I know by now that a closed door—car or house—is no obstacle.

We walk into the side entrance of the library, and now I have a good excuse to stare, because everyone is staring, looking for whoever they might schmooze up to. I've been the schmooz-ee more than a few times. Being a producer forces you to do that. And of course I've perpetrated the schmoozing many a time. Being a producer forces you to do that, too.

Eleanor hands a champagne flute into my left hand, and touches the brim of hers to mine. "Cheers."

I smile and raise my glass. I'm not tired of standing yet—I sit too damn much as it is—so Eleanor and I gaze around at the crowd like we've gone to the zoo. A flash of red zips past me and when I look over it's Naomi swooping onto someone with her hand out. I've seen her darn near shake a man's hand right off, no limp-wristed girly handshake for her. I spot some people I know and they acknowledge me and wave, or nod, and then they lean to their companion and whisper. I can well imagine. *Oh look, Milo Short is here. He still can't talk since his stroke, though. So sad.*

Finally, a few of them break away from the pack to come greet me, approaching with the sad little head-tilt of "poor you" I remember after Bee died.

When an old casting director of mine breaks eye contact to laugh at her own story, clearly on her third or eighth glass of champagne, I elbow Eleanor and cross my eyes at her. Eleanor laughs, which is fine because the casting gal thinks it's for her own story which is incoherent and has something to do with a Tony award statue and a bathroom stall.

Eleanor jumps in when the gal—I think her name is Leslie—pauses for air. "I'm sorry, I think we should excuse ourselves and sit down. Nice to see you, though."

At our own table near one of the pillars supporting the glass dome, Eleanor takes a moment to stare up. Tiny circles of light speckle the inside of the dome, which rises three stories over our heads. "It looks like a starry sky. You know I hardly went to the beach this summer?" Eleanor turns to me, and she tugs the skin near her eye again. "I was working so much. I'm not sure the last time I saw real stars."

I smile back, thinking about trying to reply, like my therapy lady Marla would have me do. But I don't want to try it here, out in public, and end up groaning like an imbecile, or spouting nonsense.

Eleanor fills the silence, toying with the stem of her glass, rolling it back and forth. "Oh, do you know I might have found Vivian's records? Did you know she died young? In Michigan, of all places. Not even thirty years old."

Now I feel warm, all right. I clear my throat and try to be subtle about loosening my tie, but it's so awkward left-handed I quickly give up. Eleanor hasn't noticed; her eyes have a faraway look, like she's mentally in Michigan.

Then she turns to face me, tilting her head and squinting a little, as if in concentration. "Was she an actress, maybe? Vivian, I mean? Seems the most likely way you'd have known her. Maybe she was in one of your very early shows? I suppose I could get the cast lists of those shows easily enough and look. There must be an archive of playbills somewhere. Not that it matters, really. It's just one of those irritating things, do you know, Grampa? Like when you can't think of an answer to a riddle but you're sure it's really obvious and it haunts you until you figure it out? I feel like I'm going to lie awake at night until I can figure out how she knew you, is all. I guess if you remember we can play some Twenty Questions until I get it right."

Twenty questions, charades. My past reduced to party games.

Eleanor's makeup is all smeared up from where she was rubbing her eye. I take out my clean handkerchief and hand it to her, pointing at my own eye so she'll know what I mean.

"Oh, shoot. I'm not used to wearing much makeup either, but Eva told me if I didn't put some on and ended up being photographed I'd look like a cadaver. Will you be okay here a minute if I go try to fix this up?"

Sure, sure, I wave her away. Fine.

She shuffles away as quickly as she can manage in her shoes, which are taller than she usually wears and seem a little big, too. They keep slipping off. Probably also Eva's.

I stare down at my own hands and wonder if I shouldn't just let her know I remember Vivian. Pretending not to know has turned this into a bigger deal than it would have been. I smirk to myself. It's what they always said after Watergate. It's the cover-up that gets you.

I'll just let Eleanor know through our questions and charades that she was a secretary for Harms and that Allen didn't like her and neither did Mrs. Allen. That's it, ta-da, we can dust our hands of this. Maybe then I'll stop seeing her, too, because I won't be thinking about her anymore.

And maybe then I can concentrate on getting my words back.

Smoke and flowers, dark waves of hair, and now the pressure of a small feminine hand on my forearm.

I push back from the table, scrabbling away, shaking the pressure of that hand off my arm. How is she touching me? How can I feel her? I hear broken glass and a couple of startled yelps but in my sweaty panic all I see is a blur of candlelight and glasses and dresses.

I try to slow down my breathing before I black out, then will myself to look right at her... Not Vivian! This gal has brown eyes, and she's short. I can still smell roses and smoke but then, lots of people smoke and walk around smelling like perfume and ashtrays. Her eyes are wide and watery, and she's angled slightly away from me, a wet splash across her pink dress.

"Oh, Mr. Short, I didn't mean to scare you, I'm so sorry. I just saw the empty chair next to you, and wanted to tell you how much I admire and respect your work." She looked around to the assembled crowd. "I swear, I only lightly touched his arm, I didn't know it would scare him so bad."

Now it's my turn to look apologetic, as the crowd rushes in, some of them ministering to her dress, others asking me if I'm all right. Other than my body temperature shooting through the roof with this scare and all the gaping attention, I'm in the pink. I nod, dab my forehead with a cloth napkin, make another apologetic face at the girl, who is acting so flustered and upset you'd think I'd thrown my drink in her face on purpose.

Eleanor strides up, almost sliding in her too-big shoes. Her face is half made up now. Looks like she was washing her makeup completely off and got interrupted.

Joel has appeared now, and he and Eleanor have a whispered conference with each other and the nearest bystanders, who are either old business contacts and friends, or vaguely recognizable types who make the gala circuit something of a second job. None of them approach me. They either stare, or look sideways like I can't tell they're staring.

Finally they come back to the table, and Joel tells me he has to go because the twins' nanny has to get home. He says Eleanor will escort me back to the townhouse. "I'm going to stay over," Eleanor adds, with a weak smile. "Just to keep an eye on you."

The nurses are paid to keep an eye out, but I won't mind the company, anyhow.

Just now I want to get the hell out of here, too. Eleanor says, as the crowd around us thins out, clucking their expressions of concern over their shoulders, "I'm going to wait just a few minutes to give the driver time to get back to the door. Joel called his car phone. Then we can blow this joint." Eleanor gives me a tired sideways smile. "Slumber party at your house."

I can feel an arc of interest around us, where people are standing back, giving me and my granddaughter a moment, I guess, but they're gawking in that too-cool-for-you society way. If only I could get up and do a soft-shoe on the table just to show them what for. Back when I had good knees and strong bones, I never did. Too polite, I guess, and too busy keeping everyone else in line. Shame, truth be told. When I get my words back I'm telling that to every young person I meet, starting with Eleanor. Dance on tables, kid, just because you can.

"You know, Grampa, why don't I move in?"

I frown. Move in with me? Not that I wouldn't enjoy her company, but doesn't she want her own real life? She can't really think that being a nursemaid to her rickety, mute grandfather counts as a future.

"I mean, look, staying at Uncle Paul's apartment doesn't make sense anymore, does it? It's too big for just me, and he should get a tenant in there who can pay him some real money. I know, I know"—Eleanor waves away the objection I can't give anyway—"but really it's just embarrassing. That place was meant for Daniel and me, and there is no Daniel and me." She peers into her empty champagne flute. "Well. Let's go find that driver."

We get up and she takes my elbow, and I wrap my opposite hand over hers, and together we make a slow but steady progression away from the rapacious, glittering room.

16
Eleanor

startle awake, my mind scrambling to understand where I am.

Oh, Grampa Milo's house. I flop back onto the overfull pillows as the benefit comes back to me in flashes. The pity, the staring, Grampa for some reason freaking out and spilling his drink all over that girl. And there I went, on my third glass of champagne, thinking it was a great idea to move in.

It felt so right at the time. He could use the company, and I don't need that apartment, not really. We can work on the book much more efficiently if I'm here anytime, and can grab him at cheerful moments.

But this also means packing up my things and closing the door where Daniel and I… Well. Perhaps all the more reason to move.

I'll have to go back to the apartment today. My computer is there, most of my notes. I should check my home answering machine, too, in case Vivian's grandson called me back. I'd called him the next day after his email, but so far, no response. The silence, after he'd freely given his number, has only made my curiosity burn hotter.

I swing my feet off the side of the huge bed. Lace-edged flannel tickles my ankles. I'd scrounged up an old nightgown of Grandma Bee's last night for lack of anything else to wear besides the party dress, and used a new toothbrush we'd picked up with a quick stop at Duane Reade on the way home. Once we got back, the nurse and I helped Grampa Milo to his upstairs room—he pointed happily at his old canopy bed, indicating how glad he was to sleep there again—and we hovered in the hallway as Grampa Milo readied himself for bed. As we did so, I couldn't help but think how he was getting physically stronger, while his words remained stubbornly absent, his dominant hand stubbornly limp.

The nightgown is so soft that I believe I'll keep it, patterned as it is with rosebuds and bows. It felt odd at first, wearing my late grandmother's nightgown. Then as I pulled the bedspread up around my chin, I decided that she'd have insisted I wear it, had she been here to do so. And it's as cozy as Grandma Bee herself always was.

While I'm waking myself up, I make a mental list of what else to do today. Call Uncle Paul and tell him I'm giving up the apartment. Get the essentials I'll need here. Arrange for storage for things like that brown leather couch, my bed.

I give up on combing the tangles out of my hair with my fingers, instead wrestling it into a fat braid with an elastic that I always keep in my purse, just in case. A corona of frizz frames my forehead. I use a bar of soap I find in the shower to wash my face.

The smell of coffee wafts up the stairs as I step into the hall. I'm smacked by a retroactive wallop of loneliness. No one makes coffee at my apartment for me, because there's no one there to do it. I'd forgotten about the simple joy of having a cup already waiting.

In the kitchen, I find Esme bustling around and a full plate of eggs and toast in the center of the butcher block island.

My delight at the coffee fades as I see that Grampa Milo isn't in here. Instead we have a woman I don't know with rings of shoulder-length curls, sitting in front of a breakfast plate. She gives me a genial smile and I fidget with my flannel nightgown. I didn't expect to be in my pajamas in front of a stranger.

"Good morning. Where's Grampa?" I ask Esme.

"Good morning, Miss Eleanor. He only ate a piece of toast and went back to lie down. I think he is overtired. This here is Ms. Marla, the therapist helping Mr. Short with his words."

"Hello," she says. "I've met most of the grandkids. You must be David's daughter?"

"Yes, David was my dad." I swirl the creamer into the black coffee, and keep swirling, just for something to do.

"I'm sorry he passed."

"Thank you."

"I saw a picture the other day in the parlor and it must have been him. Lots of dark curly hair, just like you."

"We all have dark curly hair," I answer.

"Not just that, but just the look of him, the shape of your face, I just knew. Do you favor your mother, too? I've got two little towheaded blondes, because of my husband, but their eyes are dark like mine. Quite a mix." Marla sips her coffee and looks at me with her eyebrows up, waiting for me to chime in with my mother's physical attributes.

Esme clears her throat and offers Marla more eggs.

I put on what I hope registers as a serene smile. "My mom left a long time ago. It's hard for me even to remember what she looked like."

Marla gasps and puts her hand to her chest. "Oh! I'm sorry, I didn't know. Thoughtless of me to pry, I hope you forgive me."

"No, it's fine. You couldn't know."

At this, the conversation curls up and dies. A siren outside breaks the silence at last, and Marla informs us she's going to check with "dear Milo" one more time before officially abandoning today's therapy session. I'm grateful that she doesn't throw me pitying looks, or continue with stammered apologies. She clears her own place before Esme has a chance to do it and slides out through the swinging doors. Esme follows her, no doubt attending to her work elsewhere in the house.

I notice I'm breathing fast when little ripples appear in the surface of my coffee as I raise it to my face. This agitation is not Marla's fault, nor was it anyone else's any other time this has happened. Why shouldn't they ask? Everyone has a mother; everyone came from somewhere.

I know too little about my mother, and also too much. What I know for sure is she was a gentile girlfriend my father had, name of Charlotte, who was always reserved and cold in public, but my dad assured me was a laugh riot when it was just the two of them. I have to take his word for it, because she left before I went off to nursery school. My father's fumbled explanations were along the lines of "she couldn't handle it" and "wasn't ready," never defining what "it" was supposed to be. My child-self filled it in the way all children do, by nature self-centered. "It" was me. She wasn't ready for me.

My Aunt Rebekah unknowingly filled in the blanks. She got tipsy one night and got into it with my father when we were all out at the Hamptons house. They were sitting around the embers of a bonfire, and I'd gotten bored playing Monopoly with Naomi and Eva, and Joel was on the Atari. So I figured I'd come out to the fire and look at the stars. I didn't know that my dad and Aunt Rebekah were the only ones out there, until I got so close I could hear every word of their conversation.

"You owe that child a mother," was the sentence from my aunt that froze me in place.

"What are you talking about?" my dad had answered, his voice more weary than indignant or angry.

"She's growing up weird, and it's your fault there is no feminine influence in her life."

"There's so much wrong with that I don't even know where to begin. Feminine influence? If she's lacking that, look in the mirror, Bekah. You barely talk to her, and you're the closest thing she's got to a mother. And anyway, our mother is doing a wonderful job picking up your slack there, lucky for

Eleanor. She is not weird, she's shy. And anyway…my fault? How is it my fault that Charlotte left us? I gave that woman everything."

"You got her knocked up is what, and talked her into keeping it. That's what she told me."

"That 'it' is my daughter, and you better shut your mouth right now."

"She never wanted a baby, but you convinced Charlotte to go through with it and play house, and what did you think would happen, huh? That she'd squeeze the kid out and she'd be magically transformed into Mother of the Year? Honestly, it's a wonder she didn't run for the hills the first week, my God. And now the poor girl is so screwed up having been abandoned like that, and you haven't done a single thing about getting remarried to give her something like a normal life."

"I'm getting up right now before I … Don't talk to me again. Ever."

It was easy not to be noticed. My dad wasn't looking for me, and it was so dark away from the fire. He headed off for the house like he was shot from a bow. I stared at Rebekah, and then watched her put her head down and start shaking. It took a minute for me to tease out the sound from the rush of the surf; she was crying ragged sobs.

They didn't speak for a month, and it was me who begged Dad to make up with her. I never let on what I knew, but I couldn't stand the tension and the pain the two of them wore like branded skin in each other's presence, knowing it was all because of me.

I clung to the notion that my father had fought for me as a way to blunt what I'd learned, and finally just put that knowledge away in the dusty attic of things you know but don't need, next to the quadratic equation and verb tenses in French.

Aunt Rebekah and I never did manage to be close. But I had Grandma Bee, and my dad was as sweet-natured and soft with me as any mother would have been.

I slurp some more coffee and feel guilty about leaving the eggs behind that Esme made, but I have no appetite now. A chord of sympathy for my grandfather vibrates in me, at having someone pry into your past.

I SHOVE OPEN the door to the Midtown apartment and I wish I could turn back out and leave again. Just buy all new clothes, new toiletries, new books. I'd like to just throw open the doors with a sign that says "Free, take it" and start over.

But this is not what one does, so I start with the obvious and listen to my answering machine while I dig out my suitcase from under the bed.

A few messages are from book sources, and I'll have to listen again to write those down.

I find the suitcase and haul it up onto the unmade bed. Daniel's message is next on the machine, which is not surprising, given the takeout dinner call and the surprise appearance at temple.

Ellie, hi. We haven't talked in a while. It was great to see you the other night, but you looked sad and I'm concerned. Check in, okay? I'll buy you a drink. Bye for now.

I walk over to my dresser and start tossing underwear into the open suitcase, not bothering to remove the half-used bottle of sunscreen and the magazine with sand stuck to its pages.

Hello, Eleanor Short.

I stop, stock-still with a bra in my hand.

This is Alex Bryant. Sorry I didn't return your call right away, things have been busy taking care of my grandmother's estate. Estelle's estate. Whatever. You know what I mean. Anyway, sure, we can talk. I've been looking some stuff up online, and also doing some math with birthdates, and it's interesting. I have to work tonight but you can—

The machine cuts off with a shriek. He'd either run out of time, or my machine took this moment to conk out. The message had come in yesterday, he said he was working then. Would today be okay?

I decide that as it's business hours, he's probably at the office. I'd scrawled the number to the community theater offices down the side of the printed out article, and this is what I fish out of my papers now.

He answers himself, briskly: "Alex Bryant." I can hear typing in the background.

"Hi. This is Eleanor Short."

"Oh? Huh? I mean, oh. I hadn't remembered giving you this number."

"You didn't. The Internet did. I'm so sorry, this is intrusive a bit. Curiosity was getting the better of me and I figured you'd be at work. You could always hang up on me, but of course I hope you don't."

"Um, okay. Hang on a sec."

Eleanor heard him change positions in the room, then some background noise quieted as he must have closed an office door.

"OK, so I'm back. So, speaking of curious, I got curious, too. I looked you up, and found your grandfather Milo Short. Then I popped down to the local library to read up."

"Really? And what did you learn?"

"I learned he's a 'noted Broadway producer and one-time lyricist.' And what's interesting is that my mother suddenly doesn't know who her father is. And Vivian, who you say 'knew' your grandfather, gave birth to a child not naming a father. But here's the really good part."

"Yeah?" Journalism classes and magazine writing have trained my pulse to speed up with excitement at times like this. However, the doting granddaughter in me, the one who imagines her sainted grandfather could never have abandoned a pregnant lover, feels nauseated and dizzy.

"I asked my mom a bit more about Vivian. So the story goes, she went off to New York in a snit when she was young. She was a wild one, Estelle always said. Their parents died young and Vivian just said to hell with bossy old Estelle and took off for the big city. But she came back 'in a bad way,' which was the nice way to say she was nuts. That part we always knew, by the way, about her being nuts. She was that relative, you know? Every family's got one that gets talked about all hushed."

"Do I ever." No one even speaks my mother's name.

"And now it turns out that some months after returning from New York, she has my mom. And here you come calling. Interesting, as I said."

"Do we know when exactly she left New York?"

"That we don't know. Estelle might have known more exactly, but too late now."

"So the father could have been someone in Michigan, after she got back."

"Yeah, I guess," Alex adds, his voice thick with skepticism. "But if she was so determined to get out from under her big sister's thumb when she left for New York, what made her suddenly come back? Some kind of crisis, right? And what's more of a crisis in 1936 than being knocked up by someone who doesn't want you?"

I'm glad he can't see me flinch at his phrasing. This picture he's painting, of Grampa Milo fathering a child, then disavowing it and his girlfriend, it turns my stomach. All the while, Grampa always telling us Grandma Bee was his one and only, his whole life. Making such a production out of it.

"Maybe he didn't know..." I say out loud, cross-legged among the contents of my closet. I'd forgotten what I was doing.

"So you think it was him, too?"

"The timing would work." I say nothing about my grandfather pretending not to know Vivian, about how the mention of her name disturbs him.

Alex's voice, which had been cautious and consciously casual, brightens. "So let's get a DNA test. I checked. It's a simple blood test for your grandfather, my mom, and boom. We know for sure."

"I don't know about that."

"Why not? It sorts everything out."

"I didn't say this before, but my grandfather's not well. He's had a stroke."

"Oh. Wow, sorry. Is he…will he recover?"

"I don't know."

I hear the creaking of a chair, tapping on a desk. Then Alex spits out, "Don't take this the wrong way, but all the more reason we should check."

"Before he dies? Thanks a lot for your compassion."

"And thanks for yours, too, because remember how I said my mom just found out her parents weren't her parents? She and Estelle never got along that great, but she loved her father to the ends of the earth. Poor guy died in the Korean War. And now she thinks that doesn't count."

"I'm sorry to hear that, but my sick grandfather would be a poor replacement. If we find out it's true, is that going to make her feel better?"

"At least we'd know."

"Or we wouldn't, because we find out it's not him, and I put him through the stress of thinking he had fathered some child he didn't know about—"

"Or knew about and ignored."

In calling Alex, I'd hoped for an investigative ally, someone who'd look for clues with me as to the details of Vivian's life. But he and his mother have already decided that my grandfather jilted this lady, who might have just been screwing around in Michigan for all we knew. Hell, I might have had the wrong Vivian Adair from the start and this whole thing is a huge distraction from what I'm supposed to be doing. How much work have I not done on this book that my family is counting on?

"Alex, listen. Let me try to find out more. I can look up city directories and the census and such, now that we know Vivian was here in approximately what years. Maybe I can find where she worked, figure out her connection to him. I mean, to think about it, all we really know is some lady as old as Methuselah told me that Vivian knew Grampa Milo. That's really all we know for sure. I just can't go barging up to my sick, aged grandfather who by the way can't even talk since his stroke, and demand this of him."

"So why did you want to talk to me? Why did you 'go barging' into our lives?"

My pause for an answer stretches too long for Alex's patience.

"Let me know if you change your mind." He bangs his phone down.

I sit on the floor, my thumbs tracing the phone's keypad, wishing I could call him back, but not having any idea what I would say.

A knock at the door startles the phone out of my hand.

I swing the door open to find Daniel, looking at me through his fringe of dark hair, hands jammed in his pockets. "Hey, Ellie," he says, then cocks his head, confused, at the suitcase behind me on the floor.

17
Milo

suppose I wasn't so nice to that Marla girl, but I'm so tired of her damn flashcards. I'd like to tell her where to put the flashcards, but the alphabet board doesn't have a picture for that one. She gave up on me quick today. She might be about as sick of me as I am of not speaking.

I'm so bored, and nervous so much it's like I've had twelve cups of coffee. I keep trying to act like I don't care if Vivian pops up, but how could I not? Apparently hallucinations are not something a person gets used to at eighty-eight years old.

I perch on the window seat, though it's an awkward angle and no comfortable way to spread out, but at least this way I can see normal human life flow by, the dog walkers and nannies and ladies going out in their smart suits.

This way I also get to see who's coming, and look! Eleanor! Terrific. She gets out of the town car, and wouldn't you know but there's that Daniel fellow with her. Just when we'd given him up for lost.

Daniel was always all right in my eyes because he never tried to weasel an acting gig out of me, unlike every other actor I ever met. Not that I blame them, mind you. If not for weaseling I'd never have gotten any Tin Pan Alley job in the first place, mostly down to Allen's finagling. So I don't criticize a kid for chutzpah, but boy if it wasn't nice just to have a nice young man come to dinner without trying to audition for me over the brisket.

They're lugging in boxes and so is the driver, but it doesn't take them so long. Eleanor was never much for being a packrat. About the only thing of David's she kept was that watch, and a few pictures.

I come around the corner to find Eleanor and Daniel standing almost toe-to-toe, and they don't notice me right off. He's bent down by her cheek but I've come upon them in the act of her leaning away. His forehead crinkles up and then he turns away, too fast to be kind, and is out the door, nearly knocking over the driver bringing in the last box.

Eleanor gives me a weak, fake smile and comes over for a hug.

"How are you feeling?"

I waggle my hand. So-so.

"I brought my notes and things. Is it okay if I leave them on a table down here? Seems like we always talk in here, and it would save me lugging it all up and down all the time."

I nod, sure. Eleanor plops into what I now think of as "her" chair, and I give a nervous glance around. We're alone.

I take my careful little old-man steps to the chair nearest hers, and sink down carefully. Oh to be young and careless and flop one's body around like it's nothing. You forget to enjoy these things while you can do them.

Eleanor slouches down and rubs a temple. "You know, when he first left me… It hurt, of course it did. But now he keeps showing up again, just when I'm rearranging my life around his absence. I don't know what he wants from me now. How is it different? Isn't he just going to get tired of me for the same reasons? Eva says I'm supposed to take him back, but isn't he supposed to leave me alone now that he dumped me?"

There's so much I would say to her if I could. She takes off her glasses and pinches her nose, looking so much like David I'd like to cry. Sweetheart, who cares about supposed to? If you're irritated, be irritated, and tell him so. Tell him to shove off if you want. Life is short, except when it's long, and then you have so many more years to regret.

Eleanor's eyes are still closed, and she dangles her glasses from her hand, loosely over the side of the chair. "He's a good guy. A mensch, right? He's kind, and nice, and supportive. He laughs at my jokes and knows me better than anyone."

Not anyone, kid.

She goes on, "You'd think I'd go flying back to him." She shoves the glasses back on, taking two tries because the stem gets stuck in her hair. "It doesn't matter. I'm sure I'm just grumpy. I'll get over it."

Eleanor leafs through some of her papers. "Can I ask you about where you worked back then? Your first Tin Pan Alley job, I mean, the plugging. What a funny name for it..." She continues leafing through the papers, though it doesn't look like she's really seeing them. She shoots me a sideways glance and asks, "Do you remember people you worked with? You know, secretaries and whoever, Grampa?"

Yes, do you remember...Grampa?

Her voice shimmers with mockery. I don't even look around because I don't want to know where she is.

I point to a box marked "books" in magic marker, and Eleanor looks at me confused, but drags it over. Sure enough, these are research books. I figured my studious granddaughter would have them handy. I fold over in my chair and flip through until I find just the one.

Eleanor helps me pull it out of the box. The dusty old book from the '70s with the gaudy, bulbous typefaces so popular then, has a picture of my face on the cover. I can see Post-it notes sticking out of it.

Eleanor has come closer to my chair and is crouching next to me as I flip pages.

I'd last looked at this picture fifteen years ago, and slammed the book shut right away.

Now, my knobby, spotted finger lands on Vivian's chin, in the background of a candid shot taken at the Stork Club one night, before I was famous, before all that came later. I nod at Eleanor, and then I mime typing.

"Oh!" she exclaims, lighting up. "Is that Vivian? Oh, you remembered! And she was a secretary, then?"

Eleanor bends down over the picture so far that her curls obscure the page from me.

I spot her in the middle of the room, wearing the same dress she has on in the picture. *That's a pretty picture of me, even though it's not of me, is it. I'm just in the background, accidentally caught in the frame.*

Now you're not a secret anymore. Go away.

"Grampa, did you two ever…date, or anything?"

I shake my head.

Now, now, Milo.

Those weren't dates. We worked together, you and me, and half the time Allen was there. What kinda date would that be?

What about—

We did not date, Vivian. We were not an item.

"What in the world did Bernie Allen have against her?" Eleanor isn't looking at me as she says this, lifting the book from my lap to carry it back to her chair. "He said she was crazy, so his son said."

Oh, crazy, was I? Allen, calling me crazy? That's a laugh. He was so pickled most of the time I'm surprised he didn't try to ride a pink elephant right onto the stage at the New Amsterdam. Remember Boston?

No.

Oh, yes you do.

"So she worked for Harms? I wonder if I can find her in some old records. I wonder if they keep files back that far."

She's not gonna let this go. When did Eleanor get so tenacious? Ellie was the type to shrug something off and curl up in a corner and read a book. This is more Naomi's style, to worry something until she'd broken it down and conquered it. If Naomi's mother had bailed out, she'd have unleashed the hounds to find her, I'm sure of it.

"She'd have worked there in what, 1934? '35?"

I make four fingers.

"Thirty-four. Right. Let me grab a notebook."

Your memory is improving for someone who can't remember the Boston tryout.

Eleanor flops back down again. "Right, so thirty-four to…. How long was she there? Well, you weren't at Harms much longer after that, though, because you were working on *Hilarity*… But here in this picture, she's obviously there with the other people in the show. Did she follow you to work on the *Hilarity* show somehow? Was she in it?"

I shake my head, miming stenography now.

Careful, Milo, you might accidentally tell her the whole story.

"So she was a secretary for the producer or something?"

I touch my chest, and also lean across to point at Allen, round-faced and flushed in that picture, and fully in his cups, and draw a finger around the whole bunch of us at the table.

"For everyone? For the show in general, like an assistant?"

I nod. I just want this to go away. When will she know enough to let it go?

"And how long did she work with you? Show me the years, on your fingers, like before. Thirty-four to what?"

Thirty-five, I show her.

I'm looking down at the patterned, faded carpet, and I watch those round-toe shoes come into view as she moves closer. Bile rises, and my heart thuds away more slowly than it seems like it should.

"So not very long. I wish you could tell me why she left. Maybe I can guess?

Did she quit? Maybe to get married? Married women didn't work much back then, did they? Grampa Milo, can you hear me? I'm trying to figure out why she left."

Yes, Milo, why don't you tell her why I left.

Eleanor, why does it matter? Why do you have to know?

Before I can help myself, my eyes travel up Vivian's stockings, past her hem, her short fur jacket—I always wondered how she afforded that jacket—up to her smirking face.

Leave me alone, Vivian.

You're assuming I have a choice in the matter.

"Grampa? Do you see something? Is something there?"

I hear Eleanor get up. I want to look at her, smile, shrug, dance on the carpet, anything to tear my eyes away from this impossible dead girl in front of me and convince my granddaughter everything's fine, really, it's just "expressive aphasia."

Eleanor's hand is on my arm, and she crouches down. I can smell the raspberry shampoo she's liked since she was a teenage girl. Oh, Eleanor, I don't want to scare you but I can't turn away.

"Grampa, you're scaring me. What's going on?"

A tear winds down my cheek and it feels cold, to me, a little trail of ice.

Eleanor's voice wavers. "You see something, don't you?"

She stares into what must be empty space, for her, or at least I hope to God, Vivian, don't haunt her, too.

She says, voice barely over a whisper. "It's not something. It's someone, isn't it?"

She must be guessing by the way I'm staring at Vivian's face, a person's height off the floor. These kinds of things Eleanor always notices.

I grit my teeth for her to start screaming, to call the hospital, her uncle, the men in the little white coats. Off to a rubber room for me. Can't you just kill me, Vivian, is that what you are, the angel of death? Then do it already, don't let me get locked up in a bughouse, unless that's what you want. You're trying to make me crazy, too, are you? Did you hate me that much?

Eleanor squeezes my arm. "It's okay, Grampa. I'm here. Nothing's going to hurt you."

Oh, kid, if only that were true.

Vivian drops her casual smirk. Thunderclouds pass over her face; I recognize the look and my body blasts with sweat at the memory, and seeing it now scares me more than anything this impossible Vivian has yet done.

18

Boston, 1935

The actor stomped downstage and peered into the house seats, his hand shading his eyes. "I can't sing the note like that, I need another one."

Milo put his hand over Allen's forearm, gripping hard with a warning shake of the head.

Allen whispered back, "He could sing it if he wanted to, he's just a lazy guinea."

"Change the note, it doesn't make much difference now."

Allen snorted. *Hilarity* was in Boston for its first opening night, and word backstage was that it was gonna flop here, which meant it wouldn't even open in New York and Milo's lyricist career would be over before one note was even sung on Broadway.

Allen yanked his arm hard away and stomped over, Milo holding his breath like he did ten times a day that Allen was about to get them fired.

Milo put his hand half over his face, peeking through his fingers. He saw his friend snatch the music right off the rehearsal piano, and scribble ferociously on the manuscript. He slammed it so hard back on the piano that the instrument groaned a deep, echoing thud.

The rehearsal pianist, a pint-sized man named Finkelstein, cleared his throat and looked sideways at the actor, Mark Bell, who was born Marco Rubellino and slipped into his accent when angry.

"Well?" Bell demanded, and Finkelstein played the new phrase, with a lower note. Bell repeated it beautifully, and without a word of thanks to Allen, barked to take it from the top.

Allen flopped down next to Milo, again grumbling insults under his breath. Milo's specialty was the words, so he couldn't have said exactly why Allen's original music was better, but it had been. The new note was singable, but conventional. Dull, like the hundred Tin Pan Alley ditties they'd banged out at Harms.

Allen was squirming in the seat, cursing that if the show failed it would be all "that dago Rubellino's fault."

It made Milo squirm, too. If he made Allen mad enough, would he become "that kike Schwartz"?

Not that Bell was any kind of sweetheart. He'd demanded changes to every song he sung like he was Caruso and everyone had to fall at their feet in tribute to his greatness, when in fact his voice was strained and thin at the high notes, and he had to throw them out of his mouth almost.

Milo tipped his head back on his seat as he listened to Bell squawk through the new version of their song, a comic number about rival apple cart salesmen. It was supposed to be a duet with another man, but Bell had insisted he deserved a solo performance and the director had caved. Milo thought the bit lost its spark without someone to play off, but what did he know from Broadway?

He had been excited to go to Boston with the show, and his sister had squealed about it, too, begging their father to buy a camera so Milo could bring back photographs. Their father was about to say no, his face all screwed up like he was biting something rotten, when Milo jumped in to say he wouldn't have time for that anyhow, and didn't know how to work a camera besides.

Camera or no, he hadn't time to even set foot outside, and they would be heading out of town the minute the sun came up the day after the preview run, or earlier, if it flopped hard enough. The older hands on the show told him there were always changes last minute, but when pressed they admitted that it seemed like more than usual this time. Milo felt like he was always rewriting a lyric, or a new rhyme.

The only thing that hadn't changed a bit was *Let's Live On Hilarity*. He'd tinkered with it a little that first day with Allen but after that, Max Gordon insisted they not change a word. The torch song, a ballet number, a jazz tune, the big splashy number just before final curtain, all of it had been rearranged and disassembled and sometimes the original lyrics put back.

The fella writing the dialogue—Milo learned this was called "the book" even though it wasn't a real book and in fact wasn't much of a story, just an excuse for a bunch of numbers and some talking over scene changes—wasn't faring much better.

"I'm not feeling so good," Allen said, burping into his hand. "I'm gonna go lie down. Come get me if they need me again. Or better yet, just tell them to fix it themselves how they think it should go. What do I care anyhow? I'm paid either way."

He supported himself on the backs of the theater seats, and continued to use the backs of the seats to hold himself up as he drifted up the aisle to the back of the house. The sight of him like this made Milo swallow hard. If Allen spent much more time fried to the hat he'd be well and truly useless, and then what would become of their team?

On his other side, he smelled Vivian before he saw her.

"If I have to type another article for another lousy press agent I'm going to demand they pay for a new manicure," she said, holding her slim hands before Milo so she could inspect her chipped red polish.

"You wanted to come, right?"

"I know, I'm just teasing. It's interesting, being here."

Milo looked up at the inside of the ornate theater with its curlicue décor far overhead and rows of balcony boxes staring haughtily down. "Funny thing is, this theater could be in New York and it's just as cold outside as home. If not for the train ride I wouldn't think I'd left."

"I think any place has a different heart, don't you? New York is like a wild flapper chorine, dancing her fringe all over. Boston seems like a grand lady to me, wise and serene."

"Serene? You been in the same city as me?"

"Well, no one's serene around here, true."

"So what's the heart of where you come from? You told me once you moved here, and we got interrupted."

"Chicago. It's like…a big muscular boxer. Tough, you know? Not in a bad way, not always. But it's out on the prairie, really, and the winters are hard. I think even the women go around with a certain toughness, because otherwise they'd freeze to death." At this she laughed lightly, but Milo knew enough by now to realize she didn't mean it. When she laughed for real, she doubled over and cried real tears right down her face, like when Allen had dolled up in the lead actress's hat and gloves and sang her torch song in a falsetto. It was nice not to see them hate each other for a few minutes, but of course Allen didn't know she was out there, even, just hamming it up in general.

"Is that why you left, then, the winters? If so, you shoulda looked at a map."

"I'm not tough, is why I left."

"Coulda fooled me."

"Apparently I have fooled you. No, I'm not tough at all."

"Why here, though, seriously? New York might be a dancer or whatever you said but it's not the softest place to land, seems to me."

"Are you disappointed I came?"

"'Course not. Just asking."

A voice came out of the wings while Bell was sitting down on the edge of the stage, conferring with the director. "Adair! Mabel needs you to go get some stockings for the chorus girls. There are a bunch that are ripped."

"Duty calls," Vivian said with a sigh, and pushed herself up from the seat like she was a hundred.

"I'll go with," Milo decided, standing up too. "I need to get out and see this serenity you're telling me about."

Milo didn't get halfway down the row of seats when the director hollered at him, "Hey, Milo! Where you going? We might need you again, you gotta stick around. You need anything, that girl can get it, right, honey?"

The director didn't wait for an answer, and Milo shrugged. "Sorry, Vivian. Maybe next time."

But she was already turning away from him, striding fast enough out of the seats she stumbled and had to right herself on a seat back. It was her long, angry stride that Milo had seen a time or two since she'd joined *Hilarity*.

Milo moved closer to the director, figuring he might as well get a better view of the stage, though by now he knew the songs—all the versions he'd written—so well he could have sung the entire show himself backward.

"Sorry, Milo," the director said, staring at a clipboard and frowning at whatever he saw there. "I know you like that girl, but she didn't come for a tea party."

"No one said she did."

He looked up at Milo over the tops of his glasses. "Says you. Mabel tells me she's been making up excuses not to work since she got here. Headaches." He tapped his head with his pencil. "I'll give her a headache. Anyhow, stick around, we're about to run through the *Hilarity* number, orchestra, costumes, and everything. Enjoy it, Milo." He allowed a rare smile. "This is when it gets fun. Trust me."

The stage darkened, and a spotlight came up on George Murphy, dressed like a ragamuffin, reading a prop newspaper, slouched on a stoop.

Murphy raised his face in a crooning lament, as the stage began to fill with leggy chorus girls dressed in racy costumes meant to both look like rags and show off their gams.

Herbert Hoover said he knew our bleak Depression wouldn't last

The Prez said we'd be on our feet instead of on our....keister.

Franklin Delano said, "Hey, Friend! You know, happy days are 'round the bend!"

Well I say, "Sure enough! The little guy gets it in the end..."

At "end" the girls all bent forward and popped their tuchuses straight up in the air.

No more worries about money, honey, cuz we've got no more to count.

About your rent, say, pal, don't fret! That landlord will kick you out!

When a guy comes by to give you a dime, just say no to that charity!

Tell us a joke, sing us a song, and let's live on hilarity!

Now in the instrumental break, the tap dancing girls surrounded and obscured Murphy. Milo knew what was happening back there; the costume gals had rigged his rags to rip right off of him, revealing a tux underneath. The girls melted away just in time for the next few bars.

Tired of breaking your back all day to earn a dollar?

Fear not, here comes your boss to grab you by the collar!

With no time to lose and nothing to gain, I see it all with such clarity

Let's get married, sweetheart, and we can just live on hilarity!

At this Murphy grabbed around the waist a girl who had danced in from the wings, wearing a sort of wedding veil made out of newspaper. Now the tempo slowed down and Murphy danced and sang the next part with the girl in his arms, throwing in plenty of suggestive leers to make Milo's lyrics seem naughtier than they really were.

Freedom's what you got when you've not a pot to piss in

Liberty for you and me, there's all day free for kissin'!

No pennies to pinch, no floors to scrub, I say count yourself lucky, bub

If all you've got is nothing, there's nothing to be missin'!

The chorus girls kicked and shimmied, and Murphy danced and trotted his way among them. Milo laughed out loud that the words he'd scribbled in that tiny office with Allen, for fun on a slow day, were now being belted out by none other than Broadway star George Murphy, fresh off of his turn in *Roberta*, while a dozen dancing girls frolicked around him.

Murphy's voice vaulted and somersaulted through the house as he drew out the long notes of "missin'" far longer than seemed strictly natural, then took a big, obvious breath in the middle to go a little longer, which made Milo laugh each time.

The company exploded in a frenetic dance as Murphy melted back into the crowd for the big finish, where he climbed back onto the stoop. He began the final refrain slower, almost tenderly, before picking up the pace on the final two lines.

I suppose I'd like something to eat besides the sole of my shoe
And a roof would keep out the rain, but who makes me smile? It's you!
Working's a chore, eating's a snore, who cares if a paycheck's a rarity?
If I get hungry I'll eat my words, so darling, let's live on hilarity!

The chorus girls collapsed into their final poses of admiration for Murphy and his paper-veiled girl, clutching one another on the stoop. In the silent moments that followed, the echoing notes trailed into the air, and Milo was sitting close enough to hear the dancers' panting, and see their heaving chests.

Goose bumps chased each other right up his arms.

The director broke the silence. "Outstanding, everyone. Really terrific. Girls, remember to keep those smiles big as can be during the release, Murphy, you could be faster getting that contraption off, we need this to skip right along…"

Milo tuned him out, trying to get back those last seconds when everything was sharp and bright like sun through crystal, and all his fear had fallen away, if only long enough to savor that, for the first time, everything made a kind of sense.

THE NEXT NIGHT at Jimmy McHugh's house, everyone involved in *Hilarity* got drunker or sicker or both with each tick of the second hand toward the time when the next day's morning paper would be handed to an errand boy outside the *Boston Post* on Milk Street, who'd hotfoot it to the house and the first real review would be read aloud, so all could hear at once if they were to be failures.

Milo was asking the rehearsal pianist, Finkelstein, if it was always like this.

"Like what?" he asked, swirling his ice cubes in his whiskey.

"Everyone's so nervous. It feels funny in the air, even. Like there's either going to be a parade or a brawl at any minute."

"Oh, that. Sure, normal. Makes not much difference to me as I'm just one of the hired hands. Two hired hands!" He held up his hands with long, delicate fingers, much as he could with a rocks glass in one fist. "You know I used to work on Tin Pan Alley? With McHugh over there. He helped me get this job. Thought he might cut me in on some of his songs, too, but that ain't never gonna happen."

"Cut you in?" Milo put his own drink down, deciding against adding gin to his queasy stomach.

"Yeah, you know, on the songwriting credit. I helped him out with one or two melodies. Course it wasn't much help, so I can't complain. Still, it sure woulda been nice."

"Is that his wife with him?"

"Nah. That's Dorothy Fields, in from California. She's the daughter of Lew Fields, you know, the vaudevillian. She's writing with Kern now, but she worked with McHugh a lot, a while back. Remember 'I Can't Give You Anything But Love'?"

"Oh yeah! Sure, great tune." Milo cocked his head. "They seem awful cozy."

They weren't doing anything all that much that Milo could see. But she was turned toward him, standing very close, and they were sharing glances, eye-to-eye, like they had a secret language that didn't even need words.

"Some people think they've been making more than music together, if you catch my meaning. They barely see their own spouses. But who knows?"

"I don't know why my mother is in such a hurry to marry us off. Seems like more trouble than it's worth to me."

"I bet Vivian would toss on a wedding veil for you… Or maybe not." At saying this, both men had swept their gazes around the room in search of her, and found her sitting almost in the lap of Mark Bell on a divan near the living room doorway. "Huh, I should have guessed. She's been hanging around his dressing room lately. Guess you're out of it, Milo."

"I was never in it, Fink. You know how it goes, I gotta find myself a nice Jewish girl; better yet, let my mother find one for me."

"You run across any with rich fathers, throw them my way, huh, pal? I'm so sick of piano playing. I'd like to just get behind a desk at some family business somewhere, only my family doesn't have any business anywhere."

"What you got against this gig?"

"I got a good ten years on you, Milo. And I'm still just fingers on the keys to them. I'm never going to get to write a show, or sing, or act. And it gets old, sitting there on that hard bench, watching everyone all around you live the life you ain't never gonna have."

Milo was about to ask how that happened, how his chances blew by him already, when Allen burst into the room, waving a paper. "It's in!" he shouted, then the paper slipped out of his hand. Vivian was quickest off the mark and snatched it up, rattling through its pages and ignoring Allen's woozy attempts to grab it back.

The phonograph stopped with a loud rip, and conversation dried up, and every face in the room turned to Vivian like flowers to the sun.

She cleared her throat and began to read, in an overly projected, affected high-class accent she must have thought fitting for the crowd.

"*Let's Live on Hilarity? Let's not.* That's the headline," she explained, and a groan rolled through the crowd. Milo put his head in his hand. He hadn't considered how a newsman might make fun of the show's name.

Vivian read on with less verve now that the acidic headline had seeped the joy from the room. *A new Max Gordon production has opened for previews at the Colonial Theatre, with some old Broadway hoofers and crooners, and a new team of songwriters the Great White Way has never heard of before, and may never hear of again.*

Allen cursed, loudly, and glanced around as if looking for something inexpensive to break.

The revue is a herky-jerky affair with some topical songs and some standard numbers meant to be crowd-pleasing, but the performances don't have the polish that one expects for a professional show, even a show in previews. Dancers at times crashed into each other, and a costume mishap for George Murphy marred what was otherwise a lively and tuneful number that gave the show its name. In particular, the lyrics to the title number were clever and comically lowbrow, with an ending both sad and unexpected.

But the efforts of these new songwriters, Bernard Allen and Milo Shirt—

Laughter raged throughout the room, charged with relief there was some other reaction to be had other than angry weeping.

Vivian tossed her hair impatiently and waited for the giggles to recede. "Pardon me, I should have corrected it as I read aloud. "... *Milo SHORT, will be wasted if the powers that be can't shape up the show with enough snap and pizzazz to keep the seats filled and the audience clapping at curtain call.*"

McHugh himself walked up then and seized the paper from her hand. "Never mind, sweetheart, we get the idea. Anyone want to read more, you're welcome to it. After I've finished, that is." McHugh turned his backside to the crowd and pantomimed wiping his ass, to more laughter that held a hint of wild, barely contained hysteria. He threw it at the ground and there was a pause long enough for about four heartbeats before several people grabbed for it once, including Mark Bell, still at Vivian's elbow. He'd been trying to read over her shoulder.

"Champagne all around! We're still alive and that's saying something." McHugh waved his hand, and waiters appeared from somewhere in the recesses of the house bearing trays of glittering champagne flutes.

Vivian and Mark Bell were holding hands by now. Milo was glad she seemed happy, but worried the director who'd barely given her a job would consider this fooling around with the talent. Then again, Bell was second-tier, and everyone was tanking up enough that no one seemed likely to notice or care.

Allen stomped over and slapped him on the shoulder hard enough that Milo's gin—he'd picked it back up with swimmy relief at not being personally thrashed in print—spilled out onto McHugh's thick rug.

"You lucky sonofabitch," he slurred.

"Lucky? Me?"

"You, in the review. About the only nice thing that ratface critic said was about you."

"Yeah, swell, only he couldn't spell my name right so everyone thinks a Mr. Shirt wrote that song. Anyhow, he said your music was tuneful. That's nice."

Allen waved his hand. "They'll call anything tuneful that doesn't sound like a bucket of rocks being dragged across stage."

"So we're doomed?"

McHugh himself appeared before them. "Doomed! Far from it, my lads." He was affecting an old country Irish accent, and waving over a waiter with champagne. "It all depends if the people stay away, boys. Sometimes bad notices are death to a show, other times it doesn't seem to matter and nobody knows why, not that they don't make themselves crazy wondering. If anyone knew, every show would be a hit. Well done, Milo Shirt." McHugh winked.

Milo shifted his weight, felt like McHugh was a schoolteacher he wanted to please. "Thanks for having us at the house. It's a nice place."

"Is it? I suppose so. I'm not here much, you know, usually the missus is in residence, but she's gone out to the country visiting friends. But when I heard Max here was in town, I wanted to throw him a nice bash. Hey, look alive, friend," he said, addressing Allen now, patting his shoulder. "By the end of tomorrow that newspaper will be garbage, but *Hilarity* will be in front of a whole new crowd. You'll see, you'll forget all about it by lunchtime."

He swept away, collecting Dorothy Fields from a conversation with Gordon on the way to the living room doorway, to greet an odd-looking man with a wide mouth, dark hair, and a very fine suit.

"Well, throw me overboard, if that isn't Cole Porter," muttered Fink, who'd materialized next to Allen.

Milo had just been handed a thin flute of champagne, the unfamiliar bubbles tickling his nose. "No fooling?"

Allen squinted. "Well, whaddya know."

Fink snorted and shook his head. "Have you ever seen his wife? She's a looker. What a waste." Allen nodded his agreement, but Milo asked, "How do you mean, a waste?"

Fink answered, still looking at Porter, "Such a great-looking woman, and rich, too, wasted on a man of his proclivities."

"What proclivities are those?" asked Milo.

Fink and Allen both turned to Milo, their faces bookends of amused disbelief.

Milo said, "What? What are you looking like that for?"

Fink and Allen traded a look. "He doesn't know," Fink said. "You tell him."

Cole Porter was in the doorway talking to McHugh, when he leaned over and planted a smooch on a nearby young man's pink cheek, and all of them laughed: McHugh, Dorothy Fields, Porter, and his friend. It looked playful, the kind of thing two men having a laugh could put over as nothing, if you were trying to be discreet.

"Oh!" blurted Milo, tugging on his necktie. "Oh. No one needs to tell me, I get it."

"Jeez, Milo, don't you ever get out of the house?"

Before Milo answered, he considered his time at school, then home studying at his mother's insistence, then working in the shop. Otherwise he only saw people he waved to in the neighborhood and at the deli, and at the synagogue. Until his job at Harms, he'd barely left the few-block radius of his parents' Bronx apartment.

"No, I guess I really don't," Milo answered.

"Welcome to the world, Milo," Allen said, throwing his arm around Milo and planting his own smooch on the side of his face.

Milo laughed and pushed him. "Get off, you smell like rum."

"Funny, because I've been drinking vodka."

"Look!" Fink pointed. "Cole's going to the piano. Hot damn, this is going to be good."

The crowd all seemed to close in slightly on Porter, but gradually and sideways, as if they didn't want him to notice how eager they were. Max Gordon was no slouch and *Hilarity* had some Broadway names, but because the production had been tossed together hastily, many of the people around were new, and properly awed, but just savvy enough to take a cue from their experienced friends and not gawk like rubes.

Porter launched into "You're the Top," taking his right hand off the keys to beckon to Irene May, who'd sung the torch song in the show. She was wearing a long light purple gown, and sashayed up to the piano to start singing the girl part.

Porter then pointed at Mark Bell, who looked like he was about to piss himself before he scrambled up to the piano and slipped a companionable arm around the waist of Irene.

Despite the thinness of Bell's voice, and the sporadic giggling of Irene, the crowd was rapt. When they'd sung all the published verses, Porter launched into the melody again himself, and started throwing out even more verses none of them had ever heard. The crowd was drunk on starshine and delight.

Fink leaned over. "I hear he does this all the time. He can make up new words to anything, his own songs, other famous ones. This guy's never going to stop writing hits, I bet. He's …"

"Indefatigable," Milo said.

"Look at Professor over here," chimed in Allen.

"What do you think I was doing all that time not leaving the apartment? I was studying."

Fink pointed to Vivian, who was sweeping out the door of the house, her scarlet mouth set in a hard line, her jaw tight; Milo had only caught sight of her green dress hem and one trailing shoe. "What's with Miss Adair, anyway?"

Milo made to follow, but Allen grabbed his arm. "Don't you dare. You're not her father, you don't need to chase her every time she storms off somewhere."

"And you don't need to tell me where I can and can't go." Milo shook off Allen's arm.

But Allen made another grab for his elbow. "What's your beef? We've got a party here stacked with talent, people good to know if we're ever gonna work again, whatever happens with *Hilarity*. Remember how I got us this job? At a party. Mixing in with these types. And that review just said to all these people in here what a swell job you did, and now you're going to vanish after some dame? Some dame who isn't even your girl, as you're always saying. She probably just went to buy some smokes or something. Let Bell worry about her, he's been trying to get his hand up her dress all night."

"I just feel kinda responsible for her."

"Why? Dammit, Milo, why?"

Milo opened his mouth to answer as Cole Porter finished up his tune on the piano. McHugh plopped down on the piano bench next to him and was showing him their review. A surge of heat crashed over Milo's neck and he tugged his necktie again. Cole Porter was reading his name! McHugh pointed back over his shoulder at Milo, Fink, and Allen. Porter raised his glass and called out, "Bravo, Milo Shirt!" to a fresh wave of giddy laughter.

He couldn't, just then, remember why he felt responsible. After all, she'd followed him to *Hilarity*, just like she'd followed him to Harms. Sure she was nice to him on his ill-fated day at Remick's, but what did he owe her for that? And why was she forever dashing off someplace anyway? He glanced around the room for Bell and didn't see him. Well, that solved the mystery right there. He probably left a few minutes later, allowing for some discreet distance, seeing as Bell was in fact married.

Milo downed the rest of his champagne and swallowed a belch that tickled his nose like a sneeze, just as McHugh waved him over to the great Cole Porter for a proper introduction.

"Attaboy, Shirt," said Fink, giving him a light shove between the shoulder blades.

Two hours passed, and Milo's face hurt from laughing and his head hurt from gin. Everything in McHugh's Boston townhouse seemed brighter, louder, and closer than it ought to be. Everything people said was funnier, every song played that much more brilliant. Allen, by this time, was asleep on the sofa, having started up with the gin earlier and with genuine zeal. Milo had worried about moving him, but Fink waved his hand dismissively; McHugh wouldn't care. Happened all the time.

Cole Porter had left some time earlier, and Milo expected the party might cool off, but his presence rang out like a sustained echoing note and buoyed the crowd, determined to forget its lukewarm review despite knowing they'd have to do another show the next day.

McHugh, perhaps conscious of this, had begun passing out strong coffee to all those left standing.

"Hey, Short." Milo turned to see the ruddy, thin face of Mark Bell. He looked around for Vivian. Bell went on, "I meant to say thanks earlier for changing that note for me. Much obliged."

"That wasn't me. I wrote the words."

"And damn fine words they are!" he shouted. "Who you looking for? You keep looking behind me, I feel like I'm getting mugged or something."

"I thought Miss Adair was with you."

"Vivian? Not me. I like the blondes. Plus I think she's older than me." Bell wrinkled his nose.

"Well, where did she go off to, then?"

"The hotel, I'm sure. Where else would she go?"

"I'm going to call it a night, Mark. Don't forget to have a coffee before you go."

Milo itched to get out, but did his duty putting in rounds of farewells, though he'd see most of the bunch of them the next day for the next show. McHugh near about shook his arm right off his elbow and gave him some more "buck up, pal" platitudes.

It was a half hour after he decided to get out before he finally did, the cold Boston air slapping him hard when he stepped outside.

He walked the blocks back to the hotel peering at every bench and in every doorway. Something about Vivian's exit gave Milo a funny feeling in his gut.

He saw no sign of her on the way back to the hotel, nor in the hotel lobby or its bar. He grilled the desk clerk with a description of Vivian.

The clerk had frowned and finally said, "Oh yes, I do remember her. She was carrying her shoes in her hand, which I thought was odd, considering the weather."

"Carrying her shoes?"

"Sure, right in off the street. She must have been walking right on the concrete. Probably got tight, I guess, but I saw her get on the elevator. I'm sure she's fine now, sir."

Milo's forehead ached from squinting to see better, and the top of his head throbbed with gin and champagne and raucous laughter and singing that still rang in his ears. If that was a cast party after a poor review, he doubted he'd survive a good one.

The elevator boy confirmed the shoeless dark-haired beauty going upstairs and making it to her correct floor, so Milo relaxed enough that he could stumble into his own doorway and fall asleep immediately and fully clothed on top of the bed.

MILO AWAKENED TO pounding on his door. He leapt out of bed and for frantic, sweaty seconds thought the marshals had come to put his family out on the street: the piano, the wireless, his mother's pots and pans.

He shoved his glasses onto his face and the room sharpened enough that memory pierced the gin-soaked haze: Boston hotel room. *Hilarity*.

He pulled open the door without looking or asking who was there.

Vivian shoved her way past, Milo noting with alarm she was only wearing a slip. "Vivian! What are you doing here?" Milo turned his head and shoved a blanket at her. "Kid, cover yourself up here. What's going on?"

He felt Vivian remove the blanket from his hand. He turned back to see her regarding it curiously, like she wasn't sure what it was. She looked down at herself and her eyebrows went up, as if somehow her dress had vanished. Then she shrugged and draped the blanket around her like a robe.

Milo turned to face her fully. Her hair was in disarray, and her makeup was still on but smeared all over, as if she had tried to wipe it off, and failed. She was not wearing shoes, but she was wearing stockings, which were shredded up, with runs zipping up her legs.

"What happened?" Milo asked, gulping hard.

"I'm not sure," she said, her voice vague and soft. "Mark and I...we had some words out on the street. He went back inside, and I got to the hotel, but that part I'm not so sure about."

"What do you mean not sure about?"

She cocked her head, looking past him to the molding on the ceiling. "I woke up like this. Wearing my slip, my stockings. My shoes were broken. Must have broken off a heel walking home. My feet are in a state, as you might imagine. I must have walked for blocks out there. Milo, I need you to tell them I can't come in today. Make up a story for me, will you? Something better than a headache, or a hangover. I know everyone else will be working hung over anyway."

"Are you? Hung over?"

"No, I didn't drink more than a couple glasses. No, this is....something else."

"What else? What happened to you, I don't understand? Did Bell try something funny?" Milo squeezed his hands into fists. If that slimy wop...

"No," she sighed, flopping onto Milo's bed. "Though he could have tried anything he liked, which I made perfectly clear."

The blanket had slipped out of place as she flopped down, exposing the lightly freckled skin over her ribs. Milo looked away. "Okay, I'll tell them something, but you've got to go back to your room now."

"No, I think not." She rolled over and curled up.

"No, really, you've got to. I don't want people to think..."

"Would that be so terrible?" she spoke without facing him. "Would it be so unthinkable?"

Milo first thought of his mother, realizing of course word of this would never reach her. How would it? Down at the kosher deli? He had a sense of being far away from his family, then, the tailor shop and the Bronx and the synagogue seeming remote and fantastical, belonging to another life and another Milo who minded the store so Max could sew and measure.

Milo dug in his suitcase for a fresh shirt at least. Before he stepped into his bathroom he turned back. "Vivian? Can I ask you something?"

There was no movement or answer from her curled-up form.

"Are you…" Milo struggled for the word he wanted. He couldn't just ask if she were nuts, a person didn't ask a girl a thing like that. Anyhow, maybe it was all just headaches, and lots of high-pitched emotion. "… Are you ill, somehow?"

"Yes," she answered, then, projecting her voice firmly as if she were swearing in court, "I am."

VIVIAN APPEARED TO be asleep when Milo left to walk back to the theater, his head jarring with every footfall, his temples exploding with each honk of a horn. At least he wouldn't have to work much, he figured, since his lyrics seemed to be in fine shape. As he approached the stage door, he realized his work on the show was essentially over. He'd expected relief, after all the frantic writing and rewriting in the last weeks, to have the end before him. What he felt was a yawning fear, like he got a glimpse of if he happened to stand too close to the train tracks on the elevated platform, and the crowd jostled him.

He strode right up to Mabel, who was the costumer but seemed to be more or less in charge of Vivian as errand girl. It was his misfortune that the director was standing behind her, and whirled around on Milo.

"I knew it," he snapped, overhearing Milo making excuses for Vivian. "She's fired. She can come with us back to New York but I never want to see that broad again." Mabel herself was glowering, muttering, "I could have gotten ten girls to take that job who might have cared enough to keep it."

"You don't understand!" Milo gulped, remembering her smeared face, her gauzy slip. She had seemed so broken and vulnerable when he left her on that bed. "She got mugged, see. Purse-snatched. Guy shoved her hard to the ground, too. I saw her leave McHugh's last night and it was all my fault, I thought she had an escort but she didn't."

Mabel's face softened. "Oh, the poor dear! Is she all right? Should we send over a doctor to her room?"

"No!" Milo answered too quickly. "I mean, she wasn't seriously hurt, I saw her just in the lobby. She was trying to come in to work, see, but she was so tired and shaken up that I told her she should go upstairs. I told her I felt sure you'd understand, and that the show was mostly done by now. Heck, the lyrics seem to be okay so if you need something, send me, right, Mabel? Milo Shirt isn't too proud to go buy more sequins."

The director's eyebrows seemed to form one flat line across his face. For every part of round Mabel's face that beamed understanding and sympathy, the director oozed skepticism. Then he drooped and huffed out a breath. "Fine. You tell her I hope she 'recovers' soon, Short."

Mabel was twittering away at his elbow. "Should she go to the police? I suppose there's not much sense in that, though maybe she should if her purse turns up. Did it have much money in it? Poor thing, no wonder she doesn't want to come in, I wouldn't either, why it would scare me out of my wits! We'll have to make sure all ladies have someone to walk with them from now on, goodness, I thought we were in a decent part of town, but these days I guess everyone gets a little desperate…"

Milo nodded his assent to everything, not hearing a word. He'd never been a liar, but here he'd gone and done it. It was a good thing, a mitzvah, one could argue. He saved Vivian's job, and surely whatever had gone wrong she hadn't done on purpose. And it had been true what he'd said about it being his fault. He'd seen her leave in a state, but he'd let Allen and Fink and the stardust of famous Cole Porter talk him into letting a woman walk alone in the wee hours of the night in a strange city. She could have been mugged, or worse, and it would have been his fault.

By the time Milo agreed to go get sandwiches for the chorus girls, he'd convinced himself the story he told was true.

ALL THE COFFEE on the Eastern seaboard couldn't have cured Milo's headache, and as the show's second night unspooled in front of him, he couldn't remember to be impressed that he'd been invited to sit in Max Gordon's balcony seats. McHugh had joined them, and Dorothy Fields.

Milo would've thought that the previous night's river of booze would have swamped the whole cast and ruined the show for good, but somehow everyone pounced on their roles with new fervor at that afternoon's run-through. The chorus girls in particular had been dancing their routines in an upstairs rehearsal space until they could've done it blindfolded, he heard the director say.

And it was showing on this second night's performance. The costumer had fixed whatever the problem was that caused George Murphy's pull-away rags to not pull entirely away the first night. Even Bell's voice sounded clearer and stronger.

But not here to witness it was Allen. Milo had been the one to bring cash down to the jailhouse to bail him out and drag him, still half-drunk, back to the hotel. He'd been arrested for public drunkenness, for having decided to take a piss under a streetlamp, which wouldn't have been so terrible except that when a copper hollered at him, Allen turned to face him and pissed all over the officer's polished black shoes, and threw in some colorful remarks on the policeman's questionable parentage and ethnicity.

Gordon had jammed a wad of bills into Milo's fist, saying, "You get that partner of yours dried out, or no one's going to want to bother with that drunken sonofabitch again in his natural born life."

Milo had been too angry to bother talking to Allen, who was still pickled at any rate. He was beginning to think longingly of his first days at Harms, just playing tunes by ear on the piano, going home at night to his mother's cooking, and making just enough money not to be embarrassed of himself.

What was so wrong with that? The manager at Harms would never take him back, but they might take him on staff at Remick's now, or some other publisher, writing lyrics even. He could wish Allen best of luck and dust his hands of the whole business, and while he was at it, put some real estate between himself and Vivian. She was a pretty girl, to be sure, and charming when she felt like it. But as he'd already said, he was Jewish and she wasn't, but more to the point, she was trouble. She tripped some kind of protective switch in him, which made him want to push up his sleeves and stand in front of her, arms wide and chin out. He didn't figure this was love exactly, seeing as how when they were apart what he felt was a kind of relief, and a low hum of fondness. He'd seen love closer up now that his brother, Max, had been seeing a girl named Miriam from down the block. Those two spent every moment together they could, to the point where she was in the shop so much people assumed she worked there, when she just wanted to be close enough to receive his smile.

No, this wasn't exactly love, Milo figured, but it was a tangle all the same.

An eruption yanked him away from thoughts of Vivian. In a moment his ears had organized the sound into what it was: a roaring ovation. George Murphy had just sung the last notes of *Hilarity*. The audience was losing their minds, standing, clapping, whistling. The dancers and Murphy were frozen in place, yet even from as far as back as Milo was in the balcony, he could see their chests heaving, knew how hard they were sweating, because he'd seen it before, up close. The lights dimmed at last, but the next bit couldn't start, the audience was still hollering, as the players on stage scrambled in the soft gray dark to get out of the way, ready for the next number.

Max Gordon leaned back from his seat in front of Milo. "Hey, Short? This here is what they call stopping the show."

19

1999

Eleanor

esting on the front stoop of the townhouse, I let the late September breeze push my hair back from my face. Now that I know my grandfather is seeing things, I feel haunted, too. Every time Grampa Milo's gaze rests too long on any one spot, my breathing starts to shallow out and I have to remind myself not to show it: project calm, serenity. For his sake, if not mine.

I've got to tell Uncle Paul what I've noticed. It's only right.

Grampa is hallucinating. He's seeing things that aren't there. His mind is going.

Several times this week, Paul turned to stare at me and ask if I needed something, what I was about to say. And each time I'd shrug and claim to be distracted, or just say "nothing," losing my nerve for confessing what I knew about Grampa's strange episodes. What if they sent him away to some institution? Or doped him into a stupor? And then Uncle Paul would just nod and go back to whatever he was doing: paperwork for Short Productions, or arguing with his wife under his breath as if Esme, the nurses, and I weren't there to notice. He's plenty distracted himself.

It's a plausible enough story that I'd be distracted, after all. Aunt Linda had popped in to the townhouse while Daniel was helping me with boxes and by the way her eyebrows shot halfway up her head it's safe to say she found his presence both surprising and fascinating, and no doubt she told Joel immediately, and via Jessica it would have spread like a virus to Eva and Naomi.

I wish I'd missed Daniel that day. Just another couple of hours and I'd have been gone. Sure, he might have tried to call for me here, but I wouldn't have to take that call; not being my own house, I don't answer the phone here. I've been switching to using my cell phone for the book calls, so I can go wherever I like, though I'm not great at keeping the battery charged, and sometimes I have to pace around to find a good signal.

Instead he turned up as I was packing, and he insisted he help me, and he reminisced, and kissed that one spot on my neck, just below my ear, that he always used to. When he reached for my hair to pull it out of the way I wanted to punch him, but I also wanted to let him embrace me. Instead, I pulled back a fraction of an inch, and pushed my hair back into place. I had the sensation then of a jarring crack inside; my two warring halves breaking apart.

No, it would have been far easier if I'd missed him, avoided his calls. Daniel is an actor-type who moves in struggling-actor circles, and it was wild chance that we met at all, back when I was trying to make it on my own and hanging out with other newly minted journalists in an East Village dive. That night a slurring drunk had sneered that I was a "cock tease" because I wouldn't cram into a bathroom stall and let him screw me standing up, and I bolted out the door before anyone would notice the flush creeping over my ears. I was searching in vain for a cab out on the piss-smelling street when Daniel said, "Are you okay?" from behind me, causing me to jump almost out of my shoes. He insisted on seeing me home on the subway, because all cabs in New York seemed to choose that moment to vanish out of existence.

I think I first went out with him because he didn't comment on how far uptown we were going. I hadn't moved out of my dad's place yet, with his clothes haunting me from the closet and his several pairs of reading glasses abandoned all over the apartment, accosting me each time I opened a drawer or moved a sofa cushion to find the remote.

That night on the train, he'd asked why I had burst out of that bar so suddenly, and alone. It wasn't my scene after all, I told him, and it had been silly of me to even bother.

He didn't reply. Just reached over and took my hand in his, and when I didn't pull back, he stayed just like that, his large hand over mine, resting on my knee.

Now, on this chilly September night, I marvel at how if a cab had appeared, or if I'd just shucked off that one jerk and clung to my friends in the bar, I'd never have even known him. After all, we'd been in the same bar for hours, we later figured, and never even saw each other. It was just luck that he'd stepped out for some air just before I came outside myself.

The big townhouse door opens behind me. Esme leans out. "Miss Eleanor? You have a telephone call. A man named Alexander?"

I try not to look too shocked as I stand up and thank her. I tell her I'll take the call in Grampa's study upstairs. As I pass the entry to the parlor, I see Grampa Milo sitting at the piano, plinking out a melody, left-handed. It takes me time to identify it; he's playing it slowly, awkwardly.

Embrace me, my sweet embraceable you…

I shake my head in wonderment at Alex's call, and here. He'd emailed me after our last call with an apology of sorts, though he was more sorry for my reaction than for what he said about wanting the DNA test.

Sorry I was so pushy before. With my mom all upset right in front of my nose, it's hard to remember that your grandfather is real and not just a fictional character. It's not like I meet lots of 'noted Broadway producers' in my line of work. Just don't forget my mom, either. She's real, too.

Gotta go, because my work nemesis is practicing for his black belt in passive-aggressive emailing, and it seems I should respond.

I couldn't help but smile a little at his humor, even as he reminded me what the stakes are, for him, for Millicent. I felt the joking camaraderie deserved a response in turn, so I joked with him about Eva's black belt in competitive parenting and her sparring with Naomi and Joel in that area, and the email chain had continued on such topics, with him never once demanding the test.

I settle in to the large chair at this desk that's now covered in Uncle Paul's paperwork, and predict that even casual, slacker Alex has run out of patience at last.

"Hello?"

"Hi." Alex clears his throat.

"What's up? I'm surprised to hear from you here."

"I hope it's okay I called this number. I sort of pretended to know you really well when I called the offices. I guess I convinced them; in fact the secretary I think called me Daniel."

"Ha, well done," I say, leaning back in the chair, propping up one knee against the edge of the desk.

"Regular sleuth I am," he rejoins, but something in his voice is strained and tight, as if he's walking a high wire while on the phone. He's going to ask me again, I know it, and for a moment I regret our easy joking, because he's begun to feel a bit like a friend. That creates an obligation of a different sort.

"What's going on?"

"I'm cleaning out at my... Estelle's house. My mom and me."

"Okay..."

"I found some things of Vivian's."

I sit up straight in the office chair. It's absurdly tall for me, and my feet barely touch the floor. "What things?"

"Clippings, playbills, souvenirs. All from New York. And all seemingly connected to Milo."

"Oh. Wow."

"Sure seems like he was important to Vivian."

"He did eventually remember her, by the way. He just told me she was a secretary of sorts, like an assistant, working on his early shows. At least one early show. Makes sense she would keep mementos from that time. Might be all it is."

"Maybe." He lightens his tone. "I know this is weird for you." He leaves unspoken the rest of his sentence: weird that we might be cousins, my grandfather might have fathered a child we never knew.

"What did your mother say about the box?"

"I actually didn't tell her yet."

"Why not?" In the background, I can almost discern waves. "Are you outside?"

"Yeah. Work gave me a cell phone so they can harass me anywhere." He continues, after a loud sigh, "I don't want to get her fixated on it any more than she already is. I keep telling her that it's just a chance."

"How is she fixated?"

"It's not like she talks about it constantly, but every now and then we'll just be like, having dinner or something and she'll blurt out how her Sunday school teacher told her she had a good ear for music. She's also been renting old movies. We watched *The High Hat* the other day. It was good stuff. I wish we could just get the test."

"Alex."

"Even with what I just found? You won't consider asking him?"

"Are there love letters from my grandfather in there?"

Lake Michigan roars away in the silence. I hear a gull squawk.

"Alex, I'm not trying to be defensive. I swear I'm not, but still, all that means is that she saved some things from that time of her life. I've got souvenirs, too. I've saved Playbills. It doesn't mean I've had sex with the lyricist."

"What do you need, then? What smoking gun would convince you to ask him?"

"Here's something else to think about. If you think I'm being weird about it, you don't know my cousin Naomi. My aunts and uncles. If they get wind of this, there will be a shitstorm. It's not going to be perceived as 'Isn't this wonderful we might have another sibling,' you know. They will close ranks. They'll lawyer up."

"They sound like lovely people."

"It's a normal reaction! We'd be asking them to rethink everything they ever thought they knew about their father, who, as I've said, is sick and perhaps on his deathbed." I lower my voice, aware that I've been nearly shouting, and anyone could be coming down the hall any moment. "You think famous people don't get crazy accusations thrown their way all the time?"

"Why wouldn't they just test and prove us crazy hicks wrong and be done with it?"

I toss my glasses onto the desk and pinch the bridge of my nose. "Maybe so, but in the meantime it would be DefCon 4 around here. It's better if only the two of us know, for now. I promise you, Alex, when we have clues that there really was a romance, and that the timing lines up, I'll find a way to ask him about it. I promise."

My heart jackhammers away, and I wish I could claw back that hasty promise.

"Fine, I'll stop bugging you for now. I'm going to the library later, by the way, looking up birth announcements in the paper, double-checking my mom's actual birthdate. And I'll keep going through those boxes where we found the souvenirs."

"Where did you find them, by the way? Where exactly?"

"Crammed into a corner of the attic, under the eaves. I almost pitched them out because they were filled with old clothes, mostly, and smelled terrible. But I figured I'd better at least take a look."

Footsteps on the stairs. Probably Uncle Paul, judging by the weight of the step.

"I have to go, but Alex? Thanks for calling me. We'll figure it out."

"Sure. Okay."

Neither of us hang up. For a moment I listen to the crash and sway of waves and the echoing hush of wind. Someone downstairs has switched the television in the parlor to baseball; about the only thing my grandfather ever watches on TV, besides the news. I wonder if distraction helps him. Maybe if his mind is on the pennant race and not on his past, not on music or lyrics or Broadway, he doesn't hallucinate.

Uncle Paul steps in, and I break our distracted silence to tell Alex goodbye, and he seems distracted in his farewell, too, as if he had forgotten I was there.

"Hey, Ellie," my uncle says, checking his watch as he comes in. "Do you mind? I need to do some work in here."

"Oh sure. I just had to use the phone and figured this one had the most privacy."

"Privacy, eh?" he says, as I stand up away from the desk to give him back his chair. I pick my glasses back up and slide them back into place.

I step away from the desk as he goes on, "Having a nice private chat with Daniel, were we?"

"Not him."

"Oh? Too bad. He's a nice kid." He falls into the chair so hard it rolls away a little, and slaps his briefcase on top of the desk. He clicks it open, and I can see his mind whirring on a thousand details. I am about to slip out, but instead I turn around and suck in a sharp breath.

"You should have cashed my rent check."

Uncle Paul looks at me over the top of his open briefcase. "Come again?"

"The rent. You sent it back."

"You're living here now, what difference does it make?"

"It makes a difference to me." My voice has gone thin and high-pitched. I sound like the kid he thinks I am.

"Honey, it's all family money. We just move it around from place to place."

"It is not! That was my money that I earned, writing articles."

Uncle Paul closes his eyes briefly and rubs his temples. "Kid, let me tell you something. Do you know where your cousin is today? London. Naomi flew to London." Uncle Paul snapped his fingers. "There goes your rent check, on one leg of that plane ride. She flew to London because she's got it in her head to bring over another *Les Mis* or *Cats*. As if we could afford the production costs! But does she listen to me? She used to listen to Pop, but not me, I'm just Uncle Paul, pushing the papers and making phone calls. I'm not the one who built this up, so what do I know?" He yanks out a file folder and slams the briefcase. "I'll tell you what I know. That people work with Milo Short Productions because of Milo Short. I got the same last name, but I can't get people to return my calls or take meetings, all of a sudden. So what am I gonna be when he's truly gone for good? What's this company going to be? Producing is all built on relationships, and I'm only just now realizing, kid, that I don't have them. All along with my fancy title, turns out I was the errand boy. You know"—Uncle Paul tips back in the chair, appraising me, lacing his fingers over his middle-age pudge—"I talked to Bernadette's people the other day, and they told me you haven't been in touch yet. Don't tell me you're afraid of her. We've had her over for dinner for crying out loud."

"I'm not! I just… I've been trying to nail down some details from Grampa's early life, is all…"

"So what details? What have you been doing, exactly? Who have you talked to, how much progress have you made? You remember that tight deadline, right? If I'm going to pitch this book as part of our whole strategy I have to know it's really coming. I went out on a limb for you, kid, when Naomi wanted to give it to some slick pro. So tell me: how much have you got done?"

I swallow hard, too hard, tasting panic at the back of my throat in the same way I did back in that poor mother's kitchen, the one with the dead child who started screaming at me, with damn good reason. But now in the face of my bossy, frustrated uncle, I curl my fists tightly, my own nails biting into my palms, and draw up taller. "That's between me and my editor. I'm working hard as I always have and I resent that you even imply otherwise."

Uncle Paul sighs roughly and shakes his head. "You want to help the family? Write the damn book."

And with that, he twirls his chair back to the desk and begins slapping papers around. He snatches the phone receiver up, and jabs the keypad with such ferocity he has to hang up and start dialing again.

I dash across the hall and slam my way into my room, standing with my back to the inside of the door, waiting for my pulse to slow down.

Diligent young Eleanor should redouble her efforts on the book, should get in touch with Bernadette Peters' people and line up that interview, hell, maybe even start outlining the damn thing. If Uncle Paul is to be believed, the future of Short Productions—if it's going to outlive Grampa Milo—may hang on a revival of *The High Hat*, with this book as a promotional tool. Help the family, he says. Help the family by writing the book.

I walk with shaky legs over to the edge of the tall bed and perch on the edge, my feet swinging free a few inches over the carpet. I put my head in my hands. No one's ever asked me to help the family before. It was always everyone else trying to help pathetic little motherless Ellie.

But real help won't come in the form of interviewing some stars for fawning quotes, this much I know.

This stupid biography project has raked up something in Grampa Milo's past. Not that the project caused his stroke, nothing so simple. My conviction of this lives in the radical oddity of his strange recovery, and his strange behavior. His leg movement came back so quickly. He's strong in other ways, yet every part of him that could help him communicate with us… there's just no progress at all, and our doctor cousin, Joel, admits, much to his own irritation, that there's no medical reason this should be true. No matter how long he stares at the alphabet board and listens to Marla sing nursery songs, his voice and his words remain elusive. I overheard Aunt Rebekah saying they're going to let Marla go, "throwing good money after bad" being her expression. They've cancelled the round-the-clock nursing, seeing as how I'm here now, anyway, and there have been no more nighttime wanderings. It's like the family has declared this our new normal. Mute and compromised grandfather, nearly ninety, and we'll just be around him until he croaks.

That's not good enough for me. I don't care that he's eighty-eight, this doesn't mean his life doesn't count. He shouldn't have to drift through his last years like a shadow.

I have an urge to book a plane ticket to Michigan and root through that box of things myself until I can tell the story. If Grampa Milo can't tell it, won't tell it, doesn't dare tell it… But I have my voice. I can tell that story.

A prickly sensation crawls up my neck and I glance around the room, as if by this audacious thought I'd conjure up Vivian Adair to silence me, too.

THE DOORBELL RINGS and I can hear the braying laughter of Eva all the way upstairs in my room.

I'm weighing my options between the black dress Eva loaned me for the benefit, and an outfit all my own. I hang up the dress back in the wardrobe, electing instead to wear my olive green, ankle-length broomstick skirt and a plain black blouse.

One side effect of moving into the townhouse is that I can no longer escape family dinners with the vague excuse of "work." Though they never really believed I was working all those times, they'd grudgingly accepted that as a writer, my hours were unpredictable, and thus granted me the courtesy of pretending to believe my plausible lie.

But now that I live here, I am well and truly stuck. The occasion for this one, I think, is Joel and Jessica's anniversary, but I might have that wrong. There never needed to be an excuse when Grandma Bee was alive, she'd just declare

"Dinner Thursday night" or "We're having a Shabbat dinner" and we'd attend because that's what one does when your grandmother asks.

Now it's Linda who organizes the dinners, even before Grampa's stroke, and she seems to like to have a reason of some kind.

I'm tugging my tights up into place when I hear a soft knock on the door. I pull it open to find Daniel standing there, wearing a bashful grin.

I hadn't invited him to this dinner. Eva had done it, when she'd chanced to run into him helping me move into the townhouse. I think she thought she was helping get us back together, curing my broken heart by bringing back my boyfriend.

"Didn't want to wait downstairs in the chaos?" I ask, walking away from the door by way of invitation.

He comes in and closes the door softly, sitting on a wooden chest at the end of the four-poster bed. As I finish futzing with my tights and slip my feet into my comfortable, broken-in flats, I catch him glancing around the room, maybe comparing my old place to this one.

This room is heavy with dark furnishings, landscape paintings, and a standing oval mirror in the corner. A vanity on the wall across from the bed is where I've plopped my hair things and sparse makeup supply. The mirror on the vanity reflects the bed itself and every time I get ready to turn out the light I'm confronted with my tired, washed out face and my frizzy late-day hair, and every night I think the next day I will move that thing somewhere else.

I sit at the stool in front of the vanity and pick through my little jewelry box until I find the birthstone my father gave me. Daniel still hasn't spoken as I begin to fumble with the clasp under my pile of curls.

He stands and I can see him approach me in the mirror until I see his midsection only. He's wearing a black silk shirt I bought for him on his last birthday.

"Let me," he finally says, reaching under my hair. As his fingers brush my neck a shiver races down my back. I hold my hair up out of his way. It takes him far too long with the clasp. I could have done it faster myself. I'm on the point of telling him so and taking the necklace back out of his hands when he says "There, all set" and brushes the sharp point of my jaw with his fingers, which skate down my neck until his hands rest on my shoulders.

Only now do I remember to let go of my hair, which lands in an unromantic lump over his hands.

I reach up and cover his left hand with my right, squeeze it lightly, then move it off of my shoulder. At this he stands back and releases me, and by the time I turn around, he has turned around, his face hidden.

"So, do you realize what you're in for tonight? A special Eva interrogation, I have no doubt."

He sits down on the trunk again, elbows on his knees, kneading his own hands. His hair has gotten a little long and it has flopped down, his expression inscrutable.

"I can withstand Eva's interrogation. I have before."

"I can't promise she won't have a whole gang of supporters tonight—"

"Eleanor." He stands up and turns to me, his jaw tight. Then he begins to pace like a little toy at a carnival that marches back and forth, waiting to get shot for a prize.

My door opens just then, with Eva sticking her head in. "Oh good, you're decent. Oh, hi, Daniel, didn't know you were up here. You coming down or what? Linda won't let them start with the drinks until you get down there, so move it."

Eva's head disappears from the door, and I jump when she screams down the stairs, "She's coming!"

Daniel stares at the open door a moment and then says, "It can wait." He gestures for me to go ahead of him.

"Oh thank God!" shouts Naomi when I appear, which is not a reaction I typically get, except when my appearance hails the beginning of alcohol consumption.

I wave at the assembled Shorts, really just a lift of the hand, and scan the room for Grampa Milo. I see him already ensconced in his usual head-of-table seat, staring into his whiskey and soda, swirling the ice around.

Daniel keeps his hand at the small of my back as we weave through the formal dining room toward the bar cart. I am not looking at relatives but I feel the electricity of their interest in the air. I know without having to look that they are studying Daniel's minutest gestures to tease out whether we are in fact together again.

Someone has put Ella Fitzgerald on the stereo, and for this I'm grateful, though her velvet voice can't keep me from reprising Daniel's grim expression just before he was about to tell me something.

I pour myself some white wine, and Daniel helps himself to a beer out of an ice bucket. I wedge myself into a corner and he joins me there. He gently clinks my glass without a word.

Eva bears down on us, as I knew she would. "There you are!" Aunt Rebekah's younger child, Naomi's younger sister, Eva has distinguished herself as the ultimate in ladies who lunch, who volunteer, who parent and who shop. She also is keen to decorate. Last family dinner I attended, she joked that she decorated another room every time she was tempted to have another baby and so far she'd redone the entire Hamptons house.

"I think it's wonderful that you're doing a book! Just amazing, and at your young age, too. Quite an accomplishment."

I glance down into the golden glow of my drink. "Thanks. I haven't accomplished it just yet."

"Oh, you will, I'm sure. Uncle Paul has faith in you. And so do we all," she adds in a rush, with a sideways glance to Naomi, who is chucking the chin of Joel's baby boy. She always was a rotten liar.

She moves closer to me, stage whispering. "So how is he doing? I mean, really? No one tells me anything." She throws a disgusted glance toward Linda. I know what she means; Grandma Bee was the source of all Short family news.

Linda never talks about anything of consequence, not because she's shallow, but because she's private. I may be the only one who understands this. Most everyone thinks she strained her brain by wearing her bun too tight.

"You could talk to him yourself," I tell her, spotting Joel and Jessica whispering to each other in another room, having handed off the babies to cooing cousins. They smile over a secret joke; Jessica brushes his cheek with a kiss. Daniel shifts a bit closer to me.

"What do you mean talk to him?"

"If you ask him the right kind of questions he's perfectly communicative. He's not a vegetable."

"I didn't say he was, for God's sake. Honestly. And I will talk to him." She looks in his direction and so do Daniel and I. He's sitting alone in the throng. Not a single person within two strides of him. This is not a big room, so that's quite a trick, really. "I just mean, how do you think he is, spending so much time with him."

She aims her rapacious gaze right at me and I take another sip of wine and glance at Daniel, though why I don't really know.

"I think he's feeling depressed and defeated, and lonely. Being unable to talk is isolating him. I mean look at that. It's like a force field. We tried going out to the benefit and he got startled almost right out of his chair. He—" No. I stop. Eva is not the one to tell about him seeing things. Seeing people.

At this, I see Grampa Milo turn his attention to the empty chair at his elbow, the one at right angles to his right hand. This might be something a person does when lost in thought, not looking at anything, but his posture looks purposeful, alert. I watch him shake his head, and try to mutter something, then glare over at the chair again.

I glance at Eva and notice her watching him.

I touch her hand to get her attention back to me. "Eva, tell me about your kids, I haven't seen them in ages, is Hannah still dancing?"

This sets her off on her favorite subject, and carries me all the way through my last swallow of wine in the glass before Linda announces it's time to sit down.

There's some awkwardness as Linda's place cards—really, we need place cards?—have placed Daniel at the opposite end of the table from Grampa Milo, so they are forced to stare at each other if they look up, the patriarch and the man who used to live with his granddaughter.

Daniel flashes me that look again, that gaze of stricken intensity, and I return my attention to the food, the linen napkin in my lap, and Grampa Milo to my left. He's trying to follow the dinner conversation but there's too much of it, too fast, words zipping like arrows across a battlefield. He keeps cupping his hand to his ear when there's something he's missed, and I spend most of the dinner repeating it, though I edit some of the more colorful commentary about Bill Clinton's exploits and whether they matter in light of his job.

Jessica declares, "I think it shows an inherent disregard for women in general, not to mention the office he holds. It throws into question his judgment on everything!"

Naomi barks a mocking laugh. "Please! Would you have preferred that shriveled raisin Bob Dole instead? Sure, plenty of respect for women except for supporting their basic rights."

Naomi's husband jumps in, pointing at her with his fork so that a piece of lettuce flies off. "Now you're oversimplifying just to score rhetorical points..."

And so it goes, for the salad and main course, until they finally start to run out of steam around the time slices of cheesecake are handed around and coffee is poured by a server brought along by the caterers.

Joel has been sitting to my right, engrossed in the debate and making asides to Jessica on his other side, but he startles me by standing up abruptly. "Pager," he announces, and strides out of the room.

"Come on, Daniel," Jessica declares, over the murmur of sidebar conversations that have sprung up around the table. "'Move your feet, lose your seat,' that's the rule in our house." She crooks a finger and Daniel smiles genially and stands up from his seat. The entire table watches in gawking silence as he takes the empty chair next to me.

"Can I eat his cheesecake, too?" he asks, sparking a round of charmed laughter before the hum of conversation cranks up again.

Under the tablecloth, Daniel seeks my hand and squeezes it. He leans in toward my hair. "Let's take a walk or something soon."

I nod to show that I hear him, though I'm not sure I want to know what's coming.

DANIEL AND I step into the night. In my head dance the visions of knowing winks and glances exchanged when we announced we were going out for some air.

In the Short family, taking a walk with a boy was about the only way to get any sense of privacy. You could never have a boy in your room, God forbid, and in the main parts of the house, the adults would make like buzzards and circle. For me it was worse yet because I had the older cousins, too.

Daniel drapes one arm around me. Our heights are perfectly proportional for the greatest ease of his hand on my shoulder; I have thought this so many times in gratitude while we were together, with a pang of remorse when we were apart.

"I'm going to L.A."

Of course he is. I should have known he would.

He goes on, as if he could hear my thoughts, "I'm not having much luck here lately. I didn't get that callback, and working as an extra now and then isn't enough to make a career. A buddy of mine is getting some commercial work out there, a couple of TV pilots. I'm not a native New Yorker like you. This was never my city in the first place, so what's really keeping me?"

The weight of this question does not escape me. He wants me to say that I am enough to keep him here.

"Oh. Well, good luck then."

"I'm waiting until Tom's lease is up, though. So I've got three months."

"Good."

"You don't have anything else to say, Ellie?"

We have turned toward the park, darkening now with the autumn's onrushing dusk. A breeze stirs the branches and swirls the crumbling leaves. What else is there?

"I'll miss you," I say, folding my arms and clenching tight, like my arms can steady my voice.

"I don't really want to go." He pulls me in for a sideways squeeze, causing me to stumble slightly, and at this we both chuckle. The sound is mirthless, empty. "I wish I had reasons to stay. And it's not just the work."

Don't ask this of me. Don't hand your life to me, I'm not capable.

He pulls me to a stop under a streetlight. Our feet crunch into a pool of early leaves not yet swept away by the wind. I notice a couple of leaves tangled in the hem of my long skirt.

"If you told me to stay, I would."

He did it. He put his future in my hands. I did not ask for this. It's not fair.

"It's your choice, not mine. It always was."

"It's supposed to be ours."

"So why did you leave me in the first place, then? And why are you coming back around now? I just got used to your absence, which was no easy trick."

"I just missed you. But I missed you when we lived together, too. Since Moira, which I apologized for up one side and down the other… But even before then. I thought one of these days you'd let me into those silences. I want to be let in, doesn't that count for something?"

What if I don't want to let you in? This thought bursts into existence, surprising even me, and I find myself glad I'm not the type to blurt every thought out loud.

"Will you look at me, Ellie?"

I glance up at the squared off chin, with its leading-man cleft I always teased him about.

"My eyes, Eleanor." He puts his finger on the underside of my chin.

In the movies, this is adorable. The shy, reticent heroine just needs this small nudge of encouragement to gaze at her beloved, and her face blooms like a flower, the string section crescendos, and they live happily ever after. It is beneath him to try this cliché with me.

My chin stays down so that his finger is pushing, and I have to resist with my neck, and I feel like a stubborn child, but so be it.

He lets go and his hands drop to his sides.

"You know I don't like looking people straight in the eye."

"I'm not 'people.' Or at least, I'm not supposed to be in the same category as the landlord, the guy at the bodega."

"I couldn't look at Nathan Lane full in the face, either."

"I'm supposed to matter more than Nathan Lane, too. You do look straight at the people you love, I've seen you do it."

"I'm not going to play this game." I turn away from him and start striding back to the house. "I'm not going to perform some stupid test to determine our whole future. If you go, it's because you want to. Stay if you want to. I don't care."

"You don't care?"

At this I stop. There was pain in his voice. Not the intentional wounded-dove voice of someone inducing guilt, no, this was genuine. I feel it too, just then, the slicing sensation across the chest.

I turn to him, and look at the buttons of that birthday-gift shirt. "I didn't mean that. I didn't. I just want to go home."

"So we'll go home."

We finish the rest of the walk in silence, not touching. I have my arms folded, he's got his hands in his pockets. It's a thing he's been scolded for on stage, always going for the pockets. It's his failsafe, what he does when he doesn't know what else to do.

"I'll head home from here," he says at the doorstep.

"You're going to throw me to the wolves alone?" I rejoin, grasping for our old banter.

"Good night."

I can sense him searching for eye contact, so I look up, make myself look, but the intensity makes me glance away, too fast.

"Good night."

I step into the darkness of the doorway and watch him go, disappearing in the dark and reappearing in the streetlights, until he rounds the corner, where he'll descend into the subway and be whisked back home.

20

Milo

hate to be tucked in like a baby, but I never mind a few more moments with my granddaughter.

She's handed me my medications and a glass of water, which she is now setting carefully on a coaster on the nightstand. She has already pulled the dusty curtains at the windows, switched on the light in the hall as a kind of nightlight. She switches on this receiver gizmo next to the bed, telling me it's one of Eva's old "baby monitors" and she'll be able to hear in her room. There's a little bell so I can ring it into the monitor if I need her. With Eleanor moving in, and the nurses having so little to do—my not speaking is nothing they can help with their sitting around—the twenty-four-hour staff is gone, leaving Eleanor's presence plus this monitor contraption to keep watch. This is some kind of improvement—fewer strangers, anyhow—but a baby monitor?

She reaches down to pull the comforter up higher, which would be tricky for me one-handed. I use my good hand to reach out, and try to lift her chin a little, so I can see her better, but she flinches. Actually flinches! As if I was about to hurt her, as if I could ever do such a thing. I draw my hand back like it's stung.

She notices. "I'm sorry, Grampa, I've had a long day and I guess I'm easily startled right now."

I try to get in her line of sight with my "what's wrong" face.

She looks around, over both shoulders, before she answers. She looks me in the eye and I notice then how blue the skin is under her eyes. "It's Daniel. He wants me to … He wants something I can't give him, and if I don't, he'll move three thousand miles away and I'll never see him again."

I can feel my sad face mirror hers. I do this a lot now, I notice, in lieu of speaking my sympathy. What is it she won't do for him? What does he want from her?

"Do you have everything you need, Grampa?"

I nod, settling back on the pillows. A soft yellow light glows from the lamp next to me. A small table holds the water, my glasses, and a couple of books.

"It was nice tonight, wasn't it?" she says.

She's just making conversation. It wasn't nice for her, I could tell the whole time, from Joel's gooey toast to his love for Jessica and his presentation of a gaudy necklace as anniversary present to the political fights to Eva pinning her in a corner, and then whatever came after…

Not so great for me, either, considering one unwanted guest.

I won't stay if I'm not wanted.

Ha, since when do you wait for an invitation? Haunting me all through dinner wasn't enough for you? I hope you didn't come back for dessert because the great-grands ate it all.

"Good night, Grampa." Eleanor kisses my forehead and walks with a step heavier than natural for her, a young woman, out into the hall, then slowly to her room.

At dinner, Vivian had been in the chair catty-corner to me at the dining table, making her usual series of infuriating cryptic comments, when everyone was ignoring me for people who could actually have cocktail chatter. It made me wish I was a real drooling invalid who would not notice or care. One of those desiccated old upright corpses you see dragged out by family members from time to time.

That's right, I talked to you when no one else would. I can't see well out in the dark outside the lamplight, but I think she's on a low bench at the end of the bed, where Bee used to sit to put on her stockings and shoes.

Fine, talk to me. Knock yourself out.

Were you surprised when I died?

I sense a change in her position, as if she's stood and is approaching my small circle of light next to the bed.

I wouldn't think it would surprise you, considering. You always said I was reckless.

You were. Always dashing off alone, in a tizzy about something. Not safe for a young woman, so we always had to chase you. Is that what you liked? The chase?

You assume I calculated every move. That's Allen's game. Not mine.

You didn't act for no reason. Nobody does that.

I didn't say it was for no reason.

Nothing you ever did made sense. How many times did you lose a job in the Depression? Or almost lose it?

I was unwell, you know that. Not that anyone cared.

I cared! I covered for you in Boston. Told them a sympathetic story so you wouldn't get canned. I helped you plenty of times.

Until you didn't.

That's not fair. You were asking for something I could not give you.

Could not? Or would not?

I'm not going to keep this up. What's the point? You want your own personal Day of Atonement? Well, see if you can turn back time, then. I mean, you can come back from sixty years ago to haunt me, so why not that, too? Of course you can't. You're just a trick of the brain torturing me until I die, well, hurry it up already. I'm eighty-eight years old and I can't talk, and no one pays attention to me anymore but Eleanor and I can't help her either when I'm like this. I'm worm food in a few years regardless, so God or the devil or whatever demon you are, just kill me off right now already.

Take arms against a sea of troubles, and by opposing, end them.

What nonsense are you talking? What's Hamlet got to do with it?

Bet you didn't know I loved Shakespeare. I played Ophelia in high school.

She steps forward from the shadows, into the light of the side-table lamp. I gasp aloud at the sight.

She's drenched, as if she's been bathing or swimming, but she's fully clothed, including a wool coat and kid gloves. That's not what makes me scream inside my head, no. It's the unnatural blue pallor of her skin and lips.

My mute screaming reaches a zenith right about the time she stretches out a cold wet glove and closes it around my wrist.

21

New York City, April, 1936

"Hey, Jailbird, got a dummy lyric for me on that Act One song?"

Allen squinted at the manuscript paper on the piano. "Yeah. How about 'Milo Short is a nincompoop, short of finesse.'"

"I like that well enough I may leave it as is. Think Gordon would mind if I wrote myself into the show?"

Milo reclined on the settee, tapping out the rhythm on his leg with a pencil. He could make up his own dummy lyrics to help him remember Allen's melody and phrasing, but he liked to hear his partner's version. Allen's wit was back in fine form since he decided to lay off the hooch finally, his stint in a Boston jail sufficiently humiliating him, not to mention everyone involved in the show. For days afterward, he'd sweated that the news would get back to Winchell, though Milo reassured him frequently they were not nearly important enough for that. They weren't, at the time.

But they were edging closer to that day when they might be important enough to take down in the society columns. Which was not so much a blessing, in Milo's view.

Hilarity had straightened itself out just in time and had run 350 performances, topping even Cole Porter's *Jubilee*, which the critics had worked themselves into raptures about. Rightly so, Milo thought, having seen the show and goggled at Porter's wit and musicality.

"Just goes to show what the critics know and nuts to them," Gordon had bellowed at El Morocco, where they all clustered after the New York opening. Milo and Allen had left early that night; Allen because he couldn't stand not to get himself fried to the hat with everyone else guzzling champagne, and Milo out of solidarity and to make sure he wouldn't detour into another club. Vivian and Mark Bell had resumed their romance with the grudging approval of the stage director, because Bell was performing better than ever. Milo had been startled to hear him declare, "That dame must be good for his vocal cords." When they left Elmo's that night, Vivian was in Bell's lap and his lips were wrapped around her earlobe.

Still flying from defying the early critics, Gordon hired Short and Allen immediately to write *The High Hat*, based on some British play involving star-crossed romance, reversal of fortune, and a dash of class satire.

Allen half-turned on the piano bench. "Hey, Short, want to grab a bite tonight? Head out to 21 or something, see what's doing."

"It's Passover tonight, I'm heading over to my parents' for the Seder. Word has it that Miriam has invited a friend. Oy."

"What's 'oy' for?"

"They want I should get married, now that Max has stomped on the glass."

"Oy, then."

"That is the strangest sound coming from you."

Milo was gritting his teeth to go into his parents' tiny apartment. He couldn't walk into that shriveled up little space without thinking of their first Bronx apartment with its gleaming parquet floors and sunken living room and the pride that Yosef Schwartz took in having raised his family out of the teeming tenements.

Returning from Boston, Milo had approached the family apartment with an engulfing sense of dread, seeing from a distance a pile of furniture out on the street and dark figures hovering near it. Having walked back from the train station even in the snow, the better to save cab fare, he'd been treated to a long trek of gradual and painful discovery. His father hadn't been making rent and they got evicted; apparently a wealthier cousin had been helping before, but either could not or would not send him another cent.

Max and his father were taking shifts guarding their things on the sidewalk and sleeping in the tailor shop, while Leah and his mother had moved in with sympathetic neighbors, sleeping on the living room floor since the Kleins themselves were all full up with family. They'd tried to send him a telegram in Boston, but it must have arrived only after he left.

Milo had taken what earnings he'd managed to save from *Hilarity* and found the family a new apartment. Smaller, and farther yet from the Grand Concourse to which his father aspired, but it was a roof and they could afford it. Leah slept on a cot in with their parents, and Milo and Max took turns on the living room sofa or floor, though like as not Max would stay over in the shop and Milo would end up staying at Allen's place if his wife was staying in the country, which was often enough.

Milo's father had taken to stalking around with a hunted look. It was as if the reeking, cramped, dark tenement life was about to pounce on him. Mr. Schwartz had always been fond of pronouncing their family had gone "from the ghetto to the Grand Concourse!" though they never lived closer than a block away from that most favored of Bronx addresses.

Then the contract came in for *The High Hat*, and instead of feeling like a success, Milo felt his stomach turn over watching his father have to accept his son's money just to get by. Max's bride's family had given him a job in their chain of dry-goods stores, and he and Miriam were able to set up housekeeping in a snug little room on the West Side, so they did all right for themselves. Milo moved out into his own place just a few blocks away, to give his family breathing room, but he knew the specter of his father's failed business took up as much space as he himself ever did. Mr. Schwartz did what tailoring work he could drum up right there in the apartment, for their Bronx neighbors. He talked often of "when I open the new place" but not a one of them believed it would ever happen.

"Why don't you?" Allen asked through a pencil he'd stuck between his teeth, at the piano, between scribbling down notes.

"Why don't I what?"

"Get married. People tend to do that, even a lousy sot like me."

"And it's made you blissfully happy."

"Hey, I got kids. I like my kids."

Milo sat up and rubbed his temples. "I'm just too busy working to think about girls. I'm supporting my parents now, and Leah, and we'll all end up in the gutter if we flop. Aren't you worried about that, too? Flopping?"

"Sure I am, but the wife's family has money."

"So that's why you married her. Very romantic."

Allen jumped up from the piano bench and stomped across the room to grab his smokes off the coffee table. "Gimme some credit here, of course not. I can't say it wasn't a bonus, but I'm not some…gigolo."

"You're not exactly the picture of romance, is all. So what did you do it for?"

Allen gestured to his body with his lit cigarette. "Do I look the part of Adonis to you? I liked Dorothy fine, and she was the first girl I knew who'd say yes. And like I said, it's what people do. I bet I know why you don't get married."

"Do tell."

"You're stuck on that Vivian girl."

"Stuck nothing. First, she's not Jewish. Second, however long she hung around me, and however pretty might she be, she is not my type. I hardly see her anymore since *Hilarity* ended and the stage director wouldn't hire her again."

"And good riddance, says me. That girl was trouble."

"Listen to you, Jailbird, talking about trouble."

Allen turned to the window overlooking Fifth Avenue. "You don't know the half of it."

"And I don't want to. So we gonna get to work, or what?"

"Yeah, yeah, let a fella have a smoke."

"When's the missus back from the country anyway?"

"Next week, she says. So there's no need to give you the bum rush. You can bunk over here if you want."

"Nah, I told you, the Seder? Plus if I'm spending rent money on my own place I might as well use it."

"Get a piano and we can work there, too."

"I'm saving up, I can't just go off and buy a piano, and I'm not taking the one from my parents' place. My mother tried to give it to me and you should've seen the look on Leah's face. Like to break my heart."

"I know, cheapskate. Even without Passover you wouldn't have gone out to 21."

"You bet. I don't have a rich absent wife, so I've gotta assume every penny I earn from this showbiz gig is the last I'll ever see."

"Well, cheer up, Mr. Milo, and maybe you'll find a rich and available Jewess at tonight's dinner."

"Shut up, will ya? I've gotta think of some words here."

Allen finally shut his trap and Milo sank back down to his best thinking position, which looked just like sleep but had been his good luck charm since they started working on *The High Hat*.

Milo Short is a nincompoop, short of finesse...

This was for a lively waltz duet between the two leads, who would spar with hate-you-love-you electricity for the whole first act.

Milo hummed the phrasing and his mind spun with words.

I'm a smart girl who knows when to give it a rest...

He smiled a little as he lay. Not bad as a start. He imagined the man's rejoinder.

But without all your chatter, I'll feel just bereft!

No. "Just" was a mere filler, and "bereft" wasn't much of a rhyme. Plus one could never count on the singer to deliver a sarcastic line with, well, sarcasm. The stage director on *Hilarity* had rapped him for that trick, saying it all had to be there in the music, and it was a lazy writer who depended on the singer to do his job for him.

"Hey," Milo said to the air, his eyes still closed. "Can I have more beats in that phrase? It's too short."

"No, you can't. That's how the music goes."

"C'mon. Couple more eighth notes or something."

"You deaf, too? I said no. You can do it, genius. Write me some more 'sparkling' words."

Milo cringed. The reviews had focused more on his words than the melodies in *Hilarity*, which were written off with faint praise like "hummable" or "passable." Milo had tried time and again to point out to Allen that the reviewers were talking through their hats because anyhow, they condemned the show as boring in Boston, and look what happened.

He knew by now he was better off to leave it alone. Once Allen got a notion in his head, there was no budging it.

MILO DUTIFULLY ATE his bitter herbs and matzoh, murmured along with the prayers and songs, the whole time wishing he could get all excited about the young lady across the table and make everyone happy. Esther herself looked none too happy to be there, and kept looking out the window each time Mrs. Schwartz tried to impress her with another quote from a *Hilarity* review, or another story of when Milo met someone famous.

Milo wanted to climb inside his shirt collars and hide, since he'd told those stories to thrill Leah, not so that his mother would run them up a flagpole for a potential bride.

When at last the hidden matzoh was consumed, and the Seder concluded, Mrs. Schwartz observed wistfully that there were no children yet at their table, casting a glance at Max and his bride that made Miriam blush powerfully.

"We could have joined the Kleins," noted Max, with a reassuring smile toward his wife. "They have little children and I'm sure had a festive Pesach."

"Feh. We can barely fit in this hovel as it is, and their apartment is no bigger," pronounced Mr. Schwartz. His words crashed down over the table with the force of a hammer strike.

Milo blinked rapidly to keep his eyes open. The lengthy dinner with all of its rituals, and the burden of being waved around in front of a single young woman, made him wish for his own narrow bed in his own quiet apartment. Not that Esther wasn't a fine gal, and not that he didn't want to settle down some time or another, but he had enough on his hands with trying not to be a showbiz failure and keeping his family out of the gutter. Also, Esther hadn't looked at him more than twice throughout the evening, which was not much of a romantic atmosphere.

"Moshe, you will see Esther home. She lives in the next block from you," declared his mother.

And so it was settled. There was no argument to be made. He took his leave from the family and they stepped out into the chilly April night. Their breath fogged the air, taking the place of conversation they might have had if they'd liked each other in the least.

"I'm sorry you got stuck with me tonight," Milo offered. "You must've had someplace else better to be."

"Not really. My parents are stuck in Bavaria now, some nonsense about their passports. They were visiting aunts and uncles. It was a kindness to have me here, else I'd have been alone."

"Oh gosh, I'm sorry to hear that."

"Too bad we don't fall madly in love and make them all happy." Esther said this with no bitterness at all.

"I was thinking the same thing. If only we could flip a switch, eh?"

"I have a beau, but my parents don't like him. He's Russian and lives on the East Side. I met him at a labor rally, and they don't like that much, either."

"Good for you. May you marry your Russian and have ten children."

"I can't marry him while they're gone. It wouldn't be right."

"No, you're right. I think this is your place, here?"

"Thanks for the escort."

Milo saw Esther disappear through her apartment doorway, and thought if admiration were something like love, he might have it. A little bit, anyway.

Once inside his own small, quiet apartment, Milo noticed the stack of mail he'd tossed on his table before heading over to work with Allen. Just peeking out from other envelopes, he spied some feminine handwriting that looked familiar.

He tore open the envelope.

> *Dear Milo,*
>
> *I've missed you, and I've been so bored without the music. I forgot how much I appreciated working around such artists! I haven't forgotten how you helped me in Boston. It didn't convince them to keep me on for another show, but I could at least save some face, and I've never forgotten that. Would you let me treat you to a friendly cup of coffee? Phone me at the number below and we can meet. It's the least I can do, considering all you've done for me.*
>
> *Yours musically,*
>
> *Vivian*

Milo smiled through his yawn, as he dropped the letter back onto the table.

Just when he thought she'd forgotten all about that day when he'd lied for her. Not until he saw her spiky, slanty writing did he realize how much he did miss having her around. He could well imagine Allen's rolling eyes, but what of it? Allen wasn't in charge of him, nor was anyone else. He'd call her, but first thing in the morning, after he'd finally had some sleep.

VIVIAN PUSHED BACK from the counter with a sigh and a feline stretch of the arms.

"You sleeping okay?" Milo asked, slurping the last of his bitter coffee and reaching for his wallet.

"No, as a matter of fact, but that's why this coffee is just the thing." She grabbed for the check. "Mine. I insist."

"No, let me…"

Milo lost the tug-of-war for the check and felt his cheeks flush. He could only imagine what his father would say about letting a girl pay for him.

"Let me walk you home?"

Vivian smiled by way of assent, and swiveled gracefully off the counter stool. Milo scooped up his hat, and together they stepped out into the bright bustling spring.

"If only it could be like this every day!" she cried, tipping up her face to the sun, her pert nose leading the way. Milo put his hand on her back to guide her around a woman pushing a pram in front of them.

"We wouldn't appreciate it," Milo observed. "I bet those guys in Florida complain about sunburn."

Milo wondered if that would make a good lyric idea, something about complaining about sunburn on a sunny day. One of the characters in *The High Hat* was a fussbudget so saw the downside of everything.

"Milo? Are you in there?"

"Sorry, got to thinking about the show. Anyway, Vivian, we talked about me the whole time. What's going on with you?"

Vivian pointed up. They were passing under the Sixth Avenue El, and the train was rumbling closer. They fell into silence as they crossed under the metal latticework, which sliced the spring sun into splashes about their feet.

Safely past, she answered, "I have nothing much to tell."

"Well, how are you getting by? If you don't mind my asking."

"Why should I mind? I just don't have much of an answer."

Milo looked over her clothing, which was natty as ever. He didn't know from dresses, but as a tailor's son he knew fine work when he saw it.

"Do I pass inspection?"

"Sorry. You see much of Mark Bell these days?" Milo shot her a sidelong glance.

"Not very much, no."

She led the way, turning down a leafy side street at a corner with Fifth Avenue. "Well, here I am," she said, indicating a tall, narrow brownstone.

Milo let out a low whistle before he could stop himself. "That's prettier than any boarding house I ever saw."

"That's because it's not. I'm watching it for a girlfriend. They just got married and they're traveling abroad," she replied, rooting around in her pocketbook. "She knew I was in between apartments, so to speak, so I'm caretaker. Ah, there's the key. Would you like to come up for a tour?"

Milo looked at her sideways.

Vivian dropped her arms to her sides, impatient. "What, do you think someone's going to rat you out to your family, that—oh, my!—you walked into the apartment of a single woman?"

"No, I just… I don't want to get you in trouble, with the landlady or something."

"Stop acting like it's the nineteenth century and come in already."

Milo looked at his feet to avoid being eye level with Vivian's derriere as she walked up the narrow stairs with an ornate wooden railing. She stopped at a second-floor apartment and pushed her way inside.

It wasn't large, but it was prettily made up in floral and soft colors. The wood furniture was curvy, the upholstery bulging and tufted. Milo saw no evidence of another human living there. They had the place to themselves. He felt overly warm, and pulled at the knot of his tie.

"I've got a beer. Want one?"

"Early for beer. But I'm likely to melt over here, so that'd be swell."

"Sit down already, you look like you want to float around the room like a dirigible."

Vivian swung her way back to her little sitting area, where Milo had perched on the sofa. She handed him the dark brown bottle and helped herself to an unladylike swig.

"Nice place."

"Yeah, it is, isn't it? Too bad I don't get to keep it forever."

Milo took another drink, regretting that he'd accepted it. Now he was stuck for a beer's length of time, or he'd have to abandon it half-drunk on her table, which seemed wasteful and ungrateful. But their relaxed chatter over the coffee had shriveled up and died.

Vivian dug in her pocketbook again until she found her cigarette case. Milo struck a match and leaned forward, grateful to do something other than sit there like a statue among the pigeons. She cupped her hand over his to steady it and took a deep inhale. Milo had a close-up look at her bright green eyes, irises flecked with gold, before she released his hand and sat back with a smile that looked serene and satisfied. Milo had the sense that he'd played right into her hands somehow.

How many times had he lit a cigarette for her, and why only now did he have to clench his fists to keep his hands from shaking?

"So, what are you going to do? When the happy couple gets back?"

"Hmm? Oh. I'll think of something."

"I suppose if you had to, you could always go back home? You got people in Chicago?"

"Ha!" She waved her cigarette so hard a bit of ash flew into the air. "And slink back to my sister Estelle who would say, 'I told you so, Vivi, I told you that was a mistake! I told you!'" Vivian performed this mockery of her sister with expert malice. "No, I've got time, they'll be touring around for ages. He's loaded, you know. Very successful of late."

"Lucky him, these days. What business is this fella in?"

Vivian puffed out a line of smoke. "Showbiz." She fixed Milo with a look that made him feel a blush creep all the way up his neck and over the tops of his ears.

He performed a double take at his watch that would have done Barrymore proud. "Oh sheesh, I gotta make a move. I'm late to meet Allen, we've got some songs cooking. Thanks for the beer, it was great seeing you, stay in touch, okay?"

He kept up the chatter, choosing to ignore the wry grin that had taken up residence on Vivian's pretty face. His dominant emotion as he gained the sidewalk outside her place, seeing no one he knew, was profound, through-and-through relief.

22

1999

Eleanor

'm just clambering into bed when a sound rends the air, a sound that's barely human. I scrabble around for my glasses and trip over the hem of my nightgown running into the hall, as a chilling understanding crashes over me. I fly down the hall as fast as I dare and into my grandfather's room.

The yellow hall light knifes through the dark and lights up his terrified face. I run to his side and clasp his hand.

"Grampa! It's me! Are you sick?"

Without his glasses he looks vulnerable and sick, just like he did in the hospital. He trembles. I put my hand on his forehead and it feels cool and normal, though his hands in mine are clammy.

"Take deep breaths," I command him. "Try to sip in the air slowly. Does anything hurt? Point to what hurts."

He doesn't seem to be hearing me, and I understand, oh, maybe this is what an old man's death looks like. I'm not ready to lose him, I don't care how old he is, how infirm, I'll never be ready, he should stay with me forever. I squeeze his hand tighter. "I'm here, don't be afraid," although he might have reason to be—I sure as hell am, my heart is galloping and I'm shaking— but this is what you say to the vulnerable. This is how you talk to children, to your father who is riddled with tumors, to your aged grandfather. You don't say, *you might be dying.* You lie, because that's the right thing to do. *Don't go, Grampa Milo, please not yet,* but I only say that in my head, keeping up the façade of being calm and strong.

His trembling eases, and his breath slows, but not in a scary, shallow way. No, this is the breathing of someone calming down. His eyes search out mine at last, and he nods, as if just registering my presence, *oh yes, Eleanor.*

He stretches one arm over to the table and fumbles around it. I hand him his glasses and he scoots his way slightly up the pillow. I help him prop up.

"I'm going to pull up a chair. Stay put." An idiotic thing to say. Where would he go?

I bring in the vanity stool from my room for lack of anything else handy, and draw it up close to his bed, taking his hand again. His knobby bones protrude; I could almost read them, like Braille. I think of the many tunes he's played, the songs he's written, the contracts he's signed bringing plays and musicals to life. The times he's patted my hair as a girl, or when he's tickled one of his great-grands. So much has passed through these hands.

"I know you can't tell me what happened," I say, and he rests his head back, closes his eyes. "But I'm going to ask you some yes or no questions." He nods his understanding. I ask him a series of questions about physical symptoms that Joel said could indicate heart attack, or another stroke. He shakes his head no for each one. "Was it a nightmare?" He doesn't answer right off, and at first I think he's asleep. But then he looks me straight in the eye, still not replying. "You saw it again, didn't you?" Tiny nod, and a darting look over my shoulder that sends a shiver down my back. I can't help but look, too, though there's nothing there at all, of course.

He leans forward then, and strokes my cheek with his good hand. It's shaking again, whether from fear, or adrenaline, or just because he's old and tired, I can't say. But the look on his face sends tears spilling down my cheeks.

This is a look of goodbye. I ought to know because I've seen it before. I'll call Joel, he'll know what to do, if this might really be the end, or maybe he can reassure me, if he has any reassurance to give.

I grab Grampa Milo's hand and bring it to my lips for a kiss. I don't speak either now, because what does a person say?

He tugs his hand slightly, and so I let it go. He closes his eyes, wearing the small sad smile of one who grieves.

THE MORNING FINDS me not having slept any more that night. Esme lets herself in, and nearly jumps out of her shoes as I approach her. I apologize for scaring her, and then explain our evening. Joel had come over late, hair still rumpled from his pillow, and checked him over, declaring Grampa Milo no worse than he had been the day before, though of course he couldn't give me the guarantee I'd been childishly hoping for. "El, I wish I could promise you a life expectancy but I can't do that," he'd said, and folded me in a tight hug.

After Joel left, I sat curled in the chair next to Grampa Milo's bed most of the night, except for when I paced anxious circuits around the room, checking his chest constantly for rising and falling. I tried to talk myself back into bed many times, reasoning that there was no actual indication that he would die in the night, and even if that were to happen, my sitting next to him would hardly prevent it.

Now that Esme has arrived, I choose this moment to shower and change out of my thin nightgown. By the time I come back downstairs, I am faint with relief that he is awake. Still in bed, but awake.

He's got a tray across him on the bed with some coffee and toast. I force a smile to bloom up through my worried frown that he's eating in bed. He's always managed to get to the eat-in kitchen, and just last night was in the dining room having his whiskey and soda at our lively dinner.

Esme explains, "Mr. Short is feeling tired today, perhaps because of his nightmare last night." She and I share a glance. We have something in common, we two. We've both witnessed him seeing things and behaving strangely, and have hidden this from most people. We are also, I suspect, both ambivalent about having made this choice. Here we are, both still keeping our secrets.

The use of the word "nightmare" pricks my memory. I sink down onto a low bench at the end of the bed, remembering that scream. A real, loud scream from my mute grandfather.

Grampa Milo catches the look on my face and he tilts his head, questioning. I shake my head and wave my hand as if to say "it's nothing," forcing another smile.

GRAMPA MILO EATS only a hard-boiled egg for lunch, and has only gotten out of bed long enough to dress, before he has climbed back in. By this time, family members have begun trooping in and out of the house, holding whispered conferences on the stairs, in the kitchen, in the upstairs library. *He's getting weaker. He's frail. He's sleeping so much. Maybe it's just a bad day. Maybe it's the end. Should he go to the hospital?*

Dr. Joel checks him out once more. He's as fine as his mute eighty-eight-year-old self has been for the last several weeks, aside from the lethargy. Uncle Paul asks my cousin if he thinks Grampa Milo is going to die soon, and Dr. Joel says maybe. The best he can say is maybe, or maybe not. And Joel looks briefly angry as he glares down at his shoes, as if his medical degree and all those excruciating hours as a resident have failed him in answering simple questions.

All the while I'm hovering at the edges of the Shorts that flow in and out, as I usually do. I hate to do so, but I tear myself away during one of Grampa

Milo's long naps that day and go to the library where I scroll through microfilm records of telephone directories, city directories, and old census data, looking for Vivian Adair. The census data is not helpful at all. She came to and left New York between the years of 1930 and 1940, and that much we knew already.

I see listings for her—at least, I think it's her—as late as 1936, which leaves him a plausible father for Millicent's approximate 1937 birth. It seems possible that someone would accidentally get left out of a directory, but accidentally added when they had left? Less likely. I turn the switch hard on the microfilm so that it winds itself so fast around the spool I bet it would cut me if I touched the edge with my finger.

I will have to call Alex and tell him I can't rule out Milo, but I'll also have to tell him my grandfather may be dying, and I cannot now accuse him of fathering a bastard child.

As I step into the parlor, I see Grampa Milo sitting up, awake, and I'm delighted, but mad at myself for being gone and missing these precious minutes of alertness.

"Grampa! I'm so glad you're up. I hope you're feeling better."

He smiles but his eyes seem dull, clouded somehow. He nods, though I haven't asked him anything.

"Would you like me to put on some music for you?"

Another nod.

"Ella Fitzgerald, perhaps?"

Eva's daughter, Olivia, blurts from across the room, "Look what I found!"

In my rush to Grampa Milo's side, I hadn't noticed her there. Eva must be in residence, somewhere around, probably bossing Esme in the kitchen. Olivia kneels in front of a cardboard box of old records someone must have dragged out. My little cousin is a sprightly seven who reads well beyond her years, as Eva will tell anyone who stands still long enough to listen, and now she brandishes a 45 rpm record. I wonder if she even knows what that thing is. She does know what it says, though, and announces it to all of us. "Look! It's 'Love Me, I Guess'! Play that!"

Grampa Milo shakes his head violently, again and again, so much that for a moment I think it's a seizure, then he sinks down into the chair like a sullen child, glaring into midair.

I glance back at Olivia, who has put down the record, and even from this far I can watch shiny tears trembling in her wide eyes.

"Honey, Grampa Milo isn't feeling well, would you go find your mother, please?"

Olivia leaps to her feet and tears out of the room. I understand how she feels. I found the elderly terrifying too, once upon a time, even when all was normal.

Esme, Eva, and I try, but we can't get Grampa Milo to respond after this. With reluctance I head up the stairs to my room, to make the call I'm dreading.

In my journalism days—I'm thinking of these days as long past, already, though it was only a few weeks ago when I melted down—I would sometimes rehearse my perfect version of how an interview would go, before picking up the phone. Sometimes this was counterproductive, if it all went south. All the same, it was my form of pep talk, helping me get over that hurdle of picking up the phone to call a stranger and ask prying questions, something I never could get used to. I marvel now that I ever thought I could make a whole career of doing that, for decades on end.

He picks up immediately. "I was just going to call you," Alex says, voice bright with excitement even over the crackly cell phone connection. "I found something else."

"Oh?"

"Song lyrics."

I sit up from my hunch on the bed. Across the way in the vanity mirror I can see the worry run furrows across my forehead.

"Lyrics to 'Love Me, I Guess.' In Vivian's writing."

I swallow hard. "How do you know it's Vivian's?"

"Because of other notes she left behind. She kept a scrapbook of sorts and would write captions for the things she pasted in. It looks like she even tried her hand at a couple poems, about the lake. It took a while to get back to that box between work, and cleaning out the boring stuff from Estelle's like dishes, but anyway, when I finally did I found this old steno pad I almost pitched out but I happened to open it. I recognized the lyrics from the movie."

"Well, she was a secretary."

"You don't understand, this isn't just copying down, there are scratch-offs, and rewordings. It's a real live work in progress. What if she wrote that song? What if it really was her work?"

I stand up off the bed so fast I'm dizzy. "Are you calling my grandfather a thief? First he impregnates and abandons Vivian and now he stole her work and claimed it as his? What kind of people do you think we are?"

"I didn't mean that… I just… If you could see what I'm looking at. It does not look like taking dictation. It's not in shorthand or something."

"I can't talk about this now."

"Then why did you call?" His voice has grown sharp with irritation.

I'd almost forgotten I was the one who initiated the call. "Fine. Two things. First, if I'm looking at the right Vivian Adair—a secretary of that name who was living in Manhattan in the 1930s until she left sometime after 1936—I cannot say for sure that my grandfather can be eliminated as a candidate."

Alex interrupts, "And I checked my mom's birth announcement. It was in the newspaper in 1937. It's not like they could have time-traveled to backdate that, so she definitely wasn't born later." Now I can hear his voice quicken.

"Here's the other thing, though. Grampa Milo has taken a turn for the worse."

Alex is silent as I explain the previous night, though I skip over the part about the uncanny shriek that jarred me out of sleep. I focus instead on his lethargy, disconnection, lack of appetite.

I pause and scrunch my face, trying to hold it all in, though my throat aches with the effort. It's like trying to swallow a rock.

Alex begins, "I'm sorry to hear that. But that makes the question even more urgent."

"How can you say that?" I croak out, breaking the dam by speaking. "How can that be your concern right now?"

"You love your grandfather, and I can hear your heart breaking. But my mom's heart is breaking in front of me, all the time. She's an orphan."

"So am I."

"And it's horrible, isn't it?"

And so Alex has drawn a bright line connecting his mother and me. Both of us with absent, complicated mothers, fathers taken away too soon. I want to push back against this. It's unfair, it's emotional blackmail, but it also settles into my marrow the way true things always do. We are connected, Millicent and me, by circumstance at least, if not more than that.

I can't reply to this. Alex begins again, his voice now soft. "You keep assuming this will be awful for your grandfather. What if it's not? If it's even true, which it might not be. I'm not saying it's a guarantee, you know. But it's as simple as a blood draw. I checked it all out, we could find out as soon as ten days and we don't have to keep going in circles about it. You can even frame it to him, to your whole family, as an act of mercy to an old lady who's been through a shock and just wants an answer."

"A mitzvah."

"Sure, that. What you said."

Downstairs, someone begins playing the piano. On a normal day this would be my grandfather. This playing is regimented and by-the-book, rhythmically. Someone very careful to hit every note just like it's on the page. I suspect it's one of Eva's kids who has been drilled with lessons. All the Short kids are subjected to music lessons, in case one of us is a secret prodigy. We are all merely fair to medium-good.

Yes, it's Pachelbel's Canon in D, I can tell now, which is nothing Grampa Milo would have picked to play, and not for nothing to fill the heavy silence with something other than impending death.

"Eleanor? Still there?"

"Yes." I clear my throat, wipe my face with my hand. "What about the notebook? We can't package that up as a mitzvah, to ask my grandfather if he stole this woman's work and passed it off as his."

"Maybe it doesn't matter," Alex replies, though I can tell from the dull tone in his voice that to him, at least, it very much does. "Vivian's dead and gone and we can't do anything for her. But I just want to answer my mom's question."

"Just? What if it turns out he is? Then what?"

"I don't know. Honestly, I don't know. I'm sorry I got so excited before. For what it's worth I wish Estelle had never told us anything. I wish that vicious old bitch had kept her secret to herself and we'd all lived in happy ignorance. But I can't pretend not to know. We can't make ourselves stop wondering."

No, we can't. And my grandfather can't make himself talk, can't make himself stop seeing a vision of this woman who knotted up his life, somehow, all those decades ago.

"I think you should come here."

"What? Where?"

"Here, New York. Come, and bring Vivian's things. We will think positive and assume my Grampa is only having a bad spell and that he'll be okay. And that he'll have a lucid, cheerful moment and through sign language and who knows what, we will ask him what he knows. We'll tell him about the mitzvah and show him the notebook. Assuming we haven't made him keel over from a stroke at the idea he might have fathered another child."

"Wow. You're serious."

"So they tell me."

"I can't afford it."

"I'll pay for the ticket and write it off as research. My uncle owns an apartment that I think is still vacant, you can stay there."

"I don't want to take your money."

"Hell, for all we know it might be yours, too."

"Shit," he says, stretching the word out long, half-whistling it. It sounds like he genuinely hadn't thought about that part, that he might be entitled to a legacy, he and Millicent. Song lyrics aside, even. I'm glad to believe this of him, though I know my cousins and aunts and uncles won't be so understanding.

"Can you get away?" I repeat. "Can someone else handle *The Sound of Music* for a while?"

"Are you sure you want me to come?"

When I catch a glimpse of my face in the mirror, my color is high, my eyes shining and jaw firmly set. For a moment I think I'm seeing Naomi in the mirror. This is her face when she's made up her mind. It's an unfamiliar look for me.

"Yes. I'm sure. As soon as you can."

23

July 1936

The New York summer was sticking all over Milo. It pasted his shirt to him, soaked his hatband, and dripped over the paper when he bent over his notebook and tried to write. A creaky fan just moved the hot air around, but it was better than the heavy stillness when he shut it off.

Someone had let loose a hydrant outside, and Milo had half a mind to go join the frolicking kids and soak himself, clothes and all. He'd just read in the *Times* the other day that Central Park had a record temperature of 106. Ladies' rubber heels from their shoes were getting stuck in the sticky asphalt, and some poor schlemiel had left his dentures out on the windowsill and they melted, if the paper was to be believed.

Allen's place was shaded and a few degrees cooler, and there was a piano, but Milo had taken to working at home, and alone, more often. Something was unsettling him about being around Allen's place so much. Dorothy almost never came to the city anymore, though she sent telegrams and letters about this or that bill to be paid or account settled. His children had been writing him letters that were forced and strained with duty. Allen griped that his wife was probably standing over them with a ruler, ready to smack their hands if they didn't cross their t's properly.

And yet... Milo wrestled each day with whether he should be at Allen's side. Milo had been pretending not to notice the increase in bottles strewn around the apartment in Dorothy's absence, and the increasingly late hour at which Allen chose to begin his day's work.

Milo had helped Allen dry out once already, with the help of an embarrassing arrest, but how could a person keep that up forever? He couldn't be Allen's warden, could he? Plus he was visiting his parents all the more. Their father had taken to falling into silent miseries that lasted for days. Max wasn't often able to visit, working so hard for his bride's parents. Leah reported to Milo in a small, fretful voice that only Milo's presence made the place bearable. Mrs. Schwartz used to rally her daughter's spirits with forcefully bright chatter, but news of Hitler's Olympics and that lunatic's continued rise cast a long shadow all the way from Europe. New York might be relatively safe, but a person couldn't help but worry about those Jews left behind, known personally to you or not, it didn't matter.

"It's like a tomb in here," Leah had whispered to him on his last visit. Milo's sister was not given to exaggeration.

He'd thought about giving up his apartment and moving back in with them, yes, eating up the food and taking up space, but the full force of his income could go toward supporting them. The times he tried to suggest it were forcefully rejected by Yosef Schwartz, who apparently had swallowed all the pride he could stomach already, just in accepting Milo's assistance with rent and groceries while plying his tailoring at the kitchen table.

Allen would have to take care of himself. Come what may.

Come what may, a nice musical-sounding phrase. Would that work in the song? Milo stared at the paper, his vision swimming. He had better glasses now, along with a better pair of shoes. He'd bought new glasses the moment he could afford to. But if he worked too long on anything within arm's length his vision would swim and his head would ache. It would be his lot, it seemed. He wished he could just speak the words onto the page, like magic.

It was the last song to complete in the show, and it might be the death of him, if this heat didn't do the trick. It was a love song for John Garnett, whom Gordon had hooked as the male lead, no small feat as Hollywood was beckoning. No great singer was Garnett, for sure, and if you looked at him in the plain light of day you might think nothing of him at all. But the way he could put over a song was something like wizardry. And his dancing! He barely seemed to touch the floor.

Garnett was supposed to be a poor sap trying to woo a rich girl, who seemed to like him back—maybe; she toys with him all through Act One—in spite of herself. The only line Milo had yet written was the first.

You might just love me, I guess...

Allen's melody sprinkled notes like drops in a spring rain. The tune was bright, wistful, a little slow, yet picked up in the middle, and of course the dance director was demanding Allen craft a crackerjack rapid-fire tap section. That part wouldn't be Milo's problem, though. No words required to watch Garnett scamper and whirl about the stage.

So many words! In Milo's youthful ignorance, sitting around in Allen's office making up songs on slow days, he'd never dreamed he would be cranking them out so much. On days like this, when he got more sweat on the paper than lyrics, he'd wonder if his store of words was just dried up like a spent fire hose. Other people kept writing, of course, writing seemingly forever, but he wasn't like the others. He'd been dragged backward into lyric writing by Allen's ambition; he didn't belong. If he'd read the music properly at his first plugger audition he might be there still, like Finkelstein, a hired hand on the piano bench. Maybe that was all he was meant for, anyway.

After all, there was no tailor shop to go back to. Now he knew people, in fact. He was gonna get to meet John Garnett! He could plug the hell out of songs now.

He chewed on his lip and tried another line.

Though I'm not so well dressed....

The metallic shrill of his telephone nearly knocked Milo backward off his chair. He wanted to ignore it, but figured he just better answer. Could be that Leah was sick, or something like that. He wondered how people got by without phoning everyone up all the time before. Were they always showing up and banging on doors? Or did they just leave a person alone to think?

He snatched up the phone. "Yeah?"

Allen, sounding happily dissipated. "C'mon over. Let's work. Got some beer in the icebox, and you can pick up some sandwiches."

"I don't know, I'm working now."

"You'll think better with company. Tell me I'm wrong."

Milo sighed, defeated already. This was true. Despite it all, the words did seem to come easier when they worked side by side, and he'd already blown the afternoon on two lousy lines.

"Fine. Give me some time, I gotta catch the train."

"Aww, c'mon, live a little and take a cab. Or buy a car, why don't you buy a car?"

"Because my family can't eat a car. Now shut up before I change my mind."

WALKING INTO ALLEN'S place made Milo reconsider the benefits of married life with a wife actually in residence.

The place stunk like an alleyway. Half-eaten sandwiches and crusts crumbled away on plates, and various empty bottles—Milo dearly hoped these bottles were not all from that day or even that week—stood sentry on flat surfaces from the windowsills to the top of the upright piano.

Allen's blond whiskers had grown in to a scraggly shadow that looked more like dirt that needed to be scrubbed off.

"For crying out loud, look at you! You got a nice place here and you're living like a hobo."

Allen was seated at the piano and started tinkling out the melody for "Brother, Can You Spare a Dime?"

Milo began picking up the dirty plates and taking them to the sink. "I can't think in a place like this, so I'm going to clean up. Was that your big plan? Get me over here to be your housekeeper?"

Allen switched to "You're the Top."

"Yes, thank you, are you going to speak to me, or is this your new game now?"

Allen banged the keys and then whirled around on the piano bench, unsteadily, so it seemed to Milo from the entry to the kitchen. Allen said, "All right, keep your shirt on. I'm just having a little fun. I've barely seen you all week."

"And it shows."

"You got lyrics yet for 'Love Me, I Guess'? I mean, other than that line?"

Allen and Milo had come up with that one the week before.

"Nothing that's any good, not yet anyway. But it's the last song, so I think my brain is wrung out."

"What you need, friend, is a break. You've been working too hard and you can't think straight. You know how in baseball, sometimes a hitter will just miss everything sometimes? Game after game? He's thinking too much, right? Going after every pitch, getting desperate. Sometimes you gotta park your keister in the dugout." Allen jumped up. "All right, you're making me feel guilty cleaning up this slop by yourself." Allen started grabbing the beer bottles with loud clanks and stacking them along the windowsill in a kind of parade. The afternoon sun made them glow amber. It looked something like a monument.

Milo didn't care to ask how many days, or hours, that parade of booze represented. But Allen seemed spirited, not woozy or slurring, so that was something, anyway.

In short order they had the place spiffed up and already smelling better, as Allen hauled the trash out to the garbage cans outside.

Milo wandered the apartment in the meanwhile, pausing by the piano. Allen's melody for "Love Me, I Guess" was propped up on the stand, with more notations and markings. He'd been fiddling with it, but from what Milo could tell through his squinting, not so much it would ruin his lyrics, which didn't so much exist yet anyhow.

Allen banged open the door. "Aw, leave it alone for now, Short. Grab us a couple beers from the icebox and let's dig into those sandwiches."

Allen flopped onto the sofa and tossed his sandwich on the low oval table in front of him. "The wife wouldn't stand for eating out here, but we're bachelors far as I'm concerned."

"So long as you clean up after yourself. No rule that says a bachelor, even a pretend bachelor, has to live like an alley cat."

Milo felt strange eating out in the living room. Even at his own place he didn't do that, though he supposed he could. He could eat in his bed if he had the notion. Milo smiled to himself.

"What's so funny?" Allen asked through a mouthful of pastrami.

"Just that in my own place, I'm still living by my mother's rules. Not that I want to throw my old food around like this other schmuck I know, but I always sit there at my tiny kitchen table by my lonesome."

"You'll get used to it, at least until you get married and the missus will tell you what to do. But I forgot, Mr. Milo ain't never gonna do that."

"Didn't say that."

"Too bad the young lass at Passover wasn't your type, or we'd have found out for sure."

"I never stood a chance, not that I wanted to stand a chance," Milo added, pointing at Allen with his beer bottle before taking a cold swig that seemed to flood every corner of his sweaty, sticky self. Before Milo knew it, he'd glugged half of it down. "Anyhow, she's got a fella that her parents don't like much."

"That's a rough thing, being in love when people don't approve."

"You're sentimental all of a sudden."

"It's all these love songs, I guess. They get to you after a while."

"You speak from experience, eh? Your people didn't like Dorothy?"

"Wasn't Dorothy."

"Oh. Right."

The beer and the heat settled over Milo same as a heavy blanket. He leaned back on the sofa, after another bite of sandwich and long gulps of the cold bubbly brew.

After a few moments of rare quiet, Allen stood up quickly, walked to the kitchen, and returned with two more beers. He handed one to Milo, settled down next to him on the sofa, and tapped his bottleneck to Milo's.

"Saw Cole Porter at Elmo's the other night. His wife was with him. Must be some arrangement those two have."

Milo closed his eyes. "Yeah, yeah. I've heard." The humming of a fan somewhere in the room lulled him. He sat up just enough to take another drink, thinking of some other subject to bring up. Cole Porter's unusual tastes were not a subject he much longed to dwell on.

Allen spoke up again. "Girls are too much trouble anyhow. Always changing their minds about something, always wanting more money for this and that."

Milo had no response to this, and took another drink, glad to at least not be thinking about the song, though he just thought about not thinking of it. Another swig might take care of that, too.

Allen rambled on. "That's what I like about you, Milo. You look out for me, right? You got me to give up the booze, telling me, 'You're embarrassing yourself and the show!' Remember that? When you picked me up at the jailhouse? But you didn't hate me for it, either. Looking at me like some of them did, like I was gum on their shoe, like they never got a snootful and raised Cain."

Milo touched the cool bottle to his face. "Well, you're a pal, Allen. We all trip up sometimes." Milo chuckled as Allen slumped sideways against his shoulder. "All those beers catch up with you? Speaking of a snootful. Allen?"

Milo craned his head around, trying to see if Allen was even awake. He couldn't tell at that angle. He jiggled his shoulder a bit to rouse him.

When Allen didn't react right away, Milo made to get up and untangle himself.

At first, Milo didn't understand what was happening. He felt something wet, yet oddly solid, on his neck, and reached up to brush away the bug or worm or what, then that something moved, and Milo sprung off the couch, brushing wildly at his collar. He dropped the beer, which clanked against the table and fizzed itself out all over the floor, and Milo's shoe and pant leg, too.

Allen slumped into the empty space he'd left. Allen was wide awake and alert, but his face was in the process of draining itself white, his pale eyes looking up at Milo with something almost like fright.

It was only then that Milo's brain pieced together the last few moments and a sickening horror spread out from his chest. Allen had just kissed him, right on the neck, that's what that was, he'd kissed him and even sucked softly on his skin.

Milo backed away two steps, shaking.

Allen put his elbows on his knees and knotted his hands into his hair. When he spoke, his voice was hoarse. "Please forget I ever did that."

Milo couldn't speak. Allen became a stranger before his eyes.

Allen's shoulders began to shake, and he sniffed, and Milo understood he was crying now, but trying to hold it in, his thin frame quivering with the effort. With trembling hands and bile in his throat, Milo backed out of the apartment door, and ran down the stairs to the street outside.

24

1999

Eleanor

As Alex strides across the Midtown apartment, my mind clicks back and forth between the physical reality in front of me, and the memory of Daniel in this space, our place, our home where we once shared bagels and a bed and a life. It's like a projector toggling between two slides. One, a stranger in this emptied, sterile apartment. Two, my boyfriend and his strewn clothes and the kitchen pass-through counter littered with takeout boxes.

Alex goes straight to the nearly floor-to-ceiling windows and looks down. I find it endearing that he doesn't try to play it cool. He wears the astonishment as casually as a favorite graying T-shirt. His long wavy hair falls so that I can't see his face as he peers the many stories down to the street below. In the picture I'd printed out, his hair must have been pulled back, or it was taken long ago. In any case, I'd been surprised when he got out of the cab and approached me with his hand out. He was wearing a T-shirt from a band I'd never heard of, and a dark button-down shirt open over the top of that. He's tall and lanky, and prone to slouch slightly in the way of people who are used to being the tallest in the room. With his dark clothing, it gives him the look of a tree bent in the wind.

"Wow," he says. "I feel dumb for not bringing a camera."

"We can get you a disposable one. I have one somewhere, but I'm pretty sure I packed it in a box."

Alex scratches his head and looks down, his first sign of self-consciousness. "It's not some kind of fun vacation, though, I know."

"Don't worry about it. You can want to have a camera. Maybe we can catch a show, since you came all this way. I can get us tickets to *Fosse*. I've seen it before, but I never get tired of it. Or there's a revival of *Kiss Me, Kate*."

Alex still faces the view, which isn't spectacular or anything because we're not all that high up by Manhattan standards. But everything is new for him here. A view of a brick wall would be novel. "I don't want to sponge off you," he says. "I'm doing that enough."

"I already believe you're not a fortune hunter, so please stop trying to convince me. It will just make the both of us feel more awkward than the situation already calls for, and I don't know about you, but we've got enough awkward to last us a while, right? I asked you to come, and if I suggest something expensive, we'll call it book research. I don't mind, I'm happy to do it, but I don't want to make a big deal of it. It embarrasses me as much as you, if not more."

"Is it? Book research, that is?"

"How do you mean?" I ask, sitting down on a kitchen barstool.

"Will you put it in the book, then? If my mother is his child? If Vivian... had anything to do with the song?"

It hits me hard, then, that these two projects I'd managed to demarcate in my head—Vivian and my grandfather and his voice, and then there's the book—were not exactly so separate after all. Though I'd bet the whole company this is not what Naomi and Uncle Paul had in mind when they set this ball in motion.

"Eleanor? Did you hear me?"

"Let's just see if it's true first. One thing at a time."

Alex nods and picks up his bag, moving into the bedroom, which I'd pointed out when we first crossed the threshold. He could have argued with me, he could have insisted I answer directly, but instead he chooses to give me some space. Not for nothing that I want to help him. He makes it easy to want to help him.

I have to smirk at the irony. I'd taken on this project to protect Grampa Milo. I was supposedly making a stand for dignity, and then I go and dig up a love child and my grandfather's song lyrics in someone else's writing.

I trace a pattern in the granite countertop with a ragged, bitten nail and wonder if Naomi's guy would have dug up the same information anyway. It wasn't anything remarkable, what I did. I interviewed the son of his late collaborator, is what started all this. Anyone would've have done the same. Maybe Jerry Allen wouldn't have mentioned his theory about Vivian, though. He seemed to be telling that story specifically to Milo's granddaughter. Surely he would have had chances to tell that story over the years, and he never did.

If only. If only I'd never freaked out at that Bed-Stuy interview, if only Daniel hadn't broken it off. I'd have been working away in my career like always and if anyone approached me with a book I'd have waved them away: too busy. Going back further: if only Daniel had never flirted with pretty little Moira, I could have relaxed around him, trusted him, given him whatever he thought he needed, so that he didn't leave me. So he won't decide to move away to California if I can't come through with enough eye contact to make him stay.

I haven't called Daniel. He hasn't called me. He also hasn't popped up anyplace unexpectedly. It's as if he has declared: your move. Though I miss him, I haven't made that move. I realize now I probably won't. My heart clenches against my will. After all, this is my doing. I could rally for him. I could form myself to his expectations and do away with the loneliness, the absence of him, this person who knows me. I'm choosing not to. I'm choosing not to change myself just because he thinks I should.

Alex clears his throat from across the room. I raise my hand to acknowledge him, but my eyes are blurring at the countertop, the tiny specks in the granite beginning to swirl with my concentrated staring.

Objects never care whether you stare back, which is what I like most about them.

I glance past Alex at the bedroom. Through the open door, I can see that he has opened his big suitcase and removed the contents of Vivian's box, arraying them on the duvet.

"You hungry?" I ask. "We can go out for a bite. Or get some delivery."

A shrug, and somehow he manages to toss his wavy hair away from his face in a way that looks nonchalant and masculine. "I had a bag of pretzels. I can hold off."

"I feel bad for dragging you here and then the first thing we do is shut ourselves into an apartment…"

"Well, like I said, this isn't supposed to be a fun vacation. I'll save my pennies and pay my own way another time. That will be more fun, anyway."

"We're not going to talk about money, I thought."

"Right. Never mind."

When I lived here with Daniel, and for the brief time afterward alone, the bed was never made, except for maybe the duvet tossed up over the hills and valleys of rumpled sheets. When I moved out, I washed the sheets and smoothed it out so potential renters wouldn't think the place looked gross.

So even though I know this used to be my apartment and my bed, it looks so foreign all straightened up like this that I easily toss away all thoughts of Daniel and focus on what's really here, alive and tangible.

Alex hovers near the bed as I sit down slowly trying not to jostle the objects, like they're sleeping and might be disturbed. There are playbills, the aforementioned steno book, its edges curled with age and careless storage. Yellowed news clippings and black-and-white photographs stare up at me from the bed. In the center of the array as if in a position of honor is an open book, a pressed flower crumbling on its pages. I start to touch the flower but my hand freezes midair, because I have just pictured the whole thing disintegrating. Instead I crane my neck to see the book's title at the top of an open page. It's *Gone with the Wind*.

"Was the flower always in there?"

"Yes. I leafed through the book in case there were mementoes in it, or notes. That was all I found. I think it's a pink rose."

An image unbidden leaps to mind, of my grandfather in his fedora, handing a bouquet of roses to Vivian, or maybe pinning a corsage onto her dress. It could have come from anywhere, though. She could have plucked it out of a garden and taken it home.

As I extend my hand for the notebook, I see that I'm trembling. I snatch my hand back. "Maybe we'd better eat. I'll go order."

It's an odd time of day to eat, so the delivery won't take long, I know. Still, there's time now to be filled, and no clear goal, as I've decided I can't open that notebook yet. We return to the brown couch, half-covered by a throw blanket to obscure its wear and tear, and in my peripheral vision I sense the box growing larger, like something out of Lewis Carroll, until it fills the apartment and crushes us against the window.

I've left the TV, but there's no cable service, so there's nothing to watch, as I explain to Alex.

He shrugs that off. I offer to get him a beer, because I may not have planned very well to feed him lunch, but I did stock the place with basics like bread, butter, and beer.

Obtaining the beers only eats up two minutes, and so we both stare out the windows, from the opposite ends of the couch.

"It looks like rain," I finally say, glad that the sky has provided me with conversation.

"Hmmm. It rained at home yesterday. Maybe those are the same rain clouds."

"So how is it you could leave so easily? I thought it would take some time to … untangle, from work."

"Ah. That. Well, see, there's this assistant director everyone likes better. His name is Kevin and he is a musical theater kid from way back."

"Would this be the work nemesis you mentioned in email?"

"Oh yes, it would. See, he was almost famous, in a small-town way. He played all the little kid roles in local productions all over West Michigan. You needed a kid, you found Kevin. *The King and I, The Music Man, Fiddler.* And of course, *Sound of Music.* Everyone was happy as hell to let him take over."

"Can I ask you a stupid question, then?"

"Those are my favorite kind."

"How did you end up in the job if you don't sound like you even like it, it doesn't suit you, and you say people don't want you to succeed?"

"I fell into it, I guess. My band had just broken up, and the record store I was managing closed, and the previous guy had been basically casting all his girlfriends in all the good parts until it pissed off the wrong people. Which actually wasn't so bad for the theater, because he seemed to really like screwing talented people. Anyhow, he left abruptly. Kevin hadn't materialized yet, I think he was still in college. So they were up a creek kinda, and I offered to do it. Then I was swamped with work and trying to figure out all the stupid logistics of running a community theater, which I didn't know a damn thing about, and then they hired this Kevin guy. To 'help' me."

"Where'd they get the funding?" I know this much from the family business, to always wonder where the money comes from.

Alex snickers and takes a pull from the beer as rain begins to spatter the window. "I don't know exactly but they can't afford to keep us both. They're waiting for me to fail."

"What do they have against you?"

"I don't look the part, I'm not good at sucking up to rich donors. I don't have the right kind of drama background. I was in a couple plays in school but I didn't stick with it. You know, I guess I'm waiting for me to fail, too."

"Why?"

"You said it. I don't like the job. It doesn't suit me. But in order to pay rent, and eat, and not have to live with my mother, I need a paycheck of some kind, and for now it's easier to keep working than it is to try and find something, because what, I'd work at Walmart as a greeter?"

"Do you have a degree?"

"Sociology," he answered, a wry smirk unfurling. "Very useful. So, tell me your life story now. It's only fair."

"First, there's one burning question I must have answered."

"Yeah?"

"Your band's name."

He turns to face me, one lock of hair over his face until he rakes it all back with his fingers. "Tweeney Sodd."

"Ha! The Demon Barber of Fleet Street, but with a twist!"

"Mock if you will, but I thought it was awfully clever."

"Oh it is. Just please don't tell me you carried a straight razor on stage."

"No, because that would be literal, and literal is totally uncool."

"And you were the growling front man, channeling Eddie Vedder as you draped yourself over your mic stand, hanging onto it like it was keeping you from drowning in your own tortured ennui."

"I hate Eddie Vedder."

"Jim Morrison."

"We did do a killer cover of 'Light My Fire.' And you are changing the subject."

In fifteen minutes, I catch him up on my own hapless career, arranged mostly by the interference of my bossy cousins. And how I almost managed to become a solid interviewer. My quiet presence was just enough to get people talking about anything, it seemed.

"And yet, I'm totally a fraud in this," I explain to Alex. "I'm non-threatening, and not confrontational, and I let people forget they're being interviewed. It's not even by design, it's just how I'm wired, and for a while I could get by like that. But it also means I don't ask the tough questions when they should be asked, so someone who's savvy, or angry... not a stoned poet or an earnest community reformer, but the source for a real, gutsy story... then it all goes to hell, as it did in dramatic flame-out fashion not too long ago. I was never a real journalist, and I knew it all along."

I look down at the floor and clunk my beer on the table. "I envy people who know what they want, like my cousins. And why should that be so hard to know?"

Alex's answer is interrupted by the pizza, and by now the gentle rain is full-on monsoon so I tip extravagantly.

I stick the pizza on the kitchen pass-through counter. "Listen to me going on about 'oh woe is me I don't know what to do with my life' and that guy has to bike around delivering food in a frigging rainstorm for a few dollars an hour."

"Other people's problems don't mean yours don't exist. Anyway, maybe he loves his job."

Naomi has said as much to me more times than I can count, after pointing out all the ways the Short family is charitable, which is all true as far as it goes, but the guilt is comforting to me. It's like my ticket of admission to the life I have; it's all good as long as I feel properly conflicted. Of course, I feel guilty about this, too.

We make small talk about the flight over the pizza, and finally I've eaten all I can manage, and Vivian's box of keepsakes is still there, still large in my imagination.

Alex shoves the pizza box into the fridge with the leftovers, and helps me gather up napkins, rinse the plates. We line up our four empty beer bottles neatly along the tile backsplash.

He dusts off his hands and turns to me. "Are you ready now?"

"No. But here goes."

I stop in the bedroom doorway, and Alex bumps into me lightly. He steps back and just waits there. I brace my hands in the doorframe as if he's about to shove me through, though he has not moved or said a word.

I swallow, and my tired eyes unfocus a little and I let them. The rain tinks against the glass, the sky now the color of concrete, and looking about as solid, too.

"What if this turns my grandfather into a stranger?"

"Whatever all this means, it was sixty years ago. People don't carry around their same selves for six decades. He's still the same grandpa, to you."

I pull in a long, steadying breath and let it gust out, before I step fully into the room.

25

1936

Milo leaned against a lamppost, stretching his collar to let in some air. He tried to pick out which window was Vivian's in the brick building. He'd circled the block now three or four times, having tried to form the resolution to walk up and ring the bell each time he rounded the corner.

He should make himself go home, just go to his own apartment and work on the song and forget Allen for now, just work, hard work could cure anything, just like hard work got his parents out of the ghetto and into the Bronx while Milo still had baby teeth. Hard work got them to write all those songs on that impossible deadline for *Hilarity*... Allen. He couldn't shake off Allen. He was everywhere he looked, even in his nose, Allen's shaving lather blended with the tang of summer sweat.

Filmy curtains blew lightly in the open windows of what Milo guessed was Vivian's place. The curtains weighed nothing and they writhed like dancers. A man in a hurry then pushed his way out of the front door to the building, swinging it hard in his rush. Milo trotted up to the doorstep and grabbed the door before it swung closed. He found the second floor, found the hall, and was trying to remember which door, until he noticed the mezuzah on one door frame. He went to the other and knocked, much harder than he'd meant to.

In the crack under the door he saw the shadow of her feet and nearly turned around and left, but she opened the door with alacrity. "Milo!" she cried. "Come in, just give me a moment to put myself together."

Milo dutifully stared the opposite direction as Vivian walked away from him in a cloud of roses and cigarette smoke.

His heart seemed as loud in his ears as the roar of the El and he wondered for a crazy moment if Vivian could hear it.

"Take off your hat and stay a while, why don't you?" she sang out, sweeping back into the room. Milo turned and caught her in the act of fastening the belt of her shirtwaist dress. She was bare-legged and shoeless. "I'm going to be very daring and naughty by not putting my stockings on now. You would not believe what that feels like to have all that fabric covering every inch of your legs! They get jealous that my arms are free and bare." Vivian flapped her arms briefly, birdlike, and laughed. The girlishness was endearing. "I would ban stockings if I were president. At least in summer." Vivian seemed to only just notice him. "Oh! You look terrible, what's wrong? Are you sick?"

Milo shook his head, putting his hat down on a fussy wood-carved table draped in lace.

"Here, let me get you a cold drink. I've just made some lemonade. Sit, please! You've come to my rescue so many times, I think it's only fair I return the favor."

Vivian interrupted her lemonade-fetching to take Milo by the wrist and lead him to a curvy divan near a phonograph. She inspected the record, flipped it over, and an orchestra poured out into the room. In a mere heartbeat she returned, placing the lemonade on the small round table next to the divan. She knelt in front of Milo, and with her slender fingers, stopped him from straightening his necktie. Instead, she tugged on the knot and began loosening it for him. "Now, we are not going to stand on formality, seeing as I'm not even wearing my stockings. Estelle would be horrified."

"Who's Estelle?" Milo managed to ask, not trusting his shaky hands to pick up the glass. Something inside him shivered at letting this woman take his tie off. Her caretaking wasn't soft, like his mother's. It was commanding, and strangely hypnotizing. She tossed the tie on the floor, over her shoulder.

Before she rose, Milo caught a glimpse of lacy slip under her dress.

"Estelle's my older sister. My parents died of influenza. Well, really my mother died of the flu, but my father found a way to die quickly enough by getting drunk on a construction job. Anyway, so that left Estelle and me, and oh, she's a tough nut, that one. You know she told me that going to New York would kill me?" Vivian trilled a tinkling laugh. "Imagine! Do I look dead to you?" Vivian put one hand on her hip, one eyebrow raised, and pursed her glossy red lips, just lightly. She'd done her makeup in a hurry, it seemed, because the line was uneven around her mouth.

Vivian settled herself on the other end of the divan, and tucked her bare feet under her. Milo was distracted by even part of her being nude, wondering when he'd ever seen a girl other than Leah without stockings. At the shore? The Shorts weren't beach people, and he probably hadn't been to Coney Island since he was a boy, though it was only a short train ride away.

Vivian stretched her arms, languid and long, over her head. "I'm forever telling myself, 'Estelle would be horrified.' It's *such* fun. So what's gotten into you, then?"

Milo's mouth fell open, the whole sordid story heavy on this tongue, primed to fall out, to be expelled, to get it out of his mind and out of his body. "It's Allen, see…"

He turned to face Vivian, her face bright and flushed in the July sun that rioted around them, the breeze from the open windows stirring her gentle brown curls.

No. Vivian was no blushing innocent but there were some things you did not tell a woman.

"We had a fight."

"Oh no. Over the show? Or over the drinking. He's drinking again, I knew it, that lousy souse."

Vivian took his tragic silence as answer.

"Curse that man, doesn't he understand what he's doing to everyone else? If he can't handle his liquor he needs to leave it alone before he ruins the show. This is your big chance for a show where you're promoted, you're important! Not just a last-minute afterthought."

"The show is okay, actually, the last part is my own part. It's the words to the last song, they're not coming."

"Ah, so you're stuck and he's drunk. A fine kettle of fish if ever there was."

Milo smiled sadly. "That sounds like a lyric." He chanted, "'A fine kettle of fish if ever there was.'"

"So it does. What can I do, poor Milo Short? You preserved my reputation in Boston, and saved me from joblessness and destitution no less than twice."

The beers and the heat and the apartment made Milo thoughtless. "You might be destitute again when the honeymooners get back."

Vivian jumped off her seat and stomped in her bare feet over to her kitchen. "I need a drink and I'm getting you one, too."

"I didn't mean to upset you. But I don't think I can save you this time, so what are you going to do?"

Vivian smacked the bottle on the counter. "I wasn't asking you to, and none of your business. I have plans. I always have plans."

After a moment, Vivian smacked a clear drink down in front of Milo so hard that it sloshed over her hand and she wiped it on her dress, leaving a smear of wet across her bosom. "Men love to tell a woman how to live, don't they? You think I should crawl back to Estelle, don't you? I'd rather throw myself in the East River. Do you know I stood on the Brooklyn Bridge once and wondered if I could hike my dress up high enough to get over the rail? But no. I have plans, don't you worry."

Milo sat forward, gripping his drink hard. "Geez, kid, you wouldn't do that, would you? Jump off a bridge?"

"Don't be ridiculous. Why would I need to do a thing like that?"

She took down her drink in one gulp and dragged the back of her hand across her face, smearing her lips.

Milo took out his handkerchief. Vivian flinched just slightly when he reached for her face. He took her chin in his left hand, just gently, and dabbed at her smeared lipstick with his handkerchief.

"Geez. I'm sorry, kid."

"For what." Vivian swept back into the kitchen and tried to pour herself a drink. She seemed unable to manage pouring, so she swigged right out of the bottle.

"For getting you worked up."

"I need a bath. It will calm my nerves. Enjoy the phonograph, have a drink, and I'll see you in thirty minutes." At the thought of Vivian in the altogether, in her tub, Milo felt a red flush creep over his ears, and he bit his lip hard against an urge to moan aloud.

After that tantalizing announcement, she walked by him, her pace somehow regal and assured, despite her bare feet, wet dress, and red lips half wiped clean.

26

New York, 1936

With nightfall came rainfall, the sound like a soothing hush of a mother calming a baby, and the air turning so delicious that Milo wanted to stick his head out the window and gulp down huge chunks of it.

He may have been delirious, but if he was, that suited him fine.

Vivian had emerged from the tub with her skin pink and eyes bright, wearing no makeup at all that Milo could see, her hair damp around the frame of her face. She'd come out in a long white gown, wearing a filmy robe over top. At first, Milo had flushed crimson to the tops of his ears, because he knew this was a nightie. But after peals of gay laughter, Vivian had persuaded him that she was more covered up wearing the long gown than she was in her normal day dresses, and that it was the coolest, most pleasant thing in her wardrobe.

"Pleasant" it may have been for her, but Milo found it intensely distracting and he could not look at her straight on for too long lest he take complete leave of his senses.

THEY'D SUBSISTED ALL afternoon on sandwiches, lemonade, and gin, while they talked over the latest gossip from *The High Hat* and other Broadway shows, and cracked each other up reading Winchell's columns out loud in the best rapid-fire newsman voice either of them could muster. They talked over their favorite songs, and Vivian confided that she'd once thought of becoming a singer until she realized her voice was only fair, and it would take much more than a fair voice to get on stage.

"I've heard many a merely fair voice put over a song huge on stage," Milo had retorted, with his sock feet stretched out in front of him and his shirttails out.

"Ah, but you also have to hustle. I didn't even have enough hustle for the perfume counter."

She could not be roused to sing for him, even after another glass of gin.

In a lull of their conversation, when the rain hushed down, and automobiles splashed by, Vivian asked to see his lyrics for the new song. "Could I see what you have so far?"

Milo's memory flashed on an image of his notebook, abandoned at Allen's place, on top of the upright piano. His stomach churned up to recall the scene, and now he'd have to get the notebook back. He shook his head as if to clear it. "I don't have anything but the first two lines."

"Seems to me like you need some help."

"Aw, not now, kid, I'm not feeling up to much work right about now."

"If not now, when? I know an excellent musical secretary."

She rummaged through a large handbag until she came up with a pencil and a steno book, then perched on the edge of a tufted chair, crossed her knees, and assumed a parody of secretarial readiness. "I await your dictation, Mr. Short."

"I don't have a thing to dictate, Miss Adair."

"Just as well. This is an eyebrow pencil." She laughed, and tossed the pencil aside. "Let me get a proper pen and get this thing done, shall we?" Vivian swept grandly out of the chair, toward a rolltop desk near the door.

"I told you, I don't feel like working now."

"We'll make it fun. And look, this way you won't have to keep hanging around that souse, Allen. Get the songs done and you'll only have to see him at the theater, and then you can wash your hands of him."

Even that morning, Milo would have shouted down any notion of washing his hands of his friend. He might not have signed up to be his brother's keeper, and keep him off the sauce for a lifetime, but he'd never have turned his back on Allen, who in point of fact had dragged Milo into his current success. In that way, he had Allen to credit for the fact that his family was all snug in a Bronx apartment with its own bathroom and running water, and not cheek-by-jowl with a dozen other families crammed into a tenement.

Without Allen's pushing and nudging, Milo would still be plinking away tunes for a few dollars a week. In fact, Milo recalled as he swirled the dregs of his drink, Allen had helped him keep that job even though he could barely see the sheet music.

Milo's stomach flipped over. Everything now looked different, sinister. Did Allen have...*designs* on him? Was that why he was so willing to make allowances for a guy who couldn't see so well, when there were no doubt any number of starving piano players who'd have been able to do the job regular? Was that why he'd gotten them canned at Harms, because he needed Milo at his side? And not just at his side, but dependent on him? Because without a composer, and with no connections outside the ones Allen provided, Milo wasn't worth spit, clever rhymes or not.

Every reference to Cole Porter, all the times Allen needled him about his love life, was he trying to figure out if Milo was ... was game for that kind of business?

And now they were stuck together. A team, Short and Allen, Allen and Short. Their success was together and that's what people would want more of if *The High Hat* was another hit, and how could it not be? With John Garnett in the lead?

Allen had trapped him into his funny predilections. Naïve Milo Short who barely understood what all that meant, and for certain didn't want to think about it.

"Milo? Are you coming up with genius lyrics, is that why you're so quiet?"

Milo sat up on the couch, tossed his glasses on the table, and put his head in his hands. Then he thought about that being how Allen was sitting, just as Milo got the hell out of his apartment. He grimaced; would he ever be rid of Allen's thin lips crawling around on his neck?

The soft rustle of fabric made him open his eyes. Vivian had crouched down next to him. She smelled of roses and soap with a hint of gin. Her face was all concern, her big green eyes wide, her eyebrows knit together, making a little V-shaped crease just above her nose. She reached one hand into the crook of his elbow.

"Milo, what's wrong? You look terrible. Is everyone all right at home? Is Leah sick?"

Milo's voice, when it came out, was abraded and raw, as if he hadn't spoken in weeks. "I can't talk about it."

"Then don't."

Her green eyes grew huge as she approached him, and her long dark lashes flickered down, her lips touching his, just barely, that for a moment he thought he imagined it. Then he knew he wasn't imagining it, and her lips were real, and so was she, and Milo felt he was waking from a century long sleep when he reached for her waist and lifted her like she weighed nothing, onto his lap.

He craned his neck to reach her face, and he was dissolving into her. He put his hand up into her hair, so soft, that hair, that he couldn't stop stroking it. She groaned a little into his mouth, and Milo sat back, startled. Had he hurt her?

She smiled, a brief chuckle, though not unkind. Vivian put her hand behind his head and pulled him forward, groaning again, this time so intentionally that Milo got it, oh yes, that's a good thing, and then he groaned too in the same moment, and a kind of delirium took him over. He hoisted them both up like he was a sideshow strongman. Her gown was dragging down and he was worried he'd trip on it, as he bore her back toward her bed.

He laid her down, and then frowned at her robe, the complicated ribbons and lace both blurry and confusing. She gave a low, purring chuckle and pulled it loose herself. Her gown swooped low over her bosom, revealing a valley between her breasts that Milo instinctively kissed.

And then he was pushing her gown up, up as far as he could, and she yanked on his belt, and between the two of them, they tossed and pulled and discarded and unbuttoned as much as was necessary, and when Milo saw under the gown itself she'd been wearing nothing at all he wanted to weep, so instead he buried his face in her neck where it met her shoulder so if he did weep she wouldn't see, wouldn't laugh at him, and then Vivian's lips brushed his neck, too, which startled Milo for a moment back to the afternoon, and Allen.

Milo reared up, and loomed over Vivian's heaving, creamy body. Then he swooped back down over her like he was ravenous, which in fact, he was.

VIVIAN TICKLED HIS chest hair with her red nails. "I love you, too."

Milo sat up on one elbow, and felt like he was half in a dream.

Vivian stretched and turned over to face away from Milo, and began patting the bedside table. "You don't remember saying it, do you?"

"What?"

"Saying 'I love you.' Then again, perhaps you were a little distracted."

Milo remembered nothing but a wave of sensation so intense he instantly understood every crime of passion, every farkakte thing every person ever did for the opposite sex.

"Damn, my cigarettes are in the other room." Vivian stood up out of bed, nude, and Milo averted his eyes. She laughed shrilly. "Oh goodness, we're well past modesty. But suit yourself if it makes you feel better. There, I'm decent now."

Milo looked back. "Decent" was arguable. She'd put on the filmy robe but skipped the nightie. She glided out of the room and in short order returned with two lemonades and her cigarette case pinched under her arm.

Milo drank his lemonade in three gulps, not realizing until he felt the kick in the chest she'd spiked them with the gin. Vivian held her glass to her forehead and closed her eyes. "Be a love and fetch me the matches? And the ashtray. They're on the side table, by your side."

Milo reached over and picked up a matchbook and ashtray, both from the Stork Club. Another memory, angry Vivian and soused Allen, back when he was still cranking out *Hilarity* lyrics.

His thirst overcame his languid exhaustion, and he hauled himself off the bed to get a plain old drink of water. In the kitchen, though, he spied the gin, and with a shrug, he picked it up to bring it back to the bedroom.

"Hey!" Vivian called out. "Bring that steno pad in here! Let's see if you're feeling... inspired, shall we?"

Milo paused in her sitting room, gin in one hand, glass in the other, eyeing the steno pad where she'd dropped it on the floor next to the divan. So far all that sweat and worry by himself had granted him only two lousy lines. "Sure, why not," he muttered, so quietly she couldn't have heard where she lay stretched out on the bed in her gossamer robe.

Inspired Milo was, as it turned out.

He lay sideways across her bed in his undershirt and shorts, hanging his head backward off the edge, enjoying the blood rush and the gin or maybe both and who cared?

Vivian had taken command of the pen, seeing as how she was marginally less pickled, and Milo would've been embarrassed about a girl being more sober than him, if he'd been sober enough to remember to care.

Milo sang to himself in his squeaky, wavering tenor, for lack of a piano.

"*You might just love me… I think. Did you just give me a….*"

"Wink!" shouted Vivian. She was cross-legged on her side of the bed, like a schoolgirl playing jacks. Her robe covered all the important parts, but her bare legs and toes peeked out from under the diaphanous fabric.

"Yeah, wink. I was gonna say that, give a fella a chance. *Did you just give me…a wink? But I'm no swell, can't you tell, my charms might simply…shrink?*"

"Oh, I like that. But can charms shrink? Do you think? Ha, now I'm doing it! Maybe the charms should evaporate."

"Try to rhyme evaporate, I dare you."

"Extrapolate!"

"Okay, I'll give you that one. Now you fit extrapolate and evaporate in those syllables."

"Um…" Vivian paused, scribbling, then sat up straight. "*Don't you extrapolate my charms might evaporate?*"

Milo sat up fast, his head swimming, a not-unpleasant sensation in a girl's bed. There are few unpleasant sensations he could have in a girl's bed, Milo figured. "Excellent rhyme, doesn't fit the phrasing. But more to the point, I got you to sing for me." He smiled, and pointed a finger at her in mock triumph. "Your voice is just like your laugh. It's … lyrical."

Vivian gave Milo a small, sad smile that made him hold his breath. Then she said, "That would be a …miracle."

"Empirical," Milo answered.

"Satirical."

"Spherical."

Vivian nudged his calf with her bare foot. "Hysteer-ical!" Her burst of laughter rang like chimes, then receded as she shook her head. "No, we must get back to business. We're writing you a hit song, Mr. Milo, and I will not be distracted. Not evaporate, then, but charms should do something else." She crossed off the abandoned rhyme.

Milo flopped down again and warbled thoughtfully, "*I'm no swell, you can tell, my charms will evaporate, you think?*"

Vivian jotted something, then tapped her pencil against her lips. "Maybe it doesn't have to be 'charms.' Maybe it's something else entirely. *My dear, in a year, your estimation of me, will sink.*"

"Maybe. 'Estimation of me' sounds clunky. Hard to sing. I like the 'sink' though, that's a good thought. It's why I picked 'wink,' because it has lots of easy rhymes."

"Aren't you very clever."

"I'm also very tired. Let's take a break, eh, kid?"

Vivian tossed the pad on her floor. "A break it is, but you don't get to call me kid anymore."

"Awww, don't get sore."

"I'm not sore at all. I'm just twenty-six years old."

Milo rolled over and crawled like a cat to stretch out next to her. "Then you have lived twenty-six exquisite years." Milo threaded his arm behind her neck and pulled her close to his chest.

27

New York, 1936

Milo wondered why his mother was in his apartment, shaking him. He snapped his eyes open to a fuzzy brown blur, with a voice that was not his mother's. "Milo. Wake up. I have to go."

Vivian. He was in Vivian's bed. Someone was banging a kettle drum in his head, his mouth tasted like a rug, and he thought he might dump the contents of his gut all over her bed sheets. How could Allen do this all the time?

Allen. Curse that damn Allen anyhow.

"Milo!"

He shook his head and with effort focused on Vivian, who was pulling on a sky-blue dress. "It's time to get up, don't you think?" He fumbled for his glasses, and when her smiling face came into sharp clarity, he returned her amused grin.

She approached him, turned her back, and said, "Zip, please." Her dress was only zipped up partway. She tipped her head down slightly, and waited.

Milo at first fumbled with the tiny zipper. Then he pulled it smoothly closed over her satiny slip, smooth bare back, and sharp shoulder blades. He rested one hand on her shoulder, the other on her hip. He was about to pull her back toward him, and reverse the action on the zipper, when she stepped away briskly, whirling around fast enough her skirt hem swirled around her knees.

"I'm not sure it would do, to leave you here alone, and in this state, while I step out." She raised her eyebrow at "state," causing Milo to look down and inspect his unshaven, smelly, nearly naked self. That unromantic reality jarred him out of the sensual fog he'd been in for countless hours. A pang darted through his chest, as though something precious had been irretrievably lost. He began to search the floor for his clothing.

Vivian continued explaining, though Milo had not asked her to, nor objected to leaving. "It's true what I said that no one cares about a man visiting here. But there is a landlady who might let herself in to fix something, or just to be nosy. And I don't need her spreading stories."

When Milo continued to collect his clothing without comment, Vivian sat at a dressing table and began to make up her face.

Milo found his pants in a crumpled heap on the floor. As he pulled them on, he wondered anew how Vivian would get by once the newlyweds returned to claim their home. By the time he stuffed his shirttails into his pants, he'd vowed to find Vivian another job, a job with an understanding boss. Hell, maybe if *The High Hat* took off, he could hire her as his own personal secretary. That would solve everything.

In her sitting room, he found his tie on the floor in front of the sofa and his hat on the table. He tucked the tie into his shirt pocket. Vivian by then emerged from the bedroom, walked straight to him, and pressed her lips into his with ferocity. Then she jerked back and shoved Milo lightly with her flat palms. "Time to go."

Minutes later, Milo scurried out the door and jogged down the steps, running back over the events from the day in his mind, shaking his head at all that had happened, all that he'd done. Milo Short would never be the same after a day like that.

MILO SLAMMED HIS way back into his own apartment. His phone was ringing as he walked in, but he ignored it, locking himself in and drawing all his curtains.

Today would be all about work. He'd finish that last blasted song and get away from Allen for good. He couldn't remember much of what he'd written the night before, to say nothing of whether any of it was decent. Not for nothing it was progress, though, and that counted for a hell of a lot. He ought to buy Vivian some flowers for her inspiration.

Milo stepped into his tiny bathroom to wash his face and shave, at least. He let the water run cold, splashing his face and letting it run over his wrists. It wasn't yet noon, but the air outside was already shimmering with heat.

After he'd cleaned himself up some, Milo changed into fresh pants and an undershirt, skipping anything else in the privacy of his own apartment. He set about making himself some coffee, then sat down at his little kitchen table to look at the lyrics with sober eyes.

That morning, Vivian had made to tear the lyrics out of her steno book and hand them over, until she realized something she needed to keep was on the reverse side of one of the pages. In her excitement to begin, she hadn't noticed. "Oh, I'll copy it over fresh for you anyway, without all my scribbles," she'd declared, and hurriedly written a clean copy for Milo, tearing it out with a flourish. She'd then tucked it, folded, into his front pants pocket, making Milo gasp.

Vivian's handwriting was angular and sharp, aggressively slanted, but perfectly readable. Beautiful, really. Much nicer than Milo's crabbed-looking scrawl, anyhow.

He shook his head. How pickled had he been? Half the rhymes he didn't even remember. Either they were Vivian's ideas, or he was so tight he had invented rhymes he could not recall. He took it as a warning against hitting the bottle so hard lest he go the way of Bernard Allen.

A gentle knock shook his concentration. Milo put the paper down and yanked open the door, half hoping to see Vivian there, finished with her appointment—

He stumbled back two steps. Allen, reeking of booze and sweat and smoke, did not wait for an invitation before crashing through the doorway.

"Why aren't you answering your telephone, Short?"

"I wasn't home."

Milo stood as far away from Allen as his modest apartment would let him.

Allen flicked a glance at him, then began pacing the short length of the room. "I'm not coming near you, don't worry. I'll never touch you again, not even shake your hand. Here, you left your notebook." He dropped the notebook on Milo's sofa, and backed away, raising his hands as if someone were aiming a pistol at him.

Allen continued, "I'm just gonna beg you to finish the show. Just let's finish this show, and maybe we can work together again some more, if I promise not to go near you. We can work separate, and get together when we have to at the theater rehearsal rooms, or when my wife is at home, because that's the other thing, I sent her a telegram begging her to come home to the city. I'm doing lots of begging around now. I threw out all the booze and I swear I'm going off it now, for good and permanent.

"Only, I can't be alone, I see that. I can't be alone, ever, because if I do, I do terrible things."

Allen screwed up his fists and pushed them hard into his eyes.

"Hey," Milo said, "take it easy."

"Just tell me we can still work together. Please. It's bad enough what I did, but if I ruined the only good thing in my life, our songs, I'll never forgive myself. Never."

"Sure, okay, we can still work together. I don't hate you."

Allen choked back one sob, and took one step toward Milo. Seeing his friend recoil, Allen halted, drooped, and took a long, slow step back.

Allen cleared his throat and took out a damp handkerchief. He wiped his face roughly. "My wife should get back in a couple days. Maybe you can come over for some coffee and we can finish the last song."

Milo nodded, and Allen seemed to be waiting for something, but when nothing else happened, he dragged himself to the door and out without a backward look.

When the door clicked shut, Milo exhaled, realizing he'd been holding his breath almost the entire time Allen was there. The poor schmuck was so wretched, so miserable, that Milo couldn't shun him forever, especially considering he owed his whole career to Allen. But could they really work together, like before? Could Milo sit beside him on the piano bench like they always used to? Could he sit on that couch and make polite conversation with Dorothy Allen, knowing what he knew?

Vivian may have thought that drowning herself was preferable to slinking back to her sister, but just then Milo envied her ability to shake everything off and vanish into some Midwestern city. In that moment, he'd have liked nothing better than to dust his hands of the whole lot of them. But where else would he go? Where else would he even know how to live? And more to the point, he could never leave his family, who were by now almost entirely dependent on him.

Milo sat back down at his kitchen table, picking up the pencil he'd dropped in frustration, before going over to Allen's place. For a moment before he began writing, he stared at that pencil, and imagined himself then, not twenty-four hours before, no notion at all of what lay ahead.

He turned his attention back to Vivian's writing. He squinted now at the words, the night's memories fighting back through his hangover. He frowned with the struggle toward clear recollection. Some of these rhymes were Vivian's, it seemed. But how many? Which ones, exactly?

An errant image, of sheet music with the credit line "Lyrics by Milo Short and Vivian Adair" flashed into his mind. He laughed and shivered at once. Preposterous! An erstwhile secretary and errand girl cut in on the credit. Max Gordon, and the director, they'd dismiss it as nonsense, no doubt, lust-crazed Milo wanting to impress a girl, or take pity on her. And Allen…with what he thought of her, Milo dared not imagine his reaction to her name on their song. They might not even let him do it, it's not like he went down to the music publisher himself to file paperwork or whatnot. He just wrote the songs and sheet music turned up in stores, somehow or other.

And what they would think of him for needing help from that dame! They'd truly believe he'd gone soft in the head if he couldn't even finish one show without some girl… His name would be mud, and in a business built on connections, your name was everything.

Milo ran his finger down the paper. He still needed several more lines, and he could tell right off others were just not singable, and that's not something a person can fix unless you've written songs before and watched actors try to put them over. And he'd have to continue to refine and polish, with Allen at the piano, then during rehearsals and maybe even at the tryouts. Hell, he wasn't even one-quarter done, no matter how much Vivian may have helped him, for one night, in his drunken creative frenzy.

Milo shook his head and remembered the brewed coffee, rising to get himself a cup before it turned bitter. It didn't matter. The point was to finish the job, rid himself of *The High Hat* once and for all.

28

1999

Eleanor

The cab lets us off at the corner. Alex places the box on the curb and holds his hand out to help me step out of the car, as if he'd been doing this all his life. He has to stoop so low, tall as he is, it almost looks like a bow. Despite our serious mission, I allow myself a brief smile at the accidental courtliness.

After sorting through Vivian's things, Alex and I had sat on the floor in front of the big windows, as I pointed out landmarks and tried to orient him to the city. We agreed with little discussion to bring the box to Grampa Milo the next day. I didn't bother with any more protests that Vivian might have been just a secretary, just a fan. I'd offered again to get Alex tickets to a show, played awkward concierge and tried to recommend things he could do in the city, but he waved them all off, promising he'd come back another time.

Our knees bumped into each other once or twice as we sat cross-legged, but I didn't feel like scrabbling away, establishing a moat of personal space. It might have been because Alex had already begun to assume a sort of cousinly friendliness with me. He also carried an innate stillness about him. I unwittingly found myself comparing him to Daniel, who was energetic and restless even in quiet acts of intimacy like holding hands or embracing. Alex seemed content just to sit and stare at the darkening sky, and the glowing lights of the city. He leaned back on his palms, stretched his legs out in front of him, and gazed. Whether his mind was on the city, or back home with his anxious, orphaned mother in Michigan, he didn't say. I didn't ask.

"Are you sure I should be here?" he asks me now for the tenth time, adjusting his grip on the box.

I'd insisted that Alex come, because he had as much to do with the box, with the story, as anyone. Because Vivian is long gone, but he is here, with her genes and DNA spiraling away inside him.

"We love guests," I tell him, trying to lighten his mood. "If my grandmother were alive she'd stuff you with food. I always used to tell people to only take about half of what you'll want to eat, because she'd press more on you, no matter how many times you claimed you were stuffed. Prepare yourself to be grilled by my girl cousins if they're here, only because they do that to every heterosexual male within a mile of me."

"How do you know I'm not gay?"

"Well, then you have a marvelous alibi."

"I'm actually not, but I could pretend, to fend them off..."

"Be my guest. Okay, here we are."

Alex tips his head up, his mouth open slightly with a faint grin. "Wow. It's great. Like something out of a movie."

The white limestone building is in fact lovely and historic, but so are all these buildings on this block I've been visiting the whole of my life. I swallow a "thank you" because what, like I designed the thing? It's not even my house.

I shove the door open and call out. Esme greets us, and doesn't mention this tall, long-haired stranger I've brought in, though her gaze lingers on him for an extra second or two, and the box for a second or two after that.

"Dr. Joel is upstairs with him now," Esme reports. "He is awake and fairly alert, but not in spirits."

I lead the way up the steps, but after a moment notice Alex hasn't followed me. I look back to see him rooted to the entry floor. He's looking at a chandelier above his head, a dusty, fussy thing I'd forgotten was even there. "This way," I prompt him, with a jerk of my head. Alex catches himself, and shoots me a small, shamefaced grin.

Joel's head jerks up at my entrance to Grampa's bedroom, and his gaze snaps right to Alex. "Who's this?" he demands.

Something about Joel I'd forgotten: his manners seem to evaporate when tired, and he's tired all the time as both a doctor and a father of baby twins. He's been better about this since his residency years, but these are trying times all around.

"He's a new friend," I answer, adding, "He's helping me with the book." I look at Grampa Milo and wave. He raises his good hand, and glances at Alex with a questioning face.

Joel wrinkles up his head at Alex, as if he could read the answer on Alex's face why this skinny slacker would be any help with the book. Today Alex wears black jeans, a T-shirt, and a plaid shirt open over that. It seems to be the only type of clothing he packed. Over the top of that, he's got an old leather motorcycle jacket with visible cracks and scratches.

Then Joel shakes his head and rubs the bridge of his nose. "Not sure how much book work you're going to get done today, kiddo." He rubs Grampa Milo's arm almost absently, as if his hand moved of its own accord, doing the reassuring while the rest of him was in Doctor Mode. "Don't tire him out too much, okay? He's only got a couple hours of lucidity at a time."

A thud on the mattress draws our attention. Grampa Milo scowls, and thumps his own chest in an *I'm here, right here*, gesture.

I rush to say, "I'm sorry, Grampa, we don't mean to speak for you, like you're not here. Joel's just worried for you, we all are. You took care of all of us for so long, and now it's our turn. I know you hate it, but there you go."

Joel and his long face stride out of the room, and I feel for him just then, what it must be like to never put aside "the doctor" to be just "the worried grandson."

Grampa Milo looks at Alex with his tired eyes and waves his hand like a benediction.

"This is Alex. He's from Michigan."

Grampa Milo raises his eyebrows slightly. My talkative Grampa would normally be riddling Alex with questions by now, and no doubt asking if there were any Jews in Michigan. He used to ask this of any out-of-towner who should chance to cross our threshold. He'd be just curious, just wondering how our people were faring outside the big city, but something about the question always made me cringe.

He's staring now with intensity at Alex, such that I follow his gaze instinctively. Alex turns to me, perhaps also wondering about the hard stare. It's in this way that I finally look straight into Alex's eyes, noticing for the first time their vibrant, arresting shade of green. I pull my attention back to my grandfather.

"We've got something to talk to you about," I begin.

Alex nudges me. He'd set the box down on the floor by the bedroom door as we came in. He widens his eyes at me now, as if to ask, *What, now, right now?*

"Yes, now. Could you get a chair for me from down the hall?" I point with my thumb at the door.

Ordering people around is more Naomi's thing than mine, but there's a certain serenity that has come over me since I stepped into this room, and saw my grandfather with waxy skin and hair all tufted up because no one has bothered to run a comb through it yet.

I'm reminded of something I learned when my dad was sick, something I'd managed to forget, somehow. Sickness enforces a dismissal of things that don't matter. By the end of my father's life, it seemed the fact of his own death barely rattled him, perhaps because it had been advancing long enough to lose its terrifying mystery. Except, now and then, I'd catch him gazing at me with bottomless sadness.

Alex has by now returned, dragging a chair from the office.

"You see, Grampa, it's like this. We found Vivian's family."

I settle into the chair, watching my grandfather's face for shock, anger, distress. Instead, he nods with patient solemnity, as if he'd been waiting for this all along.

29

Milo

O

f course they know all about Vivian. It seems crazy now, to think that sixty years was long enough for every trace of her to drift away like ashes.

I look past my daughter and this man, this long-haired stranger with the unsettling green eyes, and look for her in the room. But she's not here, still not here, not since the time I saw her dripping wet and blue, and I miss her; though I hardly believe this, it's true. Maybe it's because I need to see her one more time, whole and dry and okay, though of course I know Vivian is actually dead, and died long, long ago, and she was not okay when she died. No one who dies that young is okay.

Eleanor and this Alex from Michigan kid keep exchanging looks, and they seem to understand each other that way, which is interesting to me, even as I lay here mute and probably dying and almost too tired to care anymore about either of those things.

When they tell me that Vivian had a baby in Michigan before she died, you know I'm not even shocked?

Oh, Vivian, why didn't you ever tell me? I could've helped you, I would have done something. I don't know what, but something.

And this Millicent lady was Vivian's daughter, and they think maybe... Eleanor can't spit it out, poor kid, she looks like she's going to vomit, and this Alex fella reaches out his hand to steady her with a touch on her shoulder, and I think good for you, fella.

I scrabble my good hand out of the bed sheets and I seize Eleanor's hand. I squeeze as hard as I can muster and I look her straight in her golden brown eyes, those eyes like topaz, and I nod, hard. Yes, I know what you're getting at. I get it.

Alex speaks up now. "There's a test they can do these days, Mr. Short. It's just a little blood test, and someone can even come right here and do it. They mail it in, and in ten days, we can know."

Wonder of wonders.

I nod. Yes, we should, this test. We should know, though I feel like I already do. It makes so much more sense now, those last days I saw her.

Fat tears roll down Eleanor's face. "I'm so sorry to do this to you, to make you think about things like this now..."

I shake my head at her. Not her fault. All mine, really. My fault from sixty years ago, but my fault all the same.

"How are you feeling, are you in pain?"

I shake my head again. I'm not, not the kind of pain she means, anyway.

The next few minutes overflow with anguish, Eleanor for seeing me so frail and sick, mine for seeing my loss predicted in the pain of her watery eyes. This Alex stands like a pillar of salt next to her, coming to life only when she says goodbye to me with a kiss on my cheek, smelling of her raspberry shampoo.

He picks up a box on the way out, and I wonder about that box, but of course I can't ask.

And so I'm alone now, briefly, I'm alone so seldom anymore, always they're keeping one eye on me for my moment of demise.

And then she's next to my bed, and it's my turn for tears to course down my old papery face.

She's wearing a black dress, and a tiny hat with a puff of black veil; I hardly ever saw her in black. Her face is pale compared to the slash of red lipstick and her dark wavy hair, but otherwise she appears how she always used to. There's no vicious smirk, no sneer or tease in her expression. It's a softness I rarely noticed, even in 1936, and even then mostly when she didn't think I was looking. Then she'd catch herself, and a hardness would settle into her features like she was made of marble.

Oh, Vivian.

30

September 1936

Vivian had said she'd be wearing a green dress, and Milo kept jumping at every splash of green in his vision. This seemed hopeless; how did he think he would find her in this crush of humanity? There had to be thousands of people cramming together along the 72nd Street Lake in Central Park to see this Water Carnival mishegoss.

Milo had just thought it would be a nice place to spend time with her, being both entertaining and also free of charge, and furthermore, not intimate or scandalous in the least. Just two friends out watching some folk dancing, what could be more innocent?

He might never even see her in this mess, that's what. Milo shifted the package in his arm, a little something he bought for her, considering her current situation did not seem likely to leave her much pin money. He'd wrapped up another surprise in there, too: the Playbill for *The High Hat*'s New York opening next week.

Milo had put his head down and polished off the song right that day, the morning after their night together, not sleeping or eating until he was finished and satisfied. He kept some of the words from their night together, but not all. Some of them, in the bright light of sobriety, were just wrong. Clunky, or too easy. But by the time he brought the words over to the theater, where rehearsals for other parts of the show were already underway, he and Allen could play it through without interruption, to the delighted appreciation of the cast and director, and Gordon, too, when they played it for him.

With the flush of accomplishment still high in his cheeks, he'd phoned Vivian up to take her to the movies to see *Show Boat*. His mother would never have approved, but he didn't live at home, and he didn't have to tell her he was taking a gentile girl to a movie. It was just for friendliness and appreciation, anyway. Once in a while he'd phone her up, or she'd phone him, and then they'd meet for a coffee, or a sandwich, or a show. This turned out to be a pleasant way to spend the summer, while he and Allen worked on the finishing touches of *The High Hat* and steered clear of each other at all other times.

But with their recent call, Milo had gotten worried. She'd confessed, due to his persistent asking, that the girlfriend and her new groom were due back home soon, and she needed a new place. Milo had already approached the director of the show about a job for Vivian and been turned out flat; her reputation preceded her.

"I suspect I can find a room in a boarding house somewhere," she'd said with a sigh, sounding bored with the line of questioning. "Anyway, it would just be temporary, wouldn't it? I have that feeling."

Her voice sounded strangely serious on that last sentence, but maybe it was hard to tell on the phone. "Sure it is, you bet," he enthused, wanting to buck up her spirits.

Milo didn't dare tell Vivian, in case it didn't work out, but if *The High Hat* was a hit, and he made some good dough off the royalties, he'd hire her as his own personal secretary. He might be the only person in Manhattan who understood her, maybe also the only one who cared.

So they talked a few minutes and then they made a date to meet in the park for this Water Carnival, where according to the *Times*, they'd built a stage right out in the lake, and all kinds of folk dancers were going to be hoofing it out there on the water.

Milo hadn't noticed the lake yet, so busy was he looking for Vivian.

It was a husky alto shout of "Milo!" that drew his attention first, the voice with so much oomph it almost sounded like a man.

It was her swinging brown hair he spotted next, through the slanting golden light of the early autumn dusk. She was rotating her head this way and that, with a restless energy that seemed uniquely hers, even at that distance, through a crowd and with his squinty eyes.

"Vivian!" he called, and she turned and lit up like a photoflash. She barged her way through the crowd and threw herself into Milo's chest. He caught her, steadied her. "You okay?"

"Never better. This is exciting! I've never been to one of these before. I can barely see the stage from here, but I got a glimpse. It's amazing, it looks like a water lily, and there are reeds and bluebells made of wood... I hope no one falls off, and they have to fish them out! C'mon, let's get closer."

Vivian grabbed Milo's hand before he could argue, and threaded through the mob. She kept up an animated chatter with the crowd as she went, "Lovely hat, could you excuse me please? So sorry, passing through, fine night, sir, isn't it?" and people seemed to part willingly for her, as if she were moving up to her rightful place, which had been set aside by all of Central Park just for her.

As they approached the edge of the lake, the spectators were seated on blankets, or coats spread onto the ground for those unprepared, a small sacrifice on such a fine night, which still bore the faint tinge of summer, though it was closer to October, in truth.

Vivian somehow convinced a family to squeeze closer together to make room, and flung herself down on a square of trampled grass before Milo could get his own coat down.

"Vivian, you'll tear your stockings, or muddy up your dress."

"Oh, who cares? Sit down and enjoy. Oh look, they're starting!"

Milo lowered himself to the ground, tossing his coat over the package for Vivian. It was just as well she hadn't noticed it yet; it seemed a bad time to present it to her, in the throng. He should have guessed that free entertainment would have drawn them out in droves.

Milo propped himself up with his arm, positioned just behind Vivian so if she should tire, she could lean on him. She had the posture of a steel girder, though, and her face radiated interest with her grinning mouth open just slightly, with a childlike lack of awareness of her own appearance.

Following the singing was a modern ballet, then children who'd won prizes in a folk dancing competition: Russian, Polish, and Scottish dances. Milo felt himself watching something out of a fairy tale, all these dancers whirling improbably over a lake.

The fluid, rolling vowels of Italian spilled out into the night to finish the program, courtesy of the singers of Coro d'Italia.

The crowd began to move in concert, as if of one body, but Vivian seemed content to let them go on without her. As they sat, they were surrounded by a forest of legs on the move. Vivian brought her face close to Milo's; she smelled of roses. "Thank you for inviting me here."

"Here," Milo said stupidly, and without preamble, thrusting the package into her lap.

She tore open the brown wrapper, and then cocked her head. "Oh, *Gone with the Wind*! You remembered."

"Yeah, you told me that you wanted to read it, once, at your place. I mean… your friend's place."

"Oh! Look at this!"

Vivian was holding the Playbill up, trying to catch the ambient light from nearby lampposts. She began to tear through page after page so roughly Milo thought she'd rip it apart. He wondered at this voraciousness.

"Well, where am I?" she asked him, her green eyes round and questioning.

"Where are you? Kid, I'm confused, what are you getting at?"

"In the Playbill, for our song. It doesn't say my name anywhere. Maybe just on the sheet music?"

Milo's confusion gave to way to a sickening dread.

"It's not, actually. It's my name, and Allen's."

"I thought it was our song. I helped you." She lowered the Playbill into her lap, carefully, as one might a sleeping child.

Milo hadn't noticed how thoroughly Vivian's normal jaded pose had been overtaken by her childlike delight in the folk dancing and music, until that delight melted away again, leaving behind a fierce, brittle hardness.

"Yeah, you helped me take notes, you helped me once or twice with a word maybe, but look, if I gave credit to everybody who threw in a word now and then, every song would be split ten ways. Hell, Gordon's Negro cook gave us a rhyme once in *Hilarity*."

"You told me I saved the song, Milo. You said that to me." Had he said that? It seemed possible. The memories of that evening were fuzzed up by gin and the momentous occasion of his first time in a woman's bed, not to mention the thought of that evening—however pleasant—was always mixed up with Allen on the couch that afternoon. These were not things on which he longed to dwell.

"I didn't mean to confuse you, kid, but that's not the way it works. It was my song. Mine and Allen's."

Vivian stood up roughly, unsteadily, in doing so stumbling out of one shoe. "I threw over Mark Bell because that song was partly mine and it was going to be a hit."

While Milo's panicky mind tried to understand what she was saying, he looked around on the ground for her shoe, as if the shoe was what mattered. It was all he could think to do.

"What are you talking about? You said you hadn't been seeing much of him."

Her laugh was harsh, like a slap. "Oh, Milo, I've been seeing *all* of him. All the time, too. Who do you think really paid for that apartment? Did you honestly think I'd know a girlfriend rich enough to have a place like that?"

Milo gave up on the shoe. Still on his haunches, he looked up at her, mouth hanging open.

Vivian smirked. "I thought you were just pretending along with me, so we didn't have to admit it out loud, but you really bought all that? Poor little Milo. You grew up in the greatest city in the world and you know so very little."

Milo rose unsteadily, wondering why he felt ashamed when she'd been the one living as… Bell's concubine. A kept woman. He thought back to her fine dresses, the short fur jacket she liked to wear. The morning after the night they spent together, she'd given him the bum's rush with some story about a nosy landlady… Bell was probably on his way over, right then.

Milo still couldn't find his voice, so Vivian filled the silence. "Look at you, like you're going to be sick. Well anyway, it's over now, like I said. I'm not a fool, Milo. I knew that was no way to live, not forever. I knew he'd get tired of me soon enough when a dewy-eyed chorus girl turned his head. But it didn't matter, because I'd helped you write a hit song. And you said I saved the song. I know you did."

"I don't remember that… We didn't even talk about credit…"

"I didn't know we had to talk about it. I didn't know I'd have to plead for what's rightfully my share."

Milo took off his hat and scratched his head. It wasn't exactly fear of Vivian that was running him through with such a sick, scary feeling. It was a sense that something in the world had tilted sideways, bizarre, like that weird painting where clocks were melting over trees that he saw once at the MoMa: everything was going crazy wrong and he didn't know why.

"Vivian, it's just not the way it's done. I'm sorry, but—"

"It's Allen, isn't it? That bastard said no. You always do everything he wants, don't you? Loyal Milo who just hops-to at his word."

"I do not!"

"You quit your Harms job because he said so! You took the *Hilarity* job because he said so! You took on this show because he said so! Why don't you stand up and be a man for once?"

"I am a man!" Milo bellowed. "Don't you ever say that to me again!"

Vivian's expression flashed fear. Milo noticed his posture then, he was leaning forward, his finger was out and he'd apparently jabbed or shaken it right in her face. He drew back, and stared at his own hand in wonder.

Stricken, Milo looked up in time to see Vivian's face go from slackened fright to hard bright anger. Something about her eyes glinting in the yellow lamppost light made him think of a dark, many-faceted jewel.

"And a man doesn't share credit with a girl, then? He steals her work and takes her to bed and then he's off to live his life and to hell with the broad anyway."

"I'll help you get a job, I swear I will, if this show does great, how'd you like to come work for me, huh? You can be my secretary, and you won't have to worry about getting fired—"

Vivian laughed then, shrilly, so loud that people whipped their heads around to stare. "You want to buy me. Same as Bell did, only you're doing it smarter, aren't you, Short? Heaven forbid you just marry me, no, I have to *earn my keep* with you?"

"Vivian, but I already said—"

"I know what you already said! But that was before you boffed me like I was the last woman on earth, and I was stupid enough to believe that meant… But to you I'm just a shiksa whore and not worth wiping your shoes on."

Milo stepped close to her so maybe she'd stop shouting, his heart thrashing around in his chest, feeling like he was at Coney Island on a ride gone crazy. "I would never say that about you, but look, I hardly think you can talk to me about it considering whose bed that really was. How did this all get so confused?"

"When you practically tear a girl's clothes off I don't see how there's much room for confusion."

"You weren't exactly shy yourself!"

She ripped the hat off her head, balling it up in her fist. Her hair stood up like a crown. "So what, you're through with me, then?" She began smacking his chest with her hat, her voice sliding into a sneering parody of an office girl: "Unless I want to take your dictation, Mr. Short? How would you like your coffee, Mr. Short? I'll type it up right away, Mr. Short!"

He seized her wrist. "Stop! People are staring! Look, I didn't mean for this to get so crazy, can't we just cool off a minute?"

"Cool off? Honestly."

She yanked her wrist so hard out of Milo's hand that he stumbled forward. She took three limping, one-shoe strides away, then whirled back around and shouted through the night.

"You're a vine is what you are! You twisted into all my spaces, wrapped around all my branches! We are trapped together, Milo Short, we'll never be rid of each other now, and I don't mean as your *office girl*, typing your letters and doing your bidding so you can give me money in a way to ease your conscience. You and your 'I have to marry a Jewish girl' and yet you kept coming back."

Milo opened his mouth to retort: Vivian was the one who kept coming to him! Kept quitting jobs, following him around, so of course he felt responsible... But the panting Fury in front of him now wouldn't hear these words. It would be all useless noise to her, now and forever.

So he stood there, dumb and pathetic in the face of her wrath. He had a sense of shadows in the distance, shocked murmurs from a gawking few reaching his ears on the autumn breeze.

Vivian stepped backward, awkwardly, lopsided, and then she was beyond the circle of lamppost light. The stage lights had by now been extinguished, and the darkness and dispersing performers swallowed her retreating figure.

Milo bent down to pick up his coat, and in so doing, saw *Gone with the*

Wind lying in the grass. He'd forgotten all about it. He'd been so tickled that morning, walking out of the Strand on Fourth Avenue with the book for Vivian and a fan magazine for Leah. Stupid, ignorant Milo, not knowing what he was about to step into.

And Vivian, once again putting herself in trouble on his account, without him ever asking her to do so. Walking out of Harms, and that was a good job, too, with the ever-diligent and reserved Mrs. Smith typing away on her Corona while keeping one eye on Vivian, on all the girls. And now Vivian again gave up her security supposedly on his account, well, who asked her to do that? And why was it his fault? Sure they spent a night together, but she spent all kinds of nights together with Bell and why wasn't this his problem, then?

Seemed like he'd spent his last two years keeping tabs on this crazy dame, who was always dashing off someplace she shouldn't be, and for that matter following him around from place to place like some kind of puppy. Well, someone else could chase her this damn time because Milo Short was good and tired of it.

Milo found the Playbill, though someone had stomped on it and he had to brush the dirt away. He shoved it back in the book. He began to walk away when he stumbled on something: her shoe. He picked it up, snarling at the shoe as if it were to blame for the whole stupid mess.

Someone else would have to take care of her, and if she'd thrown over Bell, well then she'd have to make her own way. Or better yet, go back home to that sister. Sure, that wouldn't be fun for her, but she'd have someone to watch out for her, someone who cared. So many families he knew had been split up by emigration, by war, people dead with the flu. He'd seen the faces of the new Jewish immigrants who'd be sent to his father's tailor shop for a decent set of American clothes at a cheap rate. They would have this look of lonely terror that seemed unique to them, having fled their homelands out of desperate necessity, having left behind all they knew, sometimes family, sometimes wives and children if they couldn't afford to bring them, parents who wouldn't leave the shtetl life, the only life they'd ever known.

And here was Vivian, who'd done that to herself on purpose, thrust herself into a dirty, noisy city alone, and for what? Selling perfume? Being some man's girl on the side? She didn't leave home to marry a Jew songwriter, this much he knew.

He clutched the shoe in one hand until its strange contours hurt his palm. If he had the power, he'd throw her onto a train home himself.

He stomped up the metal steps of the elevated platform to head for home. By the time he stepped onto the train, his breathing had slowed and he felt mainly tired.

The clattering rocking of the train seemed to soothe him. He leaned his head against the window and tried to remember the sister's name. Edna. Elaine. Esther. Something with an E. How bad could the sister be, anyway?

You think I should crawl back to Estelle, don't you? I'd rather throw myself in the East River. Do you know I stood on the Brooklyn Bridge once and wondered if I could hike my dress up high enough to get over the rail?

Milo gasped and snapped to alertness, standing up to get off the train at the very next stop, needing to turn around and head back the way he came. He drew worried and disgusted stares from the others on the train, as they eyed his incoherent mutterings, none of them knowing they were frantic prayers.

31

Eleanor

n the window seat, I have both a view of the street outside, and Alex on a chair pulled up near the window. I tap a picture in the photo album on my lap.

"I think this must be her," I tell Alex, pointing at the dark-haired woman frowning behind Grampa Milo and his songwriting partner at the Stork Club. This was the same photo as was in that old biography. There must have been two copies, because I can't imagine Grampa Milo would have shared his copy with a biographer. He was always so closed-mouthed with biographers, interviewers. He used to say it was because he was tired of the same questions all the time, and how his boring old life didn't matter anyhow, just the work. I believed him, because why wouldn't I? Same as I believed him that Grandma Bee was his one and only love. Everything I ever thought I knew is slipping through my fingers.

Alex leans in. "Wow, she looks like Mom in old pictures. Or, Mom looks like her. I guess she would, wouldn't she?" He's pulled his hair back so that if you see him from the front he looks like he's got an unfortunate caplike haircut, but if you look behind him there's wavy tail between his shoulder blades.

"You know, you can let your hair down. We have seen long hair a time or two in New York. No one's going to care."

This last part isn't true, really, because Naomi would wrinkle her nose and sniff as if checking for pot smoke. But it's not like he can really hide it.

He shrugs. "Nah. It would get in my way right now anyway. I've been thinking of cutting it. I spend way too much money on shampoo."

An odd, snorting giggle escapes me before I can snatch it back. So wrong to laugh now, here, of all places. But Grampa Milo would have laughed, too, if he'd have heard the joke. He's sleeping now upstairs, has been all morning.

We are waiting for the nurse to come take his blood, and I am so fluttery and shaky I am craving a smoke, something I haven't experienced since I was trying to be cool back in college.

We made the house call appointment when Uncle Paul had said he would be out of town, checking on a show in previews. Naomi was not yet due back from London. I'd weaseled out of Aunt Rebekah the fact that she had a lunch meeting for some charity board. So it seems we will be alone today, just long enough.

The sonorous doorbell chimes and I gasp, fumbling the album. Alex catches it before it slides off my lap. He closes it reverently and hands it back to me, meeting my eyes. "Here goes nothing," he says, and then gives my hand a pat, where I'm gripping the album far harder than I need to.

As I disentangle from the window seat, I catch Esme's eye. We'd had to enlist her in this subterfuge, about which I feel well and properly guilty. The family can get mad at me all they want, but they can't fire me. This is not true for Esme.

Alex and I follow Esme into the foyer. She opens the door with her "greeting" face on, but then I watch her warm brown skin drain pale at whatever she sees behind the guest.

The nurse comes in, or I guess phlebotomist. He's a thin, reedy man with sharp cheekbones and a close-cropped haircut, who introduces himself as Leon. I'm starting the introductions when I hear Esme exclaim, "Back so soon,

Miss Naomi?"

Naomi clomps in, dropping a carry-on bag on the floor. "Who the hell is this?" she says, gesturing to the phlebotomist and finger combing her hair at the same time, and turning her attention to Alex. "And this? What's going on, is Grampa okay? Who are these people? Eleanor?"

"I didn't think you were supposed to come back yet."

"Yeah, well, here I am, and why aren't you answering me?"

"Let's talk," I tell her, and nod to Alex, who approaches Leon. I'm praying he will catch my drift, and get the blood test and get the guy out while I stall Naomi.

She shoves the swinging door into the kitchen, and it bangs against the wall and back toward me such that it almost hits my nose.

"Okay, what, El? Start talking."

"Why are you back?"

"I forgot my daughter's recital was this week until my assistant reminded me so I cut the trip short, but why does it matter when I'm back? Who are those people? Do I need to call the police to get these strangers thrown out of our house? Because I'm about five seconds from doing that."

"It's research. For the book."

"What kind of research requires that one guy to have a big black case like a doctor bag, and why does some hippie slacker guy have anything to do with your book? So help me, Eleanor, you better give me answers that make sense."

"Or what, Naomi?"

"Forget this." Naomi makes to cross the kitchen, so I stand in her path. "Move out of the way."

"No, hear me out first, please."

"I've been trying to hear you out and you keep dodging. Something is going on with those people or you'd have just told me who they are the minute I came in the door. I will put your ass on the ground, so move."

"It's a blood test."

At this Naomi stands back from me somewhat, but still in arm's reach. "For what."

"There's a possibility… a remote… we think…. I mean, there's this person, it's possible…"

"Oh God, it's a paternity test?"

Naomi shoves past me while I'm still stammering, and I stumble back against the door. She's improbably fast even in her business heels, and has gained the door to Grampa Milo's room while I'm still on the first landing. I can hear her bellowing about stopping this farce.

"Wait, Naomi! Listen to me!"

"Get out!" she's hollering. "Get out right now, or I'm calling the police."

I finally burst in to see Grampa Milo finish scribbling on a piece of paper on a clipboard, his left hand looking awkward and cramped. Leon continues with his preparation, not fazed in the slightest. He fishes out a little rubber tourniquet, and begins talking in a soothing, unruffled voice about what he's going to do, though how Grampa can hear over Naomi's bluster I've no idea.

I've put myself between Naomi and the bed and finally distinguish the basic gist of her rant: that Grampa Milo has been tricked into this and can't possibly understand what he's signing and don't you dare or she'll call the police.

I seize her by the arms and give her a brisk shake. Her face clears up from its indignation long enough to regard me with stunned, mute shock that I should lay my hands on her.

"You don't want this in the papers, do you? You want this call over the police scanner? On Page Six?"

"Are you threatening me?" She shakes her arms away from me and scrunches up her face. She's so confused that retiring little Ellie has physically grabbed her that it's not an argument she's making, it's a genuine question. Her world has gone so crazy she honestly can't understand it. It's almost funny, and some part of me thinks I will laugh about this later, when I've finished with my own panic attack.

"Of course not, I wouldn't tip them off, but police reports and scanners are public. We were trying to be quiet about this until you came in here and lost your shit."

We both turn at a snapping noise: Grampa Milo snapping his fingers, as Leon the phlebotomist tapes a piece of gauze in the crook of his arm. Grampa's glaring at Naomi, and shaking his head, for now every inch the patriarch. His turn to say, in the only way he can, "Don't you dare."

"You people are all nuts." She whirls on her heel and strides out. I follow her into the office across the hall. She assumes her more typical stance: legs wide, arms akimbo. Her color is high again, her shock burned away by her rage.

"This is outrageous. It will not stand up in court for a moment, you realize this. He's frail and a stroke victim who probably has no idea what he's even signing, and what's more you can't be sure he understands you. He can barely even sign left-handed, it won't look like a competent signature. I don't know what you hope to prove but this is a joke. I'm calling Eli right now."

She snatches up the receiver, but I press the button to hang up her call.

"How dare you?" She bats my hand away. "What the hell is wrong with you anyhow?"

"Naomi, Grampa Milo wants to know. He agreed to this."

"He doesn't know what the hell he's agreeing to." She tries to dial again, so I hang her up again. "Eleanor, I'll just call our lawyer from another phone."

"So call from another phone, but listen to me, dammit."

She slams the phone down and crosses her arms. "Fine. Talk."

I explain about the existence of Vivian, and Alex and the birthdates and all the coincidences. I leave out anything that seems hallucinatory and say nothing about song lyrics, God forbid Naomi hear about all that.

I finish up trying to appeal to a sense of charity. "So we just want to find out, just in case, just to set this poor lady's mind at ease in Michigan. It's a mitzvah."

She snorts. Naomi has a world-class derisive snort. "I cannot believe you would do this to him. Our grandfather is sick and probably dying, and you go in there and make him think, on his deathbed, that he fathered a child out of wedlock with some crazy lady, based on press clippings? Being in the same picture as him at the Stork Club? Jesus, Eleanor, were you born yesterday? This hippie kid is a fortune hunter, he just wants some easy money, or publicity. Have you figured that out? How he can go to the tabloids now?"

"What do the tabloids care, anyway? Grampa's not Tom Cruise."

"You were just talking to me about Page Six! God, you're so naïve. I knew you shouldn't have done this book. I'm calling Paul and telling him to cancel the contract. You're not even working on the book, are you? Have you written a word? You've gotten all swept up in this stupid romantic theory, manipulated by this stranger, and in the meantime the book project that's going to promote our amazing revival show is dead in the water. Once again, I'm right, but does anyone ever listen to me? And then the next thing I do is call Eli and tell him about this insane escapade so that we have a plan to quash any ludicrous claims that come out of this."

Naomi steps around the desk to get close to me, and she jabs her long nail toward my nose. "I thought you wanted to help the family, El. Well, thanks for helping us into legal fees and scandal and probably another stroke for our poor grandfather. Thanks for nothing."

Her voice cracks over "nothing," and she flings herself down into one of the guest chairs on the other side of the desk. She puts her head in her hands and stays there while the clock downstairs gongs away.

When she speaks again, her voice is crackly, like radio static. "I am trying so hard. Trying so hard to keep everything okay."

I settle into the opposite chair. I won't try to take her hand, or pat her arm. I know better. "I know you are." *So am I, in my way,* I'm tempted to argue, but she won't listen, anyway. "Look, how's this? We don't tell anyone yet. You're assuming the blood test will be damning. It might clear him, too. Let's just wait it out. If it's not him, then we can forget all about this and no one else has to be the wiser. No legal fees, no scandal. As for me, you can hate me as much as you want, either way."

"Okay, you got me with that last part." Naomi sits up, rubs her face, and collapses backward into the chair. "Kid, will you go check on Grampa? I need to get myself together a minute."

By the time I get out into the hall, Naomi has curled forward again, her blown-straight hair swinging down past her face, her expression unreadable.

32

1936

t wasn't much past dawn when Milo Short stepped heavily down off the streetcar in Times Square, on his way to the theater. Soon enough he'd be at the opening, then at parties, then swallowing boulders as he waited for the early notices to come in. Soon enough he'd be side-by-side with Allen for all of it.

He just wanted to view the marquee in peace, and seeing as how he hadn't slept all night for his pointless search for Vivian, the crack of dawn was as good a time as any. He'd been back and forth across the Brooklyn Bridge, had haunted the doorstep of her—Bell's—apartment. He'd tried hotels, he even went back to the park in case she might return to search for her shoe.

Now the newsboys were cutting open stacks of papers, and he was half expecting and all the way afraid to hear a shouted bulletin along the lines of "Read all about it: Dead girl fished from East River!"

The High Hat *opening Friday! John Garnett, Marianne West, George Lamb, Gigi Giselle.*

All of these fabulous names, and every one of them fake as the wooden sets on the stage inside. Garnett's real last name escaped him, but he knew it was foreign sounding with a whole lot of blocky consonants. Marianne's true last name was Wisocki. Gigi Giselle's real name was Bertha Lambert and she was from Indiana. Mark Bell was Marco Rubellino, and Milo himself was supposed to have been Moshe Schwartz.

Vivian Adair and Bernard Allen were some of the few real names he knew.

Milo thought the stage door might be open early, so he wandered over that way. The night had turned cold and gusty during his search, and the morning was taking its time in warming up, so he jammed his hands deep into his pockets. Not like he could sleep, even being awake all night, because inside he was vibrating like a cymbal crash.

Aw, nuts, he thought, a bum at the stage door entrance. Then he noticed the "bum" was in fact wearing one ladies' shoe.

He was at her side in a flash. "Vivian? Kid?"

When she opened her eyes a slit and stared at him, blank, he was firstly glad she was not dead. That had been his thought when he realized it was her, prone on the ground: dead, and all his fault.

She wasn't dressed for the weather. He shrugged out of his coat and wrapped it around her. Her stockings were shredded up. "What did you do all night?"

She looked at him like he was a mannequin.

"Does it matter?" With his propping arm she sat up, but slumped forward, her legs out straight in front of her, stocking feet pointing vaguely outward. *Broken* was the word that drifted into his mind.

"It matters to me."

"Ha."

"Were you out all night in the weather?"

"Walked."

"Walked where? Home? I tried to look for you."

"Here."

"You walked all that way here?"

A shadow fell over Milo's shoulder, and he turned on his haunches to see a cop staring down his nose at them. "You need some assistance, sir?" He drew out the "sir" with practiced sarcasm.

"Not at all, officer, she's just had a bit too much, I'm about to take her home."

Any notion of calling for help drained away. If Vivian kept on like this in front of anybody official she'd end up in an asylum.

"C'mere, let me take you home. You're not staying at the apartment now, since you threw him over…"

She laughed a hollow, dark chuckle. "I haven't left him. Sure, I thought about it. Hoped to do it. But part of me knew, just knew, you wouldn't come through for me. Mark is going to shine me on soon enough, anyway. There's prettier girls, younger girls, more… pliable girls. Easygoing girls who never give a bit of trouble."

"Some girls are worth the trouble."

"And some are not." She looked at Milo straight on for the first time since he'd found her. Her face softened. "Oh, Milo. You turned out to be a good egg in the end."

"What are you talking about, 'end,' what end? C'mon, stand up, I'll get you to whatever home, I don't care, just someplace off the streets here."

Vivian let herself be pulled to her feet, and walked along the sidewalk, though she seemed to always be pulling against him slightly.

"Here, let's get a cab so you don't cut your feet."

The driver paid no mind to Vivian's dishevelment, nor the fancy apartment house address. Milo overpaid because he didn't have the right change on him, and maybe a little because he felt vaguely guilty. Though what tipping a cabbie had to do with things, he hardly knew.

Vivian was picking her away across the sidewalk, and Milo swooped her up into his arms. Her head rested on his shoulder. Her hair smelled like wind, dirt, and soot from the trains.

He stood her gently on her feet on the apartment stoop. "So, where's your key?"

"I can't believe I'm back here," she said, staring at the heavy wood door. "I really thought I wouldn't be."

Milo dared not repeat anything he said the night before, even if it was all true. It would only bring her low. Lower yet. Some truths you leave alone because all they do is hurt.

Milo said quietly, in the soft voice he'd heard his mother use to Leah as they were growing up, when she'd be coughing and coughing, "Where's your key, huh? Let's get you inside."

A whining siren reached their ears, growing louder with proximity. *Some poor bastard* was Milo's thought because whatever the siren was for, police or the fire department, it sure didn't mean anything good for somebody.

The siren seemed to energize Vivian. She straightened, her complexion brightened before Milo's eyes.

For a heartbeat, Milo didn't understand what was happening. It wasn't until Vivian was halfway down the stoop, his own coat sailing out behind her, that he had even an idea of what she planned.

How was she so quick, and without shoes, too? She'd gotten to the sidewalk and gone several strides while Milo still had one foot on the steps. She was streaking down the concrete, arms pumping like an athlete. Two cars parked on the side had left a sizeable gap between bumpers and Milo saw her head turn that way, and she angled toward it. The siren grew impossibly louder.

Milo was hardly an athlete but he ran harder anyway, muttering to God for speed, now, please…

The siren pierced Milo's ears and he threw himself forward, crushing Vivian beneath him to the pavement. The fire engine swerved unsteadily around them, and Milo thought he heard indistinct shouts of outrage from the firemen, but it was hard to know, because the loudest sound was his own blood rushing in his ears.

He picked himself up off of her and rolled her onto her back to inspect for damage. Her face and upper chest above her bodice were scraped and red. The high color which had brightened her cheeks was draining away. Her eyes were staring flatly at the sky.

"Why did you do that?" she asked listlessly.

"Why did you?" He tried to lift her. They were still lying on the road, after all. She didn't answer, and refused to budge. Annoyance and fear of traffic braided together for Milo. He was heaving her into a seated position when she let loose.

A screech as loud as the fire truck shrilled in his ear. Apartment dwellers threw up their curtains all over the block to get a look, pigeons scattered, and Milo nearly dropped her.

As suddenly as she started, she stopped, like someone yanked the needle off a record. This time she let Milo pick her up without resistance, and he decided to take her home.

His mother answered the door. "Milo! Who is this? What has happened?"

"She's in a bad way. She needs people around her, and I didn't know what else to do."

"Bring her to the sofa. I will make her some coffee."

Vivian allowed herself to be laid down like a doll. Milo cast a glance at the door, which his mother had locked behind them. Not that it would stop her if she were really determined, but if Vivian did try to run out, he'd at least have a couple seconds to catch up with her first.

He joined his mother in the kitchen, where she was plugging in the percolator.

His mother turned to him and fixed him with a narrowed, steely look. "This your girlfriend?"

"No, Ma, I swear. She's sorta…attached to me. I guess I probably gave her the wrong idea."

"I guess you probably did. What is it you plan to do with her?"

"I don't know, I just can't leave her alone now."

"Why is she all scratched up?"

"I had to tackle her to keep her from throwing herself in front of a speeding fire engine."

She clucked her tongue. "I knew a girl like this once. Very sad."

Milo didn't ask for the story, not wanting to hear the tragic end.

His mother went to the cupboards, looking for coffee mugs. "I will let her stay here until this evening, but you need to have her gone before your father gets home. I should not like to explain this to him. He will not believe she is not a girlfriend, and this he will not appreciate, Moshe."

"When does he get back? And where is he, anyhow?"

"Seven o'clock. Meetings with the Jewish Relief Council. They are talking of Europe. Everyone talking Europe. Why do you fuss and worry about here, when our people suffer so? If only you knew. If only all of you knew."

"We know. Just not in the same way as you."

The percolator bubbled. "Does she like anything in it? We have only sugar just now."

"Just some sugar. I doubt she'll drink it." Milo silently added, *I hope she doesn't throw it against the wall.* This limp wraith on the couch, and the streaking figure bent on single-minded destruction, neither of these Vivians did he understand.

Milo took the coffee to her, and murmured her name. She looked at him with resignation, and turned to face the back of the couch. "I'll leave it here," he said, and rested the cup on the side table.

Then he sat in an adjacent chair, watching her, turning his hat around and around in his hand, while he thought. What he really needed, Milo decided, was a girl. Another girl would know what to do.

An hour later, Milo was wearing a path in the living room rug. Vivian had hardly moved, about as human and warm as a piece of furniture. Milo had finally drunk the lukewarm coffee rather than waste it, nearly performing a spit-take because his mother had made it so strong.

Chana Schwartz had gone to the market to buy the night's dinner, and other than the telephone ringing once (Max, asking after Leah, who was at the pictures with a neighbor) the apartment was so quiet that Milo could faintly hear conversations of people going by in the street.

Somehow he kept ending up alone with this dame.

The only time Vivian spoke was once. She turned over on the sofa, curled on her side like a child, to face Milo. "I could stay with you. We could write more songs? Help each other? I promise to be good. I know I'm not always good."

"You are good," Milo answered, sitting across from her, where he'd been tapping out rhythms from the show on the arm of his chair. He made his voice hard, imitating his father. "But you can't stay with me. It's time you went home."

"You don't want me." This was part challenge, part question. Milo couldn't bring himself to answer.

Vivian raised herself on one elbow. "Then say so. Say you don't want me, or I won't believe you."

"C'mon, kid…"

"Say it."

Milo made himself look at her straight on. "No. I don't want you."

Vivian pulled back as if bitten, then melted gradually back down to a prone position, her eyes unfocused, staring at nothing.

When there was a quiet knock at the door, Milo yanked it open and he could have kissed Mrs. Smith, if she'd have stood for such a display. He'd never have imagined the prim head secretary back at TB Harms would be coming to his aid now. He never even thought he'd see her again after that day Keenan canned him. He never even went back to visit, or bring her a pastrami sandwich like the old times. And yet here she was, answering his call, bringing her brisk efficiency to bear, no questions asked.

"I'm not sure how much I can help, but I'll try," she said, stepping past Milo without waiting to be invited, crisp and secretarial as ever.

She walked with erect, proper posture to the girl's limp form, and sat carefully on the edge of the table. She reminded Milo of a tiny bird, perched the way she was. She reached out a slim hand with red nails and stroked Vivian's arm.

"Vivian? It's me. Beatrice."

Beatrice. Milo had never heard her first name during the time they worked together. She seemed to prefer the formality of "Mrs." Or maybe that was just his assumption, since she always seemed as reserved and controlled as her hair knotted on the back of her head.

Mrs. Smith turned to look over her shoulder at Milo. "Mr. Short, would you give us a minute?"

"Sure, of course."

Milo scampered out of the apartment and down the steps, all too happy to let Mrs. Smith do whatever she would.

He rested on the stoop and watched the Bronx parade by as he lit a cigarette. From his view he could see the Majestic Theatre, likely where Leah had gone. It was showing an Astaire picture, *Follow the Fleet*. Some songwriters had been heading out to Hollywood, and Allen had been pestering him about it, too, saying the money was better, what with theaters shutting down all up and down Broadway, turning into movie houses. "They still need music, Short," Allen had implored, but Milo had shook his head quietly, concentrating instead on watching the final dress rehearsals for *The High Hat*.

Milo had heard the old hands in the business telling gleeful old stories about the older shows, about pranks played on each other in the cast, about stage mishaps that must have been horrifying at the time but in the retelling, having all survived, became hilarious anecdotes, more so when greased by free-flowing booze. Milo would like to tell stories like that, but his two shows thus far both were all tangled up with Allen and Vivian, two wretches who'd taught him more about life than he ever wanted to know.

He squinted down at his cigarette and wished he'd have been good with a needle after all, stitching away at the Schwartz and Sons tailor shop. Vivian had come to the city for excitement, so it would seem, but Milo didn't think so much was wrong with boring. Max was doing just fine with his pretty little wife and a good job.

Milo turned as the apartment building door opened gently, knowing right off it was Mrs. Smith.

She lowered herself down next to Milo on the stoop, holding out her hand. Milo handed her the cigarette and she sucked in a long, unladylike drag. When she handed it back, a ring of red lipstick was imprinted on the end.

"Well," she said, in a puff of smoke. "I told her I'm contacting her sister, which I will do momentarily."

"How did she react to that?"

"About the same. Inert."

On the telephone, Milo had told Mrs. Smith everything, nearly everything anyway, leaving out the reason he'd gone running to Vivian's apartment in the first place that one sweaty afternoon. A good girl like Mrs. Smith didn't need to know about Allen, this much he knew.

"How'd you even know about the sister?"

"Oh, us girls in the typing pool have plenty to talk about. It won't be hard to get a telegram to her, now that I've got out of Vivian that the sister married one Howard Mann and moved to this little town in Michigan named Ludington."

"Michigan? She'll freeze to death."

Mrs. Smith turned to regard him with one eyebrow raised. "Mr. Short, it's no farther north than New York. Did you flunk geography?"

"Call me Milo, I beg you. We don't work together, you don't have to act like I'm important."

"Fine, then. And you may call me Beatrice."

"It's a nice name. I once knew a Jewish girl who went by Beatrice."

"Well, now this makes twice."

Milo's mother came up to the sidewalk, and he trotted over to take her bags. He rushed through introductions while the trio went up the steps.

As they entered, he realized Vivian was nowhere to be seen. All three of them wordlessly began searching the apartment's few rooms with alarmed energy.

It was Milo who bumped into her emerging from the bathroom. Vivian took a cold look at Milo's face and deadpanned, "A girl can't freshen up without a search party?"

Mrs. Smith smiled at her with a tilt of her head. "You look so pretty, Viv. Now tell me, where can we get the address of your sister? We really need to get in touch with her, don't you think?"

At this, Vivian sat heavily into the nearest chair, a marionette with cut strings, staring at the floor between her stockinged feet.

33

New York, 1936

Allen's face lit up yellow with the flare of his match, lighting a cigarette.
"What's eating you? This is the greatest night of your life and you
look practically dead. What's with the crepe-hanging?"

In the balcony seats at the theater, they were flanked by Max
Gordon and his wife, Mrs. Garnett, Allen and his wife Dorothy, and of all people,
Mark Bell and his missus. The orchestra was warming up, and the theater was
packed to the rafters. Their first big show, hired on their own merits, not as
stand-ins for other writers who washed out. This should have been, as Allen
put it, the greatest night of his natural life.

But his parents refused to come, on account of it being the Sabbath and all,
and his mother especially made it known how displeased they were that their
son's wonderful career would make regular observance next to impossible. The
proximity of Allen and his glowering, large wife, not to mention Bell and his
prim, pretty wife, were cranking Milo's nerves. And through it all, his mind
was torturing him with nightmare visions of Vivian throwing herself under
the wheels of a train, with no one to keep an eye on her between New York and

Michigan. What was to stop her from getting out in Pennsylvania and carrying on with what she started?

Well, all the drugs helped. Mrs. Smith had called a doctor and gotten Vivian tranquilized plenty tranquil, and Estelle Mann was on her way to Detroit to pick up Vivian at the station. It was all copacetic. In theory.

A sharp jab roused him. It was Allen. "Stop looking like that, like someone shot your dog. You'll curse the show." After a lifeless pause, Allen turned in his seat and leaned close to his ear. Milo used all of his force of will not to lean away from his whisper.

"It's that broad, isn't it? Bell told me she got her hooks in you. Didn't I say she was trouble? Well, she's gone, Short. Out of your life and not your problem. So snap out of it. Soon as this show gets going, I got a job for us in Hollywood."

Milo crinkled his forehead at him.

"Yeah, Hollywood, did you think I was just telling stories before? It's where the money is, and it'll get your mind off that dame if you get out of the city. Now shut up and look alive before Gordon decides you and your long face are ungrateful."

The house lights dimmed, and a wave of excited murmurs blended into the overture.

Milo tried to let himself bob along on their excitement. The darkness helped: here he could pretend no one else was around. All those months of writing, sweating, rewriting, worrying… And here it was, a crackerjack cast belting out his words and the crowd lapping it up like honey, he could sense it. It was there in the hushed attention, in the easy laughter bubbling down the rows, in the spontaneous explosions of applause, sometimes catching the actors by surprise, such that they had to make some stage business, pacing from place to place maybe, or fiddling with a prop as the crowd simmered down.

As the melodic opening notes of "Love Me, I Guess" struck up, with the two leads gazing at one another across a pool of yellow light, Milo's throat closed up in excitement and fear.

He needn't have worried, though, because they knocked it straight out of the park and halfway to New Jersey. John Garnett was tender, Marianne West's faux-demure reactions were a hoot, the dance direction was perfect for the number. Garnett liltingly, charmingly, exquisitely professed his growing love, just in time for riotous and improbable second act complications.

As they danced their way into the release, Milo relaxed, at long, long last, and tears pricked his eyes. He almost didn't notice Allen's hand squeezing his knee.

Milo batted that hand away just as the curtain fell on the first act, and the audience roared its hearty approval.

He excused himself with just a curt nod at Gordon, racing down the balcony steps.

In the throngs of the lobby, he heard snatches of talk, like *wonderful,* and *so much fun!* and *wasn't that song just gorgeous?*

And Milo was glad he wasn't famous like Irving Berlin, because he didn't want to talk to any single person who knew him.

"Mr. Short! I thought that was you."

And there was Mrs. Beatrice Smith, smiling up at him, and Milo admired her hair loosened at last from its bun, though the tight little curls around her round face were controlled in their own way. Milo didn't know from hair, but he imagined it took her a good while to fix it like that.

"Well, hello… Beatrice. Gonna take me some practice saying it. And please, call me Milo."

"I guess I need practice, too."

The crowd around them pushed them together. Milo noticed how tiny she was; even in her shoes she barely reached his chin.

"What brings you here?"

She smirked. "I'm not exactly selling tickets, am I? I'm watching the show, Milo. I saw *Hilarity*, too. Well done. I can really tell these words are yours; even if no one had told me you wrote it, I would still know."

"Awww, gosh, thanks. People seem to be liking it."

Small talk ensued, during which Milo found out that she had intended to come with a girlfriend, but her friend had ditched her at the last moment to go out for dinner with a man she was sweet on.

Finally, she fixed him with a canny, glinting look. "See, I shocked you the other day, didn't I?"

"How do you figure?" Milo thought, *boy, you don't know from shocked.*

"When I told you I was Jewish."

"Well, it did come as a surprise, a bit," Milo allowed, inwardly cringing that he might have noticed plenty about the efficient and businesslike Mrs. Smith, if he'd cared to talk to her about more than work and the weather.

"My late husband was not Jewish, hence the Smith. And honestly, sometimes it's easier to just let people think what they will, these days."

"I get it. My last name is supposed to be Schwartz. It's funny, sometimes my folks don't seem to mind my blending in. They barely blinked at me going from Moshe Schwartz to Milo Short. But my mother is horrified that I'm not observing Shabbat tonight. And my father can't seem to decide how Jewish he wants to be. Sometimes he acts like he's never seen a synagogue, other days he's reading aloud from *The Forward* and shaking his fist at American Jewish Council rallies. I think it's strange for him, having a foot in two places. Three, if you count the East Side. And he acts like his old tenement is lurking just behind him, all the time."

Milo cocked his head at her. "Can I ask you something, Beatrice?"

"Of course."

"Didn't your people get upset when you married a gentile?"

"Until the day he died, they thought he was the worst thing that ever happened to me."

"But what did you think?"

"I think I miss him, every single day. I suppose you'd better get back. You probably have front row seats."

"Say, did you mention that your date to this soiree stood you up? And may I take it to mean you have an empty seat by you?"

"You may take that, yes."

"I'd like to see the show out in the house. It's too nervy up there with all the big shots. So, may I come sit with you, then? Is that okay, Beatrice?"

"Sure, that would be swell. And why don't you call me Bee? My close friends call me Bee."

MILO ALMOST COULDN'T watch his own show, so busy he was sneaking looks at Beatrice. Bee.

Her face had a serenity and stillness that made him think of painted portraits.

So it was a kind of magic when Bee's serenity cracked open with a raucous laugh, or a smile uncurled itself on the breeze of a quiet sigh. And with sinful pride and arrogance he reveled in the fact it was his show, his words, that made her do that.

Not just his words, though. His and Allen's, and the actors, Max Gordon and his hustle and purse strings. It seemed impossible, all these things from a chorus girl's sequins to the instruments and the spotlights... It was like an army up there, all in service of making the audience happy, making this one young lady happy, far as he was concerned.

When the curtain went down, and the audience roared, and stood, and stood longer, and there were bows, Milo felt the tears pushing at his eyes again and he just let them go because why the hell not? What was it gonna hurt?

It was no sacrifice to Milo to skip out on the party. He rushed back to the balcony long enough to share some back-slapping and explain that he had run into a girl he knew who was all on her own, and he had to do the courteous thing and escort her home safely.

Gordon elbowed him. "Make sure she's not too 'safe,' eh, Milo? Ha ha, good for you."

Allen wouldn't look at him, which was noted by the others, as Milo could tell by all the eyes sliding back and forth between them, and raised brows.

He cared not a bit as he nearly skipped down the steps, squinting until he saw a tiny gloved hand stretch above the heads of all the people leaving. As he weaved through the people to reach Bee, the name for this feeling hit him solid, right in his chest, in fact. Safe. He suddenly felt safe.

34

1999

Milo

draw my fingers down the page, watching Vivian's spiky cursive spooled out under my finger. That steno book. She'd saved it when she went away. Or maybe it wasn't her choice. She was all but catatonic, after all, when they poured her onto the train, I heard later. Bee and my mother had packed her things, including *Gone with the Wind*. I'd handed that book to Bee so maybe Vivian could read on the train. I knew for damn sure I didn't want it lying around my apartment. Then I'd phoned up Bell and explained Vivian was ill and would be heading home. Bell had, in one burst of chivalry or guilt or possessiveness, helped Bee escort her to Penn Station. I wasn't there to see her off.

It's been some days since they came in to draw my blood and Naomi went bananas about it. Eleanor came in that day to tell me that she'd smoothed it over, at least for the moment, unless and until that blood test confirmed what we'd all begun to believe was probably true. In that case, all bets were off, but that was probably always the case. Eleanor's furious, I can tell, but I can't be mad at Naomi, not really. For one thing I love all my grandkids flaws and all, and for another, it's just her way of protecting us. She can't save me from aphasia, from dying, or Bee from her heart attack or David from cancer. So she suits up for battle whenever she can.

That day I was so worn out from the excitement I slept most of the rest of the day, and Alex has been scarce around the house if there was any chance Naomi might be around, so it wasn't until today that I finally remembered that mysterious box he brought, and made myself understood enough that they would show it to me.

And the first thing I saw was that steno book, my God. Bee and Bell or whoever packed up, they might've just thrown this notebook in a trunk or box or suitcase, paying it no mind, having no idea what was in it. Vivian might have just staggered into bed back at her sister's place and never looked inside it again for all I know. After all, she died young, not so long after her return to Michigan. Return? More like exile, at least partially because of me, partially because of Bell, too. He seemed eager enough to send her packing. Vivian's instincts were probably right about him tiring of her.

I would like to ask exactly how she died, but of course I cannot, and I am too tired to try to mime or spell it with the alphabet board.

How different would it have been if she'd stayed? If she'd somehow calmed down and perked up and was able to get back to her own sharp-witted self?

She'd have seen me and Allen try to go to Hollywood, and scamper back on different trains, me because Leah landed in the hospital with what would turn out to be a fatal bout of pneumonia, poor kid. I was promising Allen that I would come back even as I boarded the train, but I already knew I'd break the promise whatever happened. Sorry, my friend. I should've just said forget it right away and spared you the disaster that was to come. Instead, I let my sister's death be my excuse and for that I'm ashamed.

I lost my nerve for a lot of things in 1936 and it took me some years to get it back. Or did I ever? Maybe not.

Allen and I were supposed to be writing an Astaire-Rogers picture, but they kept throwing out our songs and having other people change them and telling us to get lost if we complained. Allen stuck it out after I left for a while, writing with Yip Harburg, who was no slouch, lyrically speaking. He was palling around with George and Ira Gershwin by then, and when a brain aneurysm snuffed out poor George, Allen came back looking ten years older and ten drinks drunker.

Maybe I'd have had lunch with Vivian to tell her that my old rehearsal pianist friend Finkelstein had an idea for a show, from a novel by Edith Wharton, and that he thought it would make a great serious musical play if he only updated it a bit for modern times. I could have told her how everyone thought he was nuts, and me too when I went around trying to get investors for him. But then *Oklahoma!* was a smash without any sequins or leggy chorus girls and suddenly a musical play with songs that actually have something to do with the plot seemed like the smartest idea since coast-to-coast plane travel.

Then when the *Age of Innocence* knocked everyone's socks off, I figured out I liked this producing thing, whereby I could find all my favorite people to work with, and put them all in a room, and smooth-talk rich types into giving up their money, calling on my old tailor shop charm, back when making the customers happy at Schwartz and Sons was my only skill. And sometimes I could sit in with the book writer, or the dance director, and give them an idea or two, or get out of their way, and settle squabbles, too, calming people right down when they were about to tear each other's heads off. Seems some people found my presence soothing. Go figure.

Would Vivian have been happy to hear about me and Bee getting married and moving into this here townhouse? Would she have enjoyed my later shows, the peppy shows of the upbeat fifties, the weird, experimental shows of the sixties and seventies I produced off-Broadway, when people thought the world was upside down and I thought of the Depression and Hitler and figured, *eh, we'll get through*?

Would she have mourned with me as my son died too young, and we lost Bee too soon after? Would she think I'd done a good job with my kids, and looking after my granddaughter, all but orphaned?

What would Vivian have done all that time if she'd grown old, too? Would she have married eventually, and mellowed with age? Become a white-haired grandmother doing her knitting and listening to a scratchy phonograph of Paul Whiteman and thinking about the time we danced at the Stork Club?

It seems impossible, but then, but who guessed about things like the Holocaust? The moon landing? A president shot during a parade, and now these computers, and telephones you carry around in your pocket and people can call you anyplace? If I learned nothing else in eighty-eight years, I learned not to say "never" about pretty much anything.

I'd almost forgotten Eleanor and this other kid watching me stare at the notebook. I can tell what they're thinking, though they haven't said it out loud. Besides the fact they think I knocked up Vivian, they also think "Love Me, I Guess" was hers. I shouldn't be surprised. After all, I erased her from my memory, from conversation, from life. When she pops up—Bernie Allen's kid knew about her, who knew?—and I deny her again, what are they to think?

I never should have gone there that day. With sixty years of hindsight, despite my pretending that I was only blindly wandering and only accidentally found myself outside her place, despite me acting like I only needed a friendly face when I went in there ... No, that was all nonsense. Truth be told, there was some animal, frightened part of me that knew exactly what's what. That primitive, thoughtless part wanted to make it known that Milo Short was a man for sure and no arguments, and Vivian was the closest girl at hand I could prove it with.

By now I've gotten to know plenty of men with the proclivities of Allen and realized what they were up against back then, and how it would have been a particular kind of torture, all that pretending, with few options. How lonely that life must have been, how complicated it would be to read and speak and say everything in code, to be so terrified of being found out, or at least found out openly because some people knew anyhow.

Now I look back at Vivian's writing again, really look carefully, and then I bring the notebook closer to my face.

I can remember so clearly her brown curls swinging down over her cheeks, her teeth bit into her pale lips, without makeup, as she wrote, and crossed out, and wrote some more, smearing ink on her pretty, pale hands.

I sink back on the pillow and let the notebook drop from my hand. I turn my head away from the desperate curiosity in the faces of my granddaughter and the long-haired stranger, and in so doing I see her. Vivian crosses the room in her long negligee. I hear rain outside, loudly, like the windows are open. The bitter tickle of cigarettes weaves through the room, and pricks my chest like in the old days with that first deep drag, and that reek of wet summer garbage is a sour note underneath the smoke and roses that seems to be Vivian's signature scent. The sour tang of lemonade and sharpness of gin mingle on my tongue.

There you are, Milo.

I've been here all along, kid.

Not really, not the Milo I knew.

I guess I thought it didn't matter anymore.

But it did.

Why does it matter to you, even now? You're not even really here.

Whoever said it mattered to me?

I'm sorry, kid. I truly am.

Without her makeup on, Vivian looks so young. Her green eyes seem softer, less glaring, her pink cheeks glowing softly like my little Rebekah's on the rare chance I'd get to tuck her into bed. Vivian now leans over me, lets her manicured nails trail gently along my chin before she bends down and kisses me, more gently and delicately than she ever did when she was real, as if she's saying goodbye, though I'm not sure which of us is leaving.

35

1936

Milo regarded the envelope held in Bee's outstretched gloved hand. Bee was explaining how it had come to her, from Vivian, but it was meant for him. Milo could only picture Vivian raving that night in the park, running in front of that truck, all the times she seemed wild and her mind careening around from emotion to emotion, reaction to reaction.

"Milo," Bee said softly, her voice firm and kind. She shook the envelope lightly.

"Thanks, Bee," he said, finally closing his hand around it. She'd come all this way to deliver the letter, the least he could do was take it. "Will you come in? I could make some coffee."

She only shook her head and smiled in that small charming way she had, and turned to go, leaving Milo alone to read.

October 17, 1936

Dear Milo,

Have settled in here in Michigan. I'm told they sent you a telegram. Good, I'm glad to know someone thought of letting you know. My sister has forbidden me from ever writing to you, or to Mark, so I'm enclosing this in a letter to Beatrice, ostensibly a much belated thank-you note for her help. I plan to mail it myself because I don't trust Estelle not to open it and read it. As it is, she might snatch this next letter right out of my hands, or maybe get someone at the post office to show it to her. These small towns, people just know everything about you.

I spent most of the train ride assuming I would come back to Manhattan. I could rest a spell and then pick back up where I left off. But now that I've been back a while, I have come to understand that there's no point in thinking like that. I have no money of my own, and no way to find work here. There are no secretarial positions for the likes of me. It seems it is believed I am some kind of "fallen woman." Estelle takes care of me just fine, though, and gives me a little spending money so that I don't rot away entirely. And all she expects in return is my slavish devotion and undying gratitude, constantly repeated. You will not be surprised to know I am failing her in this.

Have not been feeling well. Headaches have been plaguing me since the train trip, along with my old friend exhaustion and a new friend, nausea. The girls who want to reduce should just get whatever I've got and they'd be slender in no time. Estelle lets me sleep as much as I need, however, and for this much I am glad.

I've been reading Gone with the Wind. *Thank you for sending it with me. It takes me out of myself, and I like knowing that you had this book in your hands. I'm still confused about what happened with us and the song, but my memory plays tricks.*

For example, Estelle swears I screamed at her when I left for New York that I wanted her to drop dead and rot in hell, but I don't remember it being that bad. Funny how two people can live through the exact same thing, and yet have two entirely different memories, each believing his own version is exactly correct. Are we telling ourselves lies and stories all the time? But if that's so, why don't we tell happier stories?

Will you write me back, Milo? Send it to the address below, care of Mr. Joshua DeVries. He runs the store in town, and I bet he'd hold onto a letter for me, seeing as he's no great friend of my sister. I could run an errand at the store, pick up your letter and Estelle will never have to know. And if she did find out, so what? She might tear it up, but either way I'd be no worse off than I am now. It's just that I'm a bit lonely, you see. I do so miss the music.

Now you'll think I'm trying to make you pity me. I'm not, I just have little news to report. I sleep, I read, I embroider and knit, and go for walks along the lake. Lake Michigan is pretty, and my favorite way to watch it is during bad weather. It's thrilling to witness all that power, with the waves smashing up against the pier, and roaring away on the sand. Something about that angry lake is mesmerizing.

My point is that I am fine. I thought it would kill me to come back. Yet now that I'm here, I find that I'm still here.
Yours affectionately,
Vivian

36

Eleanor

Grampa Milo drops the notebook and turns his head away, and I swear he goes whiter yet before my eyes. I gasp and grab for his paralyzed hand, the closest thing I can reach. The hand is cold, and for long moments I can't feel his pulse, nor hear him breathe.

I hear my own sob before I feel it, because I can't believe I'm again at a deathbed, though what do I expect? It's going to keep happening, all the people I love until the day it's me… Alex puts his large hand on my shoulder.

Then Grampa Milo pulls in a shuddering gasp. I sob again, in grateful surprise that this is not the moment.

Grampa Milo turns back to me, and he smiles and coughs. Alex lets go of me and goes searching for something down the hall, water, I assume, because that's what I want to give him, too, but Grampa Milo squeezes my hand to draw my attention.

"Hey, sweetheart," he whispers. "I'm still here."

"Grampa! Alex, he talked! Oh my God, he's talking!"

Grampa Milo puts a finger to his lips to shush me, and shakes his head. I lean in to hear him better, as Alex comes back with water. "Don't fuss…"

I sit on the side of his bed, mustering all my will not to slam myself down on his body and squeeze him like I'm four years old again.

"Sweetheart, I'm okay," he says once more, having taken a good long drink of water. His voice sounds as it always did: spry, Bronx accent intact, a thread of age lending him extra dignity.

"You don't have to talk right now," I manage to choke out, barely finding my own voice. "I'm just so happy you can, and that you… You scared me for a minute there."

"I still have a lot to say."

"You always did."

At this Grampa Milo shakes his head emphatically. "New stuff. You'll see. But later," he says, waving his hand in the air. "We'll be interrupted by the stampede any minute now."

This is true. Esme no doubt heard our excited cries, and is probably on the phone, and I'm sure Paul's got his driver flooring it uptown as we speak. Phone lines all over Manhattan are lighting up with the news.

Grampa Milo looks back at me. "I know you kind of like it quiet, and though I've had too much lately.… I can see the appeal, kid."

He reaches up and chucks my chin with his thumb. I grab his hand and stare at it in wonder. "It's your right hand! It works again!"

"Oh, Mr. Short!" trills an accented voice, and all of us turn to see Esme, her warm brown eyes brimming over and her hands clasped under her chin. "*Madre dio*, I've been praying for this day."

Alex leans down and says in my ear, "I should go, I don't want to be in the way. Just point me toward the subway station."

I look at up at him. "Actually…" I begin, thinking of advising him to borrow the town car when Uncle Paul arrives, or just take a cab to save himself the time, but before I even know what's coming I hear myself say, "I'd rather you stayed."

THE FAMILY ISN'T there for an hour before I tug on Alex's sleeve and tip my head toward the door to plot our escape.

Seems like everyone has materialized, even Eva's husband, Aaron, and he's hardly ever around. All the grandchildren and the tiny great-grands seem to cover every square inch of carpet, and a party of sorts has sprung up, once someone decided to break out the drinks cart, and with Esme calling for Chinese delivery. Esme is also strictly regulating how many of us are upstairs with Grampa at any one time, protecting him from suffocation under the tide of our love and relief.

When my family is not exclaiming with joy and wonder at Grampa Milo's returned voice and hand strength, they circle around Alex in an almost choreographed set of interrogations to which he replies mildly, again and again: acquaintance from Michigan, helping with the book. I swallowed hard when I saw Naomi appear. She nodded to me coldly and fired a quick menacing glare at Alex, but did not tip our hand.

When they all briefly give us a moment's peace, distracted by the wailing of a great-grandchild who has bonked her head, I lead Alex out the door, down the front stoop, and onto the sidewalk.

It's evening now, and has grown cloudy without me noticing. With the sun veiled, the autumn chill has a bite. Alex shrugs out of his leather jacket and rests it on my shoulders like a cape. I think of putting my arms through the sleeves but know it will be hilariously large, so instead I cross my arms underneath it. It smells like pot and old records.

"I'm glad he's better," Alex says, matching my slow amble. He pulls the tie out of his hair and shakes it out. This causes a couple of Upper West Siders walking their Pomeranian to double take. "I hope the results don't do him in, when we get them."

"In a couple days, I'd guess. Maybe sooner if we're lucky."

"Then what will happen?"

"I don't know. We tell him, and your mother, and see what they want to do. He can talk to us now, thank God for that. We don't have to rely on gestures and guesswork. He'll probably call the lawyer, Naomi will insist on it if nothing else. We'll probably have to test again, to convince them."

"What about the book?"

I hate the book now. I hate the day they ever thought of it, and hate that Uncle Paul pushed me into writing it. I'm not even a writer anymore. I don't know what I am.

"I suppose I'll have to mention it."

"'It' being my mother?"

"The situation, Alex. You know what I mean. I just don't know… How's that going to work? An asterisk in the 1937 chapter, oh by the way, a woman he had an affair with gave birth to his child he never raised or saw…"

"An asterisk. Nice."

"This is supposed to be a book about his work, not his love affairs—"

"Yes, speaking of that, his most famous song's lyrics written in Vivian's writing."

I can't walk another step suddenly, and I lean against the stoop of some other townhouse, staring down at my flats. The breeze prickles the skin on my bare shins. It's gotten so cold so quickly. I seem to forget, every single autumn, that the sun sets and it gets chilly. My dad used to say that's a "self-correcting mistake" but clearly not for me.

"What's on your mind?" Alex asks. He's stopped next to me, leaning on the adjacent side of the square post.

"I can't do it," I say, almost surprising myself by saying the words aloud. "The book. I can't."

"Who's going to tell the truth, then?"

"What truth is that exactly?"

"About my mother, and those lyrics."

"We don't know anything about lyrics."

"But we're going to ask him, right? Now that he's better? You said you would. You promised you would."

"He's my grandfather."

"Maybe mine, too."

I sink down into his jacket. "Don't be flip. You've just met him and you see him as a means to an end. A piece of biology."

"That's not fair."

"No? Then why won't you shut up about the notebook for a day and give me a minute with my talking, alert grandfather before you want to ride in there and give him another stroke."

He stands up off the stoop and I sense him coming around to face me, though my eyes are still on my shoes and all I see are his own scuffed and faded Chuck Taylors, toe to toe with me.

"I need my keys and wallet. You can wear the jacket, though."

I start to take the jacket off but he stays my hand with his own, pulling the jacket closed again, under my chin. "You're cold and I'm not. I'll get it later." He reaches into his own jacket pockets, taking out his wallet and keys, and walks away from me. He's going the wrong way to the subway, but I can't find my voice to call after him.

37

Milo

play the happiest melody that comes to my mind on the piano in the parlor, reveling in the full use of both my hands. *We're in the money, we're in the money, we've got a lot of what it takes to get along!*

Did we ever love that song back then, funny enough when you think how almost no one had money to throw around, or if they did they were scared half to death to lose it, or that their parents or kids or neighbors would lose it.

I have been prodded and measured and monitored and declared fit as I ever was, by my grandson Dr. Joel and plenty of others, too, down at Beth Israel, just making sure I was truly right as rain. Joel keeps shaking his head and muttering things like "astonishing" because stroke patients aren't supposed to talk and move again suddenly—bam!—just like that. Esme says it's a miracle. Our family feels a bit squirmy about religion when it comes right down to the brass tacks of it. Mostly everyone's going around saying how happy they are and leaving it at that. I'm in no rush to clarify, and I don't know what I'd say even if I had the notion.

I'm stronger, too, able to get up and around pretty much like I did before

I fell down in the first place, though it seems I won't be walking any distance outside anymore. Cabs and cars for me, which really isn't such a bad thing, though some days in this city walking is faster, even with my old-man shuffle.

Finally the throng of family hanging around me is shrinking down a bit so maybe I can finally grab a minute alone with my granddaughter the biographer, this poor kid who thought she'd just write a nice book and ended up with a mess right in her lap.

I also know it's been several days, over a week, since they snuck that man in to draw some blood from me, and this is not often far from my mind, nor Eleanor's, I can tell. And I further know that even though I'm stronger, and my voice is back, a certain visitor has not left the premises.

I scoot over on the piano bench, just a tiny bit, this impulse irresistible even though Vivian isn't real, and can't possibly need the room.

So, kid, is this your doing?

Is what? I wish you'd keep playing. I like it. I never used to hear you play.

I couldn't afford my own piano until…

Until after I was long gone.

I meant, is my voice back because of you?

You always did like to blame things on me.

Who's blaming? I'm giving you credit, if anything.

Good to know I get credit for something.

Aw, Vivian. I didn't mean for all that stuff to happen. I can't fix it now, anyway.

Can't you?

I wish you'd told me about the kid.

A girl doesn't know right away, you know. It's not like we get a telegram.

You could've told me when you knew. I would have…

My brain stumbles on that "what I would have" statement. What would twenty-five-year-old Milo have done, truth be told? The same kid who banished this scary and troublesome woman far, far away from him, even when she looked him in the eye and asked to stay? The same Milo who never wrote her back, even when she recounted her loneliness, and pleaded with him?

It feels cold next to me suddenly, and where I'd just been seeing some brown curls in my peripheral vision there is now only the indistinct blur of the parlor around me.

I close my eyes and hold my hands over the keys. It's been so long… And it was never my melody, anyway.

But I let it unwind in my memory, those old notes, and my hands go where they need to, and without really meaning to, I sing it to myself, though quietly, because no great vocalist am I.

> *I once was uptown, now I'm down, no more kid gloves, top hats*
> *or spats*
> *And yet you keep coming around, with your diamonds and*
> *fancy hats*
> *I don't understand it at all, no good can come of this!*
> *I'm not worthy, yet you, dear, just blew me a kiss…*
>
> *You might just love me… I guess.*
> *Though I'm not so … well-dressed.*
> *I can't guarantee that with me*
> *You'll always be … impressed.*
>
> *You might just love me … I think.*
> *Did you just give me … a wink?*
> *How can we go out to a show*
> *If you don't have … a mink?*
>
> *Take my advice and please heed it, get out while the getting's*
> *good*

Together we'll just be defeated; do what pretty rich girls should...

So you still love me ... it seems
We'll make the strangest ... of teams
Come take my hand, let's make our stand
And live the grandest ... of dreams!

"Grampa." Eleanor is next to the piano now, standing as if she were a torch singer, leaning on its side. "You never play that song, much less sing it."

"I'm feeling sentimental about old times, I guess."

"I have to tell you something."

"Yeah?"

"Alex called. The mail is here."

I nod my understanding. Eleanor says, "Maybe we'll look at it up in the office? It's private there. Alex is bringing it over because I had it mailed to the Midtown apartment."

"I might need a hand going up the stairs."

"You've always got my hand, Grampa. All the hands I've got to give."

We begin a halting progress, grandfather and granddaughter. It's not that I'm so weak, just out of practice. As we go up the bend in the stairs, I flash back to one of the apparitions that scared me so bad it all went black, but today the sun is bright and the room is well lit and it's just a patch of floral rug.

"You okay, sweetheart?" I ask her, patting her hand where she's got it crooked in my elbow, steadying me, and maybe I'm steadying her back, just a bit.

"Sure."

"You seem so quiet. Quiet even for you."

"Someone I know is mad at me, and I can't fix it."

"Why can't you fix it?"

She's quiet for a few more steps. I know she heard me, so I'm patient.

"Because he wants me to do something I can't do. I even think he's probably right to ask me, but I can't do it."

"Is it something awful? Morally wrong?"

"No, nothing like that. Just something that's beyond me."

"For the record, I think very little is beyond you, but I'll give you this for the sake of argument. Can you tell him that? What you just said. You even think he's right, but you can't."

"It won't matter."

"You'd be surprised. Not saying things always seems like a better idea in the moment, until you don't say it once, and you don't say it a hundred times, and the fact of your not saying it grows so big it gets bigger than everything else." We have reached my office doorway. "Listen to me on this, sweetheart. I know from secrets."

I settle into my office chair, at this desk now blanketed in unfamiliar paper, Paul's paper. Eleanor goes to stare out the window at the street, watching for Alex and his mail, no doubt. And so we wait in our own private silences.

I know that Alex is approaching when I see Eleanor move away from the window and take a seat in a chair opposite the desk. We both turn toward the doorway, and I startle just a tiny bit at Vivian leaning there, inspecting her deeply red fingernails. She's wearing a gown now, a sweeping lilac-colored thing that has a deep V-neck, small waist, and fluttery sleeves. A jewel pattern decks out the shoulders. It's more glamorous than what I ever saw her wear, because mostly in our time together we were working, so she'd be wearing a suit or day dress.

We all, even Vivian, turn toward the office door when Alex comes in, escorted by Esme, who gives us all a significant look of concern before she closes it behind her. I almost call her back to hear it the same time with us, seeing as how she helped us get this all arranged.

Alex proffers the envelope. "I didn't look yet."

I let Eleanor take it. Her hands visibly tremble, though I don't know what she's so afraid of. If she thinks the truth is scary, she should try being haunted by a dead ex-lover from six decades ago.

She frowns at it, squints, looks the page up and down.

"Excluded," she says, her voice breathy with wonder. "Excluded as biological father."

For a minute, I think we all forget how to speak the language, we're all silently defining "excluded" for ourselves, until Alex says it out loud in plain English.

"You're not the father. It wasn't you."

I can't help it; I look at Vivian. She stares back at me, coolly, inscrutable, in this fancy dress of hers, like something she might have worn to a fancy party with the likes of…

"Mark Bell," I say.

"What?" Eleanor asks. "Bell? What bell?"

"No, it's a name. Well, sort of, his real name was Marco Rubellino. He was, well, seeing Vivian at the time as well."

Alex shakes his head and looks out the window at the next white townhouse across the side street. He says, "Or Estelle was right and Vivian didn't know herself because she slept with men in Michigan, too. As family lore goes, her behavior was strange and outrageous after she came back. The timing still works if she got right down to business. I'm sorry to have taken up your time, and well, your blood, Mr. Short. It was kind of you to put our curiosity to rest. And I'll get out of your way now."

Eleanor rises from her chair, dropping the paper on the desk. "Alex, wait."

"I have to go call my mother and put an end to her suspense."

"Your jacket. Let me at least get your jacket."

I stand up behind my desk, drawing their attention in doing so. I draw on whatever gravitas I might have based on age alone and the fact that I'm dressed up in a shirt and tie today, so sick I was of deathbed pajamas. I adjust this tie, in fact, and decide I might wear one every day until I kick, just because I can.

"Jacket or no jacket, there's something else I need to tell you, and it's about the song."

This brings them both to the chairs opposite the desk, without my having to even tell them to sit down. Eleanor looks sick, and Alex is trying not to look like he's voraciously interested, but he is, he's near about to leap across the desk.

As I settle back down to my desk and look back up, I find myself staring straight at Vivian, who is looking back at me as she always used to look: haughty, pleased with herself, but now I can detect a shining in her eyes that could be triumph or tears, who can say?

I keep my eyes on her as I continue. "Vivian and I spent a night together once. She was a wonderful girl, but sick in ways we didn't know how to help back then. I'm ashamed because I knew that she liked me, and was hoping for what I couldn't give her, and spending the night together was only going to confuse her more. But I pretended not to know that. Milo Short was dumb like a fox and pretended to be too innocent to know why he was going to her apartment that day. If I'd been a decent man then, I'd have steered well clear of her, knowing what I knew, no matter what comfort I thought I needed.

"Comfort me she did, and more than that, she helped me write, too. I was stuck, see, and this was the last song for the show. My eyesight is not so good, you know this. And I was a little drunk, too, and Vivian was a good secretary, so it only made sense for her to hold the pen. But she didn't just take notes, she helped me. Yes, with the song. Trouble is, you two, I can't say how much she helped. She was taking dictation, and adding her own ideas, and it's all a jumble. It wasn't so strange to have people throw in rhymes, see, and not expect to get writing credit. But if I'm being honest, and honest is what I'm being finally, she did help me quite a bit. Fact is, I couldn't write the damn song until that night, and with her I wrote it."

Vivian is more still than I ever saw her in life. She's not sweeping around the room, lighting cigarettes, tossing her hair. She's holding her own hands, elbows bent, like a little girl in a choir.

"You know," I go on, "it wasn't so strange for songwriters to cut people in on credit for no real reason. I've seen it done as an outright favor to somebody who didn't know a C-sharp from a car horn. I've seen it done for publicity. So I could have cut her in on the credit. Allen would have pitched a fit, but then again, there was a lot eating at Allen back then and one more thing or another wouldn't have made a difference. I was wrong, and I knew it even then. Which is why I helped send her away on that train, even though she didn't want to go. Because when she disappeared on that train, so did everything else I'd done. It's too late now, but I'm sorry even so."

The sight of Vivian striding toward me should fill me with terror, given recent history. But it does not, even as she approaches on a trajectory that will brush her right between the chairs of Eleanor and Alex. In fact, to my great wonder—and I know from wonders—she looks at Alex as she grows nearer, and brushes over his shoulder with her hand, casting him a look that speaks of pride, regret, and pain, before turning her attention back to me.

My desk disappears, as does my office. It's dark around us, like on a dance floor, and she's in spotlight. An orchestra strikes up a tune, and it's a big band version of "Love Me, I Guess," Allen's melody but no words at all, just horns and clarinets and some drums and a piano tinkling away. As she gets right in front of me she doesn't stop, she puts a hand up by my face like she is going to stroke my cheek, but then walks past me. As she recedes, she looks back over her shoulder with a small soft smile, until the sheen of her dress and the glitter of her eyes fade into the velvety dark.

38

Milo

'm in my bright office again, the sun gleaming off the piano, dust motes dancing to the fading strains of melody quieting in my ears.

I sit myself gently back down. I don't feel dizzy, or frightened, or like I might black out, but I know enough about being eighty-eight that no matter what, you don't go throwing yourself down in chairs.

"So there you have it now. And put it in the book if you want to. I'll call my lawyer tomorrow about putting her name on the song. I don't know what that means financially, but it might mean something and seems only fair."

Alex seems to snap awake. "Mr. Short, that's not why I came here. We don't want money."

"Sure you do and nothing wrong with that. I've both had it and not and I can tell you, young man, having it is better."

"I don't want it anyway. Whatever work she did it was hers, not mine."

"Well, son, it might not be up to you. Your mother is Vivian's daughter and she might have something to say about it."

Alex sighs. "This was never about money, none of it was. It was just about knowing. And now we'll never get to."

"Well," interjects Eleanor, not looking Alex in the face. She stares instead at the corner of my desk. "What about Rubellino? Is he still alive?" At this I answer no. He died in the 1980s, having caught AIDS back when people thought "safe sex" meant not getting a girl in trouble. Eleanor goes on, "He's got living relatives, probably? Maybe the DNA would work that way."

I clear my throat and try to put it delicately. "He was with Vivian for a period of time. It might be worth a try."

Alex shrugs and begins to stand, taking a phone out of his pocket. "Whatever. I have a phone call to make, anyway."

Eleanor says, "Take it into my room. It'll be private."

He nods. "Right, okay, I might as well get it done with."

"Then come on downstairs and Esme will make you a good stiff drink."

He smiles cheerlessly and allows Eleanor to lead him out. She comes back in mere moments, her room here not being far from this office.

She sits down again and stares at Alex's empty chair. "You know, I was assuming he was my cousin all this time."

"I'd started to think it was true, too."

"Was it only…the one night?"

"Only the one night that mattered to the blood test. But we were friends, she and I. After how things ended up, though … She wrote me later and sounded agonizingly lonely, though her sister forbade her from writing. She had to sneak the one she sent."

"She wrote you? Do you have…"

"No. I'm sorry to say I did not keep it. Fact I burned it."

"Oh. So was Jerry Allen right? That you gave up songwriting because she messed you up?"

I shake my head, considering what to say. "No, see, it's not so simple. I know you'd like me to give you easy cause and effect. I could say it was my sister dying, I could say that Hollywood took it out of me, I could say it was because the whole *High Hat* show was all knotted up with bad memories, I could say it was because I just didn't have the words anymore, that I felt all dried up. I could say the producing opportunity fell in my lap. I could say that something happened between me and Allen that had nothing to do with Vivian. And those would all be sort of true."

"What happened between you and Allen?"

"That's between me and Allen, rest his soul."

"And here I thought you were telling all your secrets."

"Not today."

Eleanor frowns down into her lap. She frowns so much, this girl. "You said something about needing comfort, when you went to Vivian. Comfort from what?"

"Don't we all need comfort sometimes?"

At this Eleanor smiles down at the big watch on her wrist, David's watch. "Grampa, don't be mad at me, but I don't want to write the book."

"I would never be mad, kid, but why not?"

She looks me square in the face. "I only did it so that you'd be protected from some stranger prying into your life. If they gave it to me, it meant nobody else would do it. But now look at you, strong as ever. You don't need me."

"Oh, honey, you don't know the half of it. Without you and Alex here refusing to accept my brush-offs…"

"Well, you don't need me now. Not anymore, not for this. More to the point, Grampa Milo, is that I don't want to be a journalist. I never did. Aunt Rebekah and the cousins decided that part. I was happy as could be making copies at Short Productions, learning how it all worked behind the scenes, and by that I don't mean the meetings and pinstripe suits. I'm never going to be a super executive woman like Naomi, but I always loved the family business."

"Sweetheart, if you don't want to be a reporter, then don't be a reporter."

"You won't think it's a waste?"

"Nothing that makes you happy is a waste to me. We'll find something for you at the office without a pinstripe in sight, I'm sure, something that really suits you. And I'll tell Paul that you've thought better of the book."

Eleanor shakes her head, straightens in her chair, and shoves her glasses firmly into place on her nose. "No, I'll tell him. It's about time I do my own talking, wouldn't you say?"

The office door opens, and Alex fills the doorway. "I think I'd better get a flight home. She didn't take it so well."

I raise my finger to him. "I'll have Shelly get you a flight as soon as she can, first class so you don't have to sit there with your chin on your knees, and I won't hear a word of argument. Eleanor, go find this young man his jacket you mentioned and help him get his things together at the apartment. I'll have Shelly call your cell phone, Eleanor, when she has the flight."

Alex nods, helpless against the force of an old man's decisiveness.

"But I want to ask you one thing before you go, young man."

"Sure."

"How did Vivian die, exactly? I only know that she died young. After your mother was born, obviously."

"I only know the family story, and you know how those are, Mr. Short. But I remember it well because it was a cautionary tale in the whole family. She walked on the pier in a storm and got swept away. There was a lighthouse out there she liked. Estelle used to say she was a good swimmer going back to their days growing up in Chicago, but even a good swimmer can't fight the lake in a storm. My mother told me that all the time, whenever the waves kicked up high. 'Even a good swimmer can't fight the storm.'"

Alex and Eleanor trail out of the office, and I lean back in my chair, picturing Vivian on that last day. I can just see her, shoes dangling from her fingers as she watched the lake explode onto the shore and she dug her toes into the sand.

She'd want a better view, sure she would. She always did like a front row seat in life. So she'd drop her shoes and walk closer, closer yet, until the waves leapt up and soaked her knees.

Then she'd look out at the end of the pier and see the surf surging, mist leaping high as the lighthouse. That would be amazing up close, so she'd turn and walk out on the pier. Was it wood? Concrete? It wouldn't matter, she'd go out as far as she could, never one for doing things halfway.

Was she scared? I wonder, as the wave reared up over her, did she know it would sweep her away? Did she think of her little daughter in those last moments on the solid, strong pier?

Or did she throw her arms back, tip her head to the sky, and let it come?

39

July 1, 2000

Milo

The young girl's face bursts with delight when she opens the stage door and finds me on my way in. I put a finger to my lips, *shhhh, it's a secret,* and she giggles behind her hand, letting me past.

It's hard for an old man to sneak around, this I know, especially me, especially here, because everybody knows me, even if I weren't wearing my old favorite fedora.

I think that girl is in the chorus, but then again, it's an easy guess.

The house lights are dim, and this is convenient for me, for sure. I wend my way toward the back rows, so that I'm well clear of the dim halo of stage lights. I don't want to make anyone nervous, see, but I really did want to be here today. This particular day.

The director is a new guy who looks more than a little like Nat King Cole, and has a boyfriend who he likes to bring to the house for dinner. They're a hoot, those two. I always forget the director's name—oy, my memory these days—so I think of him as Nat. Lucky I don't have to call him by name too much.

Nat is talking to a pretty girl by name of Minerva-Something, and our star, Anthony Tremain, which I'm positive is a stage name.

Then Nat hops down off the stage with the lightness of a fawn, and nods to the rehearsal pianist. I can't see the fellow, so I can still imagine Fink sitting there, pounding away, accepting of his mediocre status, but playing as well as he can anyhow, because it's close to what he wanted and close is not nothing.

And then the chords come, and this Anthony young man begins to liltingly sing and soft-shoe around the stage like he weighs nothing, like a piece of fluff on the breeze. I will never get over these amazing people. If I didn't see scores of them all the time, pouring into New York, I'd refuse to believe so much talent was real. An embarrassment of riches, is what.

It's not a vocal duet but she doesn't stand there like a dummy. She flirts and sashays and beams without ever upstaging. She's terrific, plus she's got legs for days, which never hurts.

When Anthony finishes up that last refrain, swooping her down in a dip so low her hair brushes the stage, the assembled motley crew out in the seats make as much noise applauding as they can muster, which is more than you'd think.

That might be the best "Love Me, I Guess" I ever did see.

As the noise settles down a bit, I call out, "Bravo! Stupendous!" and everybody whips around to search for me in the dark. They know my voice too, they do. Plus who else says stupendous anymore? They ought to. And boffo, too.

Some wise guy with the spotlight swings it onto me. "Hey, you're going to blind an old geezer, you putz!" But I'm laughing, though I really am half blind with that light. By the time I've blinked the brightness away again, half the cast has rushed up to me, I think.

Nat, whose name I now remember is something like Evan or Kevin, gets to me first and shakes my hand out of my sleeve.

I spend some time telling them all how terrific they are, which they sop up like cats with milk, as well they should.

In a lull, I pull some papers out of my inside jacket pocket. "I got something here I'd like to share with you, but first, is Eleanor around? I'd like her to be here, too."

The stage manager says, "Oh sure, I just saw her a few minutes ago, I'll get her."

Eleanor has a title of some kind or another at Short Productions—at Naomi's insistence that the family have jobs that sound important—but she's never in her office and I'm not sure if she ever took her business cards out of the plastic wrap. Instead, she's over at the theater all the time, getting everybody to teach her everything they know, meanwhile running errands or whatever anyone asks her to do. She runs out for coffee, makes copies, and is in general happier than I've seen her during her Columbia days, or with any magazine story. I think she might have a future in casting, personally. She sat in with us during *The High Hat* revival auditions and she had some smart things to say, including about the comedic second lead who we almost overlooked. That gal learned a lot about people by mostly listening instead of talking so much.

She gave up the book project in the end, and oh did Naomi and Paul ever have a conniption fit about that at first! Naomi was mad she wasted all that time on the "wild goose chase" of Vivian, and was none too pleased about the song credit, either. It took me a fair amount of explaining to finally convince her I was not an addled and manipulated old fart, but sharp enough to finally learn from a batch of sixty-year-old screw-ups and give credit where it's due.

Paul was peeved, as if he'd done Eleanor this huge favor with the book in the first place, not to mention having to give back the advance they'd already paid. Some favor! He'd manipulated her into it, seems to me, and I told him so, too. I'm still his father and I'll tell him what's what. Anyway, they got over it, and this Arnie fella is doing a pretty good job. He was the one Naomi really wanted in the first place, anyhow. Sure, the book makes the point about sharing credit with the late Vivian Adair for my famous song, and sure, I've been warned that the publisher will want to make a splash about "the revelation," but it's not so bad. Arnie will be great on camera and will do all the talking. I had my say in the book, thankful enough I have my words back that I said all there was about Vivian, and her help with lyrics, and how we were "briefly romantic." Funny how I've only recently thought to wonder how much Bee ever guessed about Vivian and me. She probably guessed plenty; she was no dummy, my lovely Beatrice.

When Eleanor finally appears out of the wings, she's got dust bunnies trapped in her hair, which she tries to brush out, and she doesn't get them all. But she just shrugs and shades her eyes to try to look out in the seats. "Grampa Milo? You out there?"

"Here, kid." I wave at her as I'm about to take a seat at the rehearsal piano. "Have a seat."

She sits down at the edge of the stage, her legs over the side. One shoe hangs loose, dangling from her toe. It melts my creaky old heart to see her so relaxed she can let her shoe hang off her foot, have dust all over her hair, and not think a thing about it.

I go through a parody of piano playing prep, pretending to crack my knuckles and flapping invisible coattails out of my way. I do toss my necktie over my shoulder in case of it swinging onto the keys.

Before I begin, I remind them all of something. "Naomi said way back when she first brought this up to me, this here revival, that she was even thinking of asking me to write a new song. Then I fell down in the sidewalk and it was all very dramatic and no one asked me again. But I didn't forget. Not this, I didn't forget. So. Give a listen."

> *I used to pretend I was somebody rich, important and grand*
> *A lord of the manor, a fancy gentleman of consequence*
> *But all of that melted away, when you first took my hand*
> *With you, dear, in my arms, none of that makes any sense*

I'm no polo player, no aviator, no explorer of exotic lands

Latin, painting or opera, I'm not one who understands

I'm not good looking, not refined, I don't have joie de vivre

Here with you, dear, it's only me

I can't buy you fancy clothes, houses, an automobile

I can't buy you diamonds or jewels, anyway, not if they're real

There's not much I can give you, nothing unless it's free

Besides my love, dear, it's only me

The fact that you love me regardless, simply defies explanation

There's got to be someone better out there in all creation

Despite my attempts to convince you that all my prospects are vile

Here you are right beside me, bathing me in your smile

I guess I'm okay after all, maybe even better than that

Just as I am, as you'll have me, with no top hat or shiny spats

Goodbye to that life of pretending, of striving, of trying to be

Darling, I love you, as only me

My voice cracks on the last high note something awful, and at first no one breathes a word and I think, yes, this was a mistake, old man, you haven't written anything in half a century and even then you were sauced when you finished that last one, and people are nice to an old schmuck but that doesn't mean—

A piercing whistle starts it, then they all jump in with cheering and stomping and someone slaps my back and damn near knocks my glasses off.

I wave my hands at them, enough already. So they probably don't think it's terrible but it's also not *this* good.

Nat—no wait, it's Devon! That's his name, Devon!—Devon slides onto the bench next to me and looks at the music.

"These lyrics are fabulous! And the melody's not half bad, either."

He winks, and he gives me a playful nudge. He'd written it for me weeks ago, in secret, just like I asked him to. I can't help it; I like surprises. They're so … theatrical.

I notice Eleanor then squinting at the back of the house, shading her eyes with her hand.

Speaking of theatrical surprises.

Ellie springs so awkwardly off the stage that one of the cast members has to catch her and stand her back upright like a doll. She walks slowly up the aisle, her face all slack astonishment, until halfway up when she starts to jog.

I've got an excellent view from my piano bench of the lanky, loping silhouette of Alex from Michigan. Vivian's green-eyed grandson.

Eleanor stops short, and just gapes.

"Hey there," he says.

"What? How?"

He chuckles. His laugh is throaty, deep compared to his speaking voice, and this sends a little chill up my neck. Alex steps forward for a quick friendly hug, before stepping back to answer. "Apparently, your grandfather thought this Arnie guy should interview my mom, and talked this Arnie guy into arranging a little trip."

"Like he was so hard to talk into it," I interject. "He practically jumped across my desk to get your phone number."

Eleanor turns around to stare at me, and her face is glowing with one of her biggest, broadest smiles I've yet seen. In these moments, she's never more beautiful. I would orchestrate a surprise like this every single day if I could, just to get that smile out of her. "Grampa, why didn't you tell me?"

"Ta-da!" I add some jazz hands, to the merriment of the crowd all around.

I knew she and Alex had been talking on the phone. I knew that because her cousins are always eavesdropping, and also because I'm a little nosy, too. And I further knew that she would brighten like a struck match whenever she got a call. She should hide this from me in my house? When I've known her since she was born?

Alex and Eleanor walk toward the piano.

"Loved your lyrics, Mr. Short."

"You can stop with the mister already. And I hope you'll come to dinner tonight, if that writer doesn't have you too busy."

"I'm all yours," he says, but by this time he's looked back at Eleanor.

We all can't stop staring at them, and they can't stop standing there like mannequins, so finally Devon breaks the spell by announcing dinner break. Someone cuts the stage lights to a reasonable soft glow, and we disperse, all us of acting like we're not staring.

I take a seat halfway out in the house, spying on them, if I'm being honest. Eleanor and Alex walk to the edge of the stage and sit like she was before… hanging their feet off and leaning back on their hands. Eleanor kicks her feet lightly. Are they talking about the flight? New York? About Mark Bell, who, we found out recently, was after all Millicent's father? I plan to ask Alex at dinner if the Bell family was welcoming, or aghast. We had to lend him the family lawyer to get their answer, but they might have softened by now.

Now Alex hops down easily from the stage, and he holds out his hand and helps Eleanor down, as well. They walk side by side up the aisle, companionably.

They're going to pass right by me, and I'm not swift enough to hide, so I rely on my natural old man cuteness to get me out of trouble for spying.

"Hello, Grampa." Eleanor folds at the waist to kiss my cheek.

"Hi, kids. Boy, we pulled it off, didn't we, Alex? The surprise. Guess it's the producer in me, I can't resist orchestrating the dramatic reveal."

Eleanor asks him, this time staring out into the soft dark, "How long are you here? Before you have to get back home?"

"Well, the trip for the book interview is officially just a couple days, but I've got some time since I quit my job."

Eleanor mock-slaps his arm. "You didn't tell me!"

"It just happened. We finally cleaned out and fixed up Estelle's house, so I'm staying there now until we sell it, while I figure out the next thing."

I pipe up. "Happy to have you at the townhouse. Loads of room. You and your mom, just you, whatever. Right, Eleanor?"

"Of course." Eleanor adds, "Hey, let's get you something to eat. Where's your mom? I'd love to meet her. Grampa, you want to come?"

I shake my head as Alex answers, "Resting up from the flight."

"We'll do something fun today," Eleanor says. "Nice and touristy. Last time you were here we hardly even let you out."

"Will you stand over a subway grate in a white dress like Marilyn Monroe?"

"Only if you climb the Empire State like King Kong."

They say their farewells to me, and I turn to watch them go, shameless spy that I am. I can't help myself. All the world's a stage, old Will said, and he's not wrong.

As they walk up the aisle, Alex drapes his long arm behind her so his hand rests on her shoulder. Eleanor's arm slides underneath Alex's black leather coat, around his waist. They pause at the top of the aisle, out by the theater lobby. The doors are propped open, and the daytime light filtering in sets them in silhouette. They turn toward each other, and Eleanor tips her face up to look at him straight on. She takes one step closer, but there's still a line of daylight shining between them. For several heartbeats they stand there like that, still and close, but separate.

Then they step apart and move out into the lobby, disappearing from view.

Oh well. Not like it's final curtain, anyhow. We've got plenty of time. Well, they do, anyway. Me, I'm eighty-nine, so who knows?

I'm alone in the seats now. Out of habit, I glance around for Vivian. I've never seen her again since that last day in my office, and I'm surprised as hell myself but I sorta miss her, this hallucination or whatever she was. I pull out my wallet from my jacket and open it. Vivian's things are with Millicent, as they should be. But Alex gave me the dried flower. I hadn't given it to her, and it might not have had anything to do with me. Maybe she just dried it in *Gone with the Wind* because it's a big heavy book. But every time I smell roses, now… every time… I open the envelope in which I'd tucked the crumbling bloom and inhale, eyes closed. I think I must be imagining the scent; it couldn't be this strong, not for something that's been dead so many years.

At last I put the rose back and tuck the wallet away. It's time to go home.

Acknowledgments

I have quite the cast of characters to thank for helping *Vivian in Red* come to life, seeing as I started this ambitious project about a songwriter without even knowing which Gershwin brother was the lyricist. (It was Ira.)

As ever, thank you to Kristin Nelson and all the fine people at Nelson Literary Agency. I know you've got my back, and I appreciate it so very much.

Thank you, again and again, to Jason Pinter at Polis Books, for loving Vivian and Milo as much as I do, and bringing them to the world for me.

Many thanks to intrepid copyeditor Christine LaPorte.

As for my research sources, they did their very best to educate me on everything from expressive aphasia to the Bronx, and whatever mistakes there might be are mine alone. Better yet, consider it poetic license.

Much gratitude to:

The Bowery Boys podcasters—Greg Young and Tom Meyers—for their New York stories sparking my imagination.

Kelly O'Connor McNees, for talking me off the ledge when I thought I wasn't up to the challenge.

Philip Furia for insight on Tin Pan Alley lyrics and lyricists' workaday lives.

Alex Disbrow for sharing pictures of his Art Deco Bronx apartment.

Lloyd Ultan for sharing memories of the Bronx of days gone by, told in his wonderful accent.

Dr. Michael Baird for information about DNA testing in 1999.

Dr. Jayne Hodgson for insight into strokes and their effects.

Stephanie Toering for details on speech pathology and recovery for stroke victims who have lost the power of speech.

My friends who tolerated this goy's annoying questions about Yiddish and kosher and High Holidays. Amy Finkelstein, Marla Garfield, and Arnie

Bernstein, you're all mensches.

Jill Morrow and Elizabeth Graham, for their invaluable feedback and insight on early drafts.

Last, but he could never be least, Ernie Harburg, son of the great Yip Harburg (of "Somewhere Over the Rainbow" fame, and more) for talking with me about the life of a lyricist in the Golden Age of song.

About the Author

Kristina Riggle lives and writes in West Michigan. Her debut novel, *Real Life & Liars*, was a Target "Breakout" pick and a "Great Lakes, Great Reads" selection by the Great Lakes Independent Booksellers Association. *The Life You've Imagined* was honored by independent booksellers as an IndieNext "Notable" book. *Things We Didn't Say* was named a Midwest Connections pick of the Midwest Booksellers Association. Her latest novels are *Keepsake* and *The Whole Golden World*, which was lauded by Bookreporter.com as "a riveting and thought-provoking page-turner that will appeal to fans of Jodi Picoult and Chris Bohjalian."

Kristina has published short stories in the *Cimarron Review, Literary Mama, Espresso Fiction*, and elsewhere, and is a former co-editor for fiction at *Literary Mama*. Kristina was a full-time newspaper reporter before turning her attention to creative writing. As well as writing, she enjoys reading, yoga, dabbling in (very) amateur musical theatre, and spending lots of time with her husband, two kids and dog. Visit her online at kristinariggle.net or on Twitter at @KrisRiggle.